PRAISE FOR

The Whistling Season

"Doig is in the best sense an old-fashioned novelist: You feel as if you're in the hands of an absolute expert at story-making, a hard-hewn frontier version of Walter Scott or early Dickens. The landscape and characters are vivid, the prose flawless, and like the earlier masters, Doig imbues each scene and his spacious story with deep emotional understanding and a sense of possibility and personal adventure. *The Whistling Season* is a book that strives for more than beauty, which it achieves: It reaches for joy."

—O, *The Oprah Magazine*

"Along with his much praised, incantatory gifts for evoking quintessentially American prairie life and history, the National Book Award finalist brings . . . a bushel and peck of irresistible characters, each so full of spunk, wit, ambition or sheer orneriness that not one of them will lie down on the page and sleep for a moment."

—*Los Angeles Times Book Review*

"You can see the evidence of [Doig's] experience in his new novel: its gentle pace, its persistent warmth, its complete freedom from cynicism—and the confidence to take those risks without winking or apologizing. When a voice as pleasurable as his evokes a lost era, somehow it doesn't seem so lost after all."

—*The Washington Post Book World*

"Doig offers a gentle appreciation of the secrets beneath the surface of everyday life, set against a Western landscape that is described in concrete detail." —*The New Yorker*

"As well crafted as the best carpentry. *The Whistling Season* does what Doig does best: evoke the past and create a landscape and characters worth caring about." —*USA Today*

"Doig is at his best. . . . *The Whistling Season* is one of those novels that sets it own stage in the opening pages, promising unique characters, poetic passages and memorable scenes. And, perhaps more than in any of his previous volumes, Doig delivers."

—*Rocky Mountain News* (Denver)

"What a pleasure it is to sink into this story, which is told with old-fashioned sentences (simple but elegant, and ready to charm you with what they have to say) and old-fashioned storytelling prowess."

—*The Arizona Republic*

"[Doig] is capable of a sweet lyricism when describing the quotidian, and his attention to detail is meticulous."   —*The Denver Post*

"A deeply meditated and achieved art."

—*The New York Times Book Review*

"A paean to the sheltering world of local, rural schooling . . . by turns evocative and unsettlingly anachronistic."   —*The Boston Globe*

"*The Whistling Season* won me over on the first page. . . . The prose positively sings in this elegy to the one-room schoolhouse and the kind of community it once fostered."   —*Minneapolis Star Tribune*

"[Doig] is masterful at portraying the emotional complexities of family and community through the eyes of a precocious youngster. . . . The stalwart American virtue of a common public education for all comes through heroically in this novel."   —*The Seattle Times*

"*The Whistling Season* is a book to pass on to your favorite readers: a story of lives of active choice, lived actively."

—Rick Bass, *Publishers Weekly*

"Very satisfying. . . . These intriguing and unpredictable characters come together in surprising and uplifting ways. This is an affectionate, heartwarming tale."   —*Library Journal*

"This is [Doig's] best novel since the marvelous *English Creek*. . . . [*The Whistling Season*] has all the charm of old-school storytelling, from Dickens to Laura Ingalls Wilder. . . . An entrancing new chapter in the literature of the West."   —*Booklist* (starred review)

The Whistling Season

IVAN DOIG

The Whistling Season

A HARVEST BOOK
HARCOURT, INC.
Orlando   Austin   New York   San Diego   Toronto   London

To Ann and Marshall Nelson

In at the beginning
and reliably fantastic all the way

Requests for permission to make copies of any part of the work should
be submitted online at www.harcourt.com/contact or mailed to the
following address: Permissions Department, Harcourt, Inc.,
6277 Sea Harbor Drive, Orlando, Florida 32887-6777.

www.HarcourtBooks.com

The Library of Congress has cataloged the hardcover edition as follows:
Doig, Ivan.
The whistling season/Ivan Doig.—1st ed.
p. cm.
1. Brothers and sisters—Fiction. 2. Irrigation projects—Fiction.
3. Housekeepers—Fiction. 4. Teachers—Fiction. 5. Widowers—Fiction.
6. Montana—Fiction. I. Title.
PS3554.O415W48 2006
813'.54—dc22 2005025457
ISBN 978-0-15-101237-4 ISBN 978-0-15-603164-6 (pbk.)

Text set in Adobe Caslon
Designed by Linda Lockowitz

Printed in the United States of America

First Harvest edition 2007
E G I K J H F

1

WHEN I VISIT THE BACK CORNERS OF MY LIFE AGAIN AFTER so long a time, littlest things jump out first. The oilcloth, tiny blue windmills on white squares, worn to colorless smears at our four places at the kitchen table. Our father's pungent coffee, so strong it was almost ambulatory, which he gulped down from suppertime until bedtime and then slept serenely as a sphinx. The pesky wind, the one element we could count on at Marias Coulee, whistling into some weather-cracked cranny of this house as if invited in.

That night we were at our accustomed spots around the table, Toby coloring a battle between pirate ships as fast as his hand could go while I was at my schoolbook, and Damon, who should have been at his, absorbed in a secretive game of his own devising called domino solitaire. At the head of the table, the presiding sound was the occasional turning of a newspaper page. One has to imagine our father reading with his finger, down the column of rarely helpful want ads in the *Westwater Gazette* that had come in our week's gunnysack of mail and provisions, in his customary search for a colossal but underpriced team of workhorses, and that inquisitive finger now stubbing to a stop at one particular heading. To this day I can hear the signal of amusement that line of type drew out of him. Father had a short, sniffing way of laughing, as if anything funny had to prove it to his nose first.

I glanced up from my geography lesson to discover the newspaper making its way in my direction. Father's thumb was crimped down onto the heading of the ad like the holder of a divining rod striking water. "Paul, better see this. Read it to the multitude."

I did so, Damon and Toby halting what they were at to try to take in those five simple yet confounding words:

CAN'T COOK BUT DOESN'T BITE.

Meal-making was not a joking matter in our household. Father, though, continued to look pleased as could be and nodded for me to keep reading aloud.

> Housekeeping position sought by widow. Sound morals, exceptional disposition. No culinary skills, but A-1 in all other household tasks. Salary negotiable, but must include railroad fare to Montana locality; first year of peerless care for your home thereby guaranteed. Respond to Boxholder, Box 19, Lowry Hill Postal Station, Minneapolis, Minnesota.

Minneapolis was a thousand miles to the east, out of immediate reach even of the circumference of enthusiasm we could see growing in our father. But his response wasted no time in trying itself out on the three of us. "Boys? Boys, what would you think of our getting a housekeeper?"

"Would she do the milking?" asked Damon, ever the cagey one.

That slowed up Father only for a moment. Delineation of house chores and barn chores that might be construed as a logical extension of our domestic upkeep was exactly the sort of issue he liked to take on. "Astutely put, Damon. I see no reason why we can't stipulate that churning the butter begins at the point of the cow."

Already keyed up, Toby wanted to know, "Where she gonna sleep?"

Father was all too ready for this one. "George and Rae have their spare room going to waste now that the teacher doesn't have to board with them." His enthusiasm really was expanding in a hurry. Now our relatives, on the homestead next to ours, were in the market for a lodger, a lack as unbeknownst to them as our need for a housekeeper had been to us two minutes ago.

"Lowry Hill." Father had turned back to the boldface little advertisement as if already in conversation with it. "If I'm not mistaken, that's the cream of Minneapolis."

I hated to point out the obvious, but that chore seemed to go with being the oldest son of Oliver Milliron.

"Father, we're pretty much used to the house muss by now. It's the cooking part you say you wouldn't wish on your worst enemy."

He knew—we all knew—I had him there.

Damon's head swiveled, and then Toby's, to see how he could possibly deal with this. For miles around, our household was regarded with something like a low fever of consternation by every woman worthy of her apron. As homestead life went, we were relatively prosperous and "bad off," as it was termed, at the same time. Prosperity, such as it was, consisted of payments coming in from the sale of Father's drayage business back in Manitowoc, Wisconsin. The "bad off" proportion of our situation was the year-old grave marker in the Marias Coulee cemetery. Its inscription, chiseled into all our hearts as well as the stone, read *Florence Milliron, Beloved Wife and Mother (1874– 1908)*. As much as each of the four of us missed her at other times, mealtimes were a kind of tribal low point where we contemplated whatever Father had managed to fight onto the table this time. "'Tovers, everyone's old favorite!" he was apt to announce desperately as he set before us leftover hash on its way to becoming leftover stew.

Now he resorted to a lengthy slurp of his infamous coffee and came up with a response to me, if not exactly a reply:

"These want ads, you know, Paul—there's always some give to them. It only takes a little bargaining. If I were a wagering man, I'd lay money Mrs. Minneapolis there isn't as shy around a cookstove as she makes herself out to be."

"But—" My index finger pinned down the five tablet-bold words of the heading.

"The woman was in a marriage," Father patiently overrode the evidence of the newsprint, "so she had to have functioned in a kitchen."

With thirteen-year-old sagacity, I pointed out: "Unless her husband starved out."

"Hooey. Every woman can cook. Paul, get out your good pen and paper."

THIS JILTED OLD HOUSE AND ALL THAT IT HOLDS, EVEN empty. If I have learned anything in a lifetime spent overseeing schools, it is that childhood is the one story that stands by itself in every soul. As surely as a compass needle knows north, that is what draws me to these remindful rooms as if the answer I need by the end of this day is written in the dust that carpets them.

The wrinkled calendar on the parlor wall stops me in my tracks. It of course has not changed since my last time here. Nineteen fifty-two. Five years, so quickly passed, since the Marias Coulee school board begged the vacant old place from me for a month while they repaired the roof of their teacherage and I had to come out from the department in Helena to go over matters with them. What I am startled to see is that the leaf showing on the calendar—October—somehow stays right across all the years: that 1909 evening of *Paul, get out your good pen and paper,* the lonely teacher's tacking up of something to relieve these bare walls so long after that, and my visit now under such a changed sky of history.

The slyness of calendars should not surprise me, I suppose. Passing the newly painted one-room school, our school, this morning as I drove out in my state government car, all at once I was again at that juncture of time when Damon and Toby and I, each in our turn, first began to be aware that we were not quite of our own making and yet did not seem to be simply re-warmed 'tovers of our elders, either. How could I, who back there at barely thirteen realized that I must struggle awake every morning of my life before anyone else in the house to wrest myself from the grip of my tenacious dreams, be the offspring of a man who slept solidly as a railroad tie? And Damon, fists-up Damon, how could he derive from our peaceable mother? Ready or not, we were being introduced to ourselves, sometimes in a fashion as hard to follow as our father's reading finger. Almost any day in the way stations of childhood we passed back and forth between, prairie homestead and country school, was apt to turn into a fresh puzzle piece of life. Something I find true even yet.

It is Toby, though, large-eyed prairie child that he was, whom I sensed most as I slowed there at the small old school with its common room and the bank of windows away from its weather side. Damon or I perhaps can be imagined taking our knocks from fate and putting ourselves back into approximately what we seemed shaped to be, if we had started off on some other ground of life than that of Marias Coulee. But Toby was breath and bone of this place, and later today when I must go into Great Falls to give the county superintendents, rural teachers, and school boards of Montana's fifty-six counties my edict, I know it will be their Tobys, their schoolchildren produced of this soil and the mad valors of homesteaders such as Oliver Milliron, that they will plead for.

2

THE NEWS OF OUR HOUSEKEEPER-TO-BE GALLOPED TO SCHOOL
with us that next morning, or rather, charged ahead of Damon
and me in the form of Toby excitedly whacking his heels against
the sides of his put-upon little mare, Queenie.

"I bet she'll have false teeth, old Mrs. Minneapolis will,"
Damon announced as we rode. "Bet you a black arrowhead she
does." Before I could say anything he spat in his right hand,
thrust it toward me, and invoked "Spitbath shake," the most
binding kind there was.

I was not ready to stake anything on this housekeeper matter. "You know Father doesn't like for us to bet."

Damon just grinned.

"Let's get a move on," I told him, "before Toby laps us."

As soon as we topped the long gumbo hill at our end of the
coulee, the other horseback contingents of schoolchildren loped
or lolled into view from their customary directions, each family
cluster as identifiable to us as ourselves in a looking-glass. Toby
by racing ahead had caught up to a dilemma. Should he go tear-
ing off to as many troupes of schoolcomers as he could reach, or

make straight for the schoolhouse and crow our news to the whole school at once?

He settled for the Pronovosts, the newcomers who joined us every morning at the section-line gate.

"Izzy! Gabe! Everybody!" That general salutation was to Inez, riding double behind Isidor. She was in Toby's grade and sweet on him, an entangling alliance he did not quite know what to do with. "Guess what?"

Whatever capacity for conjecture existed in the three minimally washed faces turned our way, it surely did not stretch to the notion of domestic help. The Pronovosts were project people, although the distinction between those and drylanders such as us was shrinking fast. Father already was spending less time on farming and more on hauling wares from the Westwater railhead to the irrigation project camp nearest us, the one called the Big Ditch; the father of the Pronovosts drove workhorses on the gigantic diversion canal under construction there, that breed of old-time earth-moving teamster called a dirt skinner. Not just by coincidence, the Pronovost kids were skinny as greyhounds—a family their size living in a construction camp tent was never going to be overfed.

After hearing out Toby's feverish recitation, Isidor, who did most of the talking for the three of them, granted: "Pretty daggone good, it sounds like." I noticed he gave his younger brother, Gabriel, a strong look, the button-your-lip kind I recognized because I had given Damon enough of them. But from where she was perched behind Isidor's saddle, small Inez piped up:

"Is she gonna be your new ma?"

Instantly Damon reddened, and Toby, mouth open, for once failed to find anything to say.

I spoke up. "Housekeepers are all as old as the hills, aren't they, Damon."

The bunch of us clucked our horses along faster. To Toby's dismay, Miss Trent already was banging on the iron triangle that served as a bell by the time we got the horses picketed to graze out back of the school. Miss Trent was death on whisperers, so his news needed to stay sealed tight in him until morning recess. Then, though, he burst into the schoolyard in full voice.

"—all the way from Minnieapples!" he concluded on a high note to a ready audience of the Stoyanov brothers and the two sets of Drobny twins and gangly Verl Fletcher and his shy sister Lily Lee. At the edge of his following, Inez Pronovost listened to it all again breathlessly.

"She gonna make your beds?"

"Who's in charge of spankings, then—your pa or her?"

"Will she bring one of those featherdust things along with, you think?"

As the questions flew, Toby fended as best he could, all the while trying to gravitate toward the rival contingent at the other end of the schoolground, consisting of the Johannsons and the Myrdals and Eddie Turley, and gather them into his oration about the wonderful imminence of our housekeeper. Worried, I tried to keep an eye on the factions while Grover Stinson and I played catch with Grover's ancient soft-as-a-sock baseball, as the pair of us evidently were going to do throughout every recess until our throwing arms dropped off. Damon was busy taking on Isidor and Gabriel at horseshoe pitching. The clangs as he hit ringers meant he was on a streak hardly anything could interrupt. The littler kids chugged around amid the rest of us in their own games of tag and such. At the moment, peace reigned. All it would take for the schoolyard to erupt, though, would be for Toby to draw a few of the bunch trailing him with intrigued questions into range of the other group. For it was the hallmark of a Marias Coulee recess that the Slavs and the

Swedes never got along together, and Eddie Turley didn't get along with anybody.

I will say for Miss Trent, whenever Milo Stoyanov and Martin Myrdal or the Johannson brothers and the Drobny male twins or some other combination blew up and went at each other, she would wade in and sort them out but good. However, plenty of fisticuffs and taunts and general incitement could take place by the time she ever managed to reach the scene, and those of us who a minute before were neutrality personified might abruptly find ourselves on one side or the other, right in it. Has it ever been any different, from Eton on down? Over the years in that sanguinary schoolyard I'd traded bloody noses with both Milo and Martin, and Damon naturally had more than his share of tussles with each. But ever since we had become motherless, that had all changed. Some invisible spell of sympathy or charity or at least lenience had been dropped over us, granting us something like noncombatant status in the grudge fights. Neither Damon nor I was particularly comfortable with this unsought absolution—it had a whiff of pity-the-poor-orphans to it—and Toby was too young to grasp it, but the schoolyard community's unspoken agreement to spare us in the nationality brawls did have its advantages.

Here was where my worry came in. I somehow sensed that Toby's innocent bragging about our acquisition of a housekeeper might poke a hole in the spell and render us fit for combat again before we quite knew it.

Tobe's always considerable luck was holding, though, as I watched him scoot free from his first audience, cross the schoolyard at a high run, and start in successfully on the taller forest of the Scandinavian boys and overgrown Eddie.

Until Carnelia Craig emerged from the girls' outhouse.

Carnelia always spent a good deal of recess time enthroned

in there, probably to spare herself from the childish hurlyburly of the schoolyard. By a fluke of fate, with nearly two years of Marias Coulee classroom yet to be endured, she already was the oldest girl in school, and it showed. The front of her dress was growing distinct points, and her attitude was already fully formed: life had unfairly deposited Carnelia Craig among unruly peasants such as us instead of putting her in charge of, say, Russia. Admittedly, her family was of a different cut than any of the rest of ours because her father was employed by the state of Montana. He was the county agent, working out of the nearby Marias River agricultural experiment station, and her mother had taught homemaker courses before Carnelia deigned to be born. So, the Craigs were up there a bit on such social scale as we had. And in a strange way, I frequently felt I comprehended more of Carnelia's lofty approach to life, jaded as it was, than I did of my father's latest castles in the air. The reason for that was all too simple. She and I were oldest enemies.

Even yet I can't fully account for the depth of passion, of the worst sort, between us. After all, with more than a dozen years apiece in this world, together we amounted to a responsible age, or should have. But Carnelia and I were the entire seventh grade of the Marias Coulee school, as we had been the entire first, second, third, fourth, fifth, and sixth, and there was not a minute of any of it when the pair of us did not resent sitting stuck together there like a two-headed calf until that farthest day when we would graduate from the eighth grade. Until then there would be battle between us, and it was just a matter of choosing new ground for it from time to time.

As soon as I saw Carnelia halt, turn her head a bit to one side as if hearing something sublime the rest of us had missed, and then aim herself straight toward Toby, I knew the terrain of hostilities ahead. Even Carnelia's family did not have a housekeeper.

I yelped "Last catch!" to Grover while throwing him the ball and raced over to head off Carnelia.

Too late. By the time I got there she was practically atop Toby, her hands on her knees in the manner of Florence Nightingale bending over a poor fallen boy, and crooning her first insidious question:

"Tobias, will she tuck you and Damon and Paul in at night?"

"Huh uh!" Toby answered with the terrifying honesty of a second-grader. "She's gonna sleep at George and Rae's. I asked."

"Oh, is she," Carnelia noted for posterity. "Not a live-in, then," she lamented, evidently for Toby's sake and Damon's and mine. I tried to break through the circle around Toby, but Eddie Turley chose that moment to get me in a casual headlock around the neck and I barely managed to croak out, "Pick on somebody your own size, Carnelia!" By now Damon had tumbled to what was impending, and he yelled out in fury, "Carnelia hag, leave him alone!" But he couldn't reach there from the horseshoe pit in time either.

Carnelia was smart—worse, she was clever—and what she asked next sounded for all the world like a note of concern for the well-being of the Milliron household:

"But then she'll have to get up ever so early to come over and cook your breakfast, won't she, Tobias?"

"She can't cook," Toby confided sadly to what was now the entire listening schoolyard. Then he brightened. "But the newspaper says she doesn't bite."

That did it. We slunk home after that school day with even the Pronovosts barely able to contain their smirks.

⁓

"*Y*OU WERE NIGHT-HERDING AGAIN," DAMON MURMURED, AS if I didn't know.

By then it was Sunday, and my dream the night before had nothing to do—for a change—with the teasing circle of Hell that the schoolyard had been for him and Toby and me all week long, and everything to do with what lay in wait for us at Sunday dinner.

"Bad?" I said back in the same low tone he had used. Just out of hearing behind us, Toby romped with our dog, Houdini, both of them hoping for an ill-destined jackrabbit to cross their path. "Worse than usual?"

Damon considered while he reached for the next pebble of the right size. He was in one of his baseball phases at the time and had to throw rocks at fence posts the whole way along the section-line road to George and Rae's place. He wound up and fired, frowning when he missed the post. "Usual is bad enough, isn't it?"

Naturally Damon figured that my excursions while asleep were nightmares. It was nothing that simple. I rapidly thought back over this particular nighttime spell and decided against describing it to him in precise detail. I had tried that before. "I keep telling you, give me a poke when it bothers you that much."

"Paul, I'm scared to. You're like somebody one of those mesmerers—"

"Mesmerists."

"—yeah, like somebody one of those has put to sleep." Hypnosis? Even if I had the knack of administering it to myself, the nocturnal state of my mind was not subject to command.

We trudged on toward the beckoning finger of smoke from the kitchen stovepipe next door—which in homestead terms meant half a mile away—neither of us knowing what more to say. Until Damon, who could all but wink with his voice when he wanted to, intoned:

"Anybody I know? In your big dream?"

I had to laugh. "What do you think?"

"I can just see her." Squinching his face into the approxima-
tion of a prune, he mimicked: *"Cat got your tongue, boys?"*

It was like that most Sundays. Once in a great while the
Sabbath-day invitation to Father and his omnivorous boys
would come from the samaritan Stinsons, Grover's parents, or
from the reliably civic Fletcher family if school board business
needed tending to, but standardly we were asked over to our
Schricker relatives' for Sunday dinner. The meal itself we always
were surpassingly grateful for. Rae Schricker was our mother's
cousin, and with the same calm flint-gray eyes and impression
marks of amusement at the corners of her lips, she resembled
Mother to an extent that sometimes made my throat seize up.
Certainly Rae seemed to regard herself as Mother's proxy on
earth at the cookstove. Any of us would have had to grant that
Mrs. Stinson's mincemeat pie and Mrs. Fletcher's cream puffs
could not be bettered anywhere. But Rae operated on the assumption this was our one square meal of the week and tucked
ham with yams or fried chicken with mashed potatoes and gravy
into us until we wobbled in our chairs. Meanwhile, George in
his whiskery way would attempt to preside over the feast with
encouraging injunctions of his own: "Oliver, heavens, you're out
of coffee already! Toby, here you go, the wishbone!" I say *attempt*
because unlike us, George still very much had a mother, right
down there at the opposite end of the dinner table. At these
Sunday repasts Aunt Eunice, as we boys were forced to address
her, ate sparingly as a bird, preferring to peck in our direction.

"Old Aunt YEW-*niss*," Damon now crooned in rhythm to
his pitcher's motion, and bopped a post dead-center.

"Go easy," I warned, with a glance toward Toby as he raced
Houdini to catch up with us.

"Maybe she won't've heard," Damon muttered to me.

"And maybe the cat will get her tongue for a change," I muttered back. "But I wouldn't count on it."

Father was sending us over first this Sunday noon, as usual. "Tell George and Rae I'll be there in a jiffy," he instructed, his favorite measure of time. It was strange how many last-minute chores in the horse barn demanded his immediate attention when visiting with Eunice Schricker was the other choice. First, though, he had made sure to curry us up, ensuring that we scrubbed behind our ears, slicking our hair down for us with the scented stickum he called "eau de barber," and judiciously working us over with a comb the size of a rat-tail file. It was then that Damon, who hated to have his hair parted, pulled away from under the comb and demanded to know: "How is she our aunt?"

A perfectly sound question, actually. By what genealogical bylaw did we accord aunthood to our mother's cousin's husband's mother? Particularly when she showed no affinity with the human family?

"By circumlocution," Father said, which I resolved to look up. "I want you boys," he tapped Damon with the comb, "to tend to your manners over there. It's good practice for when our general domestication happens."

When, indeed. By mutual instinct, Damon and I had not mentioned to Father the teasing we were taking at school about the nonbiting housekeeper. (*"Does she come with a muzzle?" "Is she so old she's a gummer?"*) And we were managing to keep a stopper in Toby by telling him over and over that our tormentors were merely jealous. But the housekeeper matter was wearing us down day by day. The letter had gone off to Minneapolis, my best Palmer penmanship setting forth Father's much mulled-over wage offer, and all we had to show for it so far was red ears from the torrent of razzing. I longed for our

phantom correspondent, whoever she proved to be, to material-
ize as such a model of domestic efficiency that the rest of Marias
Coulee would swoon in tribute; but at the same time I harbored
doubts that I could not quite put words to. Besides, Father more
than once had warned us not to get our hopes up too high, although plainly his were elbowing the moon.

So, off we went to the lioness's den, two of us longing for
this Sunday to be over and Toby impatient for it to start. No
sooner had Rae let us in the kitchen door and slipped us an early
bite apiece of the gingerbread she had just baked, than the sort
of thing Damon and I dreaded was issued to us from the parlor.

"Is that those boys?" came that voice, snappish as a whip.
"Don't they have manners enough to say hello?"

His face full of smile and gingerbread crumbs, Toby charged
in, we two apprehensively trailing after. There Aunt Eunice sat,
as if not having bothered to budge from the week before, folded
into her spindleback rocking chair, the toes of her antique black
shoes barely reaching the floor. George as usual was seated stiffly
on the horsehair sofa at the other end of the room. As I look
back on it, the Schricker family line contradicted the principle of
inherited traits. You would have had to go to their back teeth to
find any resemblance between George, his ever-hopeful broad
countenance wreathed in companionable reddish beard, and the
elderly purse-mouthed wrathy figure, half his size, whom he felt
the need to address as "Mum." Sunday-clad in her Victorian
lavender dress, crochet hook viciously at work on yet another
doily to foist onto Rae—the parlor looked snowed on, so many
of its surfaces were covered with this incessant lacework—Aunt
Eunice was the obvious victor over any number of challenges of
time. Thus far, the twentieth century had had no effect on her
except to make her look more like a leftover daguerreotype.

George beamed in relief at us, desperate for any diversion from making conversation with his mother, and we variously mumbled or blurted our greetings back. As Damon beat an immediate retreat to the Chinese checker board kept on the tea table by the window and I edged dutifully toward the far end of the sofa, George said from the corner of his mouth: "No word yet?" I shook my head. He sighed a little, which indicated to me that he too had been receiving an earful on the subject of our housekeeper.

Right now, though, Aunt Eunice was all sparkle. "Toby, come here by me," she coaxed as if calling a puppy, and next thing, our sunshine boy was groaningly hoisted onto what there was of her knees.

Damon scowled but did not look up from where he was devising across-the-board jumps with his marbles, and I sat there trying to appear congenial. It was part of the Sunday ritual that where the other two of us drew dark mutters from Aunt Eunice about "young roughnecks" and "overgrown noiseboxes," she literally lapped up Toby. Out of her sleeve now came a lace-edged handkerchief, which she put to work on his gingerbread traces. "Poor thing, sent off from home looking like a mudpie."

Toby squirmed adorably while she clucked over him, and I mentally told him to enjoy being doted on while he could. The minute he grew too big for Aunt Eunice's scanty lap, he would be consigned to rogue boyhood with Damon and me.

"And school, dear?" she probed. "How are you getting on at school these days?"

Bless him, Toby thought to look my way before answering, and I twitched my mouth in warning. With effort, he stuck to "I have perfect attendance, same like last year."

With an *oof* Aunt Eunice discharged him from his bony

perch, meanwhile declaring, "What a pity it doesn't run in the family. That father of yours would be late for his own funeral."

"Now, now, Mum," George protested weakly. Damon, thunder on his brow, clattered marbles into place to signal Toby to join him at the checker board. It was up to me to defend Father, seldom a rewarding task: "He had to tend the workhorses, is all."

"As per usual," Aunt Eunice crowed. Now that I had drawn her attention, I could be worked on to the fullest. She lifted her chin as if sighting in on me with it, while her face took on an expression of grim relish. "So, you, Paul—"

"Yes, Aunt Eunice?" I was not going to let her corner me into the cat-and-tongue situation.

"—does that teacher of yours make you learn anything by heart? I always stood first in my class at elocution." Who could doubt it?

"I can say '*The boy stood on the burning deck*—'" Damon volunteered with deadly innocence. I shot him a look that said *Don't*, knowing how his version ran:

> —*his feet were covered with blisters.*
> *He tore his pants on a rusty nail*
> *So then he wore his sister's.*

Luckily, Aunt Eunice wanted no competition. "Your geography and physiology and spelling bees and all that will only carry you so far," she admonished, still intent on me. A Nile of vein stood out on her frail temple as she worked herself up. What was behind such ardor? Rage of age? Life's revenge on the young? Or simply Aunt Eunice's natural vinegar pickling her soul? In any case, something about me that Sunday had set her off. "I know you have your nose in a book all the time, but those are not the only lessons in store for you. When you get out in the world, Paul Milliron, you'll see." Pursing up dramatically, Aunt Eunice delivered in singsong fashion:

> *Life lays its burden on every soul's shoulder,*
> *We each have a cross or a trial to bear.*
> *If we miss it in youth it will come when we're older*
> *And fit us as close as the garments we wear.*

Not even George knew what to meet that with but abject silence.

Just in time came the bang of the kitchen screen door and further sounds of Father arriving. "Hello, Rae. It smells delicious around here. Brought you a sack of Roundup coal, not that slack stuff. Remind me to take the scuttle out and fill it for you." His theory evidently was that if he bustled enough, it would seem as if he had been here all the while. "Oh, the nourishment is about ready? Give me a minute to freshen up and reacquaint the boys with the washbasin, and we're yours to command."

He stuck his head through the parlor doorway, his face ruddy from shaving and his raven-black hair slicked back the same as ours. "Eunice, my goodness!" he exclaimed, as if surprised to find her there. "Aren't you looking regal today."

Soon after, we sat up to the table and began to do justice to Rae's fried chicken and baking-powder biscuits and milk gravy and compulsory vegetables, with the promise of that gingerbread spurring Damon and Toby and me to clean our loaded plates. Father and George talked crops and weather and horses and the doings of neighbors, the argot that farmers had been speaking since seed time on the Euphrates. For while those generous Sunday noons were presented to our cookless household as rituals with victuals, I am convinced it was the table talk that nourished Father and George in their unforeseen lives as adventurers in homesteading.

"The steam plow is going to be at Stinson's place anyway, why don't you go ahead and break that five acres on your east end? I'll throw in with you; I have that couple of acres of gumbo around the Lake District that needs doing."

"I don't know, though, Oliver. I'm stretched as it is, to handle what I planted this year."

These were not fluff-filled men. High-toned and fanciful as he could be, Father put in staggering days of manual labor, for others as well as himself. I always thought that the world got two for the price of one, when Father's personality was counted into the earthly mix. One minute he could summarily kill a rattlesnake with a barrel stave, and the next, he might be fashioning out loud a theory of the evolution of the human thumb. In an earlier time, Father would have been the kind to take ship for the farthest places; I can see him as someone like the ever-curious naturalist Joseph Banks, sailing around and around the world with Captain Cook. His inborn hunger for a fresh horizon hopelessly mismatched him for the drayage business handed down to him, in a set-in-its-ways Wisconsin city that wasn't even Milwaukee. But one last unexpected unfolding of the American map came to Oliver Milliron's rescue. As the finale of homesteading, the federal government offered a vast wager: western dry land thrown open free for the taking, if you were willing to uproot yourself and invest the requisite years of your life on that remote virgin patch of earth. With Montana singing in his ear, he had piled everything with the name Milliron on it—including Mother and us; I was five at the time, Damon four, and Toby merely a gleam in Father's eye—into an "emigrant car," one of those Great Northern Railway boxcars that held our furniture and dishes wrapped in bedding and a few Wisconsin keepsakes at one end, and pallets for us to sleep on at the other. Astutely, as it proved, a second boxcar brought the best one of Father's drays that had conveyed beer and meat through the cramped streets of Manitowoc, and his top two teams of workhorses. Marias Coulee awaited us, a promised land needing only agricultural husbandry and rain. Within a year, George and Rae followed from their becalmed life of dairy farming near Eau Claire, equally ready to try a new point of the compass.

"Neither one of you works a field enough," came a certain voice again now, sharp as a pinch. "My place looks like a cat scratched around on it when you're through with your so-called plowing."

And, I must always make myself admit, just as much a homesteader as either of the field-weathered men at that table was Eunice Schricker. George may have thought he was putting two states between him and his mother when he made his move west, but he only managed to transmit Montana fever. In no time at all she too had alit into Marias Coulee, filing her home-stead claim on the acreage next to George and Rae's, living on it in her shanty for proving-up purposes, and giving George and our father constant fits as they tried to farm it for her in any-thing resembling the way she wanted it done.

Sod was comparatively safe ground, so to speak, in these dinner-table contentions. I was hoping that the agricultural trio would stay dug in on dryland plowing until past dessert. But keeping tabs on Aunt Eunice even more than usual this perilous Sunday, I knew from the instant her chin took on that particular lift and she aimed it dead straight at Father, we were in for it.

"Household help always steals," Aunt Eunice announced, as if her opinion had been broadly solicited. "I am surprised some-one of your experience of life doesn't know that, Oliver. You watch. This housekeeper of yours, if she ever manifests herself, will be light-fingered. They all are."

Nervously, Toby looked at Father.

"Eunice, please, the poor soul hasn't even set foot across our threshold yet," Father protested. "Besides, as long as it's the dust and the clutter, she's welcome to everything we have."

"Go right ahead and make jokes," Aunt Eunice snapped. "If you end up robbed blind, don't say I didn't tell you."

"I never would," Father said levelly. "Eunice, all I am trying to do is to bring a bit of order out of a houseful of chaos. The boys pitch in as best they can, but they're not laundresses, downstairs maids, seamstresses—"

"—or cooks," Damon contributed.

"—or cooks," Father picked that up gamely. "So if it takes a housekeeper to set us to rights, why on earth shouldn't we get one?" He scanned the table in beleaguered fashion. "Is anyone else going to take mercy on that last Missouri T-bone?"

Rae passed him the final chicken drumstick. "Keep your strength up, Oliver."

Aunt Eunice was not going to be deterred or detoured. "Times change, they say," she uttered as if not believing any of it. And immediately followed up with:

> *Yet, Experience spake,*
> *the old ways are best;*
> *steadfast for steadfast's sake,*
> *passing the eons' test.*

Again, general silence met her spirited recitation.

Aunt Eunice appeared to expect no understanding from this gathering. "Oh, well," she fanned herself with a tiny veined hand, "soon I'll be dead."

That particular utterance of hers never failed to drive an icicle straight through the heart of every male in the room, except Toby. He turned as soulful as a seven-year-old could. Around most of the rest of the table, I could have predicted the responses. George's tone broke slightly as he tried to make the usual hearty assertion, "Mum, you're sound as a dollar." Then Father: if Father nicked himself shaving he thought he was two feet into the grave. Even worse, invocations of mortality, with Mother's memory so raw to him, always turned him as adrift as a castaway. Damon's eyes narrowed; if Aunt Eunice was on her way to the hereafter, it plainly seemed to him to be by a highly roundabout route.

Rae, who had been hearing Aunt Eunice predict imminent demise for years, merely lifted an eyebrow as if interested in the prospect. But then I caught her notice across the table and she turned concerned.

"Paul, you look a bit peaked."

Certainly the inside of my head had gone pale. Against my will, the floodgate of remembrance had been jarred open by Aunt Eunice's icy utterance, and my dream from the night before poured back to me.

Since that time I have had nearly half a century of indelible dreams. People are always telling me they wish they could remember exactly what their dreams were about, but I wonder if they have any idea what that means. Only the few persons closest to me know anything of the quirk that causes the roamings within my sleep to live on in me intact in every incised detail and every echoing syllable. My wife learned, in our first nights together, that my mind does not shut down at midnight; it goes visiting in the neighborhoods of imagination and recapitulation and other nocturnal regions that do not quite have names. Damon could have warned her. Everyone is familiar with the concept known as amnesia: a departure of memory. My condition, as I have gingerly explored it, is best called simply mnesia: protraction of recall. Dreams slide over into my memory, in a way that I am helpless to regulate; as well as I can describe it, my dream experiences become something like frescoes on the countless walls of the brain. Not that this mental trick will ever win me a job in a sideshow. Except for the acuity I am credited with by my supporters in state government, reward for the right guesses I have made in the administration of education down through the years, there seems to be no other particular power of mind in my mnesiac case. As often as anyone else, I lose track of my fountain pen somewhere between the ink bottle and whatever awaits signature on my desk. But I never forget a dream. They stay with me like annals of the Arabian Nights, except that mine now go far beyond a thousand and one.

So it was with the episode that had everyone at the Sunday table cocking an eye at me now. Dreams—at least mine—are scavenger hunts to anywhere, but I could sort out some of the sources of this one. When we arrived west on the train of emigrant cars and the boxcar next to ours was unloaded at the Westwater siding, out came a casket, empty; we never did know if it represented some settler's pessimism or was merely in shipment or what. The version of it delivered in my dream was not empty, and Mother was missing, and Damon and I and Toby—who did not exist at the time—were by ourselves in the doorway of another boxcar, one so high off the railroad bed we could not figure out how to hop down. Sitting out there supervisory in the buffalo grass was Aunt Eunice in her rocking chair. Father and, for some reason, his fellow school board member Joe Fletcher were laboring to lift the coffin onto the unhitched dray. "They forgot the horses," Damon kept fretting as we toed the brink of the boxcar, wanting to go to the aid of the men. Aunt Eunice was the only person around who could help us down, but she wasn't about to. "Don't let those boys at that," she bossed the men struggling with the casket's brass handles. "They'll drop it."

"At least we know you're not off your feed, Paul," Father deduced from my empty plate, his words snapping me out of the dream visitation. Leaning my way at the table, he reached to feel my forehead with the back of his hand. I had no idea what he would find there, fever or chill, but the diagnosis never took place. Instead came a terrifying wail from Toby:

"AUNT EUNICE, I DON'T WANT YOU TO D-D-DIE!"

This commotion took some while to settle down, Toby sobbing the front of Father's shirt wet and then Rae's blouse. I suspected Aunt Eunice of being secretly pleased, but outwardly she showed only impatience as she at last directed: "Oh, for heaven's sake, let me have the child."

Still full of sniffles, Toby went to her, the lifting *oof* was given, and he perched unsteadily on those venerable knees. "Mustn't cry," she ordered, dabbing him dry with the lace hanky. "Now I want you to be a good boy all week, and tell me all your doings next Sunday."

As Toby blinked and tried to muster a shiny-eyed smile, she added as piteously as before:

"If I'm spared until then."

THE LETTER WAS THERE WHEN WALT STINSON DROPPED OFF our sack of provisions and mail the Friday of the next week.

Father plucked it up as if it were the royal invitation he had been expecting. But he tapped the envelope thoughtfully against the fingertips of his other hand a few times before sitting down to slit it open with his jackknife blade.

The three of us crowded around him at his place at the kitchen table. The page full of staccato handwriting was too much for Toby. "Read it to us," he implored. Damon's lips were moving silently as he tried to scan the closely worded sheet of paper over Father's shoulder.

"I think Paul should be in charge of the elucidation," Father said as soon as he had figured out the gist of the letter.

The "Dear Mr. Milliron" salutation and the rest of the formal part of the letter I read off as if it had come from Shakespeare himself; perhaps Aunt Eunice's nagging about elocution had made more impression than I thought. I slowed up markedly, though, at the penultimate paragraph and then the ultimate:

> *The salary you have suggested is, may I say, not quite adequate to my current needs. Fortunately, however, I do see a way out of impasse on this matter. Were I able to draw my first three months of wages ahead of time, that would be a sufficiency to enable me to take my leave of Minneapolis and join your employ.*
>
> *If you will send the wage sum and the ticket price by Western Union, I will embark on the most immediate train for Montana.*
>
> Sincerely yours,
Rose Llewellyn

"Rose Llewellyn," Toby all but rolled in the sound of it. "That's a swell name, isn't it, Paul? Damon, don't you like it too?"

Damon, though, was rocked back on his heels by something else. "We have to pay her until after Christmas to even get her here?"

"Wait, there's something on the back," I said, seeing the ghost line of ink that had come through the paper. I turned the letter over and read aloud:

> *P.S. May I say, Mr. Milliron, you write a splendid hand. It is inspirational to correspond with one to whom penmanship is not a lost art.*

I tried to hide a grin of pride. Meanwhile Father, who had not been heard from during any of this, cleared his throat.

My brothers and I expectantly sank to our chairs at the table.

Father still said nothing. As we watched, he held the letter up in front of him and ran his other hand back and forth through his hair, as if massaging his next thought. I still wonder what the outcome would have been if Houdini had not chosen that moment to get up from his spot by the stove, shake himself vigorously, and plop back down in a settling cloud of dog hair and dust. Father took so long he might have been counting the motes, but eventually he straightened up in his chair, gave a little sigh, and sent the letter across the tabletop in my direction.

"Paul, get out your pen. We have to draft a telegram of surrender."

WHAT A TIRELESS INSTRUCTOR MEMORY IS. DON'T I WISH I could put it on my department's payroll. Its hours are unpredictable, however. Keeping an eye on the time today as I must, I see that the future—with whatever lasting recognition it will attach to October of 1957—is about to pay a visit. I have to make myself go out for a look.

At least the day itself seems neutral, which does not happen often at Marias Coulee. I think back to the winters here and shiver, and to the dry summers when Father and George and the other homesteaders watched as cloud after cloud dragged across the Rockies and the tufts of rain would catch on the distant peaks and be of no help to their fields. But around me now, the sky could not be more guiltlessly empty. Even the wind has nothing to say, for once. The only sound anywhere around is at the pothole pond where waterfowl, passing through with the seasons, sometimes alight. Whistler swans, my lifelong favorite, are the maestros, and geese next, but today it is a few dozen mallards that have migrated in and formed a fleet, with much quacking. Some kind of duck event and they have the prairie to themselves for it, except for me and whatever is passing over.

I search the unmarked blue sky, even though I know the human eye isn't adequate anymore. It is up there more than a hundred miles, the newspapers say. The Russian orbiter, Sputnik, that emulates the moon—and that will have such a tidal pull on our education system. Now that the Soviet Union has sped past this country into space, science will be king, elected by panic. It has already started, in the editorials and legislative rumblings. Those rumblings soon will grow into growls. If I have an enemy in this world, it is the chairman of the appropriations committee. Car dealer from Billings that he is, he knows how many times I have outwitted him. This time, even though it is a borrowed sum for an I.Q. like his, substance of debate is on his side. There will be no mercy on aspects of education that can't be argued as miracle cures in catching up with the Russians in the launching of satellites, such as one-room schools at the thin edges of the counties of Montana. A thousand such schools fall under my jurisdiction.

I have to catch my breath at this barbwire twist of my career. It is as if the person I thought was me—the Paul Milliron known to the world of education—has been eclipsed by this Russian kettle of gadgetry orbiting overhead. Yes, I was the youngest state superintendent of schools in the nation back when I was first elected—inevitably, "the boy wonder of the West" in the *Time* magazine article—and am now the longest-serving. Yes, I took the schools of Montana through the Depression without such wholesale closings. Yes, my depleted department fended tooth and nail during the Second World War when everything was rationed and teachers evaporated daily into the war effort, and again we never closed schools by swipe of the hand. But now it has fallen to me to pronounce the fate of an entire species of schooling, the small prairie arks of education such as the one that was the making of me.

I do not know where to turn. There is no help to be had from the governor's office; governors come and go, and the current one has a date with obscurity. No, I have been singled out—my office has been singled out—to deliver the word to the teachers and school boards of the one-room schools all across the state that there is no place for them in the Age of Sputnik. To some extent I know how it will go, in Great Falls this evening. The convocation of delegates from the rural school systems will include old friends, people I have known since I had my own country classroom. "Mr. Milliron, good to see you," they will say, or "Superintendent, hello again." Not a woman nor a man of them is comfortable calling me "Paul." They likely are not going to want to anyway, after today.

There is time before that yet. For the meeting of another sort where, like Toby, I can at least boast perfect attendance. Back there at memory's depot where Rose stepped down from the train, bringing several kinds of education to the waiting four of us.

3

S̶HE ALIT TO THE PLANKED PLATFORM OF THE WESTWATER depot on feet as dainty as Toby's little ones.

In those days people poured off the afternoon train—it was called that even though it was the only one all day—and peered around like sailors in uncharted latitudes as they waited for their belongings from the baggage car. Babies lulled by the rocking motion of the train were coming awake with shrieks at their new surroundings. Coal dust from the engine tender and the smell of mothballed things gotten out for long journeys clung in the air. Our eyes big with the occasion, Damon and Toby and I couldn't help but stare at the black-clad Belgian boys in the latest colony of families transplanting themselves from Flanders, nor they at us.

Father, who in strongest terms had prescribed best behavior for us at the depot, was standing on tiptoe and teetering a bit as he tried to sort anyone housekeeperly from the swelling crowd of land pilgrims and Big Ditch workmen and homestead people like us on town errands that called for Sunday clothes.

The disembarking passengers were dwindling rapidly,

though, and Father's composed expression along with them, when we heard "Coming through!" and had to move back to dodge the cart of cream cans that were the freight for the train's return run to the mainline. Ever since, I think of Rose as having materialized to us like a genie from a galvanized urn.

For when the creamery cart had passed, there she was on the top step of the nearest Pullman car, assembled in surprising finery, targeting us with an inventive smile which somehow seemed to favor all four of us equally, while at the same time allowing herself to be helped down by an evident admirer from the train.

"Mrs. Llewellyn?" Father addressed her as if wondering out loud.

"Yes, absolutely!"

Before we were done blinking she was across the platform to us, a smartly gloved hand extended. "Oh, I'm exceedingly happy to make your acquaintance, Mr. Milliron. And these are your young men!"

Naturally the three of us puffed up at that promotion in rank. Names were given, handshakes exchanged right down the line—Rose's hand, like the rest of her, was slender but firm—and our notion of the league of widowhood seriously readjusted. Aunt Eunice always excepted, in our experience widows were massive. We felt ourselves shrink in the presence of those great-bosomed old creatures shrouded in dresses as solemnly gray as the gravestones whereunder their late husbands lay. But this mourner of Mr. Llewellyn, whoever he may have been, was all but swathed in a traveling dress the shade of blue flame—Minneapolis evidently did not lack for satin—and there did not seem to be an ounce extra anywhere on her pert frame. In fact, I had noticed Father give a double look as if there must be more of her somewhere.

And she was awfully far from being old.

"Mr. Milliron, let me say at once," the words rushed from her as if she had been holding them in all the way from the train station in Minnesota, "your kind understanding in letting me draw ahead on my wages made a world of difference to my situation. Really it did. I don't know what I would have done but for your letters of—" Here adequate tribute to the Milliron corresponding hand—mine—obviously failed her, and she accorded Father a look of overpowering thankfulness for his existence.

"It was nothing," Father replied, magnificently bland, "an A-1 housekeeper is worth a bit of extra ink."

Rose blushed becomingly. Modesty's rush of blood went well with her gently proportioned cheekbones and the demure expression that came to her lips. Over that, though, there still were the warm brown eyes to contemplate, and the hairdo where wavy curls and fair forehead played peekaboo in a style slightly saucy compared with, well, our notion of widows. None of which caused disturbance in any of us, let me say, including Father. Toby was not advanced enough in life yet to think about it, but Damon and I knew Father was immune to women because he missed Mother so. "I will not go through life resenting a woman because she isn't Florence," he had made plain when George and Rae pointed out that people were known to marry again. "And a stepmother for this tribe of heathens"—he meant us—"is apt to be a cure worse than the affliction." So, he was at his most academic as he sized up—or more likely, sized down—Rose Llewellyn there at the depot. All he wanted was a housekeeper, and this one had come with proclamations to that effect all over her. Besides, there were those three months of wages and a train ticket invested in getting her here.

"Well, shall we be on our way, Mrs. Llewellyn?" His baritone was a bit brusque as he indicated to where our horses and wagon were hitched. He unrooted Damon and me and even Toby with seat-of-the-pants pushes of encouragement toward the baggage car. "The boys—the Milliron young men will gladly fetch whatever you've brought."

An exclamation that defied translation came from Rose and she gave her head a quick little shake, her dark brunette curls flipping on her forehead, as though just then remembering something. She spun half around, her gaze flying across the now nearly empty platform.

Our four sets of eyes followed hers to the tweed-suited traveler who had helped her off the train.

Like her, this individual believed in sparing nothing on appearance. A paisley vest peeked from amid the tweed. A gold watch chain was swagged across the vest. The man was not at all tall, but held himself very straight as if to make the most of what he had. He was lightly built, and an extraordinary amount of him was mustache. It was one of those maximum ones such as I had seen in pictures of Rudyard Kipling, a soup-strainer and a lady-tickler and a fashion show, all in one. Almost as remarkable, he was the only bare-headed man in Montana, the wind teasing his dramatically barbered hair. As we gawked at the stranger he appeared somewhat ruffled, and not merely by the breeze.

Rose went, took him by a wrist, and led him to us.

"Mr. Milliron, Toby, Damon, Paul," she counted off as if we were a select regiment, "may I present my brother, Morris Morgan."

"I'm sorry to intrude on the tableau," the newcomer articulated melodiously. "But I fear it's what comes of an attachment to Rose." My ears and Damon's and possibly Toby's perked up in interest at his cultured way with words. This was like hearing Father meet up with himself.

"Such luck!" Rose said as if it was an explanation for his presence. "That Morrie was able to accompany me."

"Are you also relocating to Montana?" Father inquired pleasantly enough over a handshake he obviously had never expected to make. Morris Morgan appeared not to hear that, instead glancing nervously aside.

"Rose? My chapeau? The ransom, remember?"

Rose's hand flew to her mouth and she whirled toward the train again. There the heavy-set conductor stood waiting, railway cap highly officious, while he twirled a nice new kangaroo-brown Stetson hat on an indicative forefinger.

"A terrible misunderstanding," Rose rushed to tell us in a low but musical voice. "We were under the impression that our tickets would take us all the way to here. But when we had to climb onto this"—she waved a disparaging hand at the branch-line train—"and that man came around demanding fresh tickets, goodness gracious, we had only enough for my fare. And so he grabbed—"

"—confiscated as collateral—" Morris Morgan interpolated, as if interested in the philosophy of it.

"—my poor brother's hat. Mr. Milliron, I hate like everything to ask. But might I draw ahead a trifle more on my wage? Just enough to cover Morris's fare?"

Now it was Father and Damon and I who looked around nervously, to make sure no one was overhearing this. He had soundly counseled the pair of us not to mention to anyone the outlay for a housekeeper we had never laid eyes on, while Toby had got it into his head that sending money to her saved her the trouble of stealing it from us, satisfying Aunt Eunice's warning.

You can't leave a man hatless in the middle of Montana. But Father did say, "If this keeps on, Mrs. Llewellyn, you'll have the house and we'll be in your employ." He counted out the exact fare and handed it to Rose.

Notably, she did not hand the money onward to her brother, but marched over to the conductor and liberated the Stetson herself.

"Now that that's settled," Father was determined to take charge, "Mrs. Llewellyn will ride out with us," nodding in the general direction of Marias Coulee, then inclining civilly but definitively toward the unforeseen brother, "and you we can drop at the hotel." He paused as the newly hatted figure drew himself up straighter yet and pulled out a pocket watch, one of those extravagant ones the size of a turnip, at the end of the gold chain.

Looking at Father instead of the time, Morris Morgan asked: "Does Westwater boast a pawn shop?"

"Not yet," Father was forced to admit.

"Oh dear," said Rose.

I was the one who came up with:

"George and Rae have that attic room."

Even I cannot fashion the kind of extreme dream Rose and Morrie, as we were calling him before long, must have felt themselves caught up in as our wagon wheeled away from a clapboard depot that slumbered back into the prairie twenty-three and a half hours of each day. Westwater then was one of the newest spots on earth, and possibly the most far-flung. A solitary substantial building, the brick hotel, towered three stories over the downtown intersection where buffalo had been the only traffic not many years before. Saloons had been shooed into one section of street north of the railroad tracks. Newcomers could follow their noses, in any of three directions, to the rival livery stables known as the White Barn, the Green Barn, and the Red Barn. But otherwise, the raw town rising out of the open plain seemed to be a mirage missing many of its vapors. Streets as long and open as boulevards arrowed off through the grassland, with only a sporadic house in evidence on each thoroughfare of dirt and weeds. The impression of civic scatter continued out to the flatland horizon, where isolated homestead shanties sat like potted plants. A few dabs of Westwater still lay here and there around us when Father smacked the horses into a mild trot, but pretty plainly our wagon had long since passed the city limits of our passengers' imaginations.

Bang! went something. Rose and Morrie both jumped an inch out of their Minneapolis hides.

Even from behind, the three of us relegated to sitting on sacks of coal and oats in the back of the wagon could tell Father was starting to relish this. Grownups had games of their own, Damon and I already knew and Toby would catch on to in his own good time. "Westwater does boast a shoe emporium," Father was saying past Rose to her disconcerted brother. "If you happen to be equine." With that he threw a wave to Alf Morrissey in his blacksmith shop, and Alf lifted his hammer in salute before tonging a red-hot horseshoe to a new angle on his anvil and giving it another thunderous *bang!*

The road to Marias Coulee put the railroad to shame for straight intent, and by the time Father had clipped off the first mile by giving the horses their head and his captive audience the benefit of his wisdom on several Montana matters, Toby had bounced from sack to sack until he was sitting practically on the coattails of the adults. From that close range, he could not resist. When Father stopped to draw a breath, Toby had his question ready for Rose:

"How'd you get so many pretty names?"

Swift as anything, she looked at him over her shoulder. "So many?"

"Uh huh. Rose and Lou and Ellen."

When all of us but Toby had had our laugh, Rose—smiling that effective smile once again—turned half around to him. "My poor husband always said Llewellyn is the Welsh way to spell Jones, there were so many with his same last name. Here, I'll write it into your hand. That way you'll always carry it with you."

Toby blushed with pleasure as she recited each letter and traced it with her finger into the palm of his small hand. I could tell Damon had been itching to ask something, too. But he simply nodded to himself as if Toby had taken care of it all.

"Now shut your eyes, say *kafoozalum,* and close your hand tight."

Toby did as she instructed.

"There," Rose proclaimed. "You won't ever forget me now."

"You're going to have an admirer there, Mrs. Llewellyn," Father said with a wink at Toby.

"Oh, could you make it 'Rose,' please, sir. I try not to use the other, it's just too—" She let that trail off to wherever things too sad to talk about end up.

I watched Morris Morgan fasten a considering look onto her, then give her a pat as though he was remembering her travail.

"Rose it is, then, if you'll denominate me Oliver," Father concurred. "While we're at it we may as well make it unanimous." He shifted the reins to his left hand and thrust his right toward Morrie for a confirming shake. I see them yet, each settling back on the seat of the wagon after that handclasp performed under the warm gaze of Rose. Father's weather-tanned face, with its work wrinkles running down his cheeks, like a copper coin a bit melted. Morrie smoothing his mighty mustache as if it was newly found. Neither of them possessing any notion of all they were being introduced to with those first names.

Maybe it was the loosening of address, like a necktie tugged free of its knot. Maybe it was Morrie's way of listening with monkish attention as though comparing the vocabulary of the next monastery over with his own. Maybe it was utter relief that at last we had a housekeeper, at least aboard the wagon. Or all of the above. Whatever was brimming in him, Father was expansive as he now speculated, "Morrie, I suppose you're traveling on through, once Rose gets established? I hear things are booming on the Coast."

"Actually, I thought I might seek something here."

"Ah?" said Father, clearly thrown. Homesteaders came in every shape and size, but Rose's tailored brother plainly was the exact opposite of agrarian. "What are you good at?"

"Intriguing question, Oliver," Morrie commended as if it had never occurred to him to undergo such self-examination. In a thoughtful tone he proceeded to do so for us now. "Whist. Identification of birds. A passable reciting voice, I'm told. Latin declensions. A bit rusty on Greek, but—"

"Oliver surely means your recent field of work," Rose took over. "The leather trade," she identified it as if Morrie's own job description might elude him.

Quick as a whip, though, he put in: "I handled the kid-glove end of things, didn't I, Rose."

"Our family enterprise," she said sadly, "it—" She gave her head that little shake. "After my poor husband—" This time she drew a chest-heaving breath. "Everything went."

Morrie rapidly followed that with:

"Oliver? You have provided for Rose most generously."

Drawing a breath of the same dramatic dimension as hers—could something like that run in the family?—he went on: "We were hoping you could be of assistance in my depleted situation, too. I am not afraid of work."

Father waited warily, to see if the ancient tagline might be coming: *"I can lie right down by it and go to sleep."* But Morrie seemed to mean what he had just vowed.

Finally, doubtless feeling the eyes of the audience in the back of the wagon on him, Father said only as much as seemed prudent: "I'll ask around." But the next thing we knew, here came his laugh by way of his nose. My brothers and I recognized one of his moments of inspiration. "On second thought," we heard him say. "I happen to know someone who needs a few cords of wood cut to see her through the winter."

"Oh," Rose exulted enough for both her and Morrie, "just the thing!"

Damon nudged me. Aunt Eunice and her woodpile both: Morrie was going to need his courage in the face of that work.

Shadows were growing long by the time we crossed the Westwater plain and came into sight of our homestead and the Schrickers'. Whether or not Rose and Morrie took it as a greeting, Houdini came out to meet us at the road, barking so hard he staggered in circles.

⤳

"*U*PKEEP," ROSE DECLARED AS SHE CAST AN EYE OVER OUR lodgings first thing the next morning. "That's every secret of a pleasant household, regular upkeep."

The bunch of us, Father in the lead, trailed her from room to room. She had shown up before we set off for school or Father made his way out to the horse barn—truth be told, before Toby had his shoes on or Father had his first dosage of coffee in him or Damon had the sleep wiped from his eyes or I had pulled myself together after a dream involving an eternal wait at a depot. The surprise knock on the door that early in the day froze the four of us until we remembered we now had a new standard of life, waiting to be let in. And everywhere Rose's gaze of inspection alit, ours following hers a bit apprehensively, some shortfall of housekeeping stood revealed like a museum exhibit of bachelor habits. Underfoot: we swept occasionally, but mopped never. Overhead: spider webs and soot clouded together in a way Shakespeare could have made something of. The upstairs bedroom, where Damon and I shared the big bed and Toby nestled in his corner bunk, displayed the individual clutter of each of us. If anything, we practiced downkeep. Damon's sports scrapbooks lay around open when he was working on them, and he was always working on them. Over in his nook, Toby had a growing assortment of bones from the buffalo jump we had discovered, secretly hoping, I suspect, that he could accumulate a buffalo. My books already threatened to take over my part of the room and keep on going. Mother's old ones, subscription sets Father had not been able to resist, coverless winnowings from the schoolhouse shelf—whatever cargoes of words I could lay my hands on I gave safe harbor. All three of us had arrowhead collections; Rose must have divined instantly that it wasn't safe to put a finger down on any surface without a good, close look first.

Still, people on Lowry Hill in Minneapolis must have had their own dusty corners and scatterings of things, mustn't they? Filing after Rose on her march through the house upstairs and then back down, we waited hopefully for her to say something such as "I have seen worse." She didn't say it.

Instead, as her quick brown eyes took everything in, we could tell she was building a mental list of some length. But nowhere on it, so far, was the one chore in the one room of the house that would do us some instant good. Maybe my stomach rumbled at me, or maybe I was merely determined to find out whether Can't Cook But Doesn't Bite meant what it sounded like or not. Maybe I did it to head off Damon, who tended to come awake like a bear out of hibernation, hungry and cranky. Or maybe I figured Toby deserved some morsel of reward for his overflowing adoration of Rose. In any event, after Rose pinned down Father on how long it had been since the chimney flue in the parlor was last cleaned, I was the one who said brightly, "The kitchen gets pretty hard use from us, doesn't it, Father."

He sent me a warning frown, but too late. "It's right in here," Toby said as he charged to the doorway and eagerly looked back over his shoulder for Rose. She said, "Then let's have a look," as if we were all going to the zoo.

Functional clutter is perhaps the best description of how Father managed in the kitchen. Provisions such as bags of flour and sugar and an arsenal of canned goods stood on the counter so he would always know where things were. Likewise certain frequently used pots, pans, butcher knives, large spoons, and dishes. The table showed only a passing acquaintance with meals; one entire end of it was permanently stacked with Toby's crayon drawings, Father's archive of newspapers except for the ones Damon had eviscerated for his baseball and football and boxing scrapbooks, even more of my books, and the like. As a person looked around, it was clear that culinary skills were not our strongest point as a family. In point of fact, the main ingredient of our mealtimes was disarray. Father had many knacks, but when by necessity he turned his hand to the cookstove, always running late, never versed in preparations, his results almost invariably came out boiled, soupy, lumpy, or tough as shoe leather. We truly dined only on those Sundays at Rae's table; otherwise we subsisted. Surely Rose would read our condition and be moved to say "I can fry up some eggs and bacon and hotcakes in a jiffy," wouldn't she? Damon and I waited tensely, and Toby plopped down at his place at the table as if the issue was already resolved. Hopes soared as Rose hesitated in the middle of the room, then stepped toward the cookstove.

"Does the reservoir hold good hot water?" she inquired of Father, and, studiously not looking our way, he said he guessed so.

Hot water! We were capable of that ourselves. Rose glided on past every foodstuff and utensil we possessed with no more than a glance, seeming to be an absolute tourist in this part of the house. The one item she did pause over lay stretched beside the kitchen stove.

"Houdini, if I recall. Whose claim to fame is—?"

Turning in that direction, Father asked in a confidential tone, "Houdini, what do you think of William Howard Taft as president?"

The dog's ears went up. He pushed himself up by his front legs, let out a howl, then rolled over and played dead.

"Quite the performance," Rose had to admit, though still eyeing him with the professional housekeeper's suspicion of a sizable hair-shedding animal.

"Wait till you see him catch a jackrabbit," Toby told her.

"Father?" By now the clock was in my favor, and I used it ruthlessly. "Look at the time. Hadn't we better think about something to eat?"

"Ah." Plainly he had not anticipated dealing with this issue this soon. But even more plainly, the rest of us were voting with our stomachs. Taking a deep breath, he squared around to Rose and began: "We haven't had breakfast yet and wondered if—"

"Oh, I never touch it, thanks very much anyway." With that she disappeared out to the roughed-in front porch known as the mud room to continue her assessment of the household.

Damon called despairingly to her departing back, "Around here, it's always mush."

Father gave us a defensive look and turned to the cookstove. He fired up his coffee first, then began boiling up oatmeal as we glumly watched. Rose soon was back in from whatever she had been in search of. "Wash day," she said decisively, donning an apron as deftly as a magician wielding a cape. "That would be a start."

"Paul's your man when it comes to water," Father informed her, not without a glint of retribution as he set aside my oatmeal bowl and nodded me toward the pump in the yard. Indeed I was in charge of the water bucket, doing the dishes, and Saturday-night baths. With a groan, I got up from the table to help Rose with the wash water.

I showed her the trick of operating the pump by wetting the leather piston with a couple of quick half strokes, then the long downstrokes that brought water gushing. She and I hefted the full washtub onto the stove to heat, then went back out to fill the rinse tub. As she worked the pump handle, our new up-holder of upkeep said only loud enough for me to hear:

"Mind you, this is merely a suggestion. But wash day could include Houdini."

"Doesn't work," I told her crossly, still out of sorts from lack of food. "You can't get him within a mile of a washtub."

"Didn't I see a pond?" The pothole pond Father called the Lake District was in the field between our place and Aunt

Eunice's. "Perhaps if a stick were tossed in it by the right person, Houdini would give himself a bath." The lilting way she said it, it sounded like a rare adventure. She gave me a look with a hint of conspiracy in it. "Toby might even volunteer for the chore, do you suppose?"

"I'll get him on it after school," I conceded, although I never liked being maneuvered.

My mind was mainly on breakfast, and as soon as we had the wash water going, I tore into my bowl of oatmeal, which by then was turning gluey. As I spooned the stuff into me and Father slapped together cheese sandwiches for our lunch at school, Rose swooped through time after time, either half buried under a mound of our bedding in her arms or hefting a heaped dirty-clothes basket on a practiced hip. Toby was upstairs in pursuit of his shoes, but Damon, I could tell, was awaiting his chance for something. When Rose disappeared again in search of any more fabric to wash, he whispered urgently across the kitchen: "Aren't you going to ask her?"

Startled, but not so much so he didn't remember to keep to a whisper in answering, Father fired back: "Young man, I would like to handle this my own way, if you don't mind. When I think the time is right, naturally I'll put it to her about the cooking—"

"No, no, the milking!"

"Ah, that. Clever of you to think of it, Damon."

When Rose sailed into the room again under another billow of sheets to be washed, Father began laying out to her the logical connection between the churn and the origin of the milk, therefore—

"I rather thought this might come up," Rose interrupted him. "It's been a while, but I can milk a cow." She studied Father for a moment. "Are there any other duties that come under the Montana definition of housekeeping?"

Father brightened. "Actually, there's another skill allied to all your domestic ones we had hoped to call on. We could even add a bit to your wages if absolutely necessary. It would help like everything, Rose, if you could handle the kitchen—"

"—scraps for the chickens," Rose concluded with a knowing wag of her head. "Inevitable. Poultry are not my favorite creatures and a slop bucket is never pretty, but all right, I can feed the chickens for you and I suppose gather the eggs while I'm at it." Now she peered at Father with mortal seriousness. The top of her head only reached the tip of his chin, but we were to find that there was no shortage of stature in Rose's tone when she spoke up like this. "Oliver, I must tell you—I take exception to pigs."

"Put your mind at rest, we're hog-free," Father said with an expulsion of breath. He noticed the riveted audience of the three of us. "Don't you have a schoolhouse waiting for you?"

"We're going, we're going," I said, reluctant to tear myself away. Damon grabbed up the schoolbooks he had brought home but of course had not opened, Toby pecked Father on the cheek as the other two of us manfully watched the daily goodbye kiss we had outgrown, we chorused a parting to Rose, and off we went.

That October sky was as deceptively clear as this one. Across the crisp grass of autumn, Toby and Damon and I spurred our horses with a verve we hadn't had since before Mother left our lives. Great gains came seldom, in our experience, but we could already count ours up since Rose's arousing knock on the door a mere hour ago. Damon was liberated from the milk pail. I no longer had to ferry our every stitch of clothing to Rae's wash days. And Toby had a name engraved on his heart, as he always needed, and it read *Rose Llewellyn*. All that, plus the fact that the disheveled house was in for the cleaning of its life. True, we were no better off on the matter of meals yet, but we had to trust that Father would find some way to win Rose over on that.

As we rode to school, the shadows of our horses lively behind us, the world as we knew it in Marias Coulee seemed to shine with fresh promise. The Pronovosts had loyally waited for us at the section-line fence, late as we were, providing us the earliest possible listening audience about the marvels of housekeeping. Father had harnessed his team of workhorses in record time and already could be seen on the haul road to the irrigation project with the dray, waving jauntily to us across the fields. Perhaps most miraculous, the slow song of a saw from the direction of Aunt Eunice's place confirmed that Morrie was gainfully employed. He had asked Father, "What exactly is meant by a *cord* of wood?" "Four feet wide, four feet high, and eight feet long, that's a cord," Father recited in surprise. "Intriguing," said Morrie. "I wonder whether Shakespeare was working that in, there in the line '*O, the charity of a penny cord.*'" "I have a hunch he was merely threatening to hang a nobleman," Father responded. "So. Do you know how to use a splitting maul?" In short, on a morning when even those two fussy autodidacts were in tune with the tasks of this earth, every prospect pleased.

But that afternoon at recess, I slugged Eddie Turley.

Damon of all people pulled me off him. Probably more in surprise than charity toward me, the Swede boys held Eddie back as he raged to get at me. Odds were that it was the only punch I would ever land on him, but it had been a good one, a clout to the jaw that knocked him back a step or two. That swing of my fist created an instant sensation in the schoolyard. "That's it, Paul, lay it to him!" Verl Fletcher yelped in encouragement, as if I hadn't just delivered my best. "Ooh, your poor hand," issued from Barbara Rellis, a sixth-grader but already catty. Carnelia's head popped out of the outhouse. I caught sight of Toby in the circle of smaller kids, looking amazed. Everything escalated with the speed of sound. Grover Stinson and Miles Calhoun were talking back to Eddie and his outraged contingent, and since the Swedes happened to be over there on Eddie's side, the Slavs automatically formed up on mine and chimed in. The history-book chapter on the Congress of Vienna had nothing to show us about balances of alliances.

My immediate adversary, however, was not Eddie Turley but my brother. In the strictest sense, Damon and I saw eye to eye. He had caught up to me in height, validating—in his own mind, at least—his passion for every kind of sports over my bookishness. Now he had me in a lassolike arm hold across my chest, and if I hadn't been so mad, it should have occurred to me what I was in for from Eddie if even Damon could so easily handle me. Our faces nearly touched as we traded savage whispers.

"Have you gone crazy? He's too much for you."

"I don't care. I'm through taking it about the housekeeper."

"What'd he say?"

"He asked me if she fed us from her tit for breakfast."

"Why didn't you hit him harder?"

"Thanks all to hell, Damon."

Suddenly everyone became aware of a sound like a woodpecker on glass. Miss Trent was rapping on a schoolroom window, trying to see what the excitement was. She came outside on these occasions only if fists were already flying. With long practice, all of us in the schoolyard dissolved from the scene of the fracas but stayed within range of catcall.

Eddie was staring blue murder at me, and for that matter, Damon. He had the right pedigree for it. Ambrose Turley hunted wolves and coyotes for a livelihood, and he and Eddie lived not much better than beasts themselves in a ramshackle place on the Marias River bottomland. People went out of their way to leave Brose Turley alone as he scavenged the countryside setting traps and collecting pelts. His nearly man-size son looked perfectly capable of collecting mine.

Damon was undaunted. "Let me," he insisted in my ear. "I'll get him off the notion of beating the jelly out of you, all right?"

"Thanks all to hell again. How—"

"Don't worry, it'll work slick."

With that, Damon already was strutting toward the Turley faction to parley. "Just Paul and Eddie—the rest of us keep our noses out," he negotiated with Martin Myrdal and Carl Johannson, eighth-graders who were Eddie's most sizable lieutenants. The Swede boys cast hard looks to where the Drobny brothers and the Stoyanovs, Milo and Ivo, were close behind me, but also on our side of the matter was Verl Fletcher, an eighth-grader like them who was all long arms and knuckles. "We don't mind watching Paul get what he's got coming," Martin finally sealed the bargain.

That quick, Damon sprung terms on Eddie. "No fighting it out. You're so much bigger than Paul it isn't fair. He'll take you on, but another way. Loser has to leave the other one alone the rest of the school year."

Eddie could not believe what he was hearing. He sputtered, "He hit me first!"

"That evens up for the time you hit Grover, and that time with Milo, and how many times has he done it to you, Martin?" Everybody knew Damon could have kept on naming off school-yard victims who had felt a clout out of nowhere from Eddie Turley, including most of the girls.

It sunk in on Eddie that this was not the jury to complain

to about unfair treatment. He switched to bravado. "I ain't scared of no Milliron. You name it, I'll clean up on him."

"Paul will race you," Damon stayed in charge. "Horseback."

Eddie sneered. "That the best you can do? Any sissy can sit on a horse."

Damon had him where he wanted him. With a wicked grin he specified:

"Wrong end to."

Which one of us had come up with riding backward in the saddle in our constant races with each other I can't really prove, but my money would be on Damon. It broke the monotony of the ride to and from school. For a few years there, in good weather my gamesman brother and I pretty much rode daily doubles against each other. Whoever lost in the first gallop only had to say "Wrong end to, this time" and off we shot again, crazy jockeys clinging atop the horse's hindquarters. Now that the bulk of age is on me, I can barely imagine ever being that nimble in the saddle—shucking out of the stirrups, scooting up and around on the seat of our pants, and ending up reseated as if we were going one direction and the horse the other—or that my roan Joker or Damon's pinto Paint put up with it. We didn't race wrong-end-to as much after Toby started going to school with us, as he didn't need any encouragement in the direction of breaking his neck. But every so often, when the three of us would reach the stretch of the road to school that couldn't be seen from any house, one or the other could not resist flinging the challenge, and the Milliron cavalry would be flying down the road, back pockets first.

But those were races for fun. The ante was sky-high in the contest with Eddie. "He has that steel-gray, remember," I pointed out to Damon, promoter of all this. Brose Turley, in his occupation of running down wolves, possessed a saddle string of deep-chested, rangy horses, and Eddie rode a grizzled brute of a steed that looked like it could run a gazelle to death.

"Joker's not bothered, are you, boy." Damon reached over from his own mount and rubbed the mane of my bow-necked sorrel saddle pony. Then held up a fist to me like John L. Sullivan striking a pose, grinning behind it. "One-Punch Milliron. Gonna have to put you in my scrapbook."

"Bam!" Toby, riding on the other side of me on our way home from school, was even more exultant about the haymaker I got in on Eddie. "You really gave it to him, Paul!"

I glanced at Damon, and he at me. Ahead of us, down the long gumbo hill toward home, a field of white linen had sprouted in front of our house and Rose could just be seen out there taking sheets off the clothesline. We both reined up, and I reached over and halted Toby's horse as well. "Tobe, listen. You can't tell anybody. Anybody, got that? The fight and the race and all, this has to be a strict secret." I spat in the palm of my hand. His eyes large, Toby did the same and submitted to the first binding handshake of his life.

Damon set the race—naturally, the whole schoolyard had to be in on it—for Friday after school. As every kid knew, parents somewhat lost track of the clock at the end of the school week, and we had our set of proven tactics to take advantage of that lapse. It was not unusual for an entire pack of us to jaunt off after school to a coyote den someone had discovered, so you could just bet that across Marias Coulee that Friday the excuse for late arrival home would be a mumbled chorus of "looking for coyote pups." Beyond that, the kids with farthest to ride made a flurry of staying-over arrangements. Miles Calhoun would overnight with Grover Stinson, the Kratka boys would become honorary Swedes for a night at the Myrdals'. Lily Lee

Fletcher took in Vivian Villard, whose lone small figure on the longest ride home of any of us, five miles, was a daily lesson in bravery. Meanwhile, details such as starting line and finish line and exact interpretation of "wrong end to" were being worked out by Damon and Martin. Edgy as I was about the outcome of the race, a part of me had to admire the level of conniving that went into it.

And nobody blabbed. That was the incredible thing. I cannot say a word to anyone in my department without it ending up three floors away. But the schoolchildren of Marias Coulee kept as mum as the pillars of Delphi. Oh, Miss Trent knew something was up, definitely. She trooped around the perimeter of the schoolroom in her cloppety shoes even more than usual, suspicion in every jiggle of her bumpy build. Once she even came out at recess to try to figure out what the sudden giggles and excited clusterings were about. Our pact of secrecy resisted her best effort, though. Not even Carnelia, who ordinarily would have gone a mile out of her way to tell on me, let out a peep about the race; after all, there was every chance Eddie Turley was going to make me look like the fool of all time. So, that week built and built, two clouds of anticipation in the opposing climate zones of the schoolyard, toward Friday.

On the home front, so to speak, morning by morning Rose arrived with some new plan of attack on the house. Now that our bedding and underwear and even hankies were as fresh as a garden of lilies—a shrewd boost in our morale—she chose her battles with professional élan. Every stove was scraped out and polished, and every stovepipe emptied of soot, before she moved on to sweeping and scrubbing the floors. The day after that, windows were washed until they sparkled and up went the new curtains that she had prevailed on Father to fetch from town.

Offhand miracles occurred, too: lamp chimneys suddenly were clean instead of smoke-darkened; Houdini no longer was a canine disaster area thanks to his pond romps with Toby. I mean it when I say the house positively breathed in a way different from before, for among all the other exhalations of wonder that our housekeeper provided, Rose was a woman who whistled at her work. About like a ghost would. That is, the sound was just above silence. A least little tingle of air, the lightest music that could pass through lips, yet with a lingering quality that was inescapable. There is nothing quite like stepping into a seemingly empty house and hearing the parlor—Rose's tidying was often so swift and silent that the tune was the only sound—softly begin to serenade you with "Down in the valley, valley so low." More than once I saw Father stop what he was doing and cock an ear toward some corner of the house a melody was coming from, as if wondering whether whistling really could be the housekeeping accompaniment on Lowry Hill in Minneapolis.

So, one breezelike song after another on her lips as she cleaned upstairs and down, Rose brightened the house. With the exception of the kitchen. We ate as we had always eaten, haphazardly and dully. Father right then was busier than ever with his hauling sideline, freight for the Big Ditch stacking up at the depot daily. For his part, Damon was so immersed in the scheming for the upcoming race that he didn't badger Father about the cooking situation. Toby went around looking like he was going to burst with our secret at any minute, but he put his energies into learning to whistle like Rose. And my mind was so crammed with scenarios of galloping backward—all that week my dreams featured Eddie Turley jeering at me from a secure perch between the humps of a racing camel—that I was useless for any other purpose.

It snuck up on me, then, when Rose managed to touch a

nerve in Father about our mother. At the time, I didn't want to witness it, but I happened to be in the line of fire, clamped to a book at the kitchen table trying to keep my every thought off the race. Father had come in from his day of freighting and was washing up, and Rose had just finished her day's work, too. Although not quite.

"Oh, Oliver?" She veered from her path out the door into the kitchen, her shawl already on. "I need your guidance on one matter." She sounded troubled.

"I can always make a stab at it," came muffled as he finished toweling his face. "What's the topic under discussion?"

"Your room." Rose hesitated. "I need to know what, that is, how much you want done with it."

Father didn't say anything until he'd hung up his towel. "You mean Florence's—my wife's things, I take it."

"Yes. I'm sorry to bring it up, but—"

"It's all right," he replied, although I knew better. "Just sweep and tend to the bedding in there," he told her with a slight catch in his voice. "I'll do any straightening up." He seemed to feel the need to add, "I haven't had the heart to disturb Florence's things. The time will come, but not yet."

Rose nodded, but didn't turn to go yet. With evident effort, she brought out another question:

"May I ask—how long has it been?"

"Last year." Father recognized what lay behind her asking. "And with your husband?"

"This past summer."

"Ah. That recent." Caught in grievers' etiquette, Father asked in return: "Was it sudden?"

"Very." Rose drew a faltering breath. "He—just went."

Father looked over at me as if he wished I didn't have to be in on this, but there I was. My eyes began to sting. I was not the only one in the room it was happening to, I could tell. Mother's death had been hard for all of us to bear, but we had borne it, because that is what people do. I thought of it as like the cauterizing I had read about Civil War doctors doing when they performed amputations, the fierce burn sealing off the wound. Each of us showed the scar; there was no help for that. Toby did not mope often, but when he did, it ran a mile deep. Damon's temper got away from him more than it had before. As for me, I am told that for a public figure I am an exceptionally interior person, and I can't argue with that; surely I looked at life a lot more warily after it took Mother from us. In Father's case, he had our symptoms to tend to as well as his own. In short, none of us was over Mother's death, but we had adjusted to the extent we could to that missing limb of the family.

Now Father had to find it in himself to finish the exchange with Rose, and he did. "Florence"—his voice struggled, and he gave me another difficult glance—"the boys' mother lasted a few weeks, after complications from a burst appendix."

Rose said how sorry she was to hear those circumstances, and turned to go. Before she did, she looked back at Father in her keen-eyed way, although those eyes were a bit damp. "Thank you. It helps, to know what someone else has been through."

"All right then. Good night, Rose."

"Good night."

4

FRIDAY, RACE DAY, IN MY DREAM-TOSSED STATE I OPENED THE door to Rose's now familiar knock and stood there blinking. Along the line of her right shoulder hovered a startling mustache, like a hairy epaulette.

"Paul!" she exclaimed as if delighted that I still was in existence. "Look who's with me!"

"Uh, morning, Mr. Morgan," I managed.

"Needless formality, Paul, especially at this ungodly hour of the day," he protested as if he had come all the way over to our place on this matter of manners. "Let's make it 'Morrie.'" He stepped from behind Rose and provided me the necessary handshake.

The sound of Morrie's voice brought Father straight out of the kitchen, cup in hand. Before he could get in a word, Rose was combining explanation and congratulation:

"We're in luck, Oliver! I've conscripted Morrie to clean the chicken house. It's really quite—" The way she wrinkled her nose said the rest.

Morrie raised a hand as if to fend off any objection from

Father. "Gratis. A token of thanks for the new lease on life you have provided Rose. And for that matter, me." By now Damon and Toby were charging down from upstairs, all ears. Morrie acknowledged their presence with as much of a smile as could make its way through the mustache. Then sped right on: "Montana seems to agree with me. Hard labor—that is, strenuous exertion such as cording up wood—was just what I needed to draw me out of dwelling on the recent plights of life."

Was? Father was startled by that; we all were. "You worked yourself out of a job already?"

"Three cords of freshly split wood, measured to the inch," Morrie attested, Rose beside him proudly nodding approval of his achievement. "The Parthenon is not built more exactly than Eunice Schricker's winter woodpile." He swung his arms restlessly, evidently ready to tackle more labor. "I believe destiny is fueled by momentum, Oliver. Once launched upon a fresh turn in life's path, a person ought not to slack off." He gazed at his sister as if to give credit where credit was due. "Rose never slacks off."

"Destiny has led you to our chicken coop, has it?" Father said, an uncommon glint in his eye. "Maybe you ought to fortify yourself with a swig of coffee first."

"Gladly," Morrie accepted, missing Rose's shake of her head to warn him off.

Damon and Toby and I were in a dilemma, antsy to reach school and endure through the day until the big race, but reluctant to tear ourselves away from Morrie's debut at shoveling chicken poop. Our compromise was to scamper upstairs to get ready for school and at the same time strain our ears to pick up every word from the coffee klatch in the kitchen.

"What's 'gratis'?" Damon asked me.

"For free."

"Really? The chicken house? Ugh."

"I have to say, our chickens usually don't have such elevated company," Father's voice drifted up. "Isn't there some other trade you want to take up, more on the town side of things? Westwater could use a good glover."

There was a rattle of cup and saucer, which we figured was Morrie putting Father's version of coffee a safe distance away. "By 'glover,' you mean—"

"Work gloves, lady's suede, sled mittens," Father hypothesized. "For someone like you who knows the leather trade, a glove store would seem a natural opportunity. Or were you and Rose and the late Mr. Llewellyn not in retail, before?"

Morrie sounded pensive. "International trade was more our line. When catastrophe came down on us as it did, frankly I lacked the heart to return to that kind of endeavor. I decided to seek something more, well, fundamental. Down to earth. No more of the frippery that we had made our name by. And so, when Rose—" He broke off, in that mannerism he shared with her, as though the rest explained itself without being said. Toby's shoelaces were giving him trouble and I was working on those, while Damon searched everywhere for his belt. As if in accompaniment to our efforts, Morrie suddenly resumed: "I might cite you Santayana—'the world of matter is the absolute reality.' I don't mind telling you, Oliver, I find those words have considerably more meaning here in the West than they did in the ostensible halls of learning."

Rose happened past our bedroom on her way to some chore just then, and giving us a lightning smile that said she knew what we were up to, she paused there with us to listen in on the kitchen colloquy.

"Where did you take your degree, Morrie?" As a proud graduate of Manitowoc Technical School, Father was always interested in educational pedigree.

"Knox."

Hearing that, Rose frowned, and made a move toward the stairway.

"In Illinois? A fine college, I've heard." Father caught on. "Or do you by chance mean 'hard knocks'?"

"A feeble jest, Oliver. I apologize. But it *was* at an Illinois institution—the University of Chicago."

Shaking her head, Rose reversed course from the top of the stairs and went off on her chore.

Damon had stopped what he was doing and his eyes widened. I didn't follow football as he did, but I'd heard of that school's unbeatable teams under its titan of a coach, Amos Alonzo Stagg. Even Toby had absorbed snippets from Damon's constant attention to the teams in his sports scrapbooks. In excited recognition he whispered now, "Damon, the Baboons!"

"The Maroons," Damon hissed back at him. He looked longingly across the room. "I have to show Morrie my football scrapbook."

"Not now, you don't," I told him. "Come on, let's get this day over with."

But I was the one who veered off at the bottom of the stairs to track down Rose whistling up work for herself. Next to where she hung her coat I noticed the itty-bitty sack of lunch she brought every day. Morrie had brought nothing at all. What did these people exist on?

"Morrie better find out where the pond is," I murmured to Rose when I found her. "He's going to smell to high heaven after he spends a day shoveling chicken matter."

Her lips twitched. "Houdini and I will share the secret with him, depend on it."

Father made an appearance in the kitchen doorway. "The last I knew, school still existed. Aren't you characters—"

"We're going," I blurted, Damon and Toby tumbling into line behind me to get out the door.

The ride to school was a blur, my mind on Eddie Turley and his steel-gray horse, while Damon pelted me with last-minute advice and Toby was as wound up as a music box. The schoolyard was a mass of anticipation when we reached it, everyone hanging on outside watching for us even though Miss Trent always wanted us all in our seats by the time she was done beating on the triangle.

It was barely into arithmetic time, when the sixth-graders were at the blackboard working on division problems she was giving them, when Miss Trent wheeled around with surprising quickness for someone of her shambly build.

"Tobias Milliron."

Every head in the schoolroom snapped up at her tone. "Perhaps you would like to share with the rest of us what you are so busy confiding to Sigrid."

"N-n-no, ma'am," Toby replied in all honesty.

"Do it anyway," Miss Trent commanded.

Next to me at our desk Carnelia snickered, until she realized that if Toby was nailed for whispering and had to tell what was going on, it meant no race. Up at the blackboard, Damon abruptly turned as pale as the chalk in his fist. He and I traded helpless looks. I didn't dare try to draw Miss Trent's attention away from Toby; she had been eyeing me suspiciously ever since I had turned into a center of attention at every recess.

Besides, there was the question of whether Miss Trent had it in for the Milliron family.

Oh, she was punctilious enough toward us in the classroom. Damon was not put on this earth to make life easy for any teacher, but Miss Trent was careful not to keep him after school any more often than any other classroom sinner. In my less obstreperous case, she drilled me on each subject as tonelessly as if going down a menu, and that was that. (The saving grace was that she didn't seem to care much for Carnelia either.) But if Miss Trent had her doubtful side toward us, we were doubly suspicious of her. Damon and I were convinced she was husband-hunting, quite possibly in Father's direction. Pickings were not plentiful in Marias Coulee: a handful of old bachelor homesteaders with not the best habits, a too-long-on-the-shelf widower like Brose Turley, and just a few eminently eligible ones such as Vivian Villard's dad and, naturally, Father. On last year's last day of school, when the entire school board and all the parents were on hand for the graduation of the eighth-graders, Miss Trent had made eyes at Father to the best of her limited ability. To our relief, he had not reciprocated. We trusted Father, but you never knew what a school board member could stumble into where a teacher was concerned. Damon and I simply could not countenance the thought of that familiar figure from the classroom dominating the rest of our hours too. High in the rump, low in the bosom, Miss Trent was rather bunched in the middle, accentuating the scary extent of her limbs. But the worse part was her customary bothered expression, as though she had something stuck in a back tooth. If she was even more out of sorts than usual—peeved at coming across an unmalleable Milliron anywhere she looked, say—Toby truly was in for a hard time from her.

Clop, clop. She was advancing on him relentlessly. Toby sat there paralyzed with terror that he would be kept after school and miss the race. The rest of us squirmed.

"Tobias? We're waiting."

Damon was frantic. But sometimes he got his best ideas while in that state. Behind Miss Trent's back now, he lifted his elbows and flapped them like wings.

Toby gathered that in and put it all into one grand expulsion of breath: "A man from the University of Chicago is cleaning our chicken house. For free."

Miss Trent's new expression revealed that she had not anticipated an announcement of that sort, evidently somewhere on the mythic level of the Augean stables. Plainly, though, this was not anything Toby could be making up.

"That is no excuse for whispering it to your neighbor," she said in not altogether convincing fashion. "You know the penalty, a taste of the ruler."

With that she gave Toby a swat on the hand and a warning that cured him for the rest of the day.

"Meet you at The Cut."

That was the watchword, when all of us piled out of the schoolhouse at the end of that interminable day and sprinted to our saddled horses.

The usual homeward group of us and the Pronovosts, with the various Drobnys and Stinsons and Miles Calhoun trying to look innocently tacked on, traveled at a just-fast-enough clip to get ourselves out of sight before parents started looking out of windows. We didn't want to wear out my horse. Joker kept flicking his ears at all the patting and rubbing of his mane by so many strangers.

We came down the gradient from the higher ground at the same time that the Turley bunch galloped in from the north gulch they had circled around to. "The suckers," Damon said to me, confident enough for both of us.

He had to be, because I wasn't so sure. I remember my heart beating at what felt like twice its normal rate, while the last few preparations for the race seemed to take forever. The excited babble of the gathering—Toby was letting loose everything he'd had to save up all day in school—reached me only dimly. We needed to kill time while the rest of the kids filtered in, and as they gradually popped into sight from every direction, I stared at that waiting stretch of road as though Joker's hoofprints and my shifting shadow had not gone back and forth over it every day of the past seven school years. If Marias Coulee possessed a creek, it instantly would earn promotion to valley. However, as if nature was rehearsing for something larger, the long crease in the land here south from the Marias River more closely resembles a sunken prairie, gentle enough in its gradual vee to attract the first adherents of dryland farming who ever set eyes on it. The neighboring benchlands along the river and the broad Westwater plain extend around it like an upper floor of the earth, and Marias Coulee fits at the base of the geographical stairs, complete with landing: the gumbo hill up from our place breaks off into an eroded claybank area, where the road runs flat and straight for about half a mile before climbing again to the bench country. This was The Cut. It was the ground I had known as long as anything in my life, yet its bare, beaten dirt looked as foreign and forbidding to me at that suspended moment in time as the Sahara.

Finally the Kratka brothers, the last of us and with the most roundabout route to sneak past nosy parents, came spurring madly in from the river end of the coulee, and Damon got things under way.

"We have to make it fast, before somebody comes along. Martin? Is Eddie ready to eat dust?"

For answer, Eddie stomped up to the starting line leading his snorty high-shouldered mount. That horse looked like it could step over the top of Joker and me. The terrible taste of doubt nearly did me in. I must admit, I was within the tip of my tongue of saying uncle, of finding some wild excuse to forfeit the race. But that would doom me at school even worse than losing to Eddie. And the dreams that would beset me—

I gave Joker a last pat and led him out onto the road beside Eddie's big steel-gray.

There we stood, at the line scratched in the dirt. Eddie always wore one of Brose Turley's old hats that seemed to have been fashioned out of the dried skin of some major beast. I pulled my mail-order Junior Stetson lower over my eyes and tried to concentrate on the road ahead. The racetrack, to call it that, stretched from the starting line to a single marker, distant and shining, in the middle of the road. Here was where the genius of Damon came in. At his insistence, the course was a loop, to the far end of The Cut and back.

"Flat-out, here to there," Martin Myrdal understandably had tried to hold out for when the two sides were negotiating the ground rules. A horse the size of the steel-gray could build a lot of velocity when simply aimed straight ahead.

Damon was pitiless. "What, Eddie can't steer that cayuse of his around any kind of a corner?"

"I'll race your squirt brother around in circles, if that's what it takes," Eddie blurted, snapping up the bait.

Most of us carried small lard pails as lunch buckets, and Damon and Martin now had stacked several of those, with a rock in each for stability, until they made a silver pillar. I understood why Damon demanded the momentum-breaking marker, but I still fretted about it. Rounding it, if the horses were close together, would be no easy stunt. On the other hand, if the steel-gray was half a dozen horse-lengths ahead of Joker by then, traffic at the marker was going to be the least of my problems, wasn't it.

Damon and Martin stepped forth to hold the bridles of our horses. Verl Fletcher had been picked to be the race caller because he was the one eighth-grader other than Eddie who wasn't a Swede or a Slav.

"Everybody back, give 'em room," he directed, and there was a collective groan of saddle leather as thirty horseback school-children moved off into the badland cutbanks on either side to spectate.

"Riders up," Verl called.

Eddie was watching me from the corner of his eye and I was doing the same to him. It hit me: he wanted me to be the first to get up there backward in the saddle, so he could see how. I planted myself like a post until Verl said to us, "You gonna ride 'em or walk 'em?"

Eddie lost patience, stuck his other foot than usual into the stirrup, and with a mighty grunt heaved himself upward toward his horse's rump, barely clearing the peril of the saddle horn as he wishboned over, then felt around behind him like a blind man for the reins Martin was attempting to hand to him. I swung into my saddle the right way, took control of Joker's reins, then shucked the stirrups and scooted around on my fanny so that I too was established in the leather basin of the saddle wrong-end-to. Eddie glared across at me as if I had just shaken a ballet tutu in his face.

Damon, though, rose on tiptoe beside Joker's mane to ec-statically whisper up to me, "He hasn't practiced! The dope! Can you believe it?"

"Damon, that horse of his doesn't need any practice," I whispered back.

"You worry too much."

"Gonna give you a count of three," Verl let us know.

Those next moments have stayed with me with the clarity of a clock face. My belt buckle brushed against the cantle of the saddle as I leaned in the direction of Joker's flanks. The reins were wrapped double around my right hand, held as far behind me as I could reach so as not to tug on the bit of the bridle differently than Joker was used to.

"One," Verl chanted.

There was not a sound from the entire mounted legion of Marias Coulee School, from either Eddie's adherents or mine. Clans of centaurs must have watched with similar appraisal when match races were run in the groves of Peloponnesus.

"Two."

Joker's tensed ears were sharpened to a point now, and probably mine were too.

"Three, SPUR 'EM!"

Eddie was the only one dressed for that, sporting a pair of silver jinglebobs, sharp as can openers, that likely were everyday equipment in the Turley family business of encouraging saddle horses to run down wolves. The first jab of those spurs commanded the steel-gray's attention, definitely. But not quite as Eddie had intended. The big horse hurtled into action shying right and left, fishtailing down the road as it tried to figure out the wishes of the unbalanced rider on its back. Nor was Eddie the master of handling reins behind his back yet. Joker and I managed a perfectly nice, orderly start when I pressed my shoe heels against his rib cage and gave the reins the flick he recognized, but it didn't do us any immediate good. Whatever lane of the road we tried, there was a wall of gray horse in our way, one instant the veering rump of the thing, the next practically a sideways view of Eddie as he tried simultaneously to stay upright and to saw his horse's head around to the right direction with that reversed grip on the reins. Over the hoofbeats and horse snorts I could hear cheering and shouts of equestrian advice from the onlookers up in their vantage points in the badlands, but none of it registered long enough to last. When I wasn't having to keep an eye on Eddie's galloping wrestle with his horse, I was aware only of the road flying at uncommon speed beneath me. It is surprising how near the hard ground seems when there is only a horse's tail between you and it.

Time whirled away like our dust. As well as I could judge ahead over my shoulder, we were about to reach the halfway point of The Cut. By that stage of the race the steel-gray had covered at least twice as much road as Joker and I, but we were able to catch up to within a length every time it made one of its sideways veers. Apparently that grizzled mass of horseflesh could hurl along like this all day long. I didn't have time to think of it then, but Morrie's point about the preponderate role of momentum in life was unfortunately holding true so far.

I collected my wits, at least those that hadn't been shaken out of me by the jolts that come from riding backwards in the saddle. It was time to make the one maneuver I was capable of. Then or never, and maybe it already was too late. Damon had worked this out with me. "Don't let him see how to use the cantle until you have to," my brother the race promoter had counseled. "Pretty good chance old Eddie won't have brains enough to figure it out for himself first."

So, until right then I had stayed more or less upright in the saddle the same jouncing way Eddie was, both of us loosy-goosy in the seat as we held on to stirrup leather or saddle strings or whatever we could find to grab in the absence of the usual saddle horn. Now, though, when Eddie's horse made another of its spooked tangents toward the far side of the road and Joker was able to close the gap just enough, I dropped down lower than any jockey and grabbed the curved back of the saddle frame in a bear hug with my left arm. I'd be lying if I said the cantle was the most appealing thing I ever hugged in my life. But right then it served its purpose. As one or another of us—probably the natural daredevil, Toby—had discovered in our wrong-end-to races, if you bent over far enough the width of the cantle steadied the base of your chest, and, swooping up hip-pocket-high on a person sitting the normal way in the saddle, it provided something substantial to hug on to. And this move greatly streamlined matters for the horse. With a crouched-over jockey now atop him, albeit one tucked in not the usual direction, Joker gained some more on the skittering steel-gray.

Eddie had his hands full with just his horse; the concept of affection for his saddle cantle must have been beyond him. Yet there I was, clinging secure as a cockleburr on the back of my horse, while the back of his was like a hurricane deck. Worse, surely, was the realization that Joker was steadily sneaking up every time his hard-to-rein steed careened across the road.

By now we were thundering down on the turn marker, the pillar of pails. The view over my shoulder told me what I already knew, that the road was not wide enough for both horses to make the turn at the same time. Here the advantage went back to Eddie. The way the steel-gray rocketed back and forth across our course anyway, Eddie only had to make sure the horse kept going a little farther than usual in its next veer in front of Joker and me, then rein it around hard to loop into the turn. All I could do was to keep us from getting run over by the gray, and try to catch up after the turn somehow. Joker was just far enough behind the other horse that I saw the flash of motion as Eddie set to work on shouldering into our way. He did what riders like the Turleys do on brawny hard-mouthed horses. He resorted to his spurs to enforce his reining.

As Damon and Toby and I could have told him, spurs actually were not the best idea while riding wrong end to. When you think about it, if your heels are in the vicinity of the horse's shoulders where your toes usually are, the rowels of your spurs are going to hit the horse up front toward the withers, rather than where he expects it in the flanks.

Eddie must have jabbed in an off-balance way, too, raking his horse more sharply on the off-shoulder. The big gray animal flinched away from Eddie's intended direction and abruptly angled off the opposite way. Straight into the turn pillar.

There was a tinny thunder as the steel-gray breasted through the stack of metal, and it rained lunch pails.

Ducking, I let Joker gallop on past where the pails were clattering down, then tugged hard left on the reins. Joker did not manage to make a sharp turn of it, huffing around like a laborious imitation of a cutting horse, but at least we were eventually turned and headed back down the course toward the finish line. That was more than could be said for our opposition.

What an advantage riding backward in the saddle provided at that moment: I had a perfect view of Eddie bouncing away into the badlands as his horse kept going and going. The claybank formations there north of The Cut gradually fell away into a maze of eroded shapes that in a mile or so reached the Marias River. The runaway steel-gray showed every sign of taking Eddie for a swim.

And Joker raced on, solo, until I checked ahead and saw Verl waving his arms and yelling, "Eddie flubbed the turn! Paul wins!"

Other shouts and hoots and whoops of congratulation filled the air as everyone headed their horses down onto the road for a better look at Eddie's situation. By the time I hauled Joker to a halt and got myself right side around in the saddle, Damon and Toby were beside me, each more giddy than the other over my victory, and we watched together as the steel-gray disappeared behind a mudstone hump. When it emerged on the other side, the saddle on its back was empty.

None of us were as concerned as we maybe should have been.

If wolf packs could not do the Turleys in, surely they were impervious to the lesser threat of horses and humans, our line of thinking ran. Still, the entire Marias Coulee school body plunged into the badlands in a loose cavalry charge to the aid of Eddie.

Before we could get there he came limping out from behind the mudstone, shirt torn, hat gone, chin a little bloody, scrapes on every patch of skin that we could see.

"This backwards stuff," he complained as we rode up, "is harder than it looks."

~

I FELT A FOOT TALLER WHEN I FLUNG OPEN THE DOOR TO THE next morning's knock and piped out cheerfully, "Morning, Rose."

"My! You must have got up on the right side of the bed." Pert as a picture herself, she swept in past me, untying her bonnet with one hand and carrying in her other the tiny lunch sack as usual but also a larger bag, doubtless containing more housecleaning weapons. Today the mud room, where we flung overshoes and hung all the seasons of coats and hats and caps and stashed anything else that was loose, was going to meet its match, she had forecast.

Dying to tell her about the race but knowing what particular form of suicide it would be to confide something like that to any grownup, I heard myself waffle:

"You know what?"

"No. What?" She paused and peered at me as if to see what kind of spell had come over me.

"I, uh, I had a really good night's sleep."

That was only half of it. My triumph the day before had been earthwide; the person who caught Eddie's horse and deposited the reins into his skinned-up hands as if dropping a penny to a beggar was Carnelia. So, the night's dream had all the schoolkids, led by an unnaturally civil Carnelia, honoring me by marching up to my desk with cakes. Angel food. Pound cake. Forbidden rum cake. Chocolate with vanilla frosting. My stomach was growling with the delicious memory of it.

"I'm glad," said Rose, still giving me a strange look.

"Good morning, Rose." Yawning, Father came down the hall and made his automatic turn toward the kitchen and coffeepot. It was Saturday, so Toby and Damon were sleeping in.

Rose headed him off before he could reach the kitchen doorway. "Oliver? There's something I must tell you."

"Is there." Father had to abandon his line of march, and I filed in by his side, since her tone seemed to merit a full audience.

"It's about what happened yesterday."

My heart skipped a beat.

Father rubbed his chin, trying to think what so distinguished that day from any other of this whirlwind week.

Rose drew in a declamatory breath that Aunt Eunice could have found no fault with, and launched. "I've been thinking about what Morrie said about destiny. That man. After all these years, I still learn all manner of things from him."

"He's an education, that's obvious," Father granted.

"But back to destiny," she persevered. "This." She pointed a finger straight as a pistol barrel at the floor, then up to the wall, then and around and across the ceiling, our eyes hypnotically following the orbit of that finger. "This is where I am meant to be," she declared. "At honest labor, in a household of people with their feet on the ground. All the—the airiness of our life before, Morrie's and mine, this is the cure we needed. After our little talk the other day"—the widower-to-widow one, it went without saying—"I knew I could tell you this. You have done wonders for us by bringing us here, bringing us out of—" The emphatic forefinger had ended up aimed in the accusatory direction of Minneapolis. By now we were used to filling in the blanks in any conversation with Rose, so Father and I both jumped a little when she unexpectedly did it for us: "—perdition!"

We knew in a general way that Rose's life had had hairpin ups and downs—the swanky leather trade before its demise along with poor Mr. Llewellyn, from the sound of it, then back to being a housekeeper on Lowry Hill—and Morrie must have undergone similar reversals of fortune or he wouldn't be here in Marias Coulee too. Naturally we ascribed it all to bad habits of the pocketbook. It was already clear that, around Rose and Morrie both, income and outgo ran past each other in baffling ways. In a sneaky way, though, I was finding it exciting to try to imagine a level of high living so stratospheric as to be soul-troubling. I could tell that Father similarly was trying to get his imagination around the silk-and-tweed existence our housekeeper and her brother had been too accustomed to, back east in Minneapolis and Chicago, and he wasn't doing much better at it than I was.

After a moment, Father cleared his throat. "Let me try to follow this a little more closely if I can. Yesterday seems to have struck quite a chord with Morrie and you. Am I right that in your minds, Morrie's rather noble gesture of cleaning out the chicken house is somehow tied into a replenished sense of destiny? Happening along the right path at the right time like a good Samaritan, something like that?"

"Exactly!" Rose bunched her hands beneath her apron as if congratulating herself on having cleaned up a nasty chore. Well, I remember thinking, she had a point. If it took something rough to scour away perdition, homestead living ought to do it. "Oliver and Paul," she went on warmly, "I think you know that a chicken house is not the sort of thing Morrie has been used to in life. The woodpile either. Yet he rallied himself to it yesterday when

I asked it of him, getting right in there with that shovel, tackling a task that evidently no one else has ever wanted to touch, not even minding that he ended up smelling like—"

This time she didn't finish the sentence. She squared her shoulders to face the conclusion all this had led her to. "I looked up *destiny* in your big dictionary before going home yesterday, to make sure. 'One's lot in life.' That seemed rather short shrift, so I tried *fate*, and that was better." Rose took another reciting breath. "'That in the nature of the universe by which things come to be as they are.' And so. Call it either, but Morrie buckling down as he did to a nasty chore handed to him by a quirk of fate—well, me—surely is proof that one's destiny can be shouldered in an unceremonious new way that makes up for the old. Wouldn't you say?"

"Just between us, I was simply going to move that chicken coop," Father said. "It's on skids."

"Oh."

"Was there anything else on your mind," Father made sure, the kitchen still beckoning, "before I make my escape?"

"It seems like there was," Rose pondered, "before I got off onto— Yes. The kitchen reminds me. I'm providing food today, aren't I."

At last! We had waited and waited, and Rose finally had acknowledged our plight. Father and I traded amazed gazes. There was an unprecedented tingle in me from my dream of all those cakes. At the time I would have had to get in line with Rose at the dictionary to look up *premonition*, yet something of the sort seemed to be crying out for definition.

"Food, food, food," Rose was thinking out loud as if trying to remind herself. "It's around here somewhere, I know it is. Ah!" She vanished, but not in the direction of the kitchen. And came back with the larger sack she had brought with her.

"There now," she declared with satisfaction, "I've done my delivery duty, you're my witnesses," our spirits falling with her every word. "Rae sent it over. Lunch for tomorrow, I think she said? I gather that you're all off to the whatsit, the Big Ditch?"

"We are," Father confirmed in his flattest tone and took the lunch sack. Then said with emphasis, "Rae is a culinary treasure," before turning away toward the kitchen.

"Oliver?"

Like someone in a game of grandmother's footsteps, Rose had moved appreciably nearer by the time he faced around to her again. She had on her slightly conspiratorial expression. "Could you stand some passengers? Morrie and I would be awfully interested to see the Big Ditch."

"It's a freight run," Father dismissed the notion. "We'll be on the dray; it rides like a bucking bronco on these roads."

Rose had her second round of ammunition ready. "Morrie has no more fear of freight than he does of a chicken house."

"Somehow I can believe that," Father had to face up to. "All right, I can always use an extra helping of elbow grease in the freight handling. We'll swing by for you about nine."

After he determinedly disappeared through the kitchen doorway, I lingered while Rose was putting on her housecleaning apron and warming up for the day with a barely audible aria of whistling. I no longer could resist asking:

"Rose? Lunch and all. What, ah, what is it you eat?"

Plucking up the minuscule bag, she displayed it to me as if it were the trophy of a hunt. "I always bring a nice slice of rusk." She pulled out what looked like a piece of toast overdone to brittle. "Here, try a bite."

I can still taste it. It was like eating a shingle.

5

*T*HE BIG DITCH, OUR INCIPIENT GRAND CANAL. ROSE AND Morrie were not its usual brand of tourists. Even on a Sunday, the haul road to the construction camp was plumed with dust. Land fever knows no Sabbath. Several speedy surreys passed us by, with Toby and Damon and I making a game of who could be the quickest to identify which of the livery barns in West-water each was rented from, with their wheel spokes of red or green or white. We could tell by their bull-wool black suits and odd-collared shirts that the surrey passengers were the latest of the Belgian colony drawn a third of the way around the world by the promise of the farm water the Big Ditch would bring. Near the end of our trip there was what Morrie might have called an instance of momentum of the automotive sort. A Model T, not a common sight yet, met up with us, to the hazard of both our dray and the little vehicle bouncing around in the ruts.

I would say Rose took everything in as though this were a spin in the park, if a bumpy one. She wore yet another silky dress, this one the color of her name. Morrie looked more thrown together, in some of George's old work clothes a couple of sizes big for him. Was it cologne, or did he still carry a faint whiff of his chicken-house adventure? I noticed Father glance every so often at this pair of sightseeing passengers and the three of us who had pestered a Big Ditch visit out of him, as if wondering what had happened to the simple business of drayage. But he never had any trouble holding up his end of a conversation, so matters chattered along. Until we topped the gentle rise at the north end of the broad Westwater benchland.

"My!" Rose issued.

"Good heavens!" Morrie let out.

I suppose every person ever born has gasped at meeting up with the latest earth-changing contraption coming over the horizon. But that it is a common moment stitched into fate or destiny or whatever other name Morrie might have put on it has never lessened my memory of seeing that mammoth dragline steam shovel at work on the prairie. Surely the biggest thing to come to the vicinity since the dinosaurs roamed, the long-necked steam shovel was visible from miles off in its digging of the irrigation project's main feeder canal, which was to say the Big Ditch. The raw banks of the canal stretched behind the machine for miles, like the wake of some bewitched ship capable of sailing on solid ground. On our journey toward the monster this day, as Toby gabbed over Rose's shoulder and Damon continued to pepper Morrie with questions about the gridiron exploits of the University of Chicago Maroons and Father was occupied with the reinwork it took to keep the dray out of the most jolting ruts on the haul road, I simply fastened my eyes on the rhythmically digging steam shovel, growing ever closer, until it could be seen that each of its bites into the ground pulled out what must have been at least a wagonload of earth.

My spell was broken by Morrie. When Damon momentarily ran out of either breath or football players, Morrie leaned ahead on the wagon seat to say across to Father:

"Oliver? I am no agriculturist," which was so obvious Rose tittered at it. "But don't I detect somewhat conflicting concepts of farming, between this"—he inclined his head sagely toward the Big Ditch and its incipient network of diversion canals designed to feed water to seventy-five thousand acres of new fields—"and Marias Coulee?"

"Here I thought you were a city slicker," Father retorted, "and already you can tell the difference between irrigation and dryland." He softened that a bit. "There's really no conflict to it. If crops were whiskey, it'd be a matter of chaser or straight, is all. We drylanders like ours undiluted."

"I am still stumped," Morrie persisted. Rose, sitting between them, pulled back a bit out of the way of debate. "If it takes all this," he again pointed with the crown of his hat to the miles of hydraulic engineering of the irrigation project, "to grow anything here, why don't you need something comparable for your fields?"

"Our formula is r-a-i-n."

But Morrie knew how to drive a point home when he had to, too. Saying not a word more but lifting his brow inquisitively, he put out his hand as a person would to decide if an umbrella was needed. Not a drop of precipitation had fallen during his and Rose's time in Montana.

Father had to deal with that or fold his cards.

"Dryland farming stores away rain when it comes," he cited the gospel of his generation of homesteaders. "A man of your astuteness will have noticed how deep the furrows are in Marias Coulee fields, surely? That's to catch runoff and keep it in the ground."

"For a fact? The soil can act as its own reservoir? Why then do deserts exist, do you suppose?"

"As far as I know, deserts are not plowed." Father evidently decided that if Morrie was looking for enlightenment about farming, he was going to receive it. "There's considerable science to dryland farming, don't worry about that. The state has tested it out for years on end; the county agent gives us all the latest from their experiment stations and holds deep-plowing institutes and so on. What it comes down to is that we get perfectly respectable crops on so-called arid land."

"Interesting," Morrie conceded, or maybe not, "that one implement such as the plow can tame nature that way. And history, for that matter." Rose, I noticed, was watching him apprehensively, evidently having seen her brother consort with history before. One more time he indicated to the Big Ditch and its promised acres. "I would think"—when Morrie thought out loud like this, you somehow could hear an idea taking flight, much the way the wing bones of the whistler swan can be heard sawing the air as it passes low over you—"I would think that in all the centuries for which there are records, people have sought to coax water to their land."

"Morrie, have you been listening to yourself?" Father was good-natured now in respect to Morrie's thought process. "We're coaxing the wet stuff to Marias Coulee, too, but the sky is our ditch. Now, except for one year, let's see, that would have been '04, our crop yields have been right up there with—"

Naturally the trio of us being bounced in the back of the wagon were letting most of this go in one ear and out the other. We were excited about visiting the Pronovosts, even though it had been only the day before yesterday since we had last spent time with Izzy and Gabe and Inez. But a taste of what life in a tent was like, a chance to poke around the Big Ditch construction camp with kids our age, one more opportunity for the bunch of us to crow over what had happened to Eddie Turley in the won-drous race—we thought we could not have designed a better holiday.

Life outdid us again. As our dray lurched into the hurly-burly of the construction camp, Damon was the first to inter-pret the cloud of canvas looming beyond the encampment of the workers' tents and interrupted the grownups with a yelp:

"You didn't tell us there's a circus!"

"Not the kind you're thinking of," Father said over his shoulder as he headed the dray toward a waving foreman at the supply dump. "It's that traveling preacher and his minions. Brother Jubal, he bills himself as. Short for Jubilee, I'd guess." Father leaned in to Rose and Morrie to elaborate. "He finds pretty good pickings at construction camps like this. A fair amount of hangovers and other symptoms of sin after a Satur-day night, don't you suppose? Wages here aren't bad"—Father all but underlined this as a hint to Morrie—"and that can't hurt his collection plate any.

"Speaking of collecting." Father turned his attention to us, poised to leap down into the attractions of the Big Ditch en-campment. "I don't want to have to track the pack of you down to poke lunch into you. Behave yourselves at your friends' and be back here at noontime, hear?" We promised, cross our hearts and hope to die, not to be late.

We jumped down, leaving Rose presiding on the wagon seat like a jaunty figurehead over a cargo wharf, and raced off in search of the Pronovosts. Set loose at the Big Ditch! Whatever Coney Island was, how could it match this? The construction camp more than met our expectations, with swearing teamsters and laboring horses and agitated foremen everywhere, the whole place as loud and dusty as any set of boys could want, and over it all the derrick boom of the steam shovel clanking and whirring as it ate into the prairie. "This beats a circus, doesn't it, Damon?" Toby gave his estimation as we rounded the cook tent and looked for the Pronovosts' house of canvas where Isidor had told us to. Sure enough, ahead was the tent flap open in welcome. But what we could see inside caused all three of us to halt hard. Something was wrong. The Pronovost kids were dressed up.

It turned out they were doomed to a relative's wedding in town. When Isidor and Gabriel and Inez, spick-and-span and dismayed, poured out to meet us, their mother followed to say she was sorry but they had to leave for Westwater as soon as Mr. Pronovost had the horses hitched. We stood around, two awkward squads, until the Pronovost buckboard drew up. As we were trading glum good-byes, Isidor paused before he vaulted into the wagon and said as if he had been giving it a lot of thought:

"You want to get yourselves a look at the Holy Willies. They're sure somethin'."

The buckboard was not even out of sight past the cook tent yet when Damon spoke up: "What about it? We gonna go see?"

"Father didn't tell us not to, did he," I reasoned.

"Not that I heard," Toby contributed.

⌒

"O SINNERS, STOP AND THINK BEFORE YOU FURTHER GO! TURN, and turn now!"

Brother Jubal's deep voice blasted us back a half step as we approached the rear of the big tent. One thing about a sermonizer of his sort, though: if you were undecided about some precept of his, another would be along in a moment. Shortly he was thundering, "We must learn the only happy lesson there is! Not to fight against Providence!" and we slipped in.

Isidor had not been kidding. The congregation, the Holy

Willies as he called them, were on their feet swaying as if the wind of heaven was sweeping through them. Every eye was fixed on Brother Jubal, up on the spacious platform that strenuous religion required. "Wow," Damon breathed, dragging a toe appreciatively as we crept forward. I saw what he meant. The floor of the tent was covered with straw, in the event that any of the worshippers were so stricken with spirit that they would need to get down and roll around. The hopeful three of us found the lee side of a big tent pole and clustered there.

"The Bible!" Brother Jubal was shouting as he brandished that item. "I ask you, brothers and sisters, the one question that shall be asked at the gates of salvation: what use have you made of this powerful book? If you can only answer that you have held it over your head to stop a nosebleed—well, then, I'll tell you, friends, you are in everlasting trouble."

As he restlessly paced and stopped and pivoted, I kept trying to think who Brother Jubal reminded me of. When he spun into profile in one of his pirouettes with the Bible, I figured it out: although not so old and not so paunchy, he was a spitting image of William Jennings Bryan, whom Father would have voted for in every presidential election forever and practically did. Same Roman brow, same coal-chunk eyes. Similar undertaker suit and scrawny tie. I would say Brother Jubal outdid W.J.B. in acrobatic ability, though. On the balls of his feet for as long as we had been watching, abruptly he was across that platform in a flash, pulling up just short of a small table with a pitcher and a glass on it, as he trumpeted: "From borning to burying, cradle to grave, the Bible is your only ticket out of Hell!" Toby had timidly slipped his hand in mine, something he hadn't done in a long while.

Pausing there to deposit the Good Book—somehow his pause seemed as loud as his preachment, and the congregation didn't lose any of its sway—Brother Jubal picked up the pitcher and glass and poured.

Damon whispered in my ear: "I bet you it's panther piss." Whether or not the pitcher held that notorious local brand of moonshine, Brother Jubal resorted to it for a good, long swig.

Swiping the back of his hand across his mouth in a manly way, the sweating preacher seemed to be suddenly reminded of something.

"Our hymn! We have not yet lifted our voices," although he certainly had. As one, the crowd snapped the song sheets in their hands taut.

Disappointed as the three of us were that the preaching had not yet led to any holy rolling, we always liked music. Damon gave the other two of us a grin and tapped his toe like a square-dance fiddler, and Toby giggled. Then Brother Jubal's voice all but swept our hair back again, as he led off the singing in a roaring bass:

> *Let us fight the holy fight*
> *On the wild Montana bench—*

Here the congregation chorused in:

> *Lord, oh Lord, lend us might!*

"Paul, look, there's—"

"Toby, shhh, I'm trying to listen."

In operatic fashion, Brother Jubal swelled his chest and sang on:

> *With a coyote for a bugler*
> *And the Big Ditch for a trench—*

"Damon, Paul—"

"Toby, it can wait until this is over."

Damon took the more direct approach of lightly squeezing Toby's lips together like a duck's bill, a reminder we used on each other when someone was gabbing too much.

Lord—

Toby managed to get himself unclamped from Damon's fingers.

"B-b-but, over there—"

—oh Lord—

Damon and I at last looked over to where our pesky brother was pointing, at the back of the tent across from us. To a raw-boned pair of figures whose shaggy heads stuck out over everybody else's bowed ones. Brose Turley and Eddie.

—lend us might!

The sight of them took all the fooling around out of Damon, and the power of thought out of me. Brose Turley had the music up almost to his nose, gnashing away in some semblance to singing. For his part, Eddie didn't seem to be paying much attention to the song sheet. Gawking around the tent in bored fashion, it was only a matter of time before he spotted us, and he did so now. He blinked and looked again, and it was still us. We could see him whispering urgently into his father's ear, even automatically clutching the front of his pants in the universal need-to-go gesture. Brose Turley gave him a heavy-browed look, but jerked his head to dismiss his son toward outside. Eddie headed our way.

"Let's get," I said, even though Damon and Toby needed no urging.

We made it out of the tent all right, but there was no getting ourselves out of range of Eddie. He was onto us like a staghound on wounded deer. "You damned peepers!" He caught hold of my shoulder and spun me around as if I weighed nothing. "What're you doing here? Come to rub it in?" Looming in on me with his Sunday watered-down pompadour flopping wildly, he looked bigger than he had on horseback.

"Simmer down," I tried. "Our father's here hauling freight; we just rode along."

"Yeah, sure. Where's any freight in the preacher's tent?"

"Lay off, can't you." I tried to sound as tough as I could. It didn't seem to faze Eddie. "We were just curious, is all." From the corner of my eye I could see Damon shifting his weight restlessly, one of his signs of temper. Before I could think of any way to defuse matters, I heard out of my feisty brother:

"Why're you bothering us, anyway. Don't you have to scoot back in there and get yourself saved?"

Eddie took a long step toward Damon.

"Eddie," Toby asked suddenly, short of breath just from thinking about it, "they gonna put you under the water?"

"Put me where?"

Damon undertook to set Toby straight. "These aren't baptizers—"

"Baptists," I said.

"—these are the ones who throw fits. What about it, Eddie? Thrown any good conniptions? Had any good cases of the jerks?" As if there was any chance his target didn't take his meaning, Damon crossed his eyes, groaned in a reverential way, and went into an open-mouthed spasm of shaking all over.

Red-faced, Eddie watched Damon's antics, looking as if he would go to pieces any moment. When he did, it was not the way I expected.

"My old man makes me," he said helplessly, dropping his hands. "Might help get the devil out of me, he says."

Damon quit jerking. Toby looked Eddie over sympathetically for any signs the devil was on his way out. My own expression, and I should have known better, must have told Eddie I
felt sorry for him.

Our pity or whatever it was fired him up again. His voice
went high as he threatened, "If you squirts tell anybody at
school I'll—"

"You'll what?" Damon was on the prod again. "You can't
touch Paul, remember?" He balled up one fist, and then the
other. I saw him eyeing Eddie's chin speculatively. Even I had
managed to land one there at least once, hadn't I? "And maybe
you can whip me"—Damon's common sense and courage were
arguing out loud with one another—"but you'll know you've
been in a scrap."

I stepped in. "Eddie, we won't tell. It's none of our business."

"How'm I supposed to believe that," he scoffed.

Toby turned the moment. Spitting in his small hand, he
then thrust it out toward Eddie's man-size paw.

"Work off some of that energy in the haymow, you two." Father
was unhitching the horses while Damon and I, who could just
as well have been helping him, were busy roughhousing. Toby
already was in a footrace to the house with Houdini. It was a
wonder the barn rafters were not shaking from the high spirits
the two of us were giving off. All the way home from the Big
Ditch, behind the backs of the earnest grownups on the dray
seat, we'd traded Chessy cat smiles at the thought of it: we had
something on Eddie Turley. It didn't even matter that we could
never tell anybody. We knew. There was this about it, too: as
much as anything, our secret mightily added to the Milliron
family repertoire, junior division. From then until the end of
time, all Damon would need to do to set Toby and me and him-

self to laughing would be to cross his eyes and give a meaning-ful twitch.

Right now my brother the cutup halted in mid-tussle with me and cocked an ear in Father's direction as though he had gone hard of hearing. "Hey? Oh, hay." Somehow I found that uproarious.

Draped in horse harness, Father turned around in that way parents do when they are about to tell you they mean business. But Damon already was scampering up the ladder to the hay-mow. I thought it prudent to dash over and help Father heft the welter of leather onto the wall pegs. From what I had overheard before we left off Rose and Morrie at the Schrickers', he prob-ably was nearing the limits of his tolerance for one day. His ef-forts to suggest the Big Ditch to Morrie as a logical site of employment had met polite but undentable resistance. "I find I rather like the solitude of a homestead workday," Morrie said, veteran of several such days. "George keeps coming up with chores for me to do on his mother's place; it's quite remarkable. And should you ever need a hand at anything that is too much for you, Oliver, I have two."

Father was weighing this when Rose burst out:

"Oh, Oliver? I have a favor to ask, the next time you go to town. It's about the dust."

That caused all the Millirons to look over our shoulders, back at the dray's billowing bridal train of dust that every con-veyance in Montana dragged after it, seven months of the year. Dust was such a part of our life we had never heard anyone bother to comment on it.

"I take exception to dust," Rose said decisively.

Bewildered, Father cast another look at the chronic brown fogbank we were raising with every turn of the wagon wheels. "I don't quite see what I can do about—"

"In the house, I mean. It would help with the housekeeping ever so much if dust didn't blow in all the time. The next time you're in town, couldn't you bring back some draft excluder?"

"Draft exclu—?" Even though Father liked to read a couple of pages of the dictionary every night for pleasure, it took him a few moments to work that out. "Do you by any chance mean 'weather stripping'?"

"I do, don't I. My poor husband always called it the other." We had not heard the late Mr. Llewellyn mentioned in the last day or two, but here he was again. "The Welsh have such a gift of gab, you know, and—well, it runs in our blood, too, doesn't it, Morrie."

"Like dye," he vouched, and gave her arm one of those pats.

"Surely it would take you no time at all to tack some whats-it, weather stripping, around the doors and windows," Rose persisted to Father. "As I say, it would do wonders for the house-keeping." He knew he was caught; he couldn't be against wonders of housekeeping. Helpfully, Morrie asked how many windows and doors the house had, and given the number, he announced in a feat of lightning calculation that fifty yards of the stuff ought to dustproof our house.

Whoosh. A cloud of hay cascaded down into the horse stall nearest Father and me, interrupting my reverie and making Father wince.

"Damon! Get a little of it in the manger, can't you?" Father looked in exasperation at the high-priced alfalfa mixed in with the horse manure on the floor of the stall. I was already on my way to the ladder by the time I heard him telling me, "Go up there and regulate the lunatic, while I water the horses."

"My turn," I informed Damon as I popped up into the hay-mow. Yielding the pitchfork and the field of battle to me, he flopped into the hay like someone keeling over backward into a swimming hole. He sprawled there, arms out, in sheer exuberance at our incredible luck lately, and I could not help grinning along with him as I carefully pitched hay down through the loft hole into the manger.

"Hah! Can you believe it?" he marveled, still unable to get over it. "Old Eddie, in there with the Holy Willies. You must have knocked him into Sunday with that haymaker."

"Damon, don't."

"Don't what? You play yourself down too much. One-Punch Milliron!" He pantomimed a roundhouse swing of such arc and ferocity it rolled him over in the hay. "I tell you, the look on old Eddie when you popped him. No wonder he raced like such a boob, he was still so surprised—"

The silence of the barnyard caught up with him as it had with me. We should have been hearing the sound of the pump as Father filled the horse trough.

Damon scrambled on all fours to peek over the edge of the haymow. I teetered behind him for my own fearful view of below.

Father, holding the skimming bucket for the trough that he had come back to the barn for, stared up at the white-faced pair of us.

"Climb down. Now."

The instinct was to bolt and run, but we knew better. We assembled, in a criminal rank of two, in front of Father. I could not bring myself to look at him and I did not want to look at my squealer brother. Damon stood there stupefied. "It—he— we—"

"By all report, this involves Paul," Father said stonily. "Go to the house, Damon. Now." He turned his attention to me, prisoner in the dock and guilty written all over me. "We need to have a conversation."

He marched me into the grain room, where we could sit on bags of oats for what promised to be a long session. From the direction of the doorway of the barn, telegraphic blurts followed us there.

"Paul was only—he didn't really—"

"Damon," Father roared, "I am telling you one last time. Clear out."

When the vast silence after that satisfied him, he turned to me again. "So. Am I to understand that you popped Eddie Turley first?"

"Yes, sir."

He looked pained. "Paul, for crying out loud. I thought Damon was the pugilism fanatic in this family. I should be able to have my eldest son know when to hold his temper."

"I held it for a week, honest I did. Then Eddie mouthed off too much and I let him have it."

Father sighed. "Tell me the particulars. 'Too much'?"

"He—" I paused.

"Out with it."

"—teased me about Rose."

His face changed. Maybe there was hope for me, I thought at the time. Even then I understood at some level that Father had set himself to ignore whatever might be rumored about a wifeless man employing a single woman in his household. Circumstances had helped out—Rose could be seen perfectly nicely traveling back to her room at George and Rae's after work each day, and her very own brother was on hand as chaperon if the situation required any—but Oliver Milliron, a pillar of Marias Coulee, nonetheless had to occasionally choose what not to hear, surely. He did not seem to mind that for himself. But it evidently had not occurred to him the rest of us might have to face some unpleasant chin music about our housekeeper.

He studied me. "Not to put too fine a point on this, Paul, but what exactly did Eddie say?"

I told him, exactly.

Father made a mouth. "Paltry vocabulary. Son, you have to consider the source, in that kind of situation." Something more than Eddie Turley's lingual ability was troubling him, I could see. "This famous fight of yours. I don't see a mark on you."

"No, sir."

"And Eddie?"

"He's a little marked up."

New concern flooded into Father's face. "The next time you decide to massacre one of your schoolmates, look at who's at home, will you? Brose Turley isn't to be fooled around with."

"Father, Eddie wouldn't tell him about me hitting him."

"Oh? How does he explain 'a little marked up' then?"

"He'd probably say his horse surprised him and next thing he knew, he was on the ground."

"And if you were in his position, is that what you would tell me?"

"Pretty much."

That drew me a stern look right out of the book of fathers. He proceeded to inform me in his best lecturing tone, "The schoolyard code of honor is not going to save your skin every time," although, I could have pointed out to him, it had been working perfectly fine for me until Damon blabbed. I hoped I was an absolute picture of attention while Father further stipulated: "I want the truth out of you in any case like this ever again, hear?" I nodded vigorously. A lecture wasn't a spanking or extra chores or exile to my room immediately after supper or any other degree of punishment, and it was beginning to look like I was going to get off with a lecture. "I don't want you instigating any more fights, either." Father had reached what seemed to be his final point. "No more of this 'One-Punch' business."

"No, sir."

"Is that all understood?"

"Yes, sir."

He stood up and started out of the barn, then paused.

"What's this about a race?"

That night. Spanked and sent to bed before sundown and lectured to a degree that definitely did constitute punishment, I lay there unstrung at how the world had turned over from that one moment in the hayloft. My mind, my whole being, was questions. Why couldn't Father have been safely out there operating the noisy, rusty pump at the horse trough when Damon's mouth got away from him? And why was it worse, on the Oliver Milliron punishment scale, to beat someone in a horse race than to punch that person in the jaw? For that matter, why was it worse to ride a galloping horse facing one direction instead of the other? ("What, *backwards?*" I can still hear Father's voice rising.) And what manner of added after-school chore was going to be inflicted on me, tomorrow and beyond? How I hoped it was not going to be the milking. And most of all, why couldn't this whole episode have missed me and afflicted someone else, such as, say, Damon?

That in the nature of the universe, Rose's spirited quoting from the dictionary echoed all through this, *by which things come to be as they are.* If this turn of events was a fair sample of that, fate was not anything to look forward to in life.

Damon and Toby came to bed as if tiptoeing around an invalid. After he climbed in next to me, Damon wriggled for a minute. When he finally managed to say anything, his voice trembled.

"Paul? Paul, if you want I'll go right down and tell Father the race was all my idea."

Dragging in an accomplice to my wrong-end-to crime would only spread the misery, not do away with mine. "Just shut up, will you," I said, and rolled over away from him.

On the list of questions without answers, how, if tears are silent, could I hear Damon begin to cry at that exact instant? Across the bedroom Toby already was sniffling to himself. Dry-eyed, I tried to fight off sleep, dreading what dream would come.

The next morning Eunice Schricker went out to her winter woodpile, pulled out the first stick of fresh stove wood, and found it was four feet long. Every stick in all three perfectly stacked cords was that length.

"I distinctly remember," Morrie defended when George brought him over that evening for a council on how to deal with the wrath of Aunt Eunice, "I distinctly remember your stipulation of the dimensions, Oliver." He reflected for a moment. "I did think it a custom peculiar to homestead life to store firewood in such length. I supposed it had to do with keeping snow from infiltrating the woodpile."

There still was a grim set to Father's chin from his session with me the day before, and this firmed it further. "Morrie, the next time you have a supposition of that sort, run it by me, all right?"

"Mum is madder than a wet hen," George reported, which did not come as particular news to any of us in the Milliron household except Toby. "She wants Morrie off her place, off my place, and probably off yours."

"She may think so," Father said briskly, "but she'll feel better when she sees the guilty party out there sawing all that wood into sixteen-inch stove chunks." He waited until Morrie inclined his head to attest that he understood the concept of sixteen-inch chunks. "And to perk her up even more," Father meted out further justice while he was at it, "I have just the volunteer to help bring that woodpile down to size. You'll meet Morrie at Eunice's every day after school, won't you, Paul."

"There is this about it," Rose sympathetically provided in the morning when I told her about my next phase of punishment. "Morrie won't bore you with silence."

Three cords is a lot of wood when you have to unpile it, drag each piece to the sawhorse, situate it between the crossbucks to hold it into place, find the rhythm of sawing with the person at the other end of the bucksaw, move the saw and cut again, then pile it all back up. Pretty quick I was wishing Father had sentenced me to milking duty instead.

This time around, Morrie was taking no chances. Before we started, he measured a stick to precisely sixteen inches and cut it off square. He used that and a carpenter's pencil to mark where our saw cut would be for each chunk.

"Do we have to?" I protested this time-consuming approach. "Stove wood never gets cut that close."

"From my limited experience with Mrs. Schricker," Morrie maintained, "I conclude that obsessive precision is our only possible defense against her."

Sure enough, Aunt Eunice descended on us at our labor every day, and sometimes twice a day. The first few of those peckish inspections, we stopped to listen to the list of imprecations that plentifully applied "incompetent" to Morrie and "young ruffian" to me. After that we simply kept sawing.

The ultimate afternoon, however, she came out to give us a going-over that would have to last us a while, because George was taking her by train to Great Falls to have her teeth seen to. Morrie did not know what we were in for, but this one I recognized as leading into her full Sunday-special "oh well soon I'll be dead" lamentation. Doom enlivened her every utterance as she had us know that the woodpile was the first thing she was going to check on as soon as she got back and so if we knew what was good for us we had better be on the lookout for her return, day after tomorrow. Aunt Eunice was not of a persuasion to cross herself, but her words seemed to do it for her as she delivered her patented sighing finale: "If I'm spared."

This time Morrie had halted our sawing, perhaps to try to put together the connection between our woodpile proficiency and her self-assigned fate. Now he smoothed his mustache thoughtfully and provided, courteous as could be: "You may ease your mind on that score, Mrs. Schricker."

Accustomed as Aunt Eunice was to mumbled general assurances by George and others that she was sound as a coin, Morrie's frank exercise of predictive powers surprised her. "How so?"

"If you're dead, we won't expect you."

Aunt Eunice speechless as she traipsed off in retreat was not a sight I had ever expected to witness. It started me wondering, in a fumbling thirteen-year-old way, what other rogue capacities Morris Morgan was masking behind that mustache. Perdition, Rose had said she and he and the late Mr. Llewellyn had wandered into in their fancy-glove way of life. That sounded exciting, but exactly what was it? A far cry from a woodpile, surely, yet Morrie did not seem to mind. True, he still looked like a total misfit around any kind of manual labor, with George's hand-me-down clothes draped on him and the beautiful brown hat showing sweat stains but no sensible downward crimp of the brim to ward off the sun. What was it like to work with such a man? Exasperating and exhilarating, in about equal measure.

One minute Morrie would fuss as maddeningly with the wood-pile as if he were arranging diamonds (even Toby could have stacked wood in his sleep), and the next he would be off on some mental excursion that took the breath out of me. A curlew foraging with its long-handle bill drew forth Morrie's observations about the adjustable tools of nature Darwin had discerned in the beaks of finches from isle to isle in the Galápagos. The deep-afternoon silence of our homestead dot on the prairie made him wonder aloud why Thoreau, if he wanted a full-fathomed pool of solitude, had never joined the Oregon Trail migration and come west. "Who's 'Thorough'?" I asked, and then and there learned that a person could go through life as a self-appointed inspector of snowstorms. Morrie's mind never rested, although the pair of us on the bucksaw did, more and more often, now that Aunt Eunice was off the property.

Looking back, I see that it was just as well that Morrie was dosing me with knowledge after school, because school itself had turned confusing. Each day started sour, with me still mad at Damon, which made him miserable, and that left Toby fretting about both of us. The Marias Coulee schoolyard sensed that I was in trouble at home, no doubt because of the wrong-end-to race, and so my celebrity dwindled away before it could get a good start. Besides that, at every recess Eddie Turley hung around squinting suspiciously at Damon and Toby and me even though we had given him our most solemn word, sealed with spit. It didn't help that Miss Trent strangely turned sunny in the schoolhouse, gaily leading us in song sessions instead of recitation period a couple of times that week. Did she have some kind of sixth sense toward the Millirons, I pondered, that brightened her up when any of us went under a cloud?

One way or another, I sawed away at that long week until, midway through our Friday-afternoon stint on the woodpile,

Morrie looked across at me as we pushed and pulled and asked, "What do you dream of, Paul?"

Was it possible? Did I dare believe my ears? A grownup was asking about my rampaging nocturnal mind. And if ever a dream needed a broader audience, it was this recurrent one of mine. Each stroke of the saw bit with more ferocity as I divulged to Morrie the nightly trance in which I would be walking along a road when a commotion kicked up behind a mudstone formation off to one side, and when I reached there the eroded hill was being circled by a couple of people and a pack of wolves— sometimes the people chased the wolves, then the wolves would chase the people, I took care to explain—and no matter how hard I tried to find a stick to throw at the wolves there never was any stick, and things went on like that until on one pass the wolves and the pair of people vanished around the hill together and when I shouted that I was going to come around there with a stick if all of them didn't quit this, someone's head rolled out from behind the hill, at which point I always woke up.

I looked across the sawhorse expectantly.

Morrie appeared boggled. "All I meant, Paul, was what do you dream of becoming when you grow up?"

My disappointment was massive. Morrie chucked aside the piece of wood we had just cut and set another length into place and marked it before referring back to my dream. "They're working on those in Vienna, I believe. I'm sorry I'm no guide on this, truly. But my own are more the daydream sort."

One of those. He really was like Father. Provider of moonbeams when I wanted full illumination. Downcast, I leaned into the sawing again. We had only done a couple of strokes when Morrie spoke up again. "I haven't wanted to pry. But what did you commit to earn three cords of punishment?"

"Nothing much."

"Something, surely."

"I wouldn't like for it to get around."

"Your secret is safe with me."

"There was a fight at recess—well, not much of a fight, and he's so much bigger than me that we settled it in a horse race that was sort of special, and the way it worked out, I won. And Father came down on me for that." There. The case of injustice was laid out.

To my surprise, the bucksaw stopped going. At first I thought we had hit a knot in the wood, but no, Morrie was holding us to a halt as he gazed across at me. A light I had not seen before came into his eyes, the kind of glint that comes off a lightning rod when the sun catches it just right. "Tell me about this fight and 'special' contest of yours."

The oilcloth took the beating of its life from sullen elbows that evening after supper. At my accustomed place I sat stonily propping my head with both arms as I pretended to read *Ivanhoe* to show Father it took more than a woodpile to break my spirit. Damon similarly had his face in his fists as he stared down at his domino solitaire game, not bothering to make any moves. Toby's chubby hands pressed against his cheeks while he idly kicked the air under his chair. We were like the proverbial three monkeys, except all stuck on "hear no evil." Father, going over his Big Ditch freight accounts at his end of the table, occasionally glanced around at us but kept at his bookkeeping. The knock on the door jarred all of us, as if the sound had shaken the table.

When we scrambled to peek while Father opened the door, Morrie stood there on the porch step. He was holding up a bull's-eye lantern to see by, and I swear, he and Father swept over the part about Diogenes searching the world for an honest man without either of them having to speak a word of it. Instead Morrie broached: "I'm here to borrow a morsel or two of newsprint, if I may. Rose tells me you have an abundance of newspapers."

I believe what Rose probably said was that we had a surplus of newspapers, but ours was a reading household. Father took the Sunday *Denver Post* by mail, which with luck arrived the following Thursday or Friday, and the daily *Great Falls Leader* and the weekly *Westwater Gazette,* and other people passed along their mail copies of various city papers when they were done with them; it all tended to accumulate. "You're welcome to any Damon hasn't cannibalized," Father offered. Homestead etiquette was taken care of in his next breath. "But come on in and sit a spell first."

Morrie cast a yearning glance toward the parlor, and followed Father on into the kitchen where the coffee lived.

Toby and Damon bounced into their spots at the table, practically glistening with readiness for anything that might change the mood of the household, and even I, who already had Morrie as company all those woodpile hours, went way up in spirit at this visit of his. Yet you could never quite be sure of the consequences of having Morrie around—those four-foot-long sticks of firewood, remember—and part of me stayed leery as he leapt into conversation with Father. The weather of Montana versus that of Minneapolis, the scandalous condition of the nation, the curious byways of mankind: they ranged over topics like the veteran talkers they were. The younger three of us swung our attention back and forth between them like onlookers at a tennis match, and I must say I didn't see it coming (although Father didn't either) when Morrie tossed into the mix:

"Oliver? Do you know the martial history of the Crow Indians?"

"Somehow it has escaped my notice. Why?"

"They were the daredevils of the northern plains," Morrie spoke with the lilt he gave to his most soaring notions. "And the boldest of them were their contrary warriors. You have in Paul here a contrary warrior."

I was petrified. The last thing I needed, around Father, was to be made known as a daredevil of the northern plains.

But Morrie unstoppably was going on: "I suspect you have your own tribe of them." Damon and Toby tried to look off to distant corners of the room. "You see the parallel between those dauntless young Crow warriors and your own, I trust, Oliver? They rode into battle backwards on their horses."

Father blinked at this anthropological news. "Why on earth—?"

"People do these things to transcend the ordinary, I'd say." Morrie made this pronouncement as if it was the most reasonable thing he had ever heard of. "Wouldn't you? To find their own boundaries, of bravery or willpower? To plow a deeper furrow of life, if I may put it that way?"

"Morrie," Father responded as he drew a slow circle on the oilcloth with his cup, "I know you intend well with this. I simply don't want my children breaking their necks."

"Every neck I see in this room is intact," Morrie pointed out. "And I believe Paul's adversary agreed to the terms of the race, and came out in one piece."

"You think I should close the book on this 'contrary warrior' episode of Paul's." Father weighed the matter and sounded dubious to me. I felt as if I didn't dare breathe so as not to tip the balance.

"I do. Warriors learn from survival. I've spent enough time with Paul under the adverse conditions of the woodpile and Eunice Shricker to rate him a very sobered young combatant."

It may have been the invoking of Aunt Eunice that gave Father pause about the extent of my punishment. In any case, something flickered in his set expression. After a long moment he said, "I'll take it under advisement. You would have made a good defense attorney, Morrie."

A wiggle of relief ran through the other three of us. Damon could restrain himself no longer. "Uhm, Morrie? Would you like to see my scrapbooks? I have Coach Stagg in them and everything."

"Damon, I would be honored. But—" He looked to Father to see if perhaps the evening should be closed down.

Father waved them off to where the scrapbooks lived, our bedroom. "The lot of you, except our fabled contrarian here. Paul, I need your help with a couple of duns."

My head still spinning from the turn of events Morrie had brought about, I assembled my writing materials. Wordlessly Father passed me the bills of lading that were past due, and I wrote the dunning letters. The kitchen was still except for the skritch of my pen and Father's shuffling of papers, while from upstairs the voice of the sports fiend, Damon, and Morrie's more melodious murmur drifted down. When I set the last letter aside for the ink to dry, I stayed in my chair instead of bolting for upstairs, unsure of the ground I was on with Father.

After an amount of time that I somehow knew he was measuring in his head, he glanced up from his accounts. Then put his hands on the edge of the table and pushed back a bit, as if trying to add to his perspective on the youngster across the table. "When you and Thucydides finish the woodpile," Father kept his voice down as he began, "we'll call the matter of that race square. All right? That does not mean you are free to go galloping around backwards, ever again. I am not raising the pack of you to be rodeo trick riders."

"No, sir. I didn't think so."

"What Morrie said about outdoing the ordinary is entirely valid, but there are ways to do it and still stay in one piece."

"I'm not against that, Father, honest."

"Paul. Son." His mouth worked at stifling a swallow. "I don't know how I could get along without you." He scraped his chair back and headed for the stove and coffeepot so that I couldn't see his face. "Now scat. I have to finish up this bookkeeping."

As I mounted the stairs, my lips silently tried out the two words "contrary warrior" together. *Valid, but,* according to Father. How was I supposed to put a paradox like that together? Maybe better to be Damon, whom I could hear had passionately worked his way from football to boxing in the scrapbook tour, which I supposed was fitting for the review of my case just concluded.

"It's funny, the name and all, but know who I liked best, before? Casper—

—"the Capper, yes, yes, I see it here," Morrie throatily finished for him, doubtless under the strain of keeping up with Damon's enthusiasm. "I swear, headline writers are more ruthless than Cossacks. 'Pug Takes Long Walk Off Short Pier,' indeed."

Damon would have bristled to be told so, but he had a Shakespearean taste for heroes who came to some gory end or another. The outfielder who fell from the bar car of a train. The fullback who rashly wrestled a sideshow bear. Those unfortunates, I knew from my brother's bedtime tales of them, were there in the album pages with the pugilist under discussion, who by all evidence had thrown a championship fight and ended up dumped off a dock. To me, that did not sound like the kind of contrary warrior a person wanted to be. But Damon, I remembered, had been heartbroken about no longer being able to follow the career of the scrappy Capper, and Morrie was so feelingly providing a wreath of solace I did not want to interrupt.

"He perhaps did make a misstep, so to speak," Morrie concluded gently. "Before that, he was a boxer nonpareil."

I knew that meant something like one-of-a-kind. Maybe I just had to take this as a nonpareil night. Damon, though, was dealing wholesale in comparisons, asking keenly, "Could the Capper have beat the Real McCoy, you think?"

"If bouts were fought on a first-name basis," Morrie was sent to musing, "one would have to think not." His voice had taken on the timbre I recognized from his more soaring disquisitions, and appreciative audience that I had grown to be at the woodpile, I waited outside the bedroom doorway to see where this one would go. "'Casper' versus 'Harry,' that would sound like a first-round knockout for the latter, wouldn't it. But nicknames capture an essence, an augmented personification of the individual." One-Punch Milliron listened to this with care. "No," Morrie was concluding as though he could see the match in some ring beyond this world, "the Capper would have capped the McCoy off, I'm sure of it. Eight rounds, no more."

What a picture the three of them made as I entered the room. Toby was half sprawled onto the worktable next to the pair hunched over the spread-open scrapbooks, his eyelids desperately heavy. In the lamplight Morrie pensively stroked his mustache as Damon ran a guiding finger through that holy writ of the true sports fan, the fine print, the agate type beneath the story of the event.

"I couldn't believe it when he lost to Ned Wolger, that time. Look at the round-by-round, the Capper was winning almost all—"

Damon became aware I was there. He swiftly looked around at me, his hand groping toward another scrapbook. His voice broke a little as he said, "Paul, I just put the World Series in. Want to see?"

He knew that baseball was the one sport I cared anything about. I figured I might as well thaw; Damon was going to be my brother forever, no matter what. "Sure."

But before I joined them at the scrapbooks, there was the matter of Morrie coming over tonight to act as my advocate. I had no idea how to thank him enough. "Morrie, I—"

"It's all right, Paul, you may have to return the favor sometime." His forefinger took its turn at the fine print of life, alighting into the lineup of the world champion Pittsburgh Pirates. "Honus Wagner, the Flying Dutchman, now there's an ominous nickname if there ever was one."

6

$\mathcal{W}$HEN I CAME DOWNSTAIRS IN THE MORNING, FRESH FROM a dreamless night, I could tell there still was something on Father's mind. Hoping it wasn't me, I dropped to my place at the table to try to fade into the routine of breakfast.

No breakfast was in sight.

"The time has come, Paul," Father said with determination, one warrior to another. "I am going to have it out with Rose on the cooking."

"Really?"

"Watch and see."

I ran back upstairs to shake Damon and Toby awake.

By the time they were more or less dressed and had spilled out onto the stairs to take a grandstand seat with me, here came the customary brisk knock.

We watched avidly as Father let Rose in and, just like that, was rewarded with, "Isn't this a morning to remember? Oliver, I have decided I am going to tackle the kitchen."

"You are?" Father sounded like someone who had hit the

jackpot. Damon, always our hungriest of the hungry, showed Toby and me his fingers crossed for luck.

"Absolutely," Rose vowed. "There is not a shelf in there that doesn't need scouring down."

She bustled by Father, the curls on her forehead giving a little flip as she sighted us perched on the stair treads. "Toby, Damon, Paul, good morning, good morning, and good morning. My, aren't you the early birds on a Saturday!" The lunch sack that barely would have fed a chickadee went to its accustomed place, off came her coat, and we knew it was only a matter of seconds before she would be whistling into her day's work and for all intents and purposes incommunicado. Damon groaned and Toby twitched. Father cast a harried glance up at us and cut her off halfway along the hall.

"The kitchen. That brings up something. I wanted to have a word with you."

"Certainly, Oliver."

"Ah, Rose? I—the boys and I," he shamelessly resorted to, "rather hoped that you might lend us a hand with the cooking. Naturally there could be an adjustment in wages."

Rose appeared mystified. "Did my advertisement contain a misprint?"

"No, no. We all got a rise from 'can't cook but doesn't bite,' believe me. It's just that we assumed the first part was as much a jest as the second part."

"Alas," Rose emitted, one of the few people in the modern world who could say that word and seem to mean it, "it was not."

"Can't cook *at all*?" Desperation was entering Father's voice. "How can that be?"

"I was never taught it. Housekeeping, yes, every wrinkle. I entered household service on Lowry Hill when I was just a slip of a girl, but was never on a kitchen staff. And even if I had been assigned to kitchen duty, there are obstacles."

"Such as?"

"Eggs," she confided. "I can't stand the sight of them."

"What, *eggs*? But you gather them every day!"

"They're still in their shells then, aren't they. It's the yolks that get me. And the runny stuff, what's it called, egg white. Ugh."

Floundering fatally before our very eyes, Father did make one last try at grasping Rose's cookery-free existence:

"But you were a married woman—how on earth did you and Mr. Llewellyn eat?"

"Out."

Twenty-four hours later, the still disconsolate crew of us pushed our spoons around in mush that was even less appetizing on Sunday than the other mornings of the week. Our fate stretched ahead of us, plate by usual dismal plate, into infinity now that we knew Rose honestly meant "Can't Cook." Father had to use the last card in his sleeve to cheer us up at all. "Gather up your long faces," he directed. "I have a load for the Big Ditch and you're all riding along; you can see your friends. Then Rae is feeding us dinner, although I can't imagine where she got the notion we need a square meal, can you?"

Some days are all ups and downs. October was drawing to an end with nice, clear weather, but the wind was practicing for winter as we bunched on the wagon seat next to Father in our caps and coats. Then when the dray crested onto the Westwater plain there was the insatiable steam shovel, and the hubbub of the construction camp, but where Brother Jubal's tent should have been, there was only the leftover strew of straw from the muscular worshipping. Damon said something under his breath, which drew him a sharp warning nudge from me. But Father didn't hear, and only instructed us to keep an eye on the time while we were visiting the Pronovosts and, need he add, stay out of trouble.

At the sight of us, the Pronovost kids practically tore through the front wall of their tent to race out and give us the news. Gabriel and Inez impatiently jigged in place waiting for Isidor to summon the words. Drawing himself up to his skinny best, Isidor said for the ages:

"You hear yet? Teacher run off with that preacher."

Toby looked puzzled. Damon and I grinned tentatively, waiting for the rest of Isidor's joke.

However, Isidor made the quick cross over the center of his chest that meant he was serious. "Pa's foreman seen 'em get on the train together yesterday with their suitcases. Kissin', too. If that don't count as runnin' off, I don't know what does."

It is the kind of bulletin that still freezes my heart. A teacher erased from the school year. The casualty reports that come to my office sometimes are as awful as can be. *Car slid on black ice.* Or *caught in the blizzard,* or *the teacherage caught fire in the night.* Other times they're simply bad enough. *Death in the family* or *taken ill.* Each time my department rushes the files of availables to the beleaguered rural school board, but any gap in the seam of a school year is troubling to me. A one-room school and its solitary teacher must exist on something approaching matrimonial terms, for better and for worse, and back there when Isidor's words were registering on us, I instantaneously missed Adelaide Trent even though I had never liked her. The confused mix on the faces of Toby and Damon said the same for them. All of us were far too young to know the weather of the heart that caused her to flee off with a Bible-thumping spieler. But we understood that Marias Coulee had been jilted.

Isidor was mustering the remainder of his report. "Seen her here a couple of Sundays in a row. We figured she was just here for the singin'. Guess not."

Two minutes later, Father looked around in surprise at the three of us screeching to a halt. Damon and I let Toby tell it; he was going to anyway.

"Miss Trent loped!"

"Did she." Father's eyebrows lifted commensurately. "That must have been a memorable change from her usual gait."

"Father, Toby means 'eloped,'" I said.

"Hopped on the train with that sky pilot," Damon elaborated.

Father sat down on the tailgate of the dray.

"Let me try to catch up here," he said. "Addie Trent has landed a man? And quit the country with him, just like that?"

We three nodded in unison.

"Destiny strikes again," he said wearily.

7

"GOOD MORNING, YOUNG SCHOLARS."

Three dozen sets of schoolchild ears took a considerable moment to adjust to that form of address. Until then, our day was always started with Miss Trent's all-purpose "Children, hush." After a ticktock of contemplating the unexpected new source of articulation at the front of the classroom, all of Marias Coulee school raggedly chorused back to Morris Morgan:

"Good morning, teacher."

Morrie gave a bit of a bow, his crisp white shirt so maximally washed and starched and ironed by Rose that I thought I could hear it crackle. Not that I dared hope it counted for much, but at least the school had gained sartorially in the swap of baggy Miss Trent—Sister Jubal now?—for this exemplar of tailoring. Morrie stood before us like an emissary from those farthest places in our books, where prime ministers attired themselves in tweed and vest and a tie as prominent as a chin napkin. Topped off in this case with the imperial mustache, of course.

While I sat there fidgeting, the collective gaze of the school-room rested solidly on the figure at the front of the room. In it,

I know from experience at both ends of a classroom, were measures of doubt, awe, trepidation, hope, something approaching dread and something approximating adoration—the ingredients of every first sighting of a teacher by those whose fate it is to sit and be taught. Morrie fingered a piece of chalk as he gazed back at the legion of us. My case of the fidgets grew worse. Hours on the woodpile instructed me about a good many of his mannerisms, and I could tell he was rubbing up one of his gigantic thoughts, genie-in-the-lamp style, from that chalk.

But whatever it was, Morrie managed to stow it for the time being. "The day's first lesson," he sent the hearts of Marias Coulee school down and just as swiftly up, "is for me, to learn your names." He whirled to the blackboard as gracefully as if ice-skating. "In exchange, here is mine." My pride in my penmanship leaked away with every swiftly stroked letter of his name; he wrote an exquisite hand, worthy of copperplate.

"So." Quick as the word, he turned to us again. "If you will please stand one by one and announce yourselves, I can acquaint names with faces. Let's start here with this handsome fellow at the end at the front row."

Shy with this mighty honor, Josef Kratka barely managed to find the floor with his feet and blurt his name. The other first-graders wobbled up one after the other, as little different from one another as ducklings. Then the second grade, where differentiation took hold. Inez Pronovost popped to her feet like a girl cadet, but Sigrid Peterson barely surfaced to deliver her accented syllables. Hot-eyed Emil Kratka rapped out his name as if challenging anyone to deny it. There was the faintest ghost of a smile on Morrie as Toby reared up and enthusiastically identified himself.

"Sally Emrich, teacher sir," the school's leading fussbudget led off primly for the third grade. Maybe this first schoolday under the unlikely generalship of Morrie was marching in place, but even I had to admit it had not fallen on its face yet.

From the moment Father talked himself into the idea and set about coaxing the other school board members into it as well, I was apprehensive about the whole notion of Morrie being tapped to finish out the school year. For one thing, most of that year remained ahead, and all across those months it would take only one lapse on the order of those four-foot sticks of firewood to make a laughingstock of him—and, by extension, of the Millirons. For another, he had never taught school a day in his life, up until now.

"Oh, how funny!" Rose said when Father broached the job to Morrie.

"I am rather out of practice at submitting a job application," Morrie said nervously. He looked at Rose as if she ought to back him up in this. "The leather trade, that was all in the family—"

"Gone, every trace of it," Rose sounded the sad note for him.

"It's of no matter," Father skipped over that, "we want someone in that classroom with knowledge running out his ears, not commerce. Morrie, why so coy? The job of teacher would fit you like those kid gloves you used to have dealings in."

Rose, at least, seemed persuaded by that reasoning. "If Oliver gives his word for you—"

"Oliver, you are all too readily casting me in a role with the heroic echoes of antiquity," Morrie mused. " *'Gladly would he learn, and gladly teach.'* I am not sure I have the capacity to play that dual part."

Any other time, Father might have dusted off Chaucer himself and parried with the further description of that book-laden pilgrim to Canterbury: *"But all be that he was a philosopher/Yet had he but little gold in coffer."* Instead he clapped Morrie on the shoulder. "I'll just need to run this by a few people."

The emergency session of the Marias Coulee school board precipitated by the elopement of Adelaide Trent was called to order in our kitchen that same night. As we'd expected, Damon and Toby and I were shooed off to our room, and just as inevitably we took our usual perches at the head of the stairs to overhear. Right away Joe Fletcher wondered out loud why a man of Morrie's sort was unmoored from any previous career:

"He isn't a bughouse case, is he?"

"No more so than thee or me, Joe," Father attested. "Make the mistake of arguing with him sometime and you'll wish he wasn't so sane."

Walt Stinson voiced the next suspicion. "Then how about tonsil paint? Is he in the habit?"

Father warded that off stoutly. "From everything I can see, he leaves the bottle strictly alone."

I could have told them Morrie's intoxication with the brew of knowledge was the real worry. Schoolchildren are quick as sharks to scent something amiss with a teacher, and if he rambled off too far into his excursions of thought in the classroom—well, the three of us there on the stairs would be pining for the old days in the schoolyard when the only topic we heard about was Rose. More than any razzing at recess, though, what bothered me about the prospect of Morrie as our teacher was what it could do to him. If he was branded as ridiculous, it would not stop with the student body of Marias Coulee. People were not a bad lot generally, in what opinion I had been able to form at that age, but there were always some who could drive a nail through a butterfly, too.

Beside me, Damon was on edge. He rightly sensed that having Morrie in the schoolroom every day, with all the rest of us there, would be a drastic alteration from the two of them poring over sports exploits together. Toby's reaction was the opposite; as far as he was concerned, Morrie inhabiting the teacher's chair would be the next best thing to having Rose on hand. With our hopes going off in various directions, we listened while Father used every caliber of persuasion in his arsenal to bring around his fellow school board members to the concept of resorting to Morris Morgan.

Walt Stinson was ending up where Joe Fletcher had started out, at that apparent gap between Morrie's attainments and his current situation:

"Then why's he not doing better for himself in life than chores at Eunice Schricker's place? Can't be he likes exercise that much."

"All I can tell you, he and his sister are gluttons for work." Father expended a breath that must have made the walls of our kitchen move. "Gents, we are up against it. We are short of a teacher, we have a man right here handy to the job, and the man happens to be a granary of learning. I ask you, isn't the logic looking us right in the face? Are we ready to take a vote?"

Without incident Morrie's call of the roll reached Damon's grade, the populous sixth. First up was the bashful girl in front of me who had a certain corner of all our hearts because of her long and lonely ride to school. She gave a shy little curtsy and said:

"Wiwian Willard."

Morrie's forefinger paused in its journey through the Marias Coulee enrollment register. He tapped the paper tentatively as if to encourage its help on this.

"Lillian, I'm sorry but I don't seem to have you on the roll."

"Wiwian," she said again.

"Miriam?" Morrie tried again.

A guffaw erupted from the back of the room, the den of eighth-grade boys. Morrie peered back there in interested fashion. "A volunteer, full of gaiety. Just the kind of messenger the gods like to send when enlightenment is required." He singled out the author of the gusty laugh, Milo Stoyanov, with a stare as level as a pointer. "Well? Enlighten me."

Caught off-guard, Milo looked right, looked left, then gulped out: "Vivian's her name."

With that clue, Morrie managed to spy *Villard, Viv.* on his list.

"Ah." He gave her a gesture of apology. "*Mea culpa,* Vivian, not *youa culpa.*" Everyone in the schoolroom except Damon and Toby and I blinked.

Catching a second wind, Morrie briskly elicited names from Isidor Pronovost and Miles Calhoun. Then Barbara Rellis sprang up and identified herself in her cheeky tone of voice. Every male in the room over the age of nine knew she was going to go out in the world and break hearts. Morrie nodded in satisfaction after finding her on the list, but Barbara stayed standing.

"Teacher? May I please trade my first name in for another one? Just for school."

All who knew Barbara could have told him it was not a wise move, but Morrie asked speculatively, "And what would that be?"

"Rabrab."

I saw Morrie brace for a gale of laughter from the rest of us, but none came. We were all as intrigued as he was. In the expectant silence, Morrie made a try at formulating:

"Technically, Barbara—to address you in the customary manner, for the moment—what you are requesting seems to be an antonymous nickname. If I am not mistaken, 'Rabrab' constitutes your given name, at least a majority of it, backwards. Why would you prefer that?"

"Boys get to be contrary warriors their way," she said with a devilish innocence I could have throttled her for. "I figured I could at least do it with my name."

My face felt red enough to ignite. Her usual elbow-length away from me, Carnelia Craig snickered to herself.

Morrie managed to quell the outburst of debate—whether she was Barbara or Rabrab, half the school instantaneously backed her and the other half reflexively rallied to the opposing view—and take the matter under advisement.

"Names are mighty things," he intoned, folding his arms on his chest in what I recognized as his deep-thinking mode. "They may carry the essence of our person, particularly if incised, which is to say nicked, with an apt bit of elaboration. Think of Richard the Lion-Hearted. The Divine Sarah Bernhardt. The Real McCoy," his gaze just above Damon's head for that one. "We mustn't take lightly what the world knows us by, and I commend Miss Rellis for the imagination to seek something she finds more fitting. But there is also the matter of official record," he tapped the roll call list again, "community custom, and need I say, parents."

With that word, the conspiratorial air that had preceded the wrong-end-to race returned to the room. In the hush, every one of us watched Morrie intently as he deliberated. "I need to know if there is a foundation of precedent upon which 'Rabrab' might be installed. Does anyone else go by a nickname, just here at school?"

"Me." Miles Calhoun raised his hand as high as it would go.

Morrie stared at him in consternation. "Miles, I am as certain as anything that you just now informed me that your name is—Miles."

"That's what everybody calls me. That's what I go by. But my name's Hector and that's what I get all the time at home."

"Then why—" From the corner of his eye Morrie caught my infinitesimal shake of my head. A trackless bog lay ahead of him in the fact that Hector was dubbed Miles by the schoolyard at large because of his habit of saying *by a mile,* as in "Is two against one fair, by a mile?" and "I don't believe a word you say, by a mile."

Pulling back just in time, Morrie returned to the issue at hand. With a Solomonic flair that impressed even those who did not want Barbara to get away with anything, he rendered his decision: "If you can sufficiently convince your fellow young scholars, Rabrab it can be, until different notification."

Peering once more into the ranks of the sixth grade, Morrie looked relieved at the prospect of getting the roll call back on track with Damon. I knew better. Damon had given me a wicked wink during Barbara's—Rabrab's—mischief and I could about hear what was coming, some wisecrack about reversing his name to Nomad. But before he got to pull this off, he happened to turn in the direction of his deskmate as he started to stand up.

"*Gaahhh!* She's bleeding to death again!"

Damon's yelp would have raised the hair on the dead. For all his fascination with gruesome fates of sports heroes, he shared Father's queasiness around actual blood. And there beside him sat Marta Johannson, perfectly calm, with a red rivulet running out of each nostril and darkening her upper lip. Marias Coulee school had probably more than its share of nosebleeds, usually brought on by fists, but this spontaneous one of Marta's was judged sensational. As Damon tried to scramble away from her, Grover Stinson leaned across to see past him, adjusting his spectacles for a better look. The Drobny sisters, Seraphina and Eva, smiled at Marta's plight like a pair of drawn stilettos. Several sets of feet drummed on the floor excitedly. "I think I'm going to throw up," Rabrab announced. "You do and I'll hit you one," Eddie Turley pledged. Milo let out another room-shaking guffaw.

"Everyone! Quiet, a moment."

Speeding down the aisle toward Marta, Morrie glanced to the seventh grade for interpretation as he passed.

"She gets these," Carnelia and I said together in veteran fashion.

Morrie slid down onto one knee in front of Marta, working fast. He tore a strip of tablet paper and rolled it into a tight little ball. "Push this up under your lip and hold it there, that's the way." With Marta staunching the flow, he professionally dabbed away the bloody residue with a dampened handkerchief. It was all over in record time.

Breathing a little hard, Morrie walked back to the front of the room and resolutely picked up the roll call list again. I began to wonder if he was going to get us to first period, arithmetic, before the end of his initial teaching day.

The remainder of the sixth grade, perhaps impressed with Morrie's capability around blood, reeled off names without event. Carnelia and I, the total seventh, accounted for ourselves in no time. This left the eighth grade, that logjam of big boys. Carl Johannson and Milo Stoyanov had both needed to repeat a grade along the way, and Eddie Turley had flunked two. There was a rim of fuzz on the upper lip of each of them, as if they were starting to grow moss from all their years trapped in the schoolroom. Martin Myrdal and Verl Fletcher merely were man-size ahead of schedule, and markedly brighter than the others, but their renegade moods of growing up were such that you had to watch your step around them, too. I had the impression that even Carnelia was taking an interest in how our new teacher would fare with this bunch. Permanently mad at each other though we were, she and I shared unspoken relief that we did not have to go through life amid the galoots of grade eight.

Morrie did not appear perturbed as one after another of them unfolded out of the desks that were too small for them and muttered a name. He did pause a barest moment when the roll call reached Eddie Turley. Just sitting there, Eddie looked like a menace to society. He took his time about getting onto his feet and made a face at the whole process, to show he had no problem with sneering at the new teacher.

But beginner's luck was with Morrie. When Eddie lurched back down, the last student of all happened to be Verl Fletcher. Before Verl could reclaim his seat, Morrie popped him a question:

"Verl, I must ask—do you happen to know the derivation of your distinguished family name?"

"Nope."

"No? Allow me then to tell you what a vital profession it was, that of a 'fletcher,' one who 'fletched.'"

I was the one person in the schoolroom who had ever witnessed Morrie soar off into full trapeze flight this way. The whole student body, however, instinctively understood that our new teacher had to catch onto something up there or fall far. Already Verl was looking uneasy with a family tree of ones who fletched.

Morrie advanced on the lanky eighth-grader unfazed. "You see, Verl, in days of old a fletcher was an arrowsmith, a maker of arrows. Knights of the Round Table, huntsmen, Robin Hood, they all depended on the skill of the fletcher to make that arrow straight and true." Snatching up the yardstick that Miss Trent used to whap on the blackboard to get our full attention, Morrie pantomimed an archer drawing back the arrow to let fly. "We take the measure, so to speak, of those long-ago fletchers every day of our lives. Verl, what do you notice about the length of this 'arrow'?" Morrie patiently held his archery pose.

"It's a yard?" Verl hazarded.

"Exactly! And that is where we get that unit of measure from. The cloth needed for a bowman's coat had to be as wide as that arrow was long, didn't it. Watch!" Morrie whipped off his suit coat, turned it upside down, held one corner up by his ear where the feathered end of the arrow would have been, thrust out his arm in drawn-bow fashion again with the other corner of the coattail in his fingers, and there it was, the yard-long length of cloth. Everyone in the room had seen their mothers or the clerk at the Westwater mercantile measure from a bolt of cloth that way, and now we knew why. Several of the girls who sewed, Carnelia among them, verified Morrie's domestic insight with testing motions of their shoulders. Toby and the others in the lower grades were examining their arrow arms with new respect. Verl looked somewhat dazed but newly knighted.

Putting his coat back on and adjusting his cuffs, Morrie headed toward the more usual teacherly territory at the front of the room. "You may sit down, Verl, thank you very much. That excursion into times past whence measurements come from brings us, I believe, to arithmetic period."

Rose mercilessly took charge when Morrie moved in to the teacherage out back of the schoolhouse, shaking her head over its prior level of housekeeping every way she turned.

"I take exception to flounces," she declared of Miss Trent's taste in curtains as she flung up a window to air the place out. "Absolute dust catchers. Oliver, surely the school board—"

Father gave Rose a look that seemed to say there it was again, that exceptional disposition of hers. Nonetheless he patted his pockets for something to write "new curtains" down on. Toby and Damon and I prowled the previously forbidden premises, disappointed not to find teacher secrets cropping up anywhere. Damon in particular was convinced Miss Trent, when she was away from the eyes of the schoolroom, had spent her time smoking cigarettes, insisting, "Why was her breath like that, if she wasn't?" So far, despite his best efforts he had not been able to find where she might have stashed her Woodbines. Toby divided his time between pitching in on Damon's search and shadowing Rose as she swept and swiped at dust. My role as water bearer followed me from home, and no sooner did I have the stove reservoir and the drinking bucket freshly filled than Rose was brandishing the mop bucket in my direction and saying, "Paul, would you terribly mind—?" Once more I headed out to the pump in the schoolyard.

This time I passed Morrie on his way from the wagon, dispatched to fetch a box of housewares Rose had insisted he could not get along without. Did Thoreau's luggage include a toasting fork, I wondered as I saw that item poking out of Morrie's box. "Thank goodness it is a small house," he murmured to me in passing, one servant of Rose to another.

It was late in the day, and the day was late in the season. The pewter cast of light that comes ahead of winter crept into the schoolground as I performed the last of my water errands, shadows growing dusky instead of sharp almost as I watched. From the feel of the air, night would bring our first hard frost. The schoolyard seemed phenomenally empty as I crossed it this time. I could distinctly hear my lone soft footsteps on ground that was stampeded across at each recess. Around at the front of the school where the pump stood next to the flagpole I slung the mop bucket into place under the spout, but for some reason did not step to the pump handle just yet.

I suppose it was the point of life I was at, less than a man but starting to be something more than a boy, that set me aware of everything around, as though Marias Coulee School and its height of flagpole and depth of well were the axis of all that was in sight. I remember thinking Damon and Toby might come around the corner looking for me any minute, and if I wanted this for myself I had better use my eyes for all they were worth. So, there in the dwindling light of the afternoon I tried to take in that world between the manageable horizons. The cutaway bluffs where the Marias River lay low and hidden were the limit of field of vision in one direction. In the other was the edge of the smooth-buttered plain leading to Westwater and the irrigation project. Closer, though, was where I found the longest look into things. Out beyond the play area, there were round rims of shadow on the patch of prairie where the horses we rode to school had eaten the grass down in circles around their picket stakes. Perhaps that pattern drew my eye to what I had viewed every day of my school life but never until then truly registered: the trails in the grass that radiated in as many directions as there were homesteads with children, all converging to that school-yard spot where I stood unnaturally alone.

Forever and a day could go by, and that feeling will never leave me. Of knowing, in that instant, the central power of that country school in all our lives. It reached beyond those of us answering Morrie's hectic roll call that first day, although we were that clapboard classroom's primary constituents, its rural minnows much in need of schooling. Everyone I could think of had something at stake in the school. For Father, all the years he spent as a mainstay of the school board amounted to his third or fourth or fifth line of work at once, depending on how strict the count. Along with him, the other men of Marias Coulee had built the snug teacherage with their own hands the summer before, and the graying schoolhouse itself back when the first homesteaders came. The mothers dispatched their hearts and souls out the door every morning as they sent waist-high children to saddle up and ride miles to school. Somehow this one-room school had drawn from somewhere Morris Morgan, walking encyclopedia. Now Rose had arrived on the teacherage scene and dust would never be the same in the vicinity of Marias Coulee School. We all answered, with some part of our lives, to the pull of this small knoll of prospect, this isolated square of schoolground.

There at the waiting pump I could not sort such matters out totally, but even then, I am convinced, began in me some understanding of how much was recorded on that prairie, in those trails leading to the school. How their pattern held together a neighborhood measured in square miles and chimneys as far apart as smoke signals. I would say, if I were asked now, that the mounted troupes of schoolchildren taking their bearing on that schoolhouse on its prairie high spot traveled as trusting and true in their aim as the first makers of roads sighted onto a distant cathedral spire. Yet that is the erasure, those tracks in the grass that have outlined every rural school district of this state for so long, that I am called on to make at the convocation tonight.

"I was about to send a search party," Rose met me with as I lurched in with the heavy bucketful of water. After she put it to immediate use—she could mop a floor while most women were thinking about it—Father reappeared from whatever he had been doing at the wagon and stood inside the doorway surveying the scrubbed teacherage and its fresh occupant. Stowing silk socks in the rude pinewood dresser, Morrie looked more out of place than ever. Father swallowed, as a man will who has stuck his neck out quite far, then took care of the last of business for the day. "Morrie"—he warily included Rose in his inquisitive glance—"is there anything else within the less-than-infinite power of the school board that we can provide for you?" He checked his jottings. "So far, it's curtains, fresh ticking for the mattress, draft excluder, and lamp wicks."

Morrie's answer was swift. "Maid service would be appreciated."

Father had his nose down in his list. Damon was investigating the flour bin and other kitchen nooks, Toby assisting. I am sure I was the only one who caught the look that passed between Rose and Morrie after he said that. Sisterless as I was, I had nothing to compare it to. But there was a surprising amount of give-and-take in the lift of his brow as he gazed at her and the considering tilt of her head as she returned the gaze for quite an extended moment. Enough to tell me two sexes, even related as closely as possible, must be drastically more to deal with than the male cast of our family. Watching, I could not have foretold whether Rose was going to answer Morrie with bouquet or shrapnel.

"Surely you don't think I would abandon you," came her eventual response. "I'll tend to everything, per usual."

Over his shoulder Father called out, "Damon, quit that, you're going to wear out every drawer in the place." With a quick glance apiece he rounded up Toby and me. "Get your coats on, the lot of you, it's time to break ground for home. The thrill of suppertime awaits as usual. Rose, weren't you going to ride back with us?"

She didn't seem to have heard. Then she roused herself and sent another freighted look Morrie's direction. "I'll stay."

Morrie gauged that response for a moment, then snapped to as if he had just thought of something. "Everyone stay. For supper. I insist."

The Milliron family in its entirety halted in its tracks.

Father was the first to find power of speech.

"You can cook?"

"Certainly." Morrie had shed his jacket and was rolling up his shirt-sleeves. "In bachelor fashion, but an acquaintance of mine was chef for the Harrimans for a time. Rose, you remember Pierre. No? Well, no matter, he showed me a few things about putting together a meal. Now then, I believe that is a haunch of deer out in the coolbox." By now he was rummaging through the sparsely stocked cupboard. "Here we have dried noodles—actually macaroni, but close enough. And onions—a bit desiccated, but they will serve. Venison stroganoff, how does that sound to everybody? I'll just start some water to going and Rose can set the table and—Oliver, why are you putting on your hat? Did I say something amiss?"

"I need some air."

8

"SEE?" ONLY DAMON'S REAR END WAS VISIBLE AS HE PAWED among the bison bones at the boulder-strewn base of the cliff. He and Houdini were our best diggers, that next Sunday afternoon. "See, the black ones are chipped different on the sides."

Hard to imagine, something that innocent as the starting point toward one of my worst dreams. But the mind goes its own way at night.

"Beveled, Damon, that angle of edge is called," Morrie told him. "Very discerning of you, though, to notice the difference." Kneeling there, big brown hat pulled low against the wind that followed the river through the Marias bottomland, he looked nearly prayerful as he turned over and over in his cupped palm the dark arrowhead Damon had handed up to him. In the next breath Toby came charging over and, proud as a kitten with its first mouse, presented him the intact bison horn he had just found. Carefully Morrie laid it and Damon's find alongside the lance point I had pried out of the nearby claybank. "They could have used the three of you on digging up Troy," he commended. "Superb specimens, all around."

Our audience clucked a storm of disapproval down at us. I had to laugh. "She doesn't necessarily agree." We had scared up a sage hen when we clambered to the bottom of the buffalo jump, and it strutted nervously on a ledge of rock above us, steadily scolding our presence.

"Didn't know Aunt Eunice was along with us." Damon's wisecrack drifted from where he still was head-down in the boneyard.

"I did not hear that," Morrie maintained, lips twitching. Toby had rambled off again, whistling for Houdini to come help him dig. As if suddenly remembering another dog duty, however, Houdini pointed his nose toward the sage hen, lifted one paw as if ready to advance, and growled way down in his throat. Dimwitted as it was, the plump bird took the hint and whirred off to the top of the precipice above us. I watched the flight in some admiration. It always took hard scrabbling for us to climb back up the tiered cliff face of the buffalo jump, and agile though Morrie could be in a number of ways, he no longer possessed the billy-goat surety of a boy. One more time I wondered if this was such a hot idea of Damon's.

At that moment, though, Morrie seemed as invincibly juvenile as any of us, overjoyed with the treasures we kept unearthing and handing him. This particular rock fall beneath a thrust of the cliff, with its scatter of bones so old they were turning stone color, was our mother lode of arrowheads. How many times over how many centuries had the Blackfoot tribe harvested meat here? What a thing, I thought then and still do, to have the hunting skills to aim a herd of skittish buffalo off the cliff above our heads.

But now the buffalo were a piece of the past and the Blackfeet nearly so, a remnant people cooped up on the reservation on the other side of the river, and this old killing site was fair game for boys with a streak of badger. I was happily spitting on a nice light-colored arrowhead I had just discovered, to rub off the dirt, when Morrie held up the coal-black one toward me.

"Paul? Correct me if I'm wrong, but I haven't noticed stone of this sort anywhere in the vicinity."

I paused in the spitbath I was giving to my own arrowhead. At times like this, I savvied Father's mixed emotions about Morrie and his ready erudition. Morrie always was stimulating to have around, but always gets to be a lot.

Still, I had weathered the woodpile sessions with him and come out a bit better for it, hadn't I. "Me neither," I contributed on the origin of the stone, and knowing school was now in session even though it was Sunday, duly looked inquisitive.

"It's obsidian, I swear," he mused. "Which is volcanic." That did make me blink. Our part of Montana had more than enough geography, but I definitely did not know of any local volcanoes. "How does this come to be here?" He bounced the arrowhead gently in his palm as if weighing it. "Care to take an educated guess?"

I gave it some thought. Those contrary warriors that I was an inadvertent honorary member of must have roamed around, to pick fights with enemies. "Some other tribe? In a scrap with the Blackfeet here?"

"Close. I'd say it was trade." Morrie's eyes had that deep light of the past in them. "The Missouri surely was a main route." He gestured off in the direction where the Marias and the countryside's other tributaries met the big river. "And tribes would have come from all points of the plains in pursuit of buffalo. They couldn't fight one another constantly. Every so often they would have had to mount up and resort to commerce." He made even that sound heroic, a foray across the prairie to swap a mysterious dark rock for, what, a buffalo-hide robe? I could feel the hair on the back of my neck come up a little. *All points of the plains:* without my ever having said a word to him about it, Morrie was conjuring paths beneath the paths that had arrived to my eyes back there at the schoolhouse pump.

Cupping the black arrowhead in his hand again, he looked off appraisingly at the prairie bluffs around us. "With all the crisscrosses possible, this may have been a Mediterranean of a kind." As if Father had invisibly put in his two cents' worth, he gave a slight smile of concession. "Dryland, of course."

"Morrie? On that. They're going to be getting home."

This was the day the latest in deep plowing was being demonstrated at the agricultural experiment station, possibly on the premise that it would give the dryland farmers something to dream about during the long winter, and Father and George had talked Rae into going with them to socialize afterward. Rose, to Toby's temporary dismay, chose to keep Rae company rather than wallow in buffalo bones with us.

Morrie yanked out his watch, then jumped to his feet. "Toby!" he called. "Kindly put back those big bones, please. I am instructed by your father, with Rose concurring, that any part of the buffalo coming home with you has to arrive in your pocket. Damon, good job done."

Damon hated to be called off from digging. On the other hand, archeological triumph was his this day. When Morrie had wanted to borrow a handful of our arrowheads to use in the classroom—heaven only knew what arsenal of lore he had in mind next, after the fletching performance—Damon saw no reason why the school should not have its own collection.

Now my excavation-inclined brother whipped out of his back pocket a flour sack and with the aplomb of a gem dealer scooped our specimens in. Swag bag in hand, Damon looked elated enough to reach the top of the buffalo jump in two bounds. But he remembered his manners enough to say to Morrie, "Ready?"

"Or not, as the case may be," Morrie acquiesced in a kind of sigh, stepping over the bones of a bison that had plummeted from where we were going.

I worried, but Morrie managed to stay in one piece as we scrambled back atop the cliff to where our horses were tied. Even as he stood there blowing and inhaling, he studied the surroundings. "Extravagant scenery," he declared, and from there on the high river bluffs it truly was. Farthest west, the tips of the Rockies were white with first snow, an iceberg flotilla that seemed to go on forever under the dark blue sky of late afternoon. All the hills in the world were stacked in shades of tan between there and where we stood. Almost at our feet, juniper patches pintoed down the breaks in the rimrock of the bluff, and lower still, wild roses blew gently in the wind. It added to the pleasure of the day, Damon's and Toby's and mine, that our site was showing off for our guest.

When Morrie's breathing was back in the vicinity of normal, we moved off to our horses. Before we could mount up, Houdini started to whine. Usually that bargained some petting from Toby, but this time the dog bounced away from him. Nose down, it raced toward the buffalo jump.

"Houdini!" Toby tried to call him back. "Crazy pooch." The agitated dog was searching for something, back and forth along the edge of the drop-off, whining louder all the while. "Houdini," Toby's indignation was growing, "do you want a spanking?"

"Houdini, here, boy," I took my turn, "that sage chicken is long gone."

Damon tried a more direct approach, whistling sharply through his teeth. Houdini lifted an ear, but kept on snuffling along the top rock ledge of the cliff.

One look at Morrie told me his command of subjects did not extend to canines. We had to do something, though. Toby would fret all the way home if we left Houdini. "I'll get him," I said, and started toward the recalcitrant dog. "No, Tobe, you stay back."

Seeing me coming, Houdini wagged his tail guiltily but stood his ground. Heights didn't bother me, but Houdini was a sizable mutt and I most decidedly did not want to have to wage a tug-of-war with him that close to the lip of the buffalo jump. I knelt a few feet away, patting a coaxing rhythm on my knee. "Come on, Houdini, get away from there."

The dog whined, wagged, whimpered, and refused to budge.

"What's got into you? Houdini, now I mean it, come here or—"

Bwhoom! The sound of a rifle and the instant echo of the shot rang in all our ears.

I shall always owe Damon. He leaped toward the pair of us at the brink and latched onto me by the tail of my coat as I swooped and grabbed Houdini around the neck. The load of a struggling dog, my blind exertion and Damon's, the thunder roll of the rifle shot yet in our ears, the gape of the cliff so near, everything mixed in some oldest instinctive wrestle to exist. Fate's heart is hard; ours were temporarily harder. In some common will beyond fear, the clump of us lurched back onto safe ground. Morrie had hold of Toby. We all had our footing, and my hand somehow still was over Houdini's muzzle, keeping him quiet except for the whimpering. It took a considerable moment for the fact to soak in that each of us up there had life left in us. Together we stared down off the cliff at what Houdini alone had sensed was happening.

My throat suddenly had as many kinks in it as the winding river below. There in the broad bottomland, around the nearest bend of the river, came the steel-gray horse I had run the race against, galloping as hard as ever, but this time with its rider hunched forward in the saddle as he jacked another shell into his rifle. A smaller gray creature fled ahead in a struggling lope. When it tried to veer toward one of the breaks in the bluffs, the rifle spoke again and a small geyser of dirt exploded just in front of the animal, making it turn back toward the flat ground of the bottomland, in front of the relentless gray horse.

Morrie exclaimed as though something hot had been spilled on him: "What on earth—?"

By the time the words were out of him, the pursued animal had started to labor across an open stretch of meadow, dodging desperately. Now the man on horseback had plenty of time to rein up and shoot again, but did not, keeping the chase going.

I found enough voice to tell Morrie what he was seeing.

"Brose Turley. He's wolfing."

As we watched the zigzag marathon—Damon was open-mouthed and Toby had crept down to hold on to Houdini with me—Morrie sounded more confounded than ever. "But—he runs them to death? Isn't the man licensed to trap?"

"It pulled loose. There, see everything it's dragging?" By now the chase had drawn near enough below us that the instrument of destruction on one hind leg was visible. Somehow the wolf had fought the trap stake loose, digging, lunging, the jaws of the trap surely cutting bone deep. As the wolf scrambled along crookedly on three good legs the clamped trap skittered beneath the crippled foot, and the iron stake trailed it like a flattened-out ball and chain.

Toby whispered across, "Paul, I'm goose-bumply. If that was Houdini, I'd feel so awful." He looked at me to see if that was all right, and I nodded that it certainly was. Anyone who grows up around farm animals cannot side with a wolf in the long clash of things. But you can be against tormenting any creature.

Another gunshot. This one steered the wolf away from our side of the river bluffs, toward some rocky broken country that looked across to the buffalo jump.

"He's herding it someplace," I figured out. "Don't you think, Damon?"

"Box canyon. Up over there."

Through it all, Brose Turley never looked up. Knee, rein, whole body, he aimed the big gray horse after the wolf as if jockeying in a derby.

The wolf struggled harder as the ground began to climb. Whenever it tried to head for the shelter of a rock formation, a bullet zinged in its way. Turley hazed it like that past the wings of the box canyon. Before long the wolf could find no more room to run, straight-up stone penning it in on three sides. We saw it make a staggering loop along the base of the inmost cliff, the trap in and out of sight in the harsh rock spill. Then the wolf leaped at the cliff face, paws scrambling, vaulting its full length up the steep canyon wall. And fell back.

Turley was there on the grizzled horse at once, forcing the wolf to its feet with another shot that shattered rock near its head. The animal clambered off into the rock spill, dragging its shackle.

As the brutal chase went on, Morrie had sunk to a squat beside Toby and me and our quivering dog. His voice still held incredulity as he asked, of us or the universe:

"Why doesn't he just shoot it and put it out of its misery?"

Damon, ever our expert on things gory, knew.

"Fur dealer won't give him as much if there's a hole in the pelt."

That was one answer. Another came in the night, in the

cruel clarity of my dream. I was outside a corral of bones and rock—femurs and rib cages stacked on boulders, some combination of the buffalo jump and an arena. The Turleys, father and son, shapeless hats on the back of their heads, circled the middle of the corral looking over their catch of wolves. I followed around on the outside trying to see in as Eddie advised me not unkindly, "You stay on out, Milliron. Leave this to us." He flapped his hat at the wolves to tease them and said as if making a schoolyard boast, "We know how to deal with these woofs." Brose Turley said, "Quit wasting time. Let's pelt 'em up." He had a knife out. The wolves huddled like sheep. One after another, they were dragged by a hind leg to the center of the corral and skinned alive, Brose kneeing down on the neck, Eddie holding on to the tail. As I watched the wolves being slaughtered and the pelts thrown into a pile, someone showed up beside me. "They are getting blood on everything." I heard the disapproval in Rose's voice. Rose? All along I had been expecting Morrie—dreams have that odd element of illogical anticipation. It was unmistakably Rose at my elbow, though, apron on, saying over and over, "But why do they do that?" I seemed to be tongue-tied, for I had no answer then. Each gutting slash by Brose Turley drew a whimper from a wolf. The pelt pile grew. Dead or alive or somewhere between, the wolves lay there in skinned sinew and gut piles. "But that's terrible. Don't you think that's terrible?" Rose kept saying indignantly as we peered through the bone corral. Of course it was, I would be able to tell her now, mankind at its most remorseless always is.

That night sweat was hours ahead yet, and Brose Turley held front and center in the long shadows of the box canyon as the four of us and Houdini watched now. The horseman kept the wolf on the move, its tether dragging, until finally the stake tangled in the rocks. The exhausted wolf fell over, the caught hind leg angled behind. Satisfied at last, Turley pulled out a stout forked stick about as long as a shovel from alongside his rifle scabbard and swung down from his saddle. He obviously had done this many times before.

Approaching the wolf, he feinted with the stick, the creature snapping at it with what ferocity it had left. Quick as anything, Turley slid the fork of the stick just behind the wolf's ears and onto its neck, putting his full weight into pinning the animal down. Carefully maintaining his balance, he lifted his booted foot nearest the animal. He stomped on the wolf's chest, crushing its heart.

"Beastly," Morrie spat out. We knew he did not mean the wolf.

9

$\mathcal{T}$HE HOUSE WAS COLD WHEN I FUMBLED MY WAY OUT OF BED and the wolf-butcher dream. Dancing unhappily on the bare floor as I struggled into my clothes, I checked on Damon in the dimness. He had rolled to the wall, as far away from me and my dream tumult as it was possible to get and still be in bed. I supposed I had to sympathize, although it was his proclivity for the sharp edges of things that had led us to the buffalo jump the day before.

I knew my way in the dark, step by measured step down the stairs and to the match holder in the kitchen and, in the flare of the struck match, to the lamp on the table. Father always banked the stove for the night by chocking it full of coal, and there were ruby-red embers left for me to feed a crumpled newspaper and sticks of kindling. With everything lit, I took stock of myself.

It did not require much: I felt like a wreck. Sweet dreams, hooey. *Nightly awaits that sweet address/Principality of Sleep/ Happy Land of Forgetfulness*—could a poet be any farther wrong than that? If that was the best the grown-up world had to offer on the subject, I would need to construct my own approach to what went on in me when I was not awake. *Don't let it get to you,* I sermoned myself, although there still was so much leftover ventriloquism in my head that the voice sounded like Eddie Turley telling me to how to best behave around woofs.

That made me mad—people hanging around in me when I was trying to evict them—but it also triggered the thought that, frazzled though I might be, at least I was better off than anything that met up with Brose Turley by day or night. This and a cup of cocoa when the teakettle began its tune improved my outlook a bit. If the past was any guide, little by little the disturbing dream should cool down into manageable memory. I pulled out *Robinson Crusoe* and sat to the table to read. It would be nearly an hour yet before the alarm clock went off in Father's room and our household began to muster itself toward what passed for breakfast and then another adventurous schoolday under Morrie.

I was buried in hermit life on a desert island when the front door creaked open. The wind? When wolves and bloodthirsty wolfers have been roaming the back of your mind, you don't doubt the ability of the wind to turn a door handle.

Unanchored as I was in all the waters between actuality and imagination, I knew nothing to do but try to stay motionless while I waited for whatever was coming in to come in. One instant the kitchen doorway breathed the cold rush of air from the door opening, and the next there was the whisk of a coat already being taken off.

"Will you look at us!" the whispered greeting practically pranced in. "At least there are two people in the world up and going."

Rose. As if she had alit from my dream, before it could quite pull out of the station.

Rose had a talent for arriving. Just by showing up, she turned the mood of a place around the way a magnet acts on a compass. "I saw your light all the way from George and Rae's," she kept to a speedy whisper as she came over to stand by the stove, rubbing her hands. "*One if by land,* Paul Revere?"

"Slept in a hurry, I guess," I alibied my presence at the opened book and glowing lamp. Rose herself seemed to have traded her bed for a lantern. This was her earliest ever at the house.

She must have read curiosity all over me. "Every mitten in this house needs mending," she provided. "I thought I had better do it before you need to go to school with them on." She peered at me in the lamplight, her brown eyes lively even at this time of day. "The last person I knew who gets up this early was my poor husband. He didn't sleep well either."

"Nightmares?" I whispered back tensely.

"Just worries, I would say. There at the last. And then—" Realizing that did not lead in a promising direction, she tempered it with a rapid smile. "We all have off nights," which sounded particularly confidential when whispered in the houseful of sleepers around us. "Morrie tells me you seem to have a lot going on in your head, for someone your age."

More than she was going to know. Maybe it simply proved that I was green in years, but I was not about to tell a woman she had just spent the night in my dream. "Uh, want some cocoa?"

Rose started to shake her head, but on second look at me she whispered back, "Yes, I could have some. Let me gather up the mending and I'll join you."

In a flash she raided the mud room of its mittens and, while she was at it, Toby's much-abused scarf and Father's winter sweater. Putting the pile on the table between us, she got busy with yarn and darning needle and every so often remembered to take a teensy sip of the cocoa I had fixed for her.

"Well, demonstration day was quite something!" she said as if I had asked. "Plows and more plows. Rae bowled over everyone at the potluck with her, what's that called, rhubarb cobbler?" The wavy curls bobbed on her brow as she moved her head this way and that to take advantage of the lamplight for whatever item she was mending. Her eyes were quick, back and forth between me and her task. "Oh, and did your father report that we met up with the entire other half of your class? The county agent's daughter? Cornelia?"

"*Car*nelia. Like in *carbuncle*."

"Oh now, tsk. She's not a bad-looking girl."

"You watch. She'll marry a banker." Why I said that, I have no idea. But it turned out to be true.

Rose giggled. "Such powers of prediction. You have blind-sight."

"I have what?"

"It's a knack. Some people just know how a matter will turn out, while the rest of us are in the dark."

"Huh uh. I don't think I want that."

"I'm not surprised you have it, though," she said, as if that would soothe me.

I wanted off the topic of me. "Rose?" It was taking me a while to work around to this, especially in whispers. "Can I ask you something? About Morrie?"

"I'm only in the same family, you realize, not the same make."

"All right, but how does he know all those things? I mean, how does he put them together like that?" Morrie's latest magic trick with his mouth had come when the fifth grade was listless toward the multiplication table. "*When you play a fiddle, you want music to come out, don't you, even though it takes a set of strings that once inhabited the inside of a cat."* As usual I held my breath, but at the next recess the schoolyard, that saucer of terrible swift opinion, brimmed with appreciation of catgut having its day in the scheme of things.

"Morrie is educated up to here." I looked. Rose was holding her hand six inches above her head. "Schooling suited him." Her face had a fixed expression, as if this was not an easy thing to be telling. "When it's that way, the other in the family—" That dangled in the air until she brought it down by tapping *Robinson Crusoe* where it lay open. "I always have to think twice whether this is about the opera singer or the shipwrecked sailor."

"Yes, but—" I was trying to find a diplomatic way to say that she was smart in her own style and people kept telling me I was bright enough, for a boy, yet Morrie could run rings around both of us in mental exploits, and at the same time ask her if he secretly practiced at that or what, when Father yawned a greeting to us from the doorway.

"Look at the time!" he exclaimed, as if Rose and I hadn't been up for hours examining it. "Roust those brothers of yours, Paul; the schoolbell waits for no man."

This day seemed determined to get off on the wrong foot. What with one thing and another—Damon must have spent fifteen minutes traversing the bed and finding his way into his clothes—we had to ride hard to school and even so, everyone else had gone inside and Morrie was giving the iron triangle a last chorus when we piled out of our saddles.

Instead of turning back through the doorway, though, he came out to waylay us, and sulking right behind him was Carnelia. This put me on my guard, especially when he shooed Toby and Damon on into the schoolhouse and announced to

Carnelia and me that he had an honor in store for us: he was
bestowing on us the duty of raising and lowering of the flag.

She looked as taken aback as I was. This was unheard of.
Always, *always,* the oldest students were the ones who took
turns at that high responsibility. Morrie must have decided, not
without good reason, that this civic rite was wasted on the current eighth-grade mob. From now on, he proclaimed, flag duty
would migrate from grade to grade, starting with our own,
which was to say with the discomfited duo of us.

Carnelia and I had one thought between us: the possible
wrath of the hairy mammoths of grade eight descending onto
grade seven. But the change of procedure was entirely a teacherly
doing rather than ours, a fact we would plead to high heaven in
the schoolyard if we had to. Duty having blindly singled us out,
she and I squared ourselves up in what might have been flag-
bearer fashion.

Then, like a delayed continuation of my bad dream, the
door of the boys' outhouse opened and out sauntered Eddie
Turley.

Possibly it irked Morrie that Eddie's preferred start of a
schoolday was to go to the toilet, or possibly he saw this as a
providential changing of the guard. In either case, we had an
immediate conscript into our flag detail. "Eddie propitiously is
on hand to show you the ropes." Morrie nailed him before he
could slouch into the schoolhouse. "We are running late this
morning," he concluded with a telling glance at me, "so I will
leave you to it while I take attendance."

Morrie vanished inside, and the three of us stood like
stumps while the empty prairie yawned around us. By his
picked-on expression Eddie would have just as soon walloped
me as look at me, and likely that held true toward Carnelia, too.
Was I going to be in another fistfight before I even set foot in

the schoolhouse? Fortunately for once, the one person who was a match for Eddie in candlepower of glower was Carnelia.

"All right then, Mr. Helpful." Her voice would have jabbed any living thing into action. "How are we supposed to start?"

"Could get out the flag, if you snot noses are gonna do this yet today."

Carnelia and I of course knew the folded flag was kept in its own special drawer at the cabinet end of the cloakroom. In we went, took it out as if we were handling dynamite and, neither of us quite certain of protocol, carried it between us, each using both hands. Eddie trailed after us in a kind of slinking way that uncomfortably reminded me again of wolves and wolfers.

"You *would* be late," Carnelia muttered to me on our stately way to the flagpole, "our first day doing this."

"Didn't know it was, did I, so save your breath."

No doubt it was proximity across the compactly folded flag that brought to mind Rose's remark that Carnelia was not bad-looking. Myself, I'd had to keep a constant eye on her for seven years now, and I had never seen her improve measurably. I took a good look to be sure. Same turned-up nose. Same milky complexion. Same eyes like the queen in a deck of cards. Catching me studying her, she snapped: "What do you think you're looking at, frog eyes."

"Nothing worth mentioning, toad spit. Don't let your side droop."

At the flagpole, we drew to a halt with the colored wedge of cloth still held between us. It was the splendid new forty-six-star flag, with Oklahoma now in the union. An unquestionable beauty, the fresh-dyed stars and stripes silky in our hands. Now, though, came the question dominating both our minds. Exactly how did a person thread and fasten the glorious thing securely onto the flagpole rope swinging ominously there in the breeze?

Oxlike Milo Stoyanov knew the secret, less-than-bright Carl Johannson knew, even Eddie Turley knew. But Eddie was standing there mute as the flagpole, smirking at the pair of us.

"So, what do you say, Eddie?" I tried prompting him man to man. "Ready to show us how to handle the rope here?"

"Whyn't you go at it backwards?" he mocked. "Your brain kicks in when it trades places with your butt, don't it?"

Giving Eddie a look of pure disgust, Carnelia laced into him as only she could. "Think for once in your life, horse nose. We need to get this done or we're all in trouble."

"Wouldn't be nothing new for me. Might be for you two."

Eddie Turley was one thing Carnelia and I could agree on. We both knew what an incurable pain in the neck Eddie could be when he wanted to. Panic starting to show in us, she and I faced each other with the breeze-blown rope between us. We had to invent together or else.

"I think we first of all have to put that through there and then—"

"No, dummy, that's backwards, we need to—"

"You're not the boss of everything. Let me—"

"Will you just not be so grabby and—*watch out!*"

It was not clear who had been in main possession of the flag and who hadn't. But there it lay, dumped in the dirt between us.

The pair of us stood there stricken into stone. Rules of the flag were as stark as Scripture. The flag had to be handled with utmost respect at all times. It had to be folded and unfolded in a prescribed manner. Above all, the flag must never touch the ground. Incalculable consequences blazed up at Carnelia and me from the bright heap of cloth there at our feet. For all we knew, Oklahoma now had to get back in line for statehood.

"Huh!" Eddie marveled, a foxy grin spreading over his usually vacant face.

As if our heads were on the same swivel, Carnelia and I shot a look toward the schoolhouse. There were no windows there on its front side and Morrie had closed the doors after him, so no one had seen the seventh grade of Marias Coulee disgrace itself. I snatched up the flag, rubbing the dirt off it onto my pant leg. Her mouth working silently in shock, Carnelia could only bob encouragement to me.

"Wait'll everybody hears this," Eddie could barely wait to unload on us. "Teacher's pets can't even keep the flag up out of the—"

My loud humming interrupted him. Carnelia was looking at me as if I had entirely lost my mind, but Eddie sobered up sharply as the tune sunk in on him. Just to be sure, I hummed another line of "Let us fight the holy fight . . ." in even more vigorous Holy Willy fashion and twitched a little along with it.

Eddie's face turned beet color. "You said you wouldn't tell!"

"I won't about that if you won't about this."

Eye-level on me was the Adam's apple on Eddie, and when I saw it working strongly, I had hope that he was thinking things over. All of a sudden he grabbed the flag from my hands, gritting out, "Here, see?" He sped the rope through the grommets a certain way, fastened it in a blur of fingers, and sent the flag shooting to the top of the pole. Without a word more the three of us headed for the schoolhouse, Carnelia glaring daggers at both Eddie and me.

She and I trooped to our double desk and sat there, both jittery, while Morrie orchestrated lessons among the other grades, gradually making his way to us. However, he said nothing about the inordinate length of time we had been at the flagpole, and merely handed back our essays on Magellan's voyage around the world. "Top marks, both of you."

Putting the pair of us to penmanship practice, Morrie

moved on to the heavy timber of grade eight. Since I was pretty well up on penmanship and the day's other assignments, I stole time that morning to watch him go through his pedagogical paces. That question still intrigued me, of how he managed the mental high jinks he did. I did not solve that, but I discovered something else. Having been around Morrie at his most systematic during our wood-sawing sessions, I knew perfectly well he was scraping through here in the schoolhouse much of the time on nerve and desperation, thumbing into things mere moments ahead of administering the next lesson to some bunch or another in the relentless stairstep system of eight grades in one room. Aplomb counts, however, and here I speak as a public figure whom the newspapers can never resist calling "oracular." Whatever being in charge of "the kid glove end of things" entailed in the prior life of him and Rose and the unfortunate late Mr. Llewellyn, there in the well-trodden aisles between our desks Morris Morgan looked as if composure was a middle name he had come by honestly.

So, on the day of all this Morrie did not bat an eye when the sixth-grade delegation detoured to his desk when all of us clattered in from afternoon recess. Consisting of Lily Lee Fletcher, as earnest as she was quiet, and Miles Calhoun, who had a slow-circling intelligence though you never knew where it would alight, and Rabrab Rellis in her inevitable role of mouthpiece, the group plainly represented a mysteriously broad constituency. Morrie listened level-headed as a judge while Rabrab made her case in feline whispers. Our unexpected teacher was gaining steady adherents in the schoolroom by giving almost any matter a hearing—the one thing Marias Coulee School was united on was scorn for the maxim that children should be seen and not heard—and he was about to win a quantity more. When everyone had settled into their seats, Morrie rose to his feet and announced: "I am reliably informed that due to unfore-seen circumstances"—Miss Trent's abandonment of us—"there has been no spelling bee since, in Rabrab's words, 'practically forever.' That does sound like an unduly long time." The reaction that greeted this was about as if he had thrown handfuls of chocolate bonbons into the room. "Line up, everyone. Alternate grades, is it, each side of the room?"

Surely by now Morrie knew this was a student body that would rather have a contest than the right number of toes, but even so he was nearly swept aside by the stampede. Grade by grade, desks were rapidly emptied. Carnelia departed ours as if called upon to don a breastplate and lead a crusade to the Holy Land. By habit, I stayed in my seat and pulled out the school's volume of *Just So Stories.*

No sooner had everyone else lined up along two sides of the room than I heard: "Squire Milliron?" Morrie's tone of voice could be felt on the skin. "Would you care to join us?"

I looked up in total surprise, no adequate phrase coming to mind.

For Carnelia, this was straight from heaven. "Paul can't be in the spelling bee," she reported with relish.

Morrie cocked his head. "And why is that?"

Carnelia simply pursed her lips as if the why of it was too obvious to say. Damon knew it should not come from him, and Toby, itching to speak up, was willed into silence by Damon's warning look. Around the room my friends and allies were un-sure of my wishes on this, while my adversaries did not know how to hone it against me as much as they might have liked. It was Verl Fletcher from the back of the room who finally piped out, "Because Paul every time beats the pants off the rest of us."

Morrie's head cocked further sideways. "Does he now. Paul, *eleemosynary,* please."

I rattled its dozen letters back to him so fast he blinked. In back of him Carnelia crossed her arms across her chest as if to say, *See?*

"Hmm. Try *prestidigitation*."

Similarly I flashed through that. By now Morrie was looking at me a bit grimly, as Miss Trent and her predecessors had done before him. "This entire sentence, then." General murmur and a few gasps emanated as he put to me: "*Pharoahs were heirs to hieroglyphics.*"

When I spelled it all back to him at about the pace of a crack telegrapher, he walked a tight circle by his desk and then said, "One more, but this time in synphonic fashion: *fish.*"

Had I misheard? Surely Morrie couldn't want me to tootle out the composition of the little word as if I were a mock symphony orchestra? No, he always enunciated every curve of every letter when he wanted to drill home a point, and from the roomful of mystified expressions around me, I was not the only one trying to puzzle out *syn*phonic. Was it like synthetic? In any case, I could not think fast enough to meet Morrie's catch spelling word with anything other than *f-i-s-h*, although I was greatly tempted to play to the crowd by adding on a *y*.

"Technically correct, imaginatively off the mark," Morrie gave the not unexpected verdict. "Consider this." He stepped to the blackboard and wrote *ghoti*.

Every eye in the room strained to take this in as Morrie declaimed: "Synphonic, meaning 'similar in sound.' You must watch out for words; they have tricks up their sleeves." As he spoke, the chalk in his hand flashed across the blackboard and yielded *cough*. "When you come down with a cold, this is what you have in your chest, isn't it. Not this." Beneath *cough*, he chalked *cow*. Laughter pealed from us all.

"Ah, but," the stick of chalk came up like a finger of warning, "when you feed the fire to keep warm during your affliction, the tree branch you break up and put into the stove is this." Beneath *cow*, Morrie wrote *bough*.

While that mischievous chime of rhyme was going off in heads around the room, Morrie further sobered the spelling-bee contestants and, for that matter, me. "Always be aware you are at the mercy of the whim of the word. It decides how it is pronounced and what it means. It chooses up its own letters, often in ways we wouldn't. And it can be a shameless mimic, by sneaking in one of those sound-alikes tucked away in the alphabet." He spun to the blackboard again as if those devilish letters were listening there. "Preposterous as this *'fish'* looks"—from somewhere he produced his pointer and went en garde with *ghoti* as if to slay it—"it is made up of similarities perfectly well known to our tongues. Sound it out for yourselves," he whapped through the letters, "*gh* as in 'cough,' *o* as in 'women,' and *ti* as in 'motion.'"

This seized me. Morrie had been addressing us all, from big-eyed first-graders to narrow-eyed eighth, yet it was one of those tingling moments when the entire might of learning seemed to have descended into the one-room school specifically for my benefit. True, I'd have been happier if it happened less obtrusively. I felt I had been taken down a peg, maybe several. I still did not know why. But my experience with Morrie thus far was that any mental extravaganza he went to the trouble of staging was worth some reflection.

"Paul?" His tone of voice relented on me. "I entirely see why you are excused from the spelling bee. Carry on with your reading in peace." I did my best at that, but a spelling contest with Morrie in charge proved to be as adventurous as anything Kipling was coming up with.

In no time, the schoolhouse was wild with claps and groans

and hoots and Morrie's exhortations. "Lily Lee, put your tongue to *mucilage,* so to speak." "A worthy try, Milo, and if any of us were in charge of such matters *xylophone* indeed would have a *z.*" He was a dervish of vocabulary; I wished Father were there to savor it. Beyond that, though, he elevated the spelling bee into an everybody-in tournament. For a while he paired second- and fifth-graders, and third and fourth, the younger ones valiantly reciting the letters aloud after frenzied conferences in whispers. (Toby mountaineering his way through *r-h-i-n-o-c-e-r-o-s* with the entire fifth grade breathless behind him was something to behold.) Then for one ferocious round he pitted the entire sixth grade against Carnelia and she haughtily spelled them down, one after another, until Morrie decided the time had come to take some of the shine off her. The next word he gave her was the crazy one for that celebration where people serenade newlyweds and dress them up funny and wheel them around in wheelbarrows and so forth.

"It is pronounced 'shivaree,' but be careful," Morrie warned scrupulously, "this one has a number of things up its sleeves." Did it ever! Carnelia missed it from the first letter. Damon went down on the same word—actually, the same letter—and sent me a pained look. Next, Rabrab flounced down in defeat. I sat there restless behind my propped book, wincing as everyone misspelled from the instant they opened their mouths. Isidor made a brave doomed try at the word. Now it was up to Grover Stinson, last hope of the sixth grade. Grover and I were best friends, or as close to that as the year of difference in our ages would let us be. Both of us read everything we could lay our hands on, Grover's eyeglasses unfortunate proof of that in his case, and we thought alike in a surprising number of ways. Naturally enough, then, when he gazed my way in concentration before tackling the fiendish word, I casually rubbed my eye, hoping he would connect that to *see* and from there to *c*. He blinked a couple of times, pursed up thoughtfully, and took the plunge: "*c, h, a* . . ." So it came to be that Grover was the conqueror of *charivari*.

"Well done for grade six!" rang out the commendation from Morrie, already ransacking his master primer for a next word. If he had not been as busy as a paperhanger on a divided stairway, keeping track of the contest between grades and scampering for spelling challenges at the same time, he might have avoided the trouble just ahead. But without looking up he chanted out: "That advances grade six to take on grade eight, I believe. The lucky individual who is next up for grade eight, please. Your word is the triangle that has two equal sides. It is pronounced—"

Eddie Turley, on the receiving end of *isosceles,* looked as if he had been tossed a hot coal.

I closed up Kipling in favor of this. During his ten-year journey through eight grades, Eddie had managed to provide the Marias Coulee classroom some never-to-be-forgotten moments. Once when Miss Trent sent him to the blackboard to work on a subtraction problem, he had stomped from the board complaining, "I can add some, but that takin' from is a bugger." According to the squinched-up expression on him now, so was *isosceles.*

"How's it pernounced again?" Eddie waffled as seven grades of Marias Coulee school collectively rooted for the word to leave a major bruise on him.

"*I-sos-celes,*" Morrie delicately sounded out.

"*E-y-e,*" Eddie agonized out loud, and got no farther before hoots went up and Morrie waved him out of the round.

But for Eddie to traipse out of contention to the far end of the room, he had to pass right by the triumphant sixth grade. First in line there was Grover, a sweet-as-pie smile still pasted on him from *charivari*. Eddie squinted in annoyance at this display of high spirits. "What're you grinnin' at, four-eyes?"

Grover had a touch in these matters. "Nothing," he answered Eddie, but enunciated it in slow, spoon-fed syllables the way Morrie had portioned out *isosceles*.

Eddie's face flamed. Big as a house, he whacked the smaller Grover backhand across the chest, sending him bouncing against the teacher's desk.

Reaction raced through the spelling-bee ranks like a line of firecrackers going off. The boys of grade six boiled to Grover's defense, Damon climbing over a desk in an effort to get at Eddie, Isidor determinedly balling up his fists and trying to wade toward his target, the others in a general surge that clogged the aisle. Rabrab contributed a scream.

Sensing riot, Morrie leapt in. "Everyone! Take your seats!" he shouted. It might have ended there if Eddie, fired up to take on the legion of the sixth grade, hadn't assumed the person charging up behind him was Grover on a mission of revenge. He wheeled around, delivering a roundhouse punch as he came.

By luck or instinct, Morrie bobbed low and took the blow on his hairline. "Ow!" cried Eddie as his fist met skull. All motion in the schoolroom stopped.

Morrie straightened up slowly. Hitting a teacher was a capital offense, we all knew. A teacher hitting back was entirely another matter. White-eyed, Eddie stood there shaking his hurting hand, awaiting his fate. A red place the size of a set of knuckles showed at the edge of Morrie's mussed hair. His tie flapped down his front and his collar was off-kilter. For long seconds the compact man and the taller schoolboy faced one another, the school teetering on the frozen scene. Then Morrie adjusted his collar and tie and said almost normally, "Eddie, I will deal with you at the end of the day. Everyone else, be seated and prepare for geography period."

"And then he kept Eddie after!"

Father was grave as he listened to Toby tell about the day at school. Damon and I stood by, content to be material witnesses. Toby's recitals always carried more oomph than ours. "Eddie doesn't ever get kept after!"

Rose hovered at the kitchen doorway long enough to catch the gist of the story, rolled her eyes at what Morrie had gotten himself into, balled up her apron, and left for the day.

I must have imagined it, but another worry line seemed to come into Father's wrinkle-mapped cheek as he sat at the table concentrating on following Toby's titanic tale. Freighting for the irrigation project had not yet let up—winter was holding off, to everyone's surprise—and balancing that and the workload of the homestead was enough to occupy any man twice over. Now he was something like president of the board of the Marias Coulee school for the unruly, on top of it all.

"Morrie didn't lay a hand on him?" he checked with those of us who had not been heard from yet. "Then or later?"

"Naw, darn it," Damon responded with the authority of one who had been more than willing to do the job himself.

"When we left, you couldn't tell Eddie from a setting hen," I amplified. "He had to stay there at his desk doing nothing for an hour. Morrie was at the front of the room at his. Reading Shakespeare, I think."

"All week!" Toby imparted.

Father looked relieved at the news that Eddie was unscathed, which I did not appreciate as someone who within recent memory had been spanked. But Damon wiped that off him in a hurry by saying, "I wish Morrie would just lock him in all night and then kick him on out of there. He's cluttering up everything for us tomorrow afternoon."

"How so?" One of those looks, the kind a father gives when he is about to hear something he would rather not, reached around the table to include all of us. "What's any of this have to do with any of you?"

"We're *staying* after," Damon said patiently, making the crucial distinction from being kept after school. "To get the arrowhead collection ready. Morrie asked us to, the day at the buffalo jump. You said we could, remember?"

"That was before hostilities broke out."

Damon nearly fell out of his chair in despair. "It's not our fault Eddie blew his stack! He can be there; we won't even look in his direction."

Rubbing his cheek as if consulting the wrinkles, Father weighed that argument. It tipped so suddenly in Damon's favor the three of us were caught with our mouths open. "Very well, stay after. I'll pull by on my way home from the Big Ditch. I wouldn't want to miss a chance to see arrowheads, would I."

10

*T*HE REMBRANDT LIGHT OF MEMORY, FINICKY AND MAGICAL and faithful at the same time, as the cheaper tint of nostalgia never is. Much of the work of my life has been to sort instruction from illusion, and, in the endless picture gallery behind the eye, I have learned to rely on a certain radiance of a detail to bring back the exactitude of a moment. Perhaps it might be the changeling green of a mallard's head in a slant of sun, as back there on Father's pothole Lake District. Or the gun gray of my thermos jug when I pulled over to the shoulder of the road in The Cut to sip at coffee while reliving a race: the shadow tone of a wolfer's horse.

The after-school hour when arrowheads were to take on a collected gleam was lit by honest lanternshine. During school-time the custom was to light the hanging lamps only on the darkest of winter days. But dusk set in so early that overcast afternoon, Morrie declared we must banish the gloom. The room of brown old desks was uncommonly cozy, then, as the arrow-head committee went about its work. We had delegated to Toby the task of scrubbing the treasures in a washbasin of warm water, accepting some splashes on the floor in exchange for his enthusiasm. Damon hummed magisterially as he wiped and buffed and breathed a sheen onto the pointed stones one after another. My pen hand had to be at its most proficient in lettering the label for each one. All the while, Eddie Turley squinted sourly toward us from the back of the room like a prisoner trying to see out of a dungeon.

"Ah, here now, just what's needed." Morrie came back in from the supply cabinet, where he had rummaged out a dusty entomological display case in which the specimens were past their prime. "The beetles have had their day. Damon, when you're done there, you can be in charge of exhuming. Oh, and Toby, there are pliers and a spool of copper wire somewhere in the kitchen drawers at the teacherage, if you could scare them up, please."

To a casual visitor, the scene would have looked suitable for engraving on good-behavior certificates. Lads nicely busy on their civic project in the twilight, while in the back corner a miscreant sits out his sentence for, oh, probably spitwads. And Morrie in tweed and mustache, presiding as though an after-school gathering of this sort was nothing out of the ordinary. But I was aware he was keeping a sentry eye on Eddie, just as I was keeping mine on Damon. For if you had happened to look in on Marias Coulee School at recent intervals when it served as a boxing ring, all of us there in the ring corners of that schoolroom— with the cherubic exception of Toby—were either active combatants or potential ones. I had got my famous one punch in on Eddie. Eddie had blindly clouted Morrie. Keen as he was to do so, Damon had not yet managed to sock Eddie, nor had Eddie found the right opportunity to wade into him. If we weren't all careful, the round robin of fists could go on and on.

The arrowheads arrayed there fresh and shiny kept us at

peace, however, at least those of us at the front of the room. Damon seemed to have found his life's work in evicting dead beetles into the coal bucket, gabbing all the while to Morrie about football epics he had been pasting into his scrapbooks as the autumn's newspapers caught up with us. For once, Morrie had nothing to do but look wise and say little. With time to my- self after finishing the final arrowhead label—for the darker- than-night obsidian one—I fooled with a scrap of penmanship.

Morrie cocked a puzzled look at the writing on my tablet when I went to his desk and handed it to him. "As Shakespeare said, this is Greek to me. How is it supposed to read, Paul?"

"'Fish,'" I said as if the five letters on the paper were the most recognizable thing in the world.

Morrie more closely studied my coinage of *phych.*

"*Ph* as in *phlegm,*" I came to his aid, "*y* as in *hysterical,* and *ch* as in *charivari.*"

"Well spelled, as always," he said drily, pocketing the piece of paper. "You are not quite finished with your labels, however. One last one for the front of the case. Make it read: 'Arrowhead collection donated to the Marias Coulee School, 1909, by the Milliron family.'"

Eddie chose just then to snort, visit his nose with a finger, and flick a booger contemptuously onto the floor. Fortunately, Damon was occupied with arranging everything to perfection in the display case and so did not go climbing over desks in hunt of Eddie a second day in a row. And here Toby came charging victoriously in with the wire and pliers to affix the arrowheads in the display case. We would be done in no time now, and as soon as Father ever showed up to admire our handiwork, we could head home and Eddie could sit and stew until he was blue as far as we were concerned. What waited for him at home was a matter for my Delphic cave of dreams, later.

Morrie, I noticed, had his big pocket watch out where he could see it on his desk to keep exact time on Eddie's incarceration. Minutes pass more slowly when looked at, so it was some little while before the outside door could be heard opening, the awaited tread at last in the cloakroom, and just in time I dotted the final *i* of the Milliron family label and blew on it to dry the ink. "Here, Tobe, you can show Father. Hold it in both hands so you don't wrinkle it."

Looking down at the masterpiece in his hands, Toby hurried toward the doorway. "Father, look what—" he began, as far as he got before seeing the big boots.

Over Toby's head, Damon and I gaped at Brose Turley as if he were a creature that had fallen down from the moon.

According to the scowl that met our gaze, he had not expected the sight of us either. Under the crinkled hat brim his dark mean eyes shifted from us to Morrie, and then found Eddie at the rear of the room.

"Good afternoon, Mr. Turley." As casual as those words, Morrie moved to stand between the interloper and us. He rumpled Toby's hair, and while his hand was there turned him around like a top and sent him back in our direction. "To what do we owe the pleasure of this visit?"

Brose Turley did not bother to answer. He strode down the aisle toward Eddie, his wolfskin coat brushing the desktops. Eddie seemed to shrink the closer his father came.

I heard Damon and Toby catch their breath, and they must have heard me do the same. But Morrie only called out in the same civil way, "Eddie has fifteen more minutes before I can let him go." Turley halted, shaking his head in disgust. He was directly beneath one of the hanging lamps and I could distinctly see the crisscrossed weather-beaten skin of the back of his neck, as though he slept on a pillow of chicken wire. He was a big man all the way up from those tromper boots. No wonder wolves or any other living thing I could think of did not stand a chance against him. I was scared to the roots of myself, and even Damon had lost the color in his face. Toby pressed more tightly against the arm I had looped around him and whispered, "Where's Father?"

"He'll be here," I barely found enough resource in myself to whisper back, hoping against hope that he was not out there slaughtered in the dusk, from having tried to head off this death dealer in a wolfskin coat.

Brose Turley turned around the way a statue would, every bulky bit of him in one revolving motion. Ignoring us, he zeroed in on Morrie. "I don't want you keeping my boy after. If he's done something that don't suit, belt him one right then and be done with it."

"Belting people is what has led to all this." Morrie brushed his fingertips across the bruise at his hairline. "Eddie must learn to keep his fists to himself. This is the best kind of penalty to remind him, I think."

"You think." Turley made it sound like that was Morrie's trouble. His voice was sized to the rest of him, but there was an odd clack to it as if it had been out of use a long while. Something about his face was out of kilter, too. It was as if the upper part belonged to one countenance and the lower part to some other. I only figured it out when Turley, still glowering across the ranks of desks at Morrie, opened his mouth to say more. He had false teeth, but just the uppers. The bottom of his mouth was an ugly, sharp ridge of gum line. From sentence to sentence, the choppers on top gnashed away and then the pink gums below leered out. "You go about this like an educated fool," the voice that came out of that maw was letting Morrie know. "*He that spareth the rod hateth his son.* I'll take a preacher over a teacher anytime."

I was afraid Damon might spout out something about that being just like a Holy Willy, but Morrie was quick with: "*A wounded spirit who can bear?* Proverbs 18:14, I believe. There is a lifetime of sermons in that."

Turley looked affronted to have the Bible cited back to him. "I don't know what kind of a hoosier you are, but you and this school of yours don't show me anything. If the law wouldn't get on me about it, I'd pull my boy out of here so fast it'd make your head swim. His next birthday I can do it anyway."

"Until that day, Eddie is a student here, the same as any other." Rather primly, Morrie smoothed the pockets of his suit coat as if to make sure he was as presentable as his argument. I hoped he was not going to bank entirely on manners, although I didn't see what else he could do. Was Father still on the face of the earth, and if so, why wasn't he here lending a hand?

Turley answered Morrie with his back, turning away until the full brunt of him again faced his son.

"You. Get on home."

Awkwardly, Eddie unfolded out of his desk, but stayed standing beside it.

"Daddy?"

Could we have heard right? The word that in the Marias Coulee hard school of adolescence only girls and toddlers used, coming out of the usually sneering lips of Eddie Turley? If Toby happened to giggle—or worse, Damon—I didn't know what might be ignited. But in the pitiful silence Eddie mustered himself and blurted, "Daddy? I, I can't. He has to say. He's the teacher."

Morrie stepped forward. "If you wish to, Eddie, you may go.

You have done well in staying after, and from here on you can stay in at recess and noon hour instead."

As Eddie edged past, his father gave him the same disgruntled look he had in Brother Jubal's tent. He made no move to follow his son. Gradually the hoofbeats of Eddie's horse faded away, and as hard as Damon and Toby and I were listening, we could not bring any sound of Father's team and dray in place of that. Turley seemed to have all the time in the world as he turned toward Morrie. "Now to deal with you, pettygog."

"Eddie is safely on his way," Morrie said calmly, "and that should conclude your business here."

"I'll show you business." Turley jerked his head toward us. "Get rid of these pipsqueaks. What're they doing here anyway?"

That was too much for Damon. "Just working on our arrowheads. We can be here if we want."

Brose Turley singled me out with the unnerving scowl that sucked in the toothless part of his face. "You there, bright boy. Take these other two and go."

"Nothing doing." I am not sure my voice carried elder-brother authority as I wanted it to, but it did the best it could under the circumstances. "We're staying."

Turley leered over at Morrie as if that was a joke to be shared. "If they want to see a fool get what's coming to him, let 'em." He looked as dangerously deliberate as he had been in goading the wolf into the box canyon. He indicated toward the hanging lamp right over his head. "Wouldn't take much to burn this place to the ground."

"It would take a lunatic." Morrie circled out away from us, to the clear area of floor at the front of the schoolroom, as if he was merely taking a philosopher's stroll. "Four of us have just heard who one might be."

Brose Turley grunted. "For now, a good pounding will do." He moved toward Morrie. I knew without even looking that Damon had the pliers ready to throw, and I would do what I could to jump on Turley's back, but the odds were that Turley could handle us like puffballs.

Still looking philosophical, Morrie had been standing with his hands parked in his coat pockets. He pulled them out now, sets of brass knuckles gleaming right and left.

Turley halted. "I'm barehanded."

"Much more metal than this would be needed to bring me up to your weight," Morrie pointed out mildly. He had lifted his arms as high as his midsection and was clinking the knobbed bands of brass together, clenched hand lightly tapping against clenched hand, as if passing the time with a tune until the bout began.

Turley was a man who knew how metal could bite flesh, and he edged back until he was sure he was out of range of Morrie's armored fists.

"I know how to wait," he ground out, the pink gums gnashing into each threatening word. Without so much as a glance at the wide-eyed three of us, he abandoned the schoolhouse.

"Morrie," Damon sounded dazed, "where—?"

Abruptly Morrie had a hand up, signaling silence. From outside came the sound we had been waiting for, the harness jingle of a dray team. Mixed with it, though, were hot words exchanged out there in the growing dark. Then, thank heaven, that drumbeat of a saddle horse's hooves, Brose Turley riding hard into what was left of the dusk.

Morrie had not relaxed one bit, but somehow the brass knuckles had vanished. Speaking low and rapidly, he enlisted us further in the chapter that had just happened. "Damon, Paul, and need I say, Toby. It would be best if the little tiff between Mr. Turley and myself, just now, were kept between us. Particularly my, ah, persuaders. Agreed?"

Which of my brothers was more distressed at the thought of not being able to regale Father with the whole episode the minute he came in, Toby or Damon? From the stricken look on them, it was impossible to choose. But we had no time to think about any of it. That quick, here was Father in the schoolroom, Brose Turley's footprints barely cool beneath his. The agitation we'd heard outside was spelled out on his face. Plainly he was not expecting to find Morrie still in one piece.

"I see you had a visitor." Father was breathing heavily. "I meant to be here long since, but a wheel rim popped. Did Turley cause you any trouble?"

"*Pff,*" Morrie made a dismissive noise. "The man is substantially shallow."

Father sensed that more had gone on here than anyone was letting on. He looked from me to Damon to Toby, and when that was unproductive, he focused back onto Morrie. "You don't want Brose Turley gunning for you."

"Oliver, you are entirely correct, I do not want that."

Then Father said something odd. "Pray for snow." We all looked at him as if his mind had wandered severely. "Brose Turley traps in the timber in winter," he reasoned it out for us. "Eddie lodges with the Johannsons as soon as that happens— he may be tamer without his father around, who knows? Morrie, if you can just put up with Eddie through the winter, this might all go away."

Unusually, Morrie said nothing one way or the other. Somehow Father's presence shouldered the tension out of the schoolroom. He was pressed into admiring the arrowhead display. Then he scooped up Toby. "Tobe, little man, you look like you've had a day." Father swung him up onto his shoulders. "Come on," he directed Damon and me, "it's getting late and Morrie has had a sufficiency of your company for one day. Tobe can ride home on the dray with me; you bring his horse with you."

As Damon and I crossed the schoolyard to the grassy plot where our horses were picketed, it took an uncharacteristically long time for words to catch up with whatever my brother was thinking. At last he fished out, "Boy oh boy, I didn't ever think something like that would happen, did you?"

"I'll say," and now I was the one doubtless sounding a bit dazed. "Imagine, Eddie calling him 'Daddy' right there in front of us."

"No, no! Didn't you see? Brassies on *both knuckles*! Morrie knows how to hit with either hand!"

11

LITTLEST THINGS. THE POCK IN THE KITCHEN WINDOW IN the shape of a star, halfway up; we used that as a mark in cold weather. If the window frosted over as high as that star, the temperature had gone way, way down overnight. A snowstorm generally followed. After Morrie's episode with Brose Turley, I would check as soon as I lit the kitchen lamp each morning, hoping to read winter's shivery arrival there on the windowpane. But the weather stayed obstinately mild, with only a dry chill in the air that carried no promise of snow anytime soon.

The last schoolday of that week, in physiology period, Morrie startled everyone by holding up the rattle off a rattlesnake and, as if it was the most natural teaching device to be found in the average schoolroom, illustrated the principle of stimulus and response.

Eddie still was sitting out his sentence, so I could not press the question at recess or noon hour. But when school let out I lagged enough to pass by Morrie's desk and, with no one else around, make sure.

"Wasn't that rattle fresh off the rattler?"

"Top mark for observation, Paul. This morning, actually."

Retrieving the item in question from a desk drawer, he cradled it in one hand in the manner of the gravedigger contemplating the last of poor Yorick. In class I had expected Damon to catch on to the unfaded quality of the segmented tail the same as I did, but he'd reflexively looked away as soon as he realized Morrie was holding up something where blood was involved. And I didn't want Toby fretting about a rattlesnake invading the teacherage. "The reptile greeted me just outside the front door," Morrie was saying as he tapped a fingernail against the horny object. "Remarkable jest of nature, isn't it, the creature carrying toxin at one end and a tocsin at the other."

"For crying out loud, Mor—" I burst out before remembering I was still technically under the rules of the schoolday. "Mr. Morgan," this time it came out of me singsong, I was enunciating so carefully, "it's practically winter."

"I don't see any snow," he pointed out maddeningly.

"You know what I mean. Snakes shouldn't be around. What if Brose Turley put the thing there?"

"What if it's mere coincidence?" Morrie weighed the rattle in his hand a moment more, then stuck it back in the desk drawer. "What if the unfortunate serpent simply was attracted by the heat of the house? We mustn't jump to conclusions," he chided, although it didn't seem to me to require much of a hop to reach a good one here. He stroked his mustache appreciatively as if a thought had just arrived to him by way of it. "Incidentally, Paul, don't tell him so just yet, but your father's method works like a charm. A barrel stave is first-rate for slaying a snake."

A snake, I remained convinced, that ought to have been holed up in its den that time of year.

That night, rattlesnakes drove wolves out of my dreams. I was my usual wreck by the time Rose showed up.

"Another off night, Paul?" How could she tell even before she set foot into the kitchen? Quick as a wraith, she was over to the stove to warm her hands and whisper: "I know just the prescription to take your mind from it. Three tubs of water."

I'd forgotten washday had devolved to Saturday now that she was in command of Morrie's housekeeping as well as ours. "Help me carry the wash water, pretty please," she set out the terms in her melodious low murmur, "then I'll leave you to your book," although for once I did not want to be left to that. I put my coat on, each of us grabbed a handle of washtub number one, and we crept from the house so as not to wake its Saturday sleepers.

In the start of daybreak we could see just well enough on the path to the pump. Out around us, the barn and other outbuildings loomed as if they were growing with the eastern light. Down at the corral, the horses gazed toward us through little fogs of their breath. I was mad at the weather again, another snowless morning that did not know the meaning of winter. The wind had not even started up yet, practically unheard of for Marias Coulee. Rose breathed in as if taking the air in the Alps. "How my poor husband loved mornings like this," she exulted, somehow managing to do it in the same veiled voice she had used in the kitchen. "I can just see him. He would be up and out at the crack of dawn, getting his miles in. Then he would gather me to go out to breakfast and—"

"His miles? On foot?" It was enough to make me gasp. If Damon and Toby and I couldn't saddle up Paint, Queenie, and Joker to go someplace farther than the neighbors within easy sight of us, we didn't go.

"A goodly distance, let's just say," Rose hastened to correct herself. "But every single morning, if the weather wasn't throwing a fit." As she chatted on, we could have been mistaken for leisurely strollers on a boulevard except for the galvanized tub between us. Ever since that first predawn conference of ours in the kitchen, several days ago now, it seemed natural to be at this. It intrigued me that in these circumstances Rose's experiences seeped from her, episode by episode, as if they wanted out. Like my dreams.

I listened assiduously as usual as she finished up the particular reminiscence brought on by the feel of this morning, about poor Mr. Llewellyn coming home from one of his constitutionals in the grip of a policeman unwilling to believe that a person would be out that early merely for exercise. "Imagine, that policeman would not even trust me to identify my own husband," she came to the end of the story as we reached the pump. "I had to ring up Morrie to come over and—"

. "Rose, you don't have to whisper out here."

"Oh, right."

I voluntarily did the pumping so she could save her energy for conversation. "Such times as the three of us had together," she mused. It was a rare moment of Rose at rest as she stood there, hands quietly pocketed. Slight against the great prairie around us, she nonetheless seemed where she ought to be, pegged into place in the forthright Marias Coulee dawn. I had to strain to pick out her words over the racket of the pump. "—and didn't we just think we had the world by the tail. High living. All the comforts. Money growing on bushes. But put such trifles up against real purpose in life and all you come out with is—" She halted.

"Perdition?" I panted.

"Paul, you are a mind reader. Blindsight. There is nothing like it."

Perdition sounded pretty good to me, out there on the clammy pump handle. The matter at the moment, though, was salvation, namely Morrie's. Rose seemed not to have a care in the world, chatting away as we started back to the house with the heavy tub, but my mind was going back and forth furiously over the dangers represented by Brose Turley. Twice now Morrie had made me promise not to say a word to Father in that regard. But he hadn't said anything about not telling Rose, had he? Halfway up the path we set the tub down to rest for a minute.

"Rose, you better know." Time to go back to whispering. "Morrie is maybe in for it."

"For what now?"

As rapidly as I could spill the words out, I told her the full story. She seemed less surprised about the brass knuckles than I'd expected. In fact, the only thing that seemed to startle her was my conclusion:

"Maybe Morrie ought to go. Leave, I mean," and I had trouble even saying the word. "On out to the Coast or back where you were, or—"

"Oh, I think not," she said quickly. "Life here agrees with both of us."

"It won't be so agreeable if Brose Turley gets hold of him when he's not looking."

"I'll speak to Morrie about being careful, don't you worry." She did her best to settle me down. "But if this Turley person wants him out of his way, he is going about it exactly wrong." One of Rose's patented pauses ensued. Her eyes always widened when she thought deeply. I waited, leaning her direction as a sunflower will follow the sun, for whatever illumination was sure to follow. At last she whispered, as if it were a secret between us, "Morrie can be contrary at times."

Aunt Eunice seconded that.

"Give that man bread and roses and he'd eat the petals and go around with the loaf in his buttonhole. Oliver, you have taken leave of your senses in turning the school over to him."

Her pronouncement caused Damon to kick the leg of the dinner table until Rae stopped him with a look. He knew it was against his best interest to contradict Aunt Eunice out loud, but here it came: "Morrie is a hundred times better teacher than old Miss Trent."

I leapt in just as recklessly. "Morrie knows something about almost everything."

"Morrie taught me 'rhinoceros,' Aunt Eunice!" Even Toby felt the need to take issue. "R-h-i-n-o—"

"There, you see? What manner of teacher lets the pupils call him by his first name, answer me that!" Her tiny mouth pursed full of triumph, she looked around at those trying to have a Sunday meal in peace. George was not uttering a peep behind his nest of beard. I was sure Rae felt some allegiance toward Rose, but did it extend to Morrie? That left Father, as usual, in Aunt Eunice's direct line of fire.

"We don't call Morrie that when school is on," I protested.

"And you had better not let me catch you at it if you ever do," Father said. "Exceptional lamb roast, Rae. You boys: less talk, more fork. You were saying, Eunice?"

"The greenest graduate of The Spencerian Academy"— Aunt Eunice's alma mater, needless to say—"could do a better job of it in that school."

Father kept his head down over his plate, but his voice was on the rise. "Eunice, The Spencerian Academy is twelve hundred miles from here. How was I supposed to pluck up a teacher from there overnight?"

"This is the way of the world anymore." Aunt Eunice was

addressing a higher invisible audience, maybe heaven. "Try to give someone the benefit of all one's years on this earth and will they listen? No."

Sitting there hearing Aunt Eunice call down the thunder of her accumulated years, I tried to imagine Morrie and Rose right then. Rose was spending most of every Sunday at the teacherage, and chances were Morrie would be putting dinner on the table for the two of them about now. Probably sparrow hearts and three peas apiece, but brother and sister would gaily tuck in their napkins and converse in spirited tones as usual. I could see it as real as anything, the teacherage a Crusoe isle of calm amid the turbulence of life—if it did not come under assault by snake, fire, fist, boot, and other weaponry my dreams provided. Was Rose having any luck in making Morrie be wary of Brose Turley? Was luck adequate to that?

12

I WOKE UP THE NEXT MORNING WONDERING WHY MY EAR WAS stuffed with cotton, when I had no memory of an earache. Groggily I lay there, my other ear still pressed to the pillow, trying to figure this out. Usual end-of-night sounds—the wind giving the house a last visit, if nothing else—were absent; the inner works of my ear held only that plugged silence. I rolled over and the other ear was the same, not able to hear a thing. Deaf in both ears? Numbed by the silence, I sat up in bed. How could I have lost my hearing in one night with not even a dream to warn me? Then the bedroom window's blue-silver light of crystalline reflection that was spread over the still form of Damon beside me and Toby across the room registered on me. The cottony stopper on the sounds of the outer world was snow.

Morrie opened that schoolday as if the six-inch white blanket outside was nothing out of the ordinary. I noticed, however, that he petted his mustache more than usual.

I am not the giddy sort, but that morning I floated somewhere above the eternal desk shared with Carnelia. Over breakfast

Father had vouched that a snowfall like this one, damp and clinging, was more than sufficient for tracking and trapping, and likely
would last in the mountains and foothills until spring. Brose Turley would have to go off to the high country now for his winter
harvest of pelts. Eddie himself gave us a sure sign of that when we
rode into the schoolyard and there he was, a sneering grin on him
for the first time in ages, getting in practice to lodge with the Johannson boys by roughhousing with them.

Mine was not the only case of euphoria left behind by the
fat, lazy overnight storm. Morrie found out in a hurry that the
first day of real winter substantially altered the classroom climate. Try us every way as he did on arithmetic that morning,
there was only one equation on our minds: first snowfall equaled
first snowballs, divided by sides. Giving in with grace, he called
recess some minutes ahead of time and got out of the way of our
stampede to coats, overshoes, and mittens.

Within seconds, Grover and I were pelting each other as happily as we had played baseball catch together in the months previous. Snow always turned Damon into a tundra guerrilla; he
plastered Martin Myrdal three times before Martin figured out
where those deadly snowballs were sailing in from. Toby's age
group exploded softball-sized chunks on one another, giggling all
the while. In no time, then, the schoolyard scene was as ordained
as one of those medieval clocks where a troupe of figurines march
out of one side and drive in the troupe on the other: every male
from first grade to eighth was in the middle of the playground
madly firing snowballs, and all the girls had wisely withdrawn
alongside the schoolhouse to cheer and scold. Skirmishes and
ambushes grew into fusillades. Before long there was as much
snow being flung through the air as rested on the ground.

Satisfying as the snowball free-for-all was, the god of
winter mischief suddenly offered something even better. It

came when Nick Drobny, trying to dodge a snowball and at the same time reach down and manufacture his own, slipped and fell flat on his face. The rest of us could not believe our good fortune. Everyone in Nick's vicinity shouted out the opportunity. "Dogpile!"

Knowing what was coming, Nick squealed and tried to scramble onto all fours. He did not quite manage to do so before Miles Calhoun belly-flopped on him, and Izzy landed crisscross atop Miles.

"Get off me!" Nick was shrieking—shrieking was one of the best parts of a dogpile—when Anton Kratka and Gabe Pronovost added themselves crosswise onto the others, and Verl Fletcher sailed in on top of them.

This already was a highly promising pile, with Nick struggling with all his might to escape the bottom and everybody atop squirming to squash him into the snow until he gave up. Grover and Damon and I and several others cagily circled the heap, gauging when to join in; a good rule of dogpiling was to end up as far on top as you possibly could. Then something beyond precedent happened. In her usual provocateur fashion, Rabrab Rellis had been on the sidelines dishing out remarks. Abruptly she came loping out, brown-stockinged legs long and scissoring, turned in midair, and slid across the pile of boys on her back, arms wide as if to spread the gospel of dogpile.

Rabrab did not stay there any time at all—that would have been unmitigated scandal—but her teasing flight of passage had a sensational effect on every boy standing there idle. Whooping, roaring, we flung ourselves onto the heap, the whole wet, wooly mass of us rolling and growing like a gigantic snowball, Nick still at the bottom.

In the schoolhouse, the uproar must have sounded like the outbreak of war. Morrie hopped out onto the front step, one overshoe on and struggling to pull the other one on, to find us laughing like junior madmen. He stopped work on the overshoe and peered at the writhing tangle of us. "Nick? Is this satisfactory with you?"

Nick squeaked out, "Just fine, Mr. Morgan."

Morrie went back inside shaking his head, probably counting the schooldays until spring.

I sometimes wonder if education has its own omens, as the weather does. That day and the next, while the snow was fresh, so was the mood I brought to any school subject, even the ones I already knew by heart. Sitting next to Carnelia as if we were galley slaves perpetually chained to our oar did not even bother me. Then came a change of weather, in more ways than one. As the snow dirtied up and winter went back to being nothing special, a feeling I could not name came over me, although since then I have observed enough students at that age to diagnose my case as pernicious listlessness. Whenever Morrie wasn't drilling us on something the world thought essential to seventh-graders, I drifted into reading of my own or disinterestedly killed off the night's homework right there during school. The only thing I felt a serious need to study was the trajectory of snowballs. And it did not help that Damon and Toby and I came down with one of our periodic fits of tardiness, so that each morning we would gallop in at the absolute last minute and there would be Carnelia waiting like the wrath of Betsy Ross, steaming to get the flag-raising over with.

Maybe it was her way of marking our last day of flag duty, but that final morning she worked herself into more of a huff than ever. No sooner had Damon and Toby scooted into the schoolroom and she and I plucked the flag out of its drawer than she gibed, "You'd think people with a housekeeper could get up earlier."

"Don't nag." My tone was as cross as hers. "Next thing, you'll be whinnying."

"Ha ha ha. You are such a pest. Watch you don't drop the flag again."

"Look who's talking, fumble fingers. Come on, let's just get this done." We marched to the flagpole as if shackled together. The rope would not behave straight when I untied it, so I had to try to undo that while distracted by her yakking at me.

"Mr. Morgan marked me down on the question *Use logical inference to determine an antipodean analogy of 'Noel,'*" she was telling me, as if that was my fault too. "I said *'summer holiday.'* What did you put?"

"*'Leon.'* See, on something like that you need to think backward and that gives you—"

"What's that supposed to mean? Aren't you ever going to get over that backwards warrior business?"

"Contrary, damn it."

"Don't you swear at me."

"I'm not. That was an interjection. Look it up."

If looks could kill, there would have been a double slaying at the flagpole. At least the rope finally was under control. Still glowering at each other, we fastened the flag with fingers that knew the job automatically by now, yanked the rope for all we were worth, and without a backward look finished our civic tour of duty together.

Thank goodness, Vivian was the first that morning to heed the call of nature. When she slipped back in from the outhouse, she headed straight for Morrie's desk and whispered in his ear. I heard him murmur, "The what, Vivian?"

Just after that, Morrie instructed all the grades to carry on with what they were doing while he made a trip to the supply cabinet. "Carnelia and Paul, help me a minute, please."

We trailed him out to the cloakroom. He turned to us with his arms folded on his chest, never a good sign from a teacher.

"You two are in distress, I take it?"

I give Carnelia full credit. She batted her eyes enough for both of us and caroled, "Not any more than usual, Mr. Morgan. Why?"

"Then how do you explain this?"

Morrie flung open the outer door. We stared at the flagpole. It was evident that what Vivian had whispered must have been something very like, "The fwag is fwying upside-down."

I tried to contribute. "We were awful busy, uh, talking."

Morrie's expression was steely. "I wonder if you have any notion of the woe that will come down on me, and that I in turn will bring down on the two of you, if anyone comes by and spies Old Glory standing on its head?"

As if in harness, Carnelia and I raced out, hauled down the flag, and put it upright in record time. Morrie herded us back into the schoolroom. Only Vivian was paying us any attention and when Morrie put his finger to his lips, she nodded.

Accordingly, I was not prepared at all for the miscarriage of justice—wasn't this called double jeopardy?—at the end of the day when Morrie dismissed everyone else and levied on me:

"Paul, I would like to see you, after."

There was something elegiac about the reaction in the schoolroom: *But oh, my foes, and oh, my friends*— In rapid succession, Carnelia looked panicked, furtive, relieved, then was out the door. Eddie Turley stopped for a good, long smirk. Grover pushed his glasses into place as if to reflect full sympathy. Toby was overcome, already staggered with the drama of telling Father, *"Paul got kept after!"* Damon went out of the schoolroom looking back at me in mystification, as if he had missed something in me.

I grumpily stayed at my desk. Morrie busied himself at his, squaring up papers and putting away books, for an interminable few minutes. Finally he looked up at me and in what I recognized as his philosophical tone began: "Now then—"

Now then nothing! My outrage could not be held in while he pontificated. "This isn't fair! Why didn't you keep Carnelia after instead of me? It was more her fault."

"Think about that," he said not unkindly. "It is a truth universally acknowledged that a man teacher cannot be alone with a schoolgirl on the brink of womanhood."

Carnelia?

"Besides," he added, leaving me no time to ponder that, "the flag mishap is not why I asked you to stay after. Paul, it's your schoolwork."

This was the one heresy I was totally unprepared to hear. In vain I tried to think of any subject that was giving me trouble. To my astonishment, Morrie bundled them all for me:

"You're hopelessly ahead in everything here. You know every lesson before I can give it, and you know you do. No, don't even try to play dumb on this. It's not in you."

He likely had a point there. If I couldn't feign successfully during school, I probably was no better at it while being kept after. But I needed to mount some kind of defense.

"Maybe once in a while in arithmetic, or I guess grammar, or more like geography, I know a little more than I let on. But—"

"That is exactly the sort of thing I mean." Morrie spread his hands helplessly. "Can't you see the position this puts me in? Here I am, a teacher with a pupil who is already chockful of what I am supposed to be teaching him. Every minute of that, I'm holding you back from where an ability such as yours ought to be taking you." He drew quite a breath to speak the next. "Paul, I have been around prodigies before and you are one. I see nothing to do but skip you past this grade and the next. You are ready for high school."

"You can't! I mean, please don't."

"Why ever not? You could catch up in high school courses in no time, and you're socially advanced for your age."

The reasons seemed to me beyond numbering. I babbled the first few that came to mind. "I'd—I'd need to lodge in town. I mean, I wouldn't be at home anymore. And Father—there are times he needs me for things. Mr. Morg—Morrie, I'd like to wait. Really I would."

"Well, if I at least were to advance you to the eighth grade—"

"*No!*" Anything but the jungle of galumphing eighth-graders. "Please, not that either." How many dooms did I have to fight off? "Can't I just be in the grade I'm already in?"

Morrie gestured to the vacant half of the double desk that constituted the seventh grade. "You and Carnelia, forever and always?"

"Maybe I could just sort of sit out of the way and read." That sounded feeble even to me.

He folded his arms across his chest, but not in command-ing fashion this time, and sat there studying me. At last he said, "You are a challenge, Paul, a palpable challenge." Uneasily I watched the signs in the features of his face, the twitch of his mustache, the lighting-up in his eyes. Morrie's mind was mak-ing one of its balloon ascensions. "A teacher would not dare to wish for a more ardent student," he propounded, "on those oc-casions when something manages to catch your interest. There-fore it is a matter of bringing your imprimatur more steadily to bear. *Omnia vincit ardor*, let us proclaim."

"Wh-what's that mean?"

"You shall see."

13

"*T*HIS HAD BETTER NOT HAVE ANYTHING TO DO WITH FIST-fighting or horse racing," Father warned as I sidled into the kitchen with Morrie close behind me.

Obviously he'd had an earful of report from Toby or Damon or more likely the duet of them, even though they had no more idea than he did about what my offense might have been. The one other time I had ever been kept after school was the first day in the second grade, for a raging argument with Carnelia over the territorial division of our desk. Now, with Father giving me a look that would have put a blind person on notice, I had some tall explaining to do again. Was it going to make sense to anyone besides Morrie and me? All the long way home with Morrie riding in bouncy dude fashion next to me, as he rehearsed the case to be made on my behalf I sat in my saddle like a zombie. What if Morrie's enthusiasm was wildly misplaced? What if I was getting in over my head? What if Father said no?

"Father, I—" The faces of the waiting audience there in the kitchen outdid my expressive ability. Father was stuck at the stove stirring beans and ham hocks that were more hock than ham, but the distance across the room did not temper the ominous gaze he had fastened on me. Parked front and center at the table were the twin heralds of my detention, Toby owl-eyed, Damon about to faint from curiosity. "Morrie, you tell them."

"Goodness, you two." Rose popped in through the doorway, untying her apron to go home but obviously not before she had her say. "Paul of all people. Morrie, really, you are going too far with this. When boys behave some way that doesn't suit you, can't you make them wash windows or some such rather than keeping them in after? That's what I would do."

Yielding to the trend of things, Father suspended cooking for the time being and drew a chair up for Rose. He shifted Toby into sharing half of Damon's chair and indicated the vacated seat to Morrie, then gravely sat down at his cup-worn spot at the head of the table. I took my place, uneasy with the fact that my case had escalated into a conference. Even Houdini padded in from the other room as if taking an interest.

Palms of his hands flat on the oilcloth, as if a séance were about to start, Morrie squarely faced Father at the far end of the table. "Unaccustomed as I am to this particular kind of excess in a student," he began, alarming me, but then in reasonably short fashion brought the matter down to how far ahead I was in my studies.

Father looked relieved, but puzzled. Rose nodded diagnostically, as though she had always figured blindsight led to something like this.

"You're the doctor," Father granted Morrie. "But can't you just—forgive me this, Paul—pile more homework on him? Even if he does it in class, it'll keep him occupied."

"That is scattershot, if I may say so," Morrie responded, shaking his head. "Paul needs aim; he does not need to be dispersed more than he is in several different directions." I shifted uncomfortably in my chair, wishing this could be conducted in writing. Morrie, however, was just hitting his stride. "From all that I can observe, Paul manages to stay on top of things here at home: chores, and helping you, Oliver, any of that. The ordinary run of schoolwork, I award him absolute top marks there too. But there is a neglected area, tucked away in that mind of his, that it would greatly help him to become fluent in." Here Morrie paused so long for drama's sake that even Rose puckered in impatience. When he was certain he had us all on the edge of our seats, he delivered:

"*Paul est omnis divisus in partes tres,* if I may slightly recast a pertinent phrase, Oliver. To make best use of that third realm, I firmly believe he must now plunge in and cross the Rubicon."

Enough silence met that to drown a barbershop quartet in.

Shifting my eyes around the table, I could see Rose and Damon and Toby were in need of an interpreter. Father was not.

"Latin? You want him to take *Latin*? But good grief, Morrie, for that he'd have to be in high—"

He broke that off with a glance toward his two other sons. Toby still looked blank. Damon had caught up and then some; his mouth tightened.

"Oh dear," Rose let out, winning even more of my heart. Our early-morning talks together obviously tugged at her as much as they did at me.

The entire room seemed to have been unsettled by Morrie's prescription for me. Looking troubled, Toby whispered something in Damon's ear. "It's like that jabber the Drobnys talk to each other, is all," I heard Damon whisper back.

Morrie tapped his fingertips on the tabletop as if calling the bargaining table back to order. "Not necessarily," he asserted,

addressing Father's apprehension that Latin would take me out
of the household. "My censorious sister notwithstanding, there's
always after school."

Father sat forward and turned directly to me. "Paul? You're
sure you want to take this on?"

Until that exact moment my mind was not truly made up.
"Divided into three parts" probably understated my condition. I
heard my decision along with the rest of them.

"More than anything."

Now came the part that worried me most. Father was all too
aware, and I sensed it along with him, that this carried the same
sort of financial risk as dealing with postal box 19 in Minneapolis had. "Morrie, straight out, all right? I can't pay you much."
He cast a whimsical glance toward Rose, who right then was refusing to meet the eye of anyone but Morrie. "I'm already laying out wages to a housekeeper, aren't I. I don't know what the
going rate for a tutor is, but—"

Morrie erased that in midair. "This is on the house, Oliver.
I could stand to sharpen up some, myself, on ablatives and such.
If you can spare Paul for an hour after school every day, I'll give
him a running start in life beyond Marias Coulee. Fair enough?"

"That's where he's headed, I know," Father said softly. "Fair
enough."

Shortly the gathering broke up, Morrie declining to stay for
supper with the excuse that he had a sage hen awaiting in mari-
nade and Rose saying she would have a bite as usual with
George and Rae. I remember I went through our meal and the
rest of that evening in a state of unnatural excitement, as if
everything inside me was on tiptoes. At bedtime Father surprised us, Toby most of all, by saying: "Tobe, you don't look that
sleepy, nor am I. How about a game of Chinese checkers? Houdini can be on your side."

Damon and I climbed the stairs in tandem, Father watching us all the way. As soon as we were in the bedroom, we halted and stood there face-to-face. Damon attempted a grin. "You want to go to school *after* school? How loony can you get?"

"I need to, is all." I made a floundering gesture in the direction of where his scrapbooks were forever spread open. "This is something like those. Only in my head." Still looking at me, Damon shrugged, which could have been yes or no. "You're gonna have to be in charge of Tobe, coming home," I blathered. "When it's really stormy I won't stay after, I'll come with—"

"Tobe and me can get by. Paul, it's all right."

It was and it wasn't. We both knew that. When we turned in, Damon rolled to his side of the bed, and I lay there waiting to see where dreams were going to take me now.

14

DAYS FLEW OFF THE SCHOOL CALENDAR FROM THEN ON. IF I could bodily pick up the appropriations chairman and deposit him somewhere enlightening, it would be at our schoolhouse those culminating weeks of 1909. The sun rose and set in the tireless figure at the front of the classroom.

—*"The polka dot bowtie on Jimsy stuck out, as ex—extra—"*

"Sound it out when you don't know it, Sally, remember? One syllable at a time, now try it."

"Ex-truh-vay-gant."

"Very good, merely a little work needed on each *a*. Say it after me: *extravagant*. It means 'to go beyond the limits of something.' That is why *extra* is in there, and *vagant* you can remember by its resemblance to *vagrant*, a person who wanders around. Does everyone have that fixed in mind? Proceed, Sally."

"—extravagant as spats on a rooster. Mr. Morgan, what's 'spats'?"

"Vests for your shoes. Your turn to read, Anton, please."

Even the vendettas of recess were taken in hand.

"—dumb honyock, your folks don't even speak American, they talk that broken stuff!"

"Is that so? Put 'em up, squarehead!"

"Ah, comparing knuckles, are you, Martin and Milo? If I didn't know better, I would have I thought I heard harsh words while I was sitting inside grading papers. People could get the wrong impression. I'll tell you how we are going to avoid that in the future. See this coin? If the flip comes up heads, Martin and Carl and Peter and Sven hereafter take recess when the rest of us come in. If it's tails, Nick and Sam and Ivo and Milo take recess then."

And in my case, Morris Morgan dipped me into Latin like a wick into ready candle wax.

I'm convinced Morrie was secretly as relieved as I was that no one else's parents—not even Grover's, and blessedly not Carnelia's—chose to enlist their offspring in our after-school sessions when he offered. Just the two of us every afternoon after Damon and Toby loyally waved as they rode off home together, we went to that other language as if indeed building a bridge across the Rubicon. Morrie had been right. Latin gave my mind a place to go, and to make itself at home for a good, long while. The danger to this, I realize, was that it fed my pedantic streak. But how much better a pedant Morrie made me, I like to think. "Look to the root, you must always look to the root," I heard him say whenever I was stumped by some fresh swatch of vocabulary or labyrinthine conjugation, and it caused me to see into two languages at once. *Fabula*, story; I gaped at the birth of *fabulous* and *fable*. Similarly *school* from *schola*, *recess* from *recedere*—suddenly everything I read was wearing a toga.

Father pitched in heroically. Evenings now, when his finger ran down the listings in the big dictionary, he would pause at captivating Latinate derivations and share those with me. But whatever moved me to do so, I waited until I was alone one night to look up the words paired in my curiosity as indelibly as, well, Rose and Morrie. For some reason I had expected *fate* to be Greek in origin. However, there it was, derived straight as a spear from *fatum*. And *destiny*, too, was as Roman as could be: *destinare*, to make firm.

I don't mean to award Morrie perfect marks for those weeks, only top ones. He had discovered a central virtue of the one-room school, the porosity between grades so that a lesson given in a good, clear voice to one level of students would find its way into others as well. Toby and Inez, I noticed, were all ears now whenever the grade ahead of them did its spelling. But there will always be some who are impervious. The eighth grade, for example. Morrie made real headway on Verl and maybe even a smidgin on Martin, but Milo and Carl had very little more capacity to put to use; and Eddie Turley simply stared toward the blackboard as if it were just another wall. To a remarkable degree, though, Morrie had everyone else in that schoolroom functioning, and it showed in morale.

"Mr. Morgan?" True to his name, Miles Calhoun was trying to put his hand a mile in the air to gain Morrie's attention. "It's December already."

"December already, yes, I have noticed that. It comes with ventilation, doesn't it, in Montana. But what brings up this matter of the calendar so urgently?"

"The Christmas play!"

"The Christmas play. Are we speaking of the Nativity? I see by the forest of nodding heads we are. Very well, someone please tell me how this has taken place in other years. Wait, wait, one at a time. Why do I not encounter so many hands up when the topic is arithmetic?"

Carnelia and I cowered, our memory still raw with our fifth-grade experience of having been cast as Mary and Joseph. For once we needn't have worried. Morrie appointed a play committee that proved to have acute directorial instincts. Rabrab, under the stage name of Barbara, starred as a very fetching mother of the doll-baby Jesus. Grover made a distinguished Joseph with his eyeglasses above his dark-dyed cotton beard. We three brothers were in the safe anonymity of shepherds, albeit in fashionable robes Rose whipped up for us. All the parents came, with the unmissable exception of Brose Turley. It gave me hope that he would stay boot-deep in the distant snows on through until spring.

On the final Friday, Morrie dismissed school on the cheery note that he would see us next year, and with Father at home for a change while the Big Ditch construction was shut down and Rose and Morrie off to the bright lights of Great Falls on a short holiday of their own, we came to that Christmas.

"*H*ER AND HER OLD TAFFY. BE LUCKY IF WE DON'T BREAK our teeth on it." Scooping up a mittenful of dry snow, Damon tried to pack it into a snowball to hurl at a deserving fence post and gave up in disgust.

"Remember what Father said," I warned. "Said" did not quite describe it. He had threatened Damon and me separately—although gently, because after all it was Christmas morn—over the niceties of taking our obligatory gift to Aunt Eunice and thanking her for the jar of barely chewable taffy she handed each of us every year. Sparta and Corinth cannot have exchanged tribute any more grudgingly, but Father was resolutely sunny about our prospects of truce with Aunt Eunice for this one day. "She'll be in the spirit of the season, you'll see," he assured us as he turned us out of the house on our gift mission. "I saw her in her yard just the other day and she gave me her annual smile."

"I like taffy." Toby, always our ace in the hole with Aunt Eunice, was carefully maintaining his arctic route of march between the pair of us as if under escort. "Don't you, Paul?"

"It'll strengthen our jaw muscles, Tobe. We'll be like those circus strongmen who lift anvils with their teeth and we'll owe it all to Aunt Eunice."

Damon continued to kick along in the disappointing snow on the road, as if somewhere under the thin skift there ought to exist a chance at an honest snowball. "I still don't see why we couldn't do this when we're at George and Rae's for dinner."

That part had been in Father's briefing to me. "Because this way it makes an occasion for her," I recited practically word for word. "She's an old lady and doesn't have that many occasions in her life."

"Huh!" Damon unhappily turtled his head down into his scarf and turned-up coat collar to try to escape the pestering wind. It always amazed us that the Marias Coulee wind managed to be in our faces no matter what direction we were going. "Have to put on a ton of clothes to go sit in her kitchen for ten minutes."

"Fifteen, Damon, damn it, didn't you hear Father? Come on, let's cut across."

The plowed field between the road and Aunt Eunice's place clipped considerable distance off our journey, but now we had furrows underfoot and snow that was even more fraudulent than the stuff on the road. What scrunched under our overshoes as we trudged through the stubble of the grainfield was the nasty mix of moistureless snow and windblown dirt that we called "snirt." Except for plenty of wind, ever since that first generous storm the winter had produced no real weather to speak of, only stingy snow squalls. This day was typical, Marias Coulee stretching around us like a colorless bay beneath a dishwater sky. Even so, this was a brighter Christmas than the year before, which had been our first one without Mother.

The snirty field was heavy going, and Damon was on the mark about one thing, the clothing Father had made us pile onto ourselves: wool pants over our everyday ones, and warmest coats and mittens, and wool sock–lined overshoes, and scarves, and caps with the earflaps firmly down. We were armored against the elements, no question. Surviving the social call on Aunt Eunice was going to be another matter. As we waddled across the field, I rehearsed to myself the version of "Merry Christmas, Aunt Eunice" I had worked up for her. *"Laetam natalem Christi, Amita Eunicia!"* She couldn't possibly pick a bone with Latin, could she? Beyond that, a quarter of an hour of conversation with her could well be as up and down as the footing there in the furrows. *"Aunt Eunice, in your elocution class, did you ever recite Shakespeare? Do you know he made up the word 'bare-faced' just because there wasn't one for that?"* No, better not; something that rarefied had Morrie written all over it. Our only safe exponent on anything to do with school was Toby, who still had perfect attendance.

A thin string of smoke that somehow looked querulous was whipping out of the kitchen chimney as we approached Aunt Eunice's place. In case she had her eye on us behind the curtains, Damon and I deployed Toby in the lead as we trooped out of the field into the farmyard. He was bearing our gift for her, a tin of toffee. Father had his own sense of humor where Aunt Eunice was concerned.

As we were passing the long batch of neatly stacked firewood, Damon grinned slyly in my direction. "Don't forget the part about the woodpile."

"Toby gives her the gift, I offer to bring in wood for her. That leaves you to thank her for the taffy, doesn't it, smart guy."

Outside the door of the house, one last thing needed tending to. "Wipe your noses, everybody." I set the example with the back of my mitten. Stamping snirt off our feet, we went on into the mud room, as people customarily did, to kick off our overshoes and then knock on the inner door. Toby, in the lead, was the first to see that the inner door was standing open.

He stopped short at the sight of the wide-open door, Damon bumping into him from behind, and I nearly fell over them both. The three of us stood bunched there, gawking at the vacant doorway. In weather such as this, no one would let the cold draft of the mud room into the house intentionally.

"Aunt Eunice? We're here!" Toby uncertainly started toward the doorway and I grabbed him back.

"Merry Christmas?" Damon ventured. "Can we come in?"

No answer arrived except an odd little blurty sound. It took me a moment to recognize it as the sputter of a teakettle nearly boiled dry.

"Take Toby and go get George," I told Damon. "Quick, run. I'll stay here."

The outer door banged behind them as they fled off, and I approached the opposite doorway with slow, unsteady steps. Ridiculously, I was carrying in one hand the tin of toffee, although I had no memory of taking it from Toby. Stepping up into the kitchen, I was bracing myself to search the house when I saw I did not need to look past the kitchen table.

Aunt Eunice was collapsed forward in her chair, her thin, bare arms outstretched across the table. She was wearing only a yellowed old underdress—was it called a chemise, I wondered stupidly? Her head was turned in my direction and her lifeless eyes were open wide, as though to announce *See?* to whoever stepped through the doorway and found her, unspared at last. I gulped so hard I choked on it. It was my first time in the immediate presence of death, Mother having died in the hospital in Great Falls.

I dealt with the dangerously dry teakettle by hooking it off the stove with the poker from the wood box, then went and closed the door to the mud room. Over on the washstand was the basin of water she had poured, washcloth and towel, both damp. She had been taking a spitbath to prepare for her callers. A freshly ironed dark dress with a bit of lace at the collar was laid out at the end of the table. Her white hair disarranged by her sprawl onto the table, she still fiercely clutched the handle of a rat-tail comb in her withered hand. No one could accuse Aunt Eunice of having timidly slept her way out of this world.

15

$\mathcal{D}$EAD BUT STILL FORMIDABLE, AUNT EUNICE UNBUDGEABLY hung over the tag end of the calendar of that year and the incipient leaf of the next.

Her burial, there in the week between Christmas and New Year's, dashed everyone's holiday intentions. In a frost-rimmed grave not far from Mother's, Eunice Mae Schricker was laid to rest, although you couldn't have proved it by me or those around me. Uncomfortable in his funeral clothes, Father wore the expression of a person on a forced march in tight shoes. Damon had gone blank, staring fixedly down to where the toe of his overshoe dug holes in the snirt at the graveside. Toby huddled amid us, eyes and nose a running spring of tears and sniffles. And we were not even the immediate family: over on the other side of the open grave, George looked positively wrung out. Rae appeared to be holding up just fine.

On either side of them stood Morrie, solemn as a visiting statesman, and Rose in black satin under her cloak. I noticed she was shivering, and the weather, unnaturally mild, did not account for it. I came down with my own case of the trembles when the pallbearers approached. The handles of the casket as the six dark-suited men walked it to the grave were brass ones, exactly as they had been in my dream, where Father and Joe Fletcher struggled with a casket while we boys could not get down out of the boxcar and Aunt Eunice sat in her rocker and gloated. She seemed to have the last say even there in the Marias Coulee cemetery.

The first Monday of 1910, I slouched at the kitchen table, still putting myself to rights after a dream involving three jars of taffy chunks that no one, not even the blacksmith Alf Morrissey, could manage to pry the lids off of.

I must have looked better than I felt, because Rose did not even remark on my condition when she sailed in for the day. Alas, she was not carrying a dishtowel-wrapped baking pan or pie plate as usual. One consolation Aunt Eunice surely had not intended was that all that week we ate better than we had in ages, off the casseroles and loaves and pies Rae was flooded with from neighbors and in turn sent over with Rose each morning.

"Rae said to tell you sorry, but the condolence food has played out." Somehow Rose's whisper sounded heartier this year and her cheeks practically blazed with color. Clearly she had recuperated from Aunt Eunice's spooky burial more completely than I had. Now she drew her gloves off, undid her scarf, shrugged out of her cloak, and marched close enough to review me, pretty much all at once. "So, Mr. Half of the Seventh Grade." Rose had a way of arching her eyebrow that invited a person into a portal where revelations were possible. "Ready to go back to school?"

"Sure. I guess." Actually, what I couldn't wait to get back to was after-school Latin.

"Have you made resolutions, I hope?" she whispered expectantly. "We always did." Her face took on the cast of sudden reflection I had come to know, as if she had bumped up against a mirror of the past. "One new year I resolved not to be jealous, ever again. That lasted until the girl across the street was given a Shetland pony." She startled me with a melody of laugh that got away from itself into a snort. "I still think that was an awfully unfair test of my poor little resolution."

Livened up by this, I whispered in turn, "What kind did Morrie make?"

"Oh, I don't remember. Probably to memorize the almanac, wouldn't you think?"

That set us both to snorting with laughter, which was how Father found us when he peered in the doorway.

"Happy New Year, Rose, as it apparently is. And for that matter, good morning." This was not like him to be up so early, but for some reason it did not surprise me. I suppose I just assumed the hinge of the year was pivoting any reasonable soul in some new direction, even a natural sleeper like Father. January needed some justification for its existence, didn't it? Now that the holidays were over, the Big Ditch would be gearing up furiously for the last lap of canal digging, and Father and the workhorses and the dray would have all the hauling they wanted while that went on. Yet I could almost tell by the look in my father's eye that he left bed that morning ready to tie into chores here on the homestead as well. Harness to be mended, field equipment to be fixed, the consequences of gravity on the granary roof to be dealt with—the list was as long as the will of his arm. For when a farmer comes around the corner into a fresh year, what he sniffs is spring, and plowing and planting. He might not have confessed to resolutions, but there was no lack of tasks ahead for Oliver Milliron to face with resolve. Mussing my hair companionably as he passed, he stepped around my chair to start life afresh with a boost from coffee.

"Oliver? I want to try an idea on you."

Father stopped short and turned around to Rose. "Silly me. I thought I might actually get through a morning without one of those being tried on me."

"May I?" She gestured to a chair at the table; Toby's, as it happened. This was new. Up until now, not even the most urgent housekeeping crisis had necessitated a sit-down conference.

"Have a seat." Father sank slowly to his own spot at the table, peeking aside at me to see whether I was in on this. I widened my eyes in disclaimer; the feverish look on Rose was as much news to me as it was to him. He faced across to where she sat as if hoping that whatever this was, it wasn't catching. "You seem a bit wound up. Is something wrong, Rose?"

"I would like to buy Eunice's homestead."

Father and I listened slack-jawed while everything raced out of her from there. Opportunity took the lead—"Who would ever have thought such a chance would come up?"—and was overrun by optimism—"Really, to think of land and a place of my own after everything was lost!"—and the final relay was achieved by that pair of old reliables, fate and destiny: "Oliver and Paul, I absolutely feel I am meant for this! Your letter in answer to my advertisement, the way Morrie and I have fit into life here, poor Eunice passing away—" Rose halted for the length of a breath, then resumed at a pace that was sweetly reasonable: "I feel quite on top of things and able to take this step now that I have the house in trim. There, now. What do you say?"

"I'm floored."

With that, Father bought time for strategy, although not much. He glanced in my direction again, but I still was speechless. Rose as a permanent neighbor, in place of Aunt Eunice? Too good to be true. But where did that leave housekeeping? For that matter, where did it leave bookkeeping?

Father was tackling that now: "Have you tried this out on George? Why do I even ask, of course you have. Let me re-phrase the question: what's the tab?"

"George and Rae will be content with a wee bit of down payment," she replied eagerly, "and, oh, monthly dabs after that."

Numbers may have been conspicuously absent, but we knew they added up to another hefty draw ahead on housekeeping wages, unless there was some wild miracle waiting out there. Father did his best to summon one:

"Rose, surely you must know Eunice got by on that place on main strength and orneriness, as the saying goes. It almost always takes two people to keep up with a homestead." He swept an arm around so comprehensively I had to duck a little, as he indicated a household near at hand that had needed to call in a housekeeper. "I imagine," he managed to imagine this with great heartiness, "Morrie is going in on this proposition with you?"

"No."

"No?"

"No."

Now Father set his jaw. As calmly as a frustrated man could, he pointed out to a listening Rose that her span of employment with us had not yet remotely caught up with the wages already advanced to her. Rose absorbed this and offered the thought that weren't we all lucky to have hit upon such an arrangement? If that were merely to be repeated, it would furnish her the same welcome sufficiency which to the best of her memory had amounted to four months' wages—

"Three," Father and I said together.

—and in turn she would gladly extend her guarantee of peerless care for our home for yet another year. There, now. Surely that was logical?

I felt like a deaf spectator at a Brother Jubal sermon. Meanwhile, Father sensed he was getting onto ground, in more ways than one, where he did not want to be. "A homestead is a farm," he said testily. "Say you do buy Eunice's place. You're going to farm it how?"

"I was hoping you could see your way clear to farm it for me. On, what's it called, 'on shares'?"

"Whoa right there. Why not let George have the honor of this?"

"His lumbago is getting worse. Rae tells me they will have all they can do to handle their own place."

"That sounds familiar—I have all I can do to handle this one. Sorry, but no farming on shares." Father shook his head so emphatically that Rose was taken aback.

"Oliver, why ever not? You did it for the previous occupant."

"And just between us, I would happily never set foot in that field again." Father slapped the palm of his hand down onto his end of the table as if that was that.

At her end—well, I have been in on my share of cutthroat negotiations in politics, government, and the Gomorrahs between, but I have never seen anyone lean in on a bargaining table more adroitly than Rose did now. Even though I was not at all sure this would turn out with any benefit to the Milliron side of things, I felt a tickle of admiration as she planted the tidy bend of her gingham-sleeved arms exactly onto the smudged spots made by Toby's elbows and clasped her hands as if she held something secret in them. She addressed Father with just a wisp of mischief coming through: "I would not want to call poor dear old Eunice stingy. But whatever 'shares' are, surely you could receive a more generous, well, share of them than what she provided?"

That brought thoughtful furrows to Father's brow. It would have to any farmer's. I can't really say he right then felt the tug of plow reins, with dollars per bushel at the other end, but that's close.

Eventually he brushed away something imaginary on the oilcloth in front of him and said, "I'll take the matter under advisement," and I could tell he was a hooked fish. So, by the time Toby and Damon came lurching downstairs to a breakfast even more tardy and hurried than usual, the cross-stitch pattern of the year ahead was as clear as it could get: Rose would work for us in the house and Father would work for her in the field; wages would fly in one direction and "shares" would crawl in from the other. No wonder she was whistling one tune after another as she dusted the parlor, while he clanked dishes and utensils as if his mind were anywhere but in the kitchen.

As we saddled up for the ride to school, Damon asked, "What's up?"

"Gobs. Tell you on the way."

Talk about New Year's resolutions; when Rose and Morrie came to a calendar change, they did not fool around. As everyone swarmed back into the schoolhouse that morning, trading stories about what Christmas had brought to them, a brand-new face met us. It was Morrie's, the Marias Coulee student body recognized after a first flabbergasted look. But without mustache.

The school had all it could do to take this astonishing facial vista in. Shaved, depilated, denuded, unveiled, bare-faced: no one phrase can capture the transformation in Morrie's appearance now that the magic curtain of whiskers was gone. Until that moment I had no idea of the range of disguise that comes with being human. Years came off him along with the mustache. Yet he somehow looked more clever in the ways of the human race, contradictory as that may sound: a blade in a woolly world, and the gleaming upper lip announcing so. When movies became more common, the roguish alabaster countenance of Rudolph Valentino always reminded me of Morris Morgan out from under the mustache.

One thing had not changed. He could still talk the air full. The year 1910 was ushered in by Morrie in the looping fashion of his inaugural day as teacher, except that those of us in our rows of desks were receiving wholesale introductions rather than providing them.

He told us one rigor of winter was going to be eased: on the wall by the stove now hung two horse collars, one for the boys and one for the girls, for portable warm seating on outhouse outings these freezing days. This innovation seemed particularly pleasing to the girls.

He told us spelling bees were going to be resumed but fisticuffs during them were a thing of the past.

He told us we were about to become scientific.

In illustration, Morrie produced magician-like from under his desk a tubelike instrument and held it high. "Young scholars, do any of you happen to know what this is?"

There was a stirring beside me. Carnelia, empress at heart but daughter of an agricultural extension agent until duly crowned, thought she had a pretty good idea of what the thing was. She leaned infinitesimally toward me the way we did when the prestige of the seventh grade overrode our permanent feud. With all the practice we'd had, we could say barely hearable things to each other without moving our lips. In ventriloquist fashion Carnelia tried out on me: "Pst, pest. It looks like a rain catcher."

"You might be right for once, priss puss," I whispered through my teeth. "It's your turn, put up your hand."

Carried away with himself, Morrie was not waiting for hands. He brandished the item even higher and announced heraldically, "It is a pluviometer."

Everyone looked as mystified as before.

"A precipitation gauge," Morrie enlightened us, still fondling the thing. "From the Latin *pluvia,* meaning 'rain.'" He brushed a glance over me, which made me squirm that my vocabulary had not reached that far, while Carnelia wriggled in satisfaction. "A simple but effective scientific instrument which will capture nature's every minute," Morrie was soaring onward, "and allow us to read its moist offerings. Along with the roof wind vane and these"—here he rummaged out of one drawer of his desk a gleaming new foot-long thermometer and out of another a beautiful gilt-bound ledger—"we are meteorologically equipped to set up the Marias Coulee weather station. Need I say, we shall have a new position of responsibility that you shall all take your turn at. Inspector-general of the weather."

Alternately mesmerized by what he was saying and how he looked, all eight grades of us would have followed Morris Morgan anywhere that morning, even into arithmetic. Next, though, he stepped over to a window and gazed up at the sky.

"This is a special year," he said quietly, the way an orator will when he wants you to listen especially hard. "One that comes rarely. The heavens are going to speak." Morrie rubbed the palms of his hands together. "In a tongue of fire."

He was smiling reassuringly, though, when he turned around to us. "Halley's comet. So named for the eagle-eyed astronomer who discovered it. A celestial wonder that moves across the sky in a long-tailed streak. It returns only every seventy-five years. That means it was last here before there were such things as homesteads or flying machines or photographs. Think of that." From the upturned faces of Josef and Toby and Inez and Sigrid low in the front rows, on past the glinting lenses of Grover and the motionless braids of Vivian and Rabrab, to the wall of stares that was the eighth grade, the school did.

Morrie held the pause one last perfect moment, then gestured to the windowful of sky. "It will be here with the coming of spring, and," he sent out a thoughtful look that moved among our young faces, "long from now, some of you may be lucky enough to see Halley's comet again." I did the alarming arithmetic in my head: when we were about as ancient as Aunt Eunice had been.

"So, our second scientific endeavor of 1910 shall be astronomy," he elaborated. "Closer to the time of the comet I will have quite a lot more to say on that." He gave a little smile at himself that would never have made it through the mustache. "You may depend on it." With that, he went off into an explanation of the Julian calendar and why its last several months were all off by two from the Latin numbers they were named after, and that led right into arithmetic.

What a matchless morning of school that was. And what an ordeal that afternoon turned into.

The first hint came when, out of nowhere, Morrie nailed Damon for gawking off into space while he should have had his nose into geography. "I will see you after school, young man," he levied, just like that. There was a malicious grin or two from the direction of the eighth grade, but Carnelia and I and Damon's sixth-grade classmates were dumbfounded. Academically, Damon frequently lived in midair; why pick him off, today of all days?

Damon's face fell a mile at this hair-trigger sentencing. Hardly any time later, it was followed by Verl Fletcher's after Morrie singled him out for sharpening his pencil with a jackknife at his desk instead of at the wood box. "No open jackknives around a desktop, that is the rule. You can keep Damon company, after."

Restlessness rippled through the schoolroom like waves of wind through wheat. A teacher on a discipline rampage can be a fearsome thing; every student ever born knows that. But we never expected that kind of behavior from Morrie. Nonetheless he seemed to go out of his way to pick fault with us that afternoon, scanning mercilessly into one grade after another as grammar period ground along and then a spelling test. Casualties piled up fast. Sam Drobny was caught with his eyes not entirely on his own spelling paper. Five minutes later, Morrie said Nick might as well join his brother after school, it seemed to run in the family. Perhaps to be even-handed among nationalities, Morrie shortly gigged Peter Myrdal, the youngest of the Swede clan but also the biggest fifth-grader imaginable, for making a face at Sam and Nick.

By now it was noticeable that our instructor had declared war on the race of boys. If I wasn't mistaken, Rabrab began to look somewhat miffed at not qualifying to represent the girls in the army of detention. I could not figure it out, this rash of petty infractions. Something hideous had come over Morrie. I'd read *Dr. Jekyll and Mr. Hyde*, but I thought Robert Louis Stevenson made that up.

There are times when you just know that whatever can go wrong next is about to. I hunched at my desk trying to will against it, through body language and telepathy and nearly semaphore to try to warn the innocent up there in the second row, but here it came.

"Toby!" Morrie's voice crackled. "Do you really think this is the time and place for whispering?"

"M-m-maybe not."

"You can stay after and decide definitively," the verdict was dropped on him.

Amazing. Like the Drobnys, the Millirons could practically hold a family reunion after school. Somehow lesson work stuttered on, with Morrie still on the prowl and everybody else on edge.

Then, with not more than ten minutes to go until school would let out, the terrible words:

"Eddie Turley. Attitude. After school."

Damon and Toby and I whirled around in our seats, aghast.

At first I thought Eddie was going to faint. But a Turley probably did not know how. Instead, he surged halfway up out of his desk as if about to make a break for freedom, then gulped mightily and sagged back into his seat again. Morrie had delivered the words like bullets, and for the life of me I could not see why. Attitude! Eddie's dopey sneer at the world was as natural to him as breathing; why convict him for his facial muscles, particularly when he'd inherited those from Brose Turley? This clinched it for me. Morrie had turned suicidal.

When school at last let out, while everyone else had fled to their horses and the after-school contingent disconsolately stayed planted at their desks, Morrie showed not a care. Unlike me. Even though I knew Brose Turley was nowhere in our vicinity, piling up pelts in the distant snows of the Rockies, the back of my neck felt like it had something creeping up on it. Eddie looked as dicey as I felt, with the same confused expression on him as the time I slugged him.

Looking the prisoners over, Morrie absently stroked his lip as if the mustache were still there. "Numerous as you are," he observed as though he had nothing to do with that, "I believe we are going to have a work detail. The cloakroom can always stand a tidying. Eddie, I'll ask you to fill the inkwells and then sit out your time at your desk, but the rest of you assemble out there, please."

I didn't like the looks of this. How was I supposed to bone up on declensions with my supposed Latin tutor running a chain gang of sulking boys? I went up to Morrie.

"Uhm, you seem to have your hands full. Shall I just go home and we start Latin tomorrow afternoon?"

"Not at all. *Exercitus ad Galliam iter faciet, philologe novissime*—the army will march toward Gaul, young scholar. Never fear. First, though, I'm going to appropriate you for the work detail"—I gaped at him in dismay, and he simply looked back at me coolly—"and then we can proceed to declensions."

The school's cloakroom was like our mud room at home, the catchall part of the building, only more so. With the nooks and crannies of the supply cabinet along one wall and the overshoe alley beneath the long line of coat hooks and some schoolyard playthings that had been brought in for the winter, it was a room that Rose could have tended to in, oh, three whistled tunes. It didn't require seven boys. It most definitely did not require me.

There I was, though, and I didn't know what else to do but button my lip and get this over with. Morrie handed out brooms to the Drobny twins, and Toby and Peter were given dust cloths, and the others of us were pointed to the supply cabinet. Verl stalked to one end and Damon and I paired off automatically to straighten up shelved materials at the other. Wordlessly we worked shoulder to shoulder. After a while Damon said in a low voice, "Know something funny? You're getting fuzz."

"What? Cut out the kidding."

"No, really, honest. You ought to take a look." He pooched out his own upper lip experimentally while trying to see down his nose. I took the opportunity to pinch his lips together duckbill style in the silencing treatment. All we needed was for Morrie to keep us *after* after-school, for talking out of turn.

Eventually he strode out from the schoolroom, closing the door behind him, and inspected. The bunch of us stood there in a clump anticipating the worst, given his mood of the afternoon, but he seemed satisfied. He turned to the group with an expression of speculation, looking quite a bit more like the Morrie of this morning.

"There is one further matter I'm going to ask you to attend to," he had us know. "It's Eddie."

All of us shifted glumly, awaiting one more grownup's sermon about the necessity of getting along with someone we knew to be a menace. Verl yawned. Even Toby looked halfhearted. Arms folded, Morrie waited until we had to give him stares of attention. Then he uttered:

"I want you to dogpile him. Right there where he is sitting."

Whatever blue this came out of—and none of us was about to question a chance to get a crack at Eddie, with the authority of a teacher behind it—we immediately were the troops for it. The Drobny brothers' sunken eyes shone. Verl perked up mightily, and Peter gave a happy little hellfire snort that must have come out of his Viking lineage. Damon positively beamed. I have to say, Toby and I balled up our fists in anticipation along with the rest of them.

Morrie shushed us and held us back, saying he needed to write something on the blackboard first and then would give the signal.

While the others gathered at the far end of the cloakroom and buzzed with glee as Damon assigned bodily parts of Eddie as targets for each of them, I edged to the doorway and took a look in. Eddie had his head down on his desk, refusing to look up as Morrie wrote on the blackboard. The chalked sentence stood out boldly until it seemed to hiccup at the end; I had to strain to make out the final three words. Turning, Morrie saw me and put a finger to his lips.

"All right, boys," he sang out, and in everybody swarmed, all over Eddie. Toby and Peter dove under the desk and grabbed a leg apiece. Eddie's upper parts were submerged under Damon, Sam, and Nick. Verl squashed down on him from behind. I hesitated for about a heartbeat, then joined the pile. Only Eddie's head showed out of the heap of boys. "I'll tell! My father—!" he managed to croak out. One or two of the Drobnys and doubtless Damon got their licks in on him with their elbows and knees before Morrie could hover in, ordering us to hold Eddie still. He opened a cigar box he'd had stashed somewhere and took out a pair of eyeglasses, the everyday kind sold in any mercantile. He fitted the glasses onto the struggling boy.

"I don't want them things," Eddie gagged out. "Get 'em off me!"

"Read the board," Morrie coaxed. "Eddie, *read the board*!"

Eddie peered there in confusion, batting his eyes furiously. Morrie gave it a few seconds, watching him squint, then replaced the glasses with another pair from the box.

"Eddie, please, read the board."

Eddie stared. Stared some more. At last he slowly recited: "'My name is Edwin Turley and I can read this—'" He stopped at the much smaller final three words, confused again. Every one of us wrapped across him held firm, but we all had our heads turned toward those blackboard words.

Morrie replaced the glasses with yet another pair.

Swallowing hard, Eddie read off: "'My name is Edwin Turley and I can read this with glasses on.'"

Morrie craned over the pile of us until he was squarely in Eddie's field of vision. "They are called reading glasses, Eddie. They do not need to be worn all the time, do you understand that? Just here at school, perhaps. If you don't want to take them home," he let that sink in, "they can be kept here in your desk."

Morrie peeled Nick Drobny off Eddie's chest. The rest of us untangled and fell back in a half-circle around Eddie's desk. Eddie hadn't said anything, but the glasses still were on him and he was gawking around like a newly hatched owl. Morrie was breathing as hard as any of us. "The rest of you, Eddie's reading glasses are to be a school matter." By which he meant a secret, we knew. "The girls and the others will be let in on it tomorrow. Isn't there some kind of handshake you swear on in the schoolyard?"

"Spitbath," said Toby, demonstrating.

16

$\mathcal{E}$DDIE EDGED TOWARD HIS DESK NEXT MORNING, AFTER HIS usual furlough at the outhouse, and took his seat with every eye in the schoolroom on him. Pausing in the recitation of his expectations of us for the day, Morrie waited with all the aplomb he could muster. Eddie was looking down at his desktop as if it might bite him. Gingerly he lifted it enough to feel around in there and came up with the eyeglasses. He unfolded them sharply, the way you open a jackknife, and for a moment I wondered whether he might snap them in half. However, the earpieces after a couple of tries found his ears, and the lenses bridged his landmark Turley nose; Eddie looked like a collie someone had slipped goggles onto, but he was staring defiantly toward the blackboard as if waiting for Morrie to put up there something worth seeing.

I half expected the schoolroom door to be kicked to splinters and a pink-mouthed wolfer to come charging in to tear Morrie from limb to limb for turning his offspring into a four-eyed sissy. But before long, Eddie's furtively fixed-up eyes became just one more trait in our mortal bin of them, along with

Vivian's lisp and Anton's purple birthmark and Marta's nose-bleeds, Rabrab's slyness and Carnelia's haughtiness and Milo's goofiness, Toby's excitability and Damon's crafty side and my odd accents of mind, Seraphina and Eva's dark spirit, Lily Lee's easily hurt feelings, on down through the list of things we learned to simply chalk off as part of one another in one-room life. That is to say, it would have taken more than reading glasses to gain Eddie Turley any adherents. ("Now he can see to hit better," Grover muttered at recess.) When it came to his right to work around a calamity that went by the name of a parent, however, the Marias Coulee School instinct in favor of that was as fully tuned as a Stradivarius.

At Latin, the end of that day, a portion of me refused to stick to the nominative and accusative cases of *pluvia*—Morrie still was preoccupied with the rain gauge, poring over a weather service bulletin on hydrography between my written drills on nouns of the first and second declensions—and circled around the meaning of *I want you to dogpile Eddie* instead. I kept coming out at different places, the more I thought about it. Never in a hundred years would Eddie, on his own, have resorted to something as unmanly as specs; those were for the Grovers and girls of the world. Yet what a tricky gamble Morrie took, in slipping those schoolish lenses onto the son of a man whose living was killing. I knew Morrie's move could not be termed impetuous, because he'd had to give thought to every bit of it beforehand: the various pairs of glasses, the number of boys to subdue Eddie. Was there such a thing as *petuous*? A word that meant thoroughly thinking a matter through, then risking your neck anyway? Morrie glanced up as I migrated between the Latin and English dictionaries. "Declensions are not done with the feet."

"Just looking something up."

But it wasn't there, in either language.

———

The morning after that brought something I never could have prepared for: Rose in tears. Awash in them, from the look of her when she drifted disconsonately in through the kitchen doorway, bonnet drooping from one hand.

"Here, sit down." I leaped out of my chair and provided it for her. My voice was husky but I kept it down, not wanting to panic the whole household. "What happened? Did you hurt yourself on the way over?"

Her soggy whisper could barely be heard. "It's Morrie."

I knew it. Sooner or later, gambling on outmaneuvering Brose Turley would catch up with him. From the way Rose was carrying on, he must have had the heart stomped out of him.

I asked shakily, "How bad—?"

"Just awful," she sniffled. "He is against my buying Eunice's place."

Visions of blood left my imagination, but Rose's gush of tears demanded attention. She dabbed at her eyes with the dishtowel I hurriedly fetched to her. "Oh," she moaned, "why did it have to happen? We've always agreed on matters. And for this, of all things, to come between us." She managed to look up at me, red-eyed. "Can you imagine? One minute we were talking about, I don't know, the weather, and the next we were having a—" Terminology failed her once again.

"—family spat?" I filled in without thinking. "They're nothing."

That set her to crying harder.

I scrambled to dig out another dishtowel and hand it to her. She fired the damp one onto the cupboard counter. Through the next flood she blubbed out: "You know how he can be. *'I am not avid to see you do this.'*" For a sobbing woman dealing in whispers, it was a remarkable job of mimicking.

I puzzled over Morrie's verdict. He himself was installed nice and snug there in the teacherage, apparently as proud as a pheasant in a parrot cage. Why wouldn't he want Rose to have a place of her own? Was it my imagination, or did the behavior of grownups become more baffling the nearer I grew to membership? Another freshet of tears came from Rose, and I sidled toward the doorway. "I'll get Father in here, why don't I."

"Wait." She blew her nose and blinked back tears for half a minute. With a hard swallow she began, so low I had to lean in to hear.

"Paul, I am sunk if your father were to have second thoughts about letting me draw ahead on my wages to make the down payment. I'd rather he not be told about Morrie's and my—difference of opinion." She smiled weakly and made the cross-your-heart-and-hope-to-die gesture over her breastbone. "Pretty please?"

At the rate secrets I was sworn to were accumulating, I'd soon need one of Damon's scrapbooks to keep track.

"Wh-what do you want me to do, then?"

Her chest heaved, and she looked around the kitchen like someone trying to find her way out of the woods. When her gaze came around to me again, Rose seemed marginally steadier as she confided, "I just needed to talk to someone with a head on his shoulders. To see if I sound like a total fool about Eunice's place." Suddenly her whispered tone turned fierce. "I am trying to make something of myself, and I'm not always sure how much I've got to work with. Bright as you are, I don't suppose you ever feel that way, but for me—"

"Sure I do. Half the time."

"Half—?"

"The school half. When I'm around Morrie."

A few minutes later Father surged in, stretching and yawning, and asked: "Where's Rose?"

"Hanging some dishtowels out."

$\frown$

ℛOSE AND MORRIE PATCHED THEIR QUARREL UP SOMEHOW. People do, sometimes. I know she spent the next weekend in a frenzy of housekeeping at the teacherage, and in turn Morrie moved furniture tirelessly when the day came that Rose took possession of the cold, empty house left to this world by Aunt Eunice. We all pitched in, Damon and Toby and I racing across the snirt field as early as was decent that Saturday morning, and George there for moral support while Rae stayed home and cooked a feast for us all, and even Father showed up promptly enough after his chores at our horse barn.

By the end of that long-ago January day, Rose was officially our neighbor as well as our housekeeper, Father was her sharecropper at well as her employer, and Morrie, I could tell, was determined to stay good-natured on the subject of Rose's homesteading fling, always a hard way to go about it.

17

WINTERS WERE THE TREE RINGS OF HOMESTEAD LIFE, CIR-
cumferences of weather thick or thin, which over time swelled
into the abiding pattern of memory. Everyone still spoke of the
big winter of 1906 with its Valentine's Day blizzard that kept
us out of school for a week, and eternally drifting snow that
mounted beneath the eaves of houses until it reached the sharp
hanging curtains of icicles. By any comparison, our weather of
1910 came into the world in the same fashion it had left 1909,
puny. Only the wind showed some spirit.

Day after day on our ride to school, high thin moody clouds
kept the sun dim, and we and our horses scarcely had shadows.
With nothing in nature in the way of his perfect attendance
record, Toby bounced in his saddle those dusky mornings as
happy as if he were on a carnival pony ride. Even so, the three
of us and the Pronovosts continually watched over our shoulders
at the weather, given strict orders from home to take shelter at
the nearest house, anybody's, at the first smudge on the horizon
that signaled a blizzard coming. Everyone in Marias Coulee was
used to that kind of winter behavior. But the sky of this young

year never did turn threatening, only stayed stuck on disagreeable. The few times it ever snowed Damon still could not make the dusty stuff hold together in a decent snowball, and if he couldn't, no one could.

From the ground up and the sky down, then, that set of school weeks stands in my memory as one of the strangest of seasons. Long, indeterminate days, as though each one was stretched by the wind blowing through it, yet not nearly enough time to follow everything.

The schoolroom whizzed with things to think about. There was the surprise right under my nose when Verl Fletcher and Vivian Villard developed a raging crush on one another; I trace it back to the day Morrie decided to enliven a spelling bee by having people choose up teams, and Vivian's first pick was loud and clear enough: "Werl." *Oh oh,* I thought, and justifiably so, because with his desk right behind mine and hers directly in front of me, there I was in the Cupid seat between. Luckily, I suppose, the generalized lust of a teenager was late in developing in me, and at the time I viewed such matters with comparative detachment. Still, I must have passed a hundred smitten notes back and forth for the lovebird pair that hothouse winter.

There was also the considerable challenge, as much for my brothers as for me, of becoming honorary Drobnys. Up until then in our school career, the Drobny twins, swarthy Nick and Sam in one case and even swarthier Eva and Seraphina in the other, never paid much heed to us either way, probably figuring the best thing that could be said for our type was that we were not Swedes. After the bunch of us together swarmed Eddie Turley for that optical fitting, however, the Drobny clan all but made us blood brothers. This was an unnerving development.

Recess took on gypsy overtones. Apparently Damon and I and even Toby possessed black arts we hadn't known of. Maybe Damon's generalship in the cloakroom did it, or maybe it was by virtue of my voluntary dive into the monumental dogpiling at Eddie's desk; but I suspect it was Toby fearlessly grabbing a drumstick on Eddie that day that sparked a glitter in Drobny eyes. Now we were regularly greeted on the playground with stinging whacks on the shoulder and Nick or Sam growling a comradely "Howya?" and hanging at Damon's elbow or mine like pint-sized bodyguards. For their part, Seraphina and Eva dealt vigilante justice to anyone who so much as brushed against Toby; when he got into a mild spat with Emil Kratka over turns at the swing, they pinched poor Emil purple. Friends like these distinctly narrowed our social circle. For one thing, it was rumored that the Drobnys were sewn into their long underwear at the start of winter and never took it off. Ruthless and foreign and sinister as they were, though, I still think fondly of those twofold hard-skinned twins every time I need to ambush some legislative foe of my department.

And there was always Eddie himself, way up there on the mental roster of that winter. Every time I checked over my shoulder to the back of the room, he was looking wary behind the eyeglass lenses, but at least looking. I hardly dared to believe it, yet Morrie's gamble on salvaging Eddie by fixing his eyes seemed to be paying off. Helped along, significantly, by the fact that Morrie did not happen to make an appearance during the particular recess when Eddie flattened Milo for teasing him about wearing sissy peepers.

There was no sign of Brose Turley—so much for my powers of prediction—except in my dreams.

———

"Does anyone happen to know what this is?"

This time, Morrie was holding aloft a contraption of sprockets and gears and small round objects on metal arms of varied lengths and a crank sticking out of its bright enameled hub.

Carnelia had learned from the example of the pluviometer. Her hand shot into the air and she did not wait for Morrie to call on her before blurting, "It's a planet machine."

"Close," Morrie said generously. "A mechanical model of the solar system, actually"—he could not resist giving the crank a twirl to send the orbs whirling around the enamel sun—"and planets, our own among them, of course predominate. Technically, Carnelia and everyone, this ingenious device"—another indulgent turn of the crank and Venus chased Mercury in a beguiling orbit and Jupiter romped neck and neck with Saturn and so on—"is called an orrery." And so the Earl of Orrery's invention joined Halley's predictable comet in our season of celestial science. Before he was done, I could tell, Morrie would have us staying up nights to run our fingers across the stars.

At the time, though, another part of me desperately hoped this was not a case of Morrie chewing more than he could bite off. A glance at the practically virgin Westwater Mercantile calendar on the side wall told how far his enthusiasm was racing ahead of the actual machinery of the cosmos. Halley's comet wasn't due until well into spring. Was our prophet of science going to exhaust everything skyward, and wear us out on the topic, before the fiery visitor even appeared?

Hardly. As I watched, Morrie craftily set aside the orrery, right then while every one of us in that schoolroom itched to turn that magical crank and send the solar system on its merry-go-round, reached into his bottomless desk drawer, and pulled out an apple. He took a significant bite out of it, munched it thoroughly while we all sat gaping, and then, shades of Aunt Eunice, he was reciting in full voice:

> *When Newton saw an apple fall, he found*
> *in that slight startle from his contemplation—*
> *'Tis said (for I'll not answer above ground*
> *For any sage's creed or calculation)—*
> *A mode of proving that the earth turn'd round*
> *In a most natural whirl, called 'gravitation';*
> *And this is the sole mortal who could grapple,*
> *Since Adam, with a fall, or with an apple.*

In conclusion, Morrie dropped the apple to the floor with a *thunk.*

It worked. Did it ever. An epidemic of grins broke out around the schoolroom, infecting even the brighter portion of the eighth grade. The moment set the mark for Morrie's excursions into the science of the cosmos; if he had to go to Eden to show us the field of gravity, he would.

"Gravity is everywhere around us," he informed us next with the aplomb of a ringmaster, "from the heavens to the ground under us. It is a force utterly consistent in its steadiness, on all items great and small. Watch."

Scooping the apple into his hand again, he borrowed Josef Kratka's much-bitten pencil, held the objects out equally at shoulder height, and let both drop at the same instant. When apple and pencil struck the floor precisely together, Marias Coulee School blinked with interest. Morrie immediately produced a copper penny and a silver dollar, and dropped them to the same result. "Your turn," he challenged, and grade by grade we madly tested the fidelity of gravity. A ball and an empty lunch pail fell at the same rate. So did a ball and a full lunch pail, we found to our amazement. An overshoe and a pen nib. The yardstick and the blackboard eraser. Damon and Grover came up with the most fiendish experiment, a gunnysack with as much coal as one of them could lift and a needle delicately held poised by the other. The law of falling objects held true every time, and from that foothold in gravitation, Morrie took us up and out, session by session, into the wonders of the universe. "Copernicus," he would say, as if remembering someone he once knew, "now there was a person who saw to the center of things." Then he'd conjure the master of heliocentrism back to life for us, and Kepler and Galileo, and peculiar Tycho Brahe, and lead us into the lenses of their trembling telescopes, and outward to the silver pinpoints of constellations. Heaven's wanderers, he took care to warn us another occasion, in superstitious times past had been no more welcome than tramps on earth. "Never fear, young scholars. An orbital comet foretells only itself, not the end of the world. Halley's has come and gone two dozen times that we know of, and the world seems to still be here, doesn't it." We had to grant the truth of that, but he punctuated it anyway by nailing up a framed Delacroix print of Halley's comet streaking benignly over the heads of terrified peasants in their fields. *The Star Dragon*, it was titled. "Quite a nice likeness of the comet," Morrie estimated.

If only I could bottle it for every teacher under my jurisdiction, the fluid passion Morrie put into those class hours of cosmic science. Naturally I would like to think it was the whetstone of daily Latin with me that sharpened his teaching mentality to a razor's edge those times, but that's awfully nearsighted. Much more likely, given the coming of the comet he simply performed up to the role he had been handed, the way a stand-in might deliver better than his best when allowed onto a hallowed stage. Whatever accounted for it, in those winter weeks when the dragon-tailed satellite was racing across its millions of miles toward us, Morrie teetered on the astronomical highest wire— some days more than others, but never did he plummet.

⤙

"*I* DID AWAY WITH THE WALLPAPER IN MY PARLOR LAST NIGHT," Rose typically would report in our hushed dialogues these mornings. She practically crackled with energy now that she had another house to maintain—counting her attention to Morrie's teacherage, this made three. "I took exception to purple flowers as big as cabbages."

"They reminded me of squashed bats," I whispered back. Damon and I were convinced Aunt Eunice decorated that parlor as a chamber of horrors for boys.

"Paul, do you know, I'm ever so glad I bought the homestead," Rose rushed on. "There is one thing, though. May I ask you something?"

"I—I guess so." I sat forward in my chair at the table, tensed for what deluge might come.

"Plowing." When whispered that way, it did sound mystifying. The isthmus between Rose's eyebrows scrunched into a tiny wrinkle as she reported her perplexity. "The ground just sits there. But every time I ask your father how soon he will start plowing my field, he gets a funny look on his face. So, tell me— when does plowing occur?"

"When you can't see frost on the ground by the light of the first full moon after the equinox."

"Oh."

⤙

"*P*AUL, *PAUL*, PAUL." MORRIE RESORTED TO THIS ONLY WHEN my translations were at their most dire.

It was a Friday, and both of us had already had another strenuous week of school. Daylight was lengthening by leaps and
bounds now—looking out at the snowless prairie, a person might
have declared winter was waning, except that this winter had been
on the wane from the start—and the after-school classroom was
not quite as cozy with dusk as it had been. Nonetheless, Morrie
kept company with my Latin just as if he wouldn't have preferred
to be over in the teacherage with his feet up. "Let's try it again.
Listen for the footsteps of the language, all right? *Veni.*"

"'I came.'"

"*Vidi.*"

"'I saw.'"

"*Vici.*"

"'I was victorious.'"

"*No!*" He slumped at his desk. "Why oh why, *why* would you
follow two active verbs with a passive one?" Possibly he had a
point. I shrewdly switched to:

"'I got the better of the fight.'"

Pain entered his expression.

"But why not?" I defended. "You keep telling me to look to
the root, and *victoria* means 'victory.'"

"Perfectly reasoned," he said tiredly, "except that you are resorting to the root of a noun when we happen to be dealing with
a transitive verb. *Vinco, vincere,* et cetera—as in in*vinc*ible—in
case it has escaped your attention?"

I brooded. This had the flavor of Father negotiating with
Rose. Try to be logical, and the next thing you knew, terms had
shifted shape and left you pawing the air.

Sympathy was not in Morrie's repertoire today. Something
like a groan came either from his desk chair or him along with his
next instruction to me. "The pertinent verb. Look it up." I made
the trek to the Latin dictionary one more time and came back.

"'I conquered,'" I conceded. "Morrie?" We had arrived at an understanding that I did not need to call him "Mr. Morgan" in the after-school sessions if no one else was around. "Have you ever been to Rome?"

"Hmm? Rome? Yes, twice—or was it three times," he said absently. As if reminded, he glanced up at me. "The leather trade involved travel, you know."

The thought of going to the Roman heart of things made me breathless. "Did you see the Colosseum and all?"

"Of course. It is a few thousand years past its prime, but still impressive. You can feel the layers of time there," he mused. "Antiquity is a strange commodity. Dilapidation adds to its worth." He caught himself. "We are straying from the topic here." Pulling my pages of homework to him, he did a rapid appraisal. "Conjugations do not particularly bother you, do they."

I shook my head. *Amo, amas, amat,* all that—much easier playmates than the Drobnys, as far as I was concerned.

"And," he cast a glance over last night's assignment again, "you seem to be quite up on declensions."

I nodded. I gobbled those.

Morrie sat back in his chair and the indeterminate groan came again. "Then why are your translations stiff as a corpse?"

The answer to that was out of my reach. Novice that I was, I didn't fully comprehend he was galloping me through Latin at such an intense pace that my vocabulary was always being left in the dust. With Father's help, I was memorizing ten new words a night. Morrie could spring that many on me in just a couple of his damnable sentences to be translated.

"Here's one for you." I thought I caught an impish gleam in him as he stepped to the blackboard and wrote it out: *Lux desiderium universitatis.* It did not look hard, which made me suspicious. "It is one of my favorites," Morrie was saying. "Quite a nice Copernican line." Copernicus was not there to decipher it into English, I was. Morrie looked at me sternly. "A hint. It does not have to be translated into precisely three words, nor does it need to be cumbered up with passive verbs and whatnot into a dozen or more. There's a lovely balance in the middle, to this one. Translate away, *discipule*."

I worked on it for some while. Knots of language entranced me even then, even through my fumbling and bad splices and hauling in heavy bowlines where I should have been threading slipknots. Finally, I cleared my throat and spoke: "'Everything wants to have light.'"

Morrie pursed his lips, lifted his eyebrows, and eventually shook his head.

"Uh, 'wishes' it," I backpedaled, "'is homesick for' it —"

"Latin is the subject you are purportedly studying at this moment, I believe, Paul, not guesswork," he closed me off. "I want you to keep at this line; it will do you good." Morrie pinched the bridge of his nose, one of his thinking postures. "In dealing with a language you must have an organizing principle. Just remember, in translating always work outward from the word to find its best equivalent in English. You must appropriate another sense of the word if necessary—"

"What's that mean, anyway?" I was grouchy by now, tired of getting ambushed by both languages. "You told me you were 'appropriating' me when you glommed onto me for the cleanup crew for the supply room, and now it sounds like it means you want me to grab off one word for another. I thought 'appropriate' was nice manners or something."

"It is a homonym, something spelled the same as another word but with a different meaning." He considered for a moment. "In fact, when all is said and done, I suppose it is a multinym."

Oh, fun, I despaired to myself, now a word could have any number of meanings.

This was just the kind of thing that always lit Morrie up. "Appropriate behavior, yes," he was merrily counting off on his fingers, "and as a verb of possession, to claim for one's own use, or maybe better, to take possession of. 'Glom onto' is not a bad colloquial rendition, actually. And, not to forget—" He dug in his pocket and flipped a penny to me. "Here, yours to keep. What have I just done?"

"Given? Donated? No, wait, I get it—an appropriation, like the legislature in Helena does with people's money?" Little did I know, then, what an adversary a predatory species called *appropriations chairman* would prove to be in my life.

"Top mark," Morrie granted, and for the first time all session he looked vaguely satisfied with my progress. "Now then, back to *Lux desiderium universitatis*—"

"WHOA." The command was accompanied by the harness jingle of the dray team pulling to a halt at the front of the school and the familiar screech of the hand brake being set. "Slack up, Blue, old fellow." Father always used a stentorian tone on the horses. "Steady there, Snapper." This was a *finis* to our Latin session neither Morrie nor I had anticipated. Well, at least I had gained a penny on the day.

"Young Cato's chariot awaits," Father announced as he joined us in the schoolroom. "I thought I'd swing by and give Paul a lift home."

"Always glad to see the president of the school board," Morrie greeted him. "Among other glories of office, in charge of replenishing the coal bin, am I right?"

Father found something in a pocket to write *coal* on, and they visited man-to-man while I went to my desk and gathered my books. I was more than ready to go, but Father was gazing around the room as if visiting a museum. "By the way, Morrie. I don't seem to recall an orrery or a rain gauge in our school budget."

Morrie was grandly dismissive of that. "Don't give it a thought. I have provided them myself. Oliver, you are looking at me crossly."

"It's irregular, to say the least," Father was plainly uncomfortable, "for the teacher to be dipping into his own pocket for classroom equipment. You could have come to the board and—"

"—Walter Stinson would have wanted to know the total history of the orrery and of the solar system as well, and Joe Fletcher would have wondered if a tin can wouldn't catch as much rain as a pluviometer. They are good men, but gradual in making up their minds, aren't they." Morrie gestured upward, his customary field of interest. "Halley's comet and the attending science coincide like this only rarely, as you know. I cannot wait on budget considerations." All at once a helpless smile played across his face. "I have been accused before of being prodigal with my funds. It's not a hanging offense."

"Something has been bothering me," Father came out with, and the way this was going, I set my books back down. "This school and our children are absolutely the best thing Marias Coulee has to offer, but it's plain as day you're used to a higher mental plane." Father's gaze probed around the schoolroom again until coming to rest on the man at the teacher's desk. "Yet here you are. If you don't care a fig for wages or other attainments, what do you gain from this?"

"I'm surprised you need to ask," Morrie responded, indeed blinking a bit. "A job of this nature is a preventative."

It became Father's turn to blink. "Against what, may I ask?"

"The acid of boredom. Surely you have experienced something of the sort, Oliver. The drayage business in the well-worn streets of Manitowoc?"

Father became aware I was closely following this back and forth. I much wanted the debate to go on—Latin had whetted my appetite for verbal thrust and parry—but he called a halt. "Speaking for the school board," he accorded Morrie, "we're lucky you find life here unboring enough. We hope you'll take the school for us again next year."

Morrie looked pleased enough to purr, although he only said, "The possibility exists." I was way ahead of him on possibility: Greek from him, after school next year—after Rome, Athens!

"Paul," Father broke in on my thoughts, "get yourself together, we'd better be on our way."

"Before you depart." Morrie rose and beckoned Father over to the weather ledger. "I have a matter of agricultural interest to show you."

With Father reading silently over his shoulder, he paged through the weekly precipitation readings since the start of the year. I knew it was dehydrated arithmetic in more ways than one. My turn as inspector-general of the weather had not come around yet, but Damon said he could have spit more than the pluviometer held during his.

Morrie flipped the last page and said in the expectant tone he used when he called on one of us in class, "Oliver?"

"It's not news that this is a dry year, so far."

"I would say more like arid."

"Now, now, Morrie. Any land agent worth the silver in his tongue will tell you aridity is insurance against flood."

Morrie's expression conveyed that if Father wanted to jest his way out of this, that was up to him. He clapped the weather ledger shut. "I confess I can't read Montana seasons," he said with a grunt, "they all seem to be one long brown patch. Exactly when do you plow?"

The lunar law as recited for Rose was recited again.

"Fascinating," was all Morrie said.

Father was quiet on the wagon ride home. I enjoyed the privilege of sitting up there in the dray seat beside him, and the day decided to put on a show as the sun went down, a seep of golden-orange between the strata of clouds over the white, white Rockies. It seemed singularly unfair to me that the irrigation project was hogging all the water—the snow there in the mountains that would fill its dam and canals—but I didn't think Father cared to hear that from me right then.

Home was hardly soothing when we got there, what with the maelstrom of Toby and Houdini wrestling on the parlor rug, and Damon all over the kitchen table making flour paste and butchering newspapers for his scrapbooks. Snatches of whistling traced Rose's route elsewhere in the house as she busily closed up her housekeeping day. Father slung the gunnysack of comestible and postal goods onto the cupboard counter and shook out the makings of supper. Ham hocks and beans again, I foretold with a sigh, and claimed a corner out of Damon's clutter to deposit my books. With water on to boil, always the first step in Milliron cuisine, Father settled to his place at the table and thumbed into the mail. He still seemed preoccupied.

Not Damon. He gave me a full devilish grin while scissoring the next sports article out of his newspaper heap. "How was *dusty fiddles* today?" He had been calling Latin that ever since Christmas, when I'd made the mistake of citing the linguistic birthright of "Adeste Fidelis" to him.

"Only the brave survive it," I told him in Roman fashion. "Who's this mug?" A beetle-browed prizefighter scowled straight up at me out of Damon's newsprint litter. "I'd hate to meet him in a dark alley."

"Rube Killian." Damon spun the scrapbook to show me the freshly pasted headline: KILLIAN HOLDS CROWN IN MIDDLE-

WEIGHT SLUGFEST. "He's 'the Ashtabula Assassin.' That and 'Killer Killian,' and 'Ruination Rube.'"

"Swell." The plentiful murderous nicknames of Damon's rogues' gallery reminded me. "Father, we need to look up *multinym* tonight."

He did not hear me. The reading finger was going over a letter.

"Damn."

From Father, this was volcanic.

Toby and Houdini stopped their din. Damon let the scissors drop.

"Oliver?" Rose called, and along with it appeared anxiously in the doorway. "Is something wrong?"

"The inspector is going to pay us a visit."

"Inspector?" Rose shot a look around the room as if a phantom were on the premises. "Inspecting—?"

"The school, what else."

Morrie flapped a hand at the letter the next morning, Saturday. "Oliver, forgive me, but I see nothing in this that specifically pertains to my tenure as teacher. The 'unusually high level of turnover'?"

The bunch of us were in the teacherage en masse. Rose had ridden over with us, and Father could not in good conscience leave Damon and me and therefore Toby out of a matter that all but screamed *the school!* Now, as if it were an inconsequential bit of arithmetic, he alluded to Morrie's query. "Ah, that. Marias Coulee has had—what is it, four different teachers now in four years?"

"Five," Damon corrected him, while I pointed out, "You're forgetting to count Morrie."

"Miss Trent was the worst," Toby announced as if he had

just decided, evidently still stung by the memory of the ruler slap on his knuckles for the misdemeanor of whispering.

"They keep getting married off." Father passed a hand in front of his face helplessly. "We figured we had that cured with Addie Trent." He cocked a glance at Morrie in sudden suspicion. "I didn't think to ask. You don't happen to have a fiancée in the wings in Minneapolis, do you?"

"I am not matrimonial at the moment, am I, Rose."

"Not that I've ever been aware of."

Morrie deposited the letter on his table and we all stood back looking at it as if it might be rabid. Across the years since, any number of such letters have gone out over my signature, and I am never unaware of the impact of the title of office, Superintendent of Public Instruction. Then, innocent of officeholding, I merely stared at the dangerous piece of paper with everyone else. Rose shook her head crossly, no doubt wishing she could sweep the thing out of the room.

Morrie rallied first. "At least this bogeyman does not sound imminent." He peered and read off: "'Due to a backlog of schools to be inspected, a member of our staff will visit Marias Coulee School on a schedule yet to be determined.' I can tell, Oliver, you still do not welcome the prospect. Why?"

"For openers," Father drew the kind of breath needed for recital, "a state inspector can grade a teacher out of a job. 'Lack of competency.'" He said it like an epitaph Morrie might not want to be buried under. "And worse than that, the Superintendent of Public Instruction can dissolve a school board."

Morrie, and for that matter Damon and I, gave him a look. Father was nowhere near finished, however. "That's only the half of it. The state can do away with a school, like that." He snapped his fingers.

"*Close* the school?" Morrie spoke the shock of all of us.

Father could recite it all too well. "It takes a 'finding,' they call it, by the state superintendent. But yes, in a worst case, he can take over a school and shut it down if he finds it's not up to the mark. What they do then is skim away the state supplemental appropriation for the school and put it to a dormitory in the nearest town instead—move the kids in there for schooling. They've resorted to that over east in the state, Ingomar and those places. Indian kids, they do it to them wholesale."

Dormitory. To Damon and me, it sounded like Alcatraz.

"Well, then, Oliver." Morrie tweaked his shirt cuffs as if he and Father were sprucing up to go out and slay the dragon. "You and I had better be at our best for that inspector, hadn't we."

"Every jot and tittle. Starting with your *bona fide*s."

"His what?" Rose hurriedly asked, as if it was something that might need sprucing up.

"Oliver is referring to my educational and occupational particulars, I believe, my dear."

"Oh, those."

"The University of Chicago, first and foremost," Father spelled out, "but anything instructional in your days in the leather trade would further enhance your record, wouldn't it?"

"There were lessons in it, never fear," Morrie said airily, not quite meeting the look from Rose.

"In other words," Father still was making sure to sound fully like a school board president, "mind your *p*'s and *q*'s with that inspector, and I intend to do the same." He sighed. "Not that it's all up to us. There's also the matter of the Standards."

"The—?"

Father bleakly enlightened Morrie. "The standard state tests. To see how the students measure up against all the other schools."

"Oh dear," Rose said for us all.

———

"If old Inspector gives Morrie any trouble, we can sic Nick and Sam on him," Damon half joked as we crawled into bed.

"Worse, Eva and Seraphina," I said.

⌒

A WEEK TIPTOED BY, HOWEVER, AND ANOTHER, AND STILL the Department of Public Instruction bogeyman did not descend on us. Imminent peril has difficulty staying imminent if it doesn't at least show a glimpse of itself. Gradually, Father began to have other things on his mind. All of them had the same meaning: springtime.

The school came down with it, too. At recess one clear blue day, Grover and I broke out the spongy baseball. (Sam and Nick hung around our first game of catch for a minute or two, then tagged off after Damon to the horseshoe pit and the satisfaction of iron striking iron.) Rabrab was the earliest of the girls to show up in fawn-colored stockings instead of winter's elephantine gray leggings. The air itself changed as robins on their sharp errands hurtled past the schoolroom windows.

And our kitchen window was free of frost the morning Rose bustled in and huskily asked: "When do you think—?"

"Won't be long now," I whispered back.

Sooner than I knew. Father had quit sighing heavily every time the words "plowing on shares" came up, and I suspect was secretly looking forward to it. So, with spring officially on the calendar that coming Sunday and the weather perfectly mild and the moon within a parenthesis width of being full, he rolled out the plow and sharpened the plowshare.

The whole menagerie of us circulated in the yard of Rose's homestead that sunlit Sunday morning. Rae came over to provide Rose female companionship, and George to hem and haw that he wanted to see how Father's plowing went before he began his own. Luckily, the ground looked less dubious than George did. Thaw had taken the last muddy remnants of snirt, and the bare brown soil now had the thin crust common to dryland farming. A person could never be too sure about the mood of dirt, though. We all watched Father walk out into the field the philosophic way farmers do, and kneel to one knee to lift a handful of earth and rub it between his palm and his thumb as though it were the finest of fabric. He came back wreathed in a smile. "I'd say it's begging to be plowed."

"Earliest I can remember," one of George's observations as obvious as his beard.

"One thing about an open winter," Father said as if he had been through a hundred such seasons, "a person can get into the field. How about giving me a hand with the moldboard? I'm going to go for broke and set the blade in the deepest notch."

The scene is etched forever in me. With spring flirting on the tattered arm of winter that fine morning, the women chatted bareheaded in the sun and the men grunted and clattered things as they adjusted the cut of the plow. Damon and I also served, standing and waiting. We had helped to harness up and there the team of big horses stood, hitched to the riding plow. Father had instructed Damon to hold the reins—Snapper and Blue were the most patient horses there ever were, but reins still had to be held—and he self-consciously grinned at me with the mass of horse might in his hands. With my loftier organizational skills, I was entrusted with the toolbox and the oilcan and the water jug and other sundries that would become a small depot for Father as soon as he singled out some mysterious spot at the edge of the field for it. Only Toby was exempt from agricultural duty, and he was busy manhandling Houdini and trying to keep track of his hat. We passed hats along as we outgrew them, and as another mark of spring Toby had graduated to Damon's old but still nice one, although it was big on him and he kept running out from under it in his jousts with the dog. I made a mental note to stuff a folded ribbon of newspaper under the hatband for him when we got home. I knew it was my imagination, but clear as anything I could hear Aunt Eunice saying, "Poor tyke, has to go around in a hand-me-down that fits on his head like a bowl."

Morrie showed up. I knew he would. How could he not? He had topped off the school week with a whirlwind session on the vernal equinox, and here it was, about to guide the plow.

Toby and Houdini nearly collided with him as they romped past with a yelp and a happy growl. I called after Tobe to take it easy, but hat and tail were disappearing around the plow on their next orbit. "Living proof that perpetual motion is possible," Morrie remarked. Father and George greeted Morrie to the extent their wrench work under the plow would let them, and he wisely joined Rae and Rose. I knew he and Rose had made up, but it struck me this was the first time he had set foot on the homestead since the day she moved in. Perhaps because of that, they gave each other long, serious smiles before saying anything.

"You're looking lovely for a toiler of the soil," he at last arrived at, and backed it up with a kiss on her cheek.

She linked her arm through his. "Who would ever have thought it?"

"Not I, obviously." Morrie gazed at Rose's field as if trying to read a map in a forgotten language.

"Oh, it's a dream come true." Turning her head my direction, she laughed and wrinkled her nose for celebrating anything nocturnal around me. "If you'll pardon my saying—"

Toby's scream ripped through us all.

18

FIRST I SAW THE HAT, WHERE IT HAD ROLLED BENEATH Blue's belly. Toby must have tried to swoop it out, stepping too close in under the horse's flank at that unluckiest moment when Blue resettled a rear hoof. The toe of his shoe pinned under the hoof with nearly a ton of horse atop it, Toby stood shrieking for his life on the other side of the workhorses from us all, out of reach. Houdini's frenzy of barking did not move Blue, trained to stand still no matter what.

Damon turned out to be the savior. By the time any of us could bolt to Toby's aid, Damon tugged on the reins just enough to make the team of horses back up a step or two. The instant Toby's foot was freed he keeled to the ground, howling out his pain. Morrie reached him first, scooping the broken-looking boy away from any more hooves. He cradled Toby there in the bare dirt of the farmyard, and I flew in on my knees to grab Houdini and keep the agitated dog from wallowing Toby.

"Tobe! Tobe!" By then Father had leaped the tongue of the plow and surged to us. Rose was there in a flash, too, looking nearly as stricken as Toby did. Damon's pale face hovered in

next; past him, I could see that the reins were in George's mitt of a hand now. Rae was the most practical one of the bunch of us, twirling her handkerchief into a tight twist of cloth and making Toby clamp it like a bridle bit between his teeth: "Bite down on this, Toby, you hear me? It'll help against the hurt. Bite as hard as you can, that's the boy, bite it good." As he gritted down on the rolled handkerchief his sobbing was muted, but he still quivered from the pain.

All of us were aware of the blood darkening the leather of his shoe.

Morrie looked sallow and somber and—I had never seen this on him before—helpless as he tried to hold Toby in some way that would ease the agony. Father had to make our decisions, and his voice came choked but definite as he did so. "We need to get him in the house here. Old bedding." Rose and Rae rushed toward the door. "Damon, run to our place and saddle Joker for Paul. Jump to it."

As Damon hurtled into the stubble of the field between Rose's place and ours, Father got a grip on Houdini with one hand and my shoulder with the other. "Get yourself out of those workshoes and put your riding boots on—one horse accident is enough. Then go like blazes to the Big Ditch camp. They have a telephone there. Tell the doctor we don't know how bad this is, but there's a crushed foot involved, understand?" He set me loose and aimed me in the same motion, and I was plunging after Damon's tracks in the field toward home.

I was too consumed with the responsibility that had been put on me to break down in any way until I was in the saddle and Damon let go of Joker's bridle and reeled out of our way as if letting a charging bull pass. By the time Joker's pounding gallop brought us to the section-line gate, I was crying. I flung myself off and fought the taut wire gate open and danced Joker through. Horses can express surprise, and I felt the tremor of confusion through the stirrups as I reined him toward the Westwater plain instead of the direction of school. We clattered up the long, straight road leading toward the Big Ditch. Somehow amid my weeping I crooned the necessary praises to Joker, over and over telling him, "Good horse, Joker boy, keep it up," as I worked him into a cruel lather. Gates, gates, gates were in our way; there were three more after the first one and I hated each worse than the others. Between those barbwire barriers I rode in what seemed a waking dream, seeing Toby curled like a wounded creature on bloody bedding in Rose's bedroom. In Aunt Eunice's old bed. In the house where I had seen death. I cried until I was out of tears. At last, we topped the rise to the Westwater plain and the snout of the steam shovel stood in sight, the brown cut of the canal ran straight across the prairie ahead, the tents of the construction camp clustered like an oasis.

Red-eyed and snuffling and shrill, I alarmed the nearest foreman enough that he grabbed onto my saddle strings and ran alongside Joker, heading us to the office tent at the supply dump. He hustled me inside to a hand-crank telephone. He could tell by looking I didn't know how to work it. The crank received some mad twirls from him, then he pulled me in close to the mouthpiece. "Central, there's a boy hurt," he shouted down the line as people did then, "cut me through to the doctor. I'm going to put someone on who'll tell him how to get there."

THE DOCTOR FROM TOWN WAS LIKE WESTWATER ITSELF, young and barely dry behind the ears. He bustled in as his Model T gave dying coughs in Rose's yard, and kept delivering abject commiseration to her on the assumption she was Toby's mother. No sooner was that straightened out than it took him somewhat too long to grasp that Father was the homesteader from next door, not simply some tongue-tied farmhand who worked for Morrie. His bedside manner wasn't much better as he clucked to Toby about "that bad horsey." Toby, who had logged more miles on horseback than that shavetail doctor had ever seen, was too terrified to take offense at toddler talk, but Damon and I were outraged for him. It did not help that while the gore was being swabbed off his monstrously swollen purplish foot, Toby yelled bloody murder.

Father was wild with worry and off-balance, as he always was around anything medical. I am convinced it was the presence of Morrie, someone well dressed who could phrase a pertinent question about metatarsals, that put the green young physician on his mettle. After an examination full of "mmm" and "hmm" he took Father and Morrie aside—Rose and Damon and I right at their heels—and announced that all the toes were broken and significant other bones as well, but possibly things could be made to knit straight.

"'Possibly'?" Morrie spoke the word as if wringing its neck.

The doctor frowned. "There's extreme swelling and the foot is one mass contusion. I just have to do the best I can in feeling out breaks."

He etherized Toby, then began setting bones. We waited in the kitchen. Even after Rose's scourings, to me it still had the faint vinegar presence of Aunt Eunice. I couldn't tell if Father felt it too, but he stood staring wordlessly out the window to where George, lumbago and all, had taken over the plowing. Rae was home fixing food for us. That much of life had to go on. Rose had said she needed some air—she still was pale—and Morrie stepped out with her. Alone with ourselves, Damon and I sat at the table like persons incarcerated. Every so often we traded white-eyed looks; neither one of us had any doubt that our lives had changed along with Toby's. We just didn't know how much.

When the doctor at last was finished, we were allowed to look in on Toby. His left foot, colossally bandaged and splinted, stuck out of the bedding so starkly it was hard to be in the same room with it. Father stared at it, one hard swallow after another bobbing in his throat, then he wheeled on the doctor. "What are we looking at ahead?"

"Mmm, weeks. Maybe a month, maybe two, before he—"

"That's not what I meant," Father spat the words. "Is he going to be crippled?"

For the first time, the doctor sounded gentle. "There's a decent chance he won't be if complications don't set in. He needs to keep that foot in bed, nice and still, for a good long while."

"Can we take him home?"

"I don't see why not. Now might be a good time, before the ether wears off."

⟿

"*R*OSE, I DON'T KNOW HOW I'M GOING TO MANAGE THIS."

"I do."

Already life was so out of kilter in the household that the four of us were marooned at our kitchen table in the middle of that fine, bright first afternoon of spring. Toby had been installed in Father's bedroom down the hall and was fitfully dozing his way through the after-effects of the ether every time one of us checked on him. It was Father who was stark awake and distraught. With two farms on him, Big Ditch freight staring him in the face, and an injured son who needed day-in, day-out care, clearly more wheels had come off his world that day than he knew how to deal with. If some people thought the Milliron family was bad off before, they should see us now. No matter how Damon and I tried to sit up straight and show Father we could shoulder our share of things, we still amounted to schoolboys. The more Toby's bedridden circumstances sunk in on me, the deeper my mood went with them. It did not take much figuring out to know I had seen the last of after-school Latin.

Minutes before, Morrie had taken his leave of us, fervently offering, "If there's anything I can do, *anything,* just say the word." The only word presenting itself in any of us at the moment was that doubt-proof "do" from the lips of Rose. It made Father peer across at her as if wondering where she got a monopoly on such certainty. Occupying Toby's spot at the table, she had her elbows planted on the oilcloth and her hands clasped neatly as a locket. I had the feeling this was something I had seen before.

"It sounds like you'll let me off the hook on the 'shares' proposition, then," Father was saying, a whiff of relief in his strained voice, "and that will free me up to—"

"Not enough, it wouldn't." Rose sounded so perfectly reasonable it took the three of us a little time to realize she had no intention of yielding on the plowing arrangement. "You already need to be out of the house on all your other work this time of year," she was laying out to Father nice as pie, "so you are up against being two places at once even if you didn't farm for me, aren't you. Then you may as well, wouldn't you say?"

Rearing back in his chair, Father was about to protest the heartlessness of that—I was, too—when Rose trumped everything. "I'll care for Toby. I'm here all day anyway." She drew a breath as if steeling herself. "Dust will just have to accumulate if it wants to."

"You'd do that? Take this on for us?" Father looked like a man reprieved. "Rose, the boys and I would be grateful beyond—"

"Oh, it's nothing," she said, as if she did this sort of thing every day. "Don't you worry."

For some moments the other three of us sat there taking up space. Somewhere beyond etiquette and just short of moral imperative, something more needed to be said in a situation like this. I knew it and squirmed with it; Damon knew it and kicked the table leg with it; most of all Father knew it and had to summon the words from down around his shoetops. "We'll figure out some way to sweeten your wages a bit."

Rose waved her hand as if that were inconsequential. However, she did not turn it down.

"That leaves nights," Damon spoke what I was thinking.

"I'll be night nurse, of course." Father went to work on that with a frown. "We'll have to rig up something for me to sleep on, in there with him."

"Father?" I saw no need to let anything this hopeless go on. "You're quite a sound sleeper."

About three heartbeats after that, Rose offered, "Oliver? I can stay over. With Toby. At night."

By the expression on Father, the reprieve seemed to have been yanked back halfway. I watched him glance at Damon and me and then toward the hallway in the pattern that sent boys upstairs, then give up on it. The issue was quite clear, whether or not the two of us were there to gawp at it. A man and a woman, unsanctioned by wedlock, under the same roof night after night, all of that. Father already had shrugged off plenty of community opinion where Rose was concerned. How much shrugging did he have left in him for something of this nature?

Now he mauled the edge of the oilcloth with a thumb while he tried to find the right words to put together, and finally he hunched forward to the table. "That's an even more generous offer, and I appreciate it, Rose. But I don't think it's a good idea for you to be—"

Damon and I were looking at each other.

"I'll go," I said after a moment.

"I could, I guess." He nibbled his lip at the thought.

"You couldn't either," I scoffed. "You'd sleep through breakfast. You'd sleep through *school.*"

"Go where?" Father asked in exasperation. "What are you two running off at the mouth about?"

"To Aunt Eu—to Rose's house, to sleep. We can haul Toby's bunk down to your bedroom, so she can be in there with him. You can have my place, with Damon." I saw Damon undergo a fleeting seizure at the prospect of sleeping with Father, snorer supreme, but heroically suppress it.

Matters were getting away from Father faster than he could see them coming. He opened his mouth to speak, but I beat him to it. "Why wouldn't that work?" I asked, as if all this was reasonable as moves on a checkerboard, which was pretty much the way I thought of it at the time.

"Everybody has to sleep someplace," Damon clinched the matter.

"There now, you see?" Rose opened her clasped hands as if this solution had been concealed in there all the time. "Don't you worry," she told Father again. I wondered why he didn't seem reassured at hearing it a second time.

"—and then, Tobe, you and I were on this kind of teetertotter, only it was a sawhorse and we were on each end of a giant stick of firewood, and one of us would go down and the other would go way, way up, high as the top of the house, and we kept seesawing like that, higher and higher, until we heard somebody say, 'You boys have won the teetertotter prize!'"

Sanitizing my dreams for Toby took some doing; it was good training later on for writing my Department of Public Instruction annual reports. What really occurred in that dream was that I was on the teetertotter alone and it went up and down on its own in a manner that mystified me and the voice had called out, "Paul Milliron, you are going to break your fool neck." My amended version did the trick for Toby, who wriggled in excitement against his pile of pillows and let out, "Wow, Paul."

"And do you know who it was?"

"Aunt Eunice?"

"You guessed it. And she had a whole wheelbarrow of candy for us—"

"Taffy, I bet."

"Uhm, fudge, more like." In my dream it was firewood and Aunt Eunice was belaboring me that she wanted every stick sawed to the exact length of a rat-tail comb. "Anyway, here she came, big as life, and told us, 'Dig right in.' Damon was there, too"—I raised my voice on this part so it would carry to the kitchen, where he was bent over his geography book; the specter of the inspector, as Father called it, had even him doing homework—"and Aunt Eunice not only fed us fudge until we were about to bust but took all three of us on her lap at once. How, I don't know."

Abruptly Toby's lower lip pooched out. "I miss her."

I didn't. Rather, I didn't have to, for Rose's homestead still held an inordinate amount of its previous occupant as far as I was concerned. How could a woman that tiny linger in every pore of a house? Especially the bedroom, where every night now I crept between the covers like a trespasser in what had been female territory since time immemorial. Rose had done away with Aunt Eunice's doilies on everything, thank heavens, but that whole fussy room still carried an atmosphere of having been crocheted into existence rather than carpentered. What unnerved me even more was that the place felt occupied by leftovers of existence. It was not simply that death had a dominion at the other end of the house, where I had walked in on Aunt Eunice as she was going cold. No, the immense parade of Eunice Schricker's years still was passing through that borrowed bedroom for me. I had worked it out that she was Toby's exact age the last time Halley's comet flew past Earth, and from there she had gone on to declaim at The Spencerian Academy and then cornered a husband and gave the world George and single-handedly nagged a Wisconsin town and in old age traipsed west to lord herself over Marias Coulee, vociferously crisscrossing other lives all the way. Then came Rose and her jampacked record of life with Morrie and poor late Mr. Llewellyn, next in the gallery of existences that was that restless bedroom. And here I was, tenant of the moment, with the night-heightened destinies and fates of everyone I knew swirling around whatever my own were. A person would need an orrery as big as mankind to keep track of it all.

Needless to say, my dreams went after such thoughts like a wolfer after wolves.

Ragged as my nerve ends were from bunking at Rose's homestead, I did my utmost to stay sunny during my bedside shifts with Toby. He was studying me somberly now in the aftermath of my dream recital.

"You're so lucky, Paul. I just go to sleep, bam."

"You'll grow into dreams when you're bigger, don't worry about that."

He dandled a hand down to the snoozing mound of dog that had become nearly permanent beside his bed. "I think Houdini has dreams sometimes."

"Probably good ones, too," I agreed. "Catching rabbits while he's lying down."

Toby made a face at my mention of lying down. Bed rest was thought to be the cure for everything then. He, however, was the world's most restless patient. Rose was putting the majority of her daytime into keeping him occupied and Father sat with him evenings and Damon and I pitched in after school, and still Toby was like someone confined to a zoo cage. Now he plucked at the bedding and I saw the glisten of tears in his eyes.

"Paul, tell me something. Am I ever gonna get up?"

"Sure you are. You heard the doctor yesterday. Just another couple of weeks yet." Then crutches. Then a long stint of careful footsteps, which did not come naturally to a boy like him. I didn't say any of that.

"I still can't go to school for a while after," he pouted. His face darkened. "It's gonna be awful to flunk a grade. I'd be in the second grade with Josef and Maggie and Alice and Marija, and they're little kids."

I was caught off-guard. Rose and Father were making sure he did the schoolwork sent home to him, and Morrie himself managed to drop by at least a couple of times a week, but evidently all of that did not weigh the same to Toby as classroom lessons. Myself, I would gladly have lain flat on my back for hours on end and let people spoon-feed education into me, if the subject could be Latin.

"For crying out loud, Tobe, what makes you think you're going to flunk? If you need more help with your schoolwork, I can—"

"I'm not there, am I," he screeched, "for the spelling bees and the comet stuff and reading out loud and all the rest, I'M ABSENT! I DON'T HAVE PERFECT ATTENDANCE ANYMORE, I DON'T HAVE ANY ATTENDANCE!"

"Is that what's eating you?" I tousled his hair; he needed a haircut, but he so hated being barbered that none of us had the heart to give him one. "Morrie is not going to flunk you just because you're not there in the second row every minute, honest. I'll tell you what." I lowered my voice. "I'll get him to show me your grades there in his record book. He's not supposed to," I made this up frantically as I went along, "that's one thing the inspector inspects, whether a teacher blabs grades, but I'll work on Morrie and I bet he'll do it for you. Then I'll tell you if you're flunking or not, how's that? But it can't be anything but a secret, all right?"

Toby attempted to shake his head and nod at the same time, whatever it took to vow secrecy.

"I have to scoot on out of here," I told him, looking at the time. "I won't forget, about Morrie and your grades."

I made a beeline for the kitchen, passing Damon at the table, where he was trying to be invisible behind his geography book. "Your turn," I said under my breath.

Damon whispered back, "If I have to read him *Heidi* one more time I'm gonna puke."

"Trade with Rose, then. Milk the cow while she does the reading." That shut him up. "Clear out of here, okay?" I shooed him toward Toby's bedroom. "I need to cook."

"Cooking" was a generous description of it, I realize. But with Father in the fields until the end of each day, I had fallen heir to the can opener and the pot of boiling water for potatoes or beans and the ham hocks and beef briskets and anything else that passed for victuals. Dismal as my supper efforts might be, no one seemed to think they were any worse than Father's best.

⁓

$\mathcal{M}$ORNINGS NOW, I CROSSED THE FIELD IN THE DARK TOward the window glow of our kitchen where I knew Rose was puttering until I arrived, whistling softly to herself. I carried a bull's-eye lantern to find my way across the fresh furrows, a chocolate sea perturbed into long regular waves by Father's plowing and seeding, but in the middle of Rose's field I would put down the lantern for a minute and step away from it until my eyes adjusted to the dark, and then scan the sky. The moon went about its business, the stars were set in place, but search as I would, I could find no sign of a miraculous spark traveling from millions of miles away. Sir Edmund Halley and Morris Morgan said the comet was coming. They had better be right, I thought to myself, and picked up the lantern.

The pertinent morning of this, I was barely through the kitchen door before the faint suggestion of a tune broke off and in its place the whisper: "Is anything up?"

"Rose, that field only was planted last week."

"Ah. I lose track of time. The days are so—" She darted to the stove where the teakettle was going off at an alarming rate. I couldn't tell exactly what description she might have given our daily household situation, but *strewn* came most readily to mind. Still and all, for a situation where she was camped out at our house, amid our bachelor habits all the time, things weren't going as badly as they could have. I'd had sizable second thoughts about the prospect of Rose and Father talking past each other, and Damon and I ineptly trying to referee, around the clock. Except for anything to do with farming, though, the two of them were getting along well enough within the same confines to surprise me.

I ferried our cups from the drainboard and spooned in the cocoa and poured the hot water. When we settled at the table and Rose had taken a hummingbird sip, I whispered the usual: "How'd Tobe do last night?"

"He didn't want to go to sleep." The little knit of consternation was between her eyebrows. "How can one boy come up with so much to worry about? The latest thing bothering him is that he won't get well in time for the comet."

It indeed was going to be a close race, whether Toby mended before he drove us all crazy. I sighed. "I've told him twenty times we'll chop a hole in the roof if we have to for him to see the damn comet."

When I glanced up after taking a slurp of cocoa, Rose was gazing at me with concern. "You're getting circles under your eyes. Isn't my bed comfortable?"

I mumbled something about not being used to such luxury and hoped she would let it go at that. Not Rose. She gave me a knowing smile, as clinical as it was sympathetic, and here it came. "You miss Latin after school, don't you."

That observation had been made to me so many times by so many different persons I was ready to pull my hair out. Because this was Rose, I merely grimaced and muttered, "After-school is shot until Tobe is himself again, that's all there is to it." I shoved back from the table and said crossly, "I have to wake up the bear den," meaning Father and Damon.

I just about made it to the doorway before the murmur cut me off. "Paul?" I turned around, and there was one of those glints in Rose's eye.

"And so." When she said that, you could never tell where things were heading. "Don't necessarily tell Morrie where you got the idea. But there's always before school."

"MORRIE? DOES *COPULATE* MEAN WHAT I THINK IT DOES? In English, I mean."

The morning I asked that, he had a terrible time keeping a straight face. Between yawns and cups of coffee that would have given Father's a run for its money and trying to prepare for the

Department of Public Instruction inspector coming to lop his head off, he was doing his best to administer Latin to me before everyone else showed up for school. At that hour I was chipper as Chanticleer, which probably was no help to a bleary teacher who had to come an hour early every day to unlock the schoolhouse and light the overhead lamps and stoke up the stove and then face me and my translations. Morrie hadn't yet uttered a peep of complaint, however, and now he looked more than passingly interested in my question. "Dare I ask why you ask?"

"Just wondering." I dabbed my finger onto the open page of the Latin collection of readings he had most recently provided me. "Besides, it's right here."

Morrie blanched, then scrambled over to my desk to take a look. *"Navem capere, copulas manus ferreas injecebamus,"* he read aloud hastily, then translated with relief: "'To capture the vessel, we threw ropes with grappling irons.' The grappling is not that severe in the English form. But look it up."

By the time I was through doing so, Morrie had banged the triangle for the start of school and everyone was filing in. This day as others, Toby's desk stayed significantly empty as the rows around it filled, and that absence continued to make itself felt a number of ways between our fellow students and Damon and me. Rabrab made sure to give us each a dramatic dose of pity every time she passed. At the other extreme, Martin Myrdal leered in our direction whenever it occurred to him. Recesses were touchy, because Martin's was not the only tongue in the schoolyard that would like to have got at Damon and me with gossip from home about Rose's nightly presence under our roof. Ah, but with the Drobnys at our sides, we comprised a Slavic splinter state no one wanted to risk hostilities with. So it went, between sympathy and scandal. I caught Eddie Turley looking at us speculatively a few times, but so far I had managed to stare him down—I didn't want Damon to get into it with him.

"What were you looking up?" Grover whispered as I passed his row on my way back from the dictionary.

"Have to tell you later." I slid into my seat just as Morrie wondered aloud if we happened to know who Archimedes was. Good, it was going to be one of those days. I settled back to digest my morning's Latin, not even particularly minding the existence of Carnelia next to me, and listened to Morrie start in on how you could move the world if you had a lever long enough.

Five minutes into the school day, he was in full spate when the door behind him opened quietly. The visitor was well into the room before Morrie became aware of him, although that was not the case with the rest of Marias Coulee School. A suck of wind went through us all.

"A visitor, do I detect from your faces?" Morrie said resolutely, straightening his tie. More than half expecting the inspector all this while, he turned around.

Brose Turley stood there.

It was nothing like what my dreams had been forecasting all those months. The schoolroom door did not splinter and fly off its hinges. The wolfman of the high country did not come garbed in shaggy winter mackinaw and bloodstained mittens. Far from it. He had materialized there at the front of our schoolroom in everyday trapping attire, which in my first instant of seeing him seemed even more horrible. The heart-destroying boots. The greasy slouch hat made of who knows what. The well-used haft of the skinning knife sheathed at his belt. Brose Turley seemed to be enjoying his school visit; he strutted a few steps closer to our ranks of desks, looking us over as if we were a carnival sideshow.

Like everyone else, I swung around to check on Eddie. The eyeglasses were off, hidden in his desk, and with remarkable presence of mind he was rubbing the telltale place on the bridge of his nose. Had he somehow heard the hoofbeats of the big gray horse when the rest of us didn't, or simply sensed his ogre of a father?

"Mr. Turley, good morning." Morrie recovered to the extent of manners, but his voice had a real edge to it. "Do you need to speak with Eddie about something that cannot possibly wait?"

"Lot more than that. I want him home." Brose Turley relished the next words in the pink of his mouth before slowly rolling them out. "From here on." Sparing Eddie nothing, he squinted down the aisle of desks to his alarmed son. "On your feet, boy."

I saw, and I am sure Damon saw, the ever-so-slight motion as Morrie brushed his fingertips along the side pockets of his suit coat. If brass knuckles resided there, this time they did not emerge. Morrie drew himself up and wielded authority. "This has gone far enough. School is in session. You can't just—"

"Look it up, teacher man. This is his birthday. Old enough to leave school, and that's what he's gonna do."

Morrie appeared stunned. We all were. To show Turley he would not let him run a bluff, he strode to his desk and whipped out the student register. His head down, he flipped through until we could tell he had come to the eighth grade's page. After a bit, he looked up at Brose Turley. "Eddie should have some say in this."

Turley shook his head, one wag each direction, like some animal ready in ambush, switching its tail. All eight grades of us stared at the spectacle occurring over our heads, so silly and savagely sad at the same time. There was fear in the room, and there was hatred. Brose Turley—or for that matter, Father—would have had to pry my cold, dead hands from my desk to withdraw me from a place of learning. Damon, Grover, Isidor, Gabe, Verl, Vivian, Carnelia, Rabrab, Miles, Lily Lee, any number of us in that classroom felt the same way, and even those among us who were not as keen on school knew that from a parent, this was not right. Yet this trespasser into our schoolhouse had the law on his side, something not even Morrie could remedy.

He was trying common sense on the situation. "For heaven's sake, be reasonable," he implored Turley. "It's only a matter of weeks until the end of school. Eddie can graduate—"

"He's doing that this damn minute." Turley made a swipe at the air; it couldn't be called a beckoning gesture, only a signal of impatience. "Come on here, you. Don't make me have to tell you again."

Like an invalid, Eddie uncertainly lifted himself up out of his desk. He bit his lip and kept his eyes down, away from all of ours. One shuffling step after another, he trailed after the blunt back of his father and walked out of the schoolroom to a life of skinning dead creatures.

Morrie crashed a fist down on his desk. All of us sat motionless, in roomwide paralysis.

At last he caught a breath and said in a low voice:

"Everyone, never forget what you've seen here today."

At recess, Milo blustered that he wished it had happened to him, but even he looked a little green around the gills from what had been witnessed.

"Some birthday for Eddie," Grover observed.

"By a mile," Miles agreed.

"What's the old so-and-so gonna make Eddie do, you suppose?" Verl pondered.

"Housework," Rabrab trilled. "Can't you just see Eddie in an apron?"

"The old man is gonna put him to tending the trap line," said Isidor the realist. "He'll have Eddie peeling pelts off his catch till he can't see straight."

"Why couldn't he just leave him alone until the end of school?" Marta voiced the thought in many minds.

Slowly but surely the verdict worked out by the Marias Coulee schoolyard court of justice was that Eddie, leaver of bruises on the majority of us, perhaps did not deserve fond remembrance, but no one deserved Brose Turley.

Riding home, neither Damon nor I said anything until we came to The Cut. All at once I heard out of him, with a crestfallen note in his voice: "You're so lucky, Paul."

"Why? What's the matter?"

"I never did get to punch Eddie."

19

MORRIE WAS LOW FOR DAYS AFTER THAT. I WOULD POP
into the schoolhouse early as usual, primed to the tips of my ears
for Latin, and he would grunt to himself over my translations
and then stick me off in some netherworld such as the ablative
case while he graded papers and looked morose.

It was the morning I was flailing through the thicket of
prepositional attachment to pronouns but never to nouns—what
were the Romans thinking, putting something like *pax vobiscum*
in the same language with *cum laude?*—when he finally burst out:

"Hopeless."

To say the least, I was startled. "Imperfect," I might have
said myself about my ablative efforts so far. Maybe even "inaus-
picious." But totally without hope? I sent Morrie a hurt look.

"No, no, not you. Read this." He came down the aisle and
skimmed a sheet of tablet paper to me, which proved to be Milo
Stoyanov's essay on homestead life.

In our family there are seven of us, Papa, Mama, Gramma,
Katrina that is just little yet, Marija, Ivo, and I. I and

Ivo and Marija go to the Marias Coulee school. I ride
Roanie and Marija holds on behind but don't like to.
Excepting for horses like Roanie and milk cows the animal
everybody raises is hogs, a few. Everybody has chores
including children. Marija's chore is gather the eggs. Mine
is get in wood and empty the slop bucket. The food we eat
is mostly deer, antelope, fish, and foul.

Morrie stared out the window. "Sisyphus. I will trade tasks
with Sisyphus, straight across." He stood there snapping his
sleeve garters in agitated fashion, all the while muttering. "Why
Montana? Why didn't I ship out to Tasmania?"

I wished the school inspector would walk in the door right
then, which at least would have stirred the blood around in
Morrie.

Still with his back to me, all at once he said in a forced
voice:

"There's something you'd better know, Paul. I am handing
in my resignation as teacher."

Shock ran through me from my ears to my toes. This was
one thing I had never dreamed of, even on my worst nights. I
could only babble back, "You can't."

The sole sound in the schoolroom for some moments was
the *plick plick plick* of the sleeve garters being beset. From the
back, in his tailoring and calfskin shoes, Morrie looked naturally
rooted here in a place of learning; but he had spoken those
words that I still was trying to get my mind around.

"I feel I must," he softly answered. "Matters are not turning
out commensurate to my endeavors. Not for the first time, I
might add."

He faced around to me now. His deflated attitude alarmed
me. How could destiny leak out of a person so fast? "Don't say

anything to anyone," I heard him through my daze. "Not even Damon," by which I understood he meant particularly not Damon. "The school does not need more fuss and bother. I'll ride home with the two of you at the end of the day and tell your father first."

I was a mound of distress as school got under way that day. When Carnelia elbowed me and under her breath demanded to know if whatever was wrong with me was something she might catch, I whispered back savagely, "I hope so."

At the front of the classroom Morrie soldiered on, a bit subdued but still throwing off a good many more sparks than most teachers. But my world had fallen apart. Not merely my world, either. I could not imagine the fate of the school without him up there, bobbing and weaving through the fields of knowledge.

At recess, the Drobny brothers were just the company I was fit for. We were kicking a gym ball against the back of the schoolhouse, doing our murderous best to bust its seams, when around the corner came a delegation. Headed by Rabrab, the leading lights of the sixth grade were all there, Grover and Miles and Lily Lee and Damon and Isidor and—*Damon?* He was hanging at the back of them, trying to look inconspicuous, but failing with me.

Immediately on my guard, I eyed the group up and down. "What's this, the Feed the Cannibals League?"

"Paul, don't be like that." When she wanted something, Rabrab had a look like the fox coaxing the baby bunny out to play. She had that look now. She glanced at my partners in gymball mayhem. "We need to talk to you without big ears around."

"Nick and Sam know how to keep a secret, don't you." I whacked the nearest twin on the shoulder in solidarity.

Rabrab stared the Drobny boys into an oath of silence—

they knew a fellow assassin when they saw one—then returned her full sly attention to me. "It's Mr. Morgan. He's down in the dumps about something."

"Top mark for observation."

"All right, smarty, we all saw it happen. But Mr. Morgan has to get over that. He can't help it if Eddie Turley has a father that would gag a maggot. We decided"—she generously indicated her fellow conspirators, with Damon still laying low at the back of the pack—"he needs something else to occupy his mind."

"Oh right, Rab. Stamp collecting, maybe?"

"Nobody asked you to be sarcastic, Paul," Rabrab said, as if I should not try her patience too far. "You remember the Christmas play, don't you?" Mystified as to how Christmas had come into this, I nodded. "We figure the school could have something like that for Halley's when it comes," she spelled matters out for me, her backers nodding like dipsomaniacs. *Damn,* I thought. If I'd been able to tell Damon about Morrie's mind being made up, everyone could have been spared these shenanigans. "Not exactly a play, maybe," Rabrab still was busily conjuring, "but something. Anything like that would pep up Mr. Morgan—he has comet on the brain."

"Well then, why don't you troop in there and see what he says?"

"We think you're the one to."

I felt caught between. The quick way out was to tell the bunch of them Morrie was finished as our teacher. But he had implored me not to. But if I went in there after recess the way they wanted me to and stood up in front of everybody and said the school would like to put on some kind of something-or-other to mark Halley's comet, what could Morrie do but say, "I regret to inform all of you—"? But this, but that. It was playing me out, juggling those. All I could think to do was to delay; I had just been reading in my primer about the slowpoke general Quintus Fabius Maximus Cunctator, who avoided battles with Hannibal at every opportunity, and it seemed to work for him.

Accordingly, I squared myself up to Rabrab and the others as if shouldering my duty and wildly procrastinated:

"Well, gee, I don't know, but I guess I could, only if you let me do this my way. Mor—Mr. Morgan might think we're putting him on the spot if I get up in the middle of school and ask. It'd be better if I had a chance to talk him into it, off on our own. Just so happens, he's coming over to our place after school."

"He is?" Damon was outraged I had not told him that.

                             ⌒

"QUIT PULLING MY LEG, MORRIE." FATHER DUG INTO HIS MEAL with vigor. "You can't quit. This is excellent pork stroganoff, by the way." The one gain of the day was that Morrie had pitched in with me on supper and for once we were eating civilized food. Even Rose took a couple of bites.

"Oliver, you are not hearing me. I have decided to resign my teaching position."

"But you can't," Father said around another forkful.

"Yes, don't tease, Morrie," Rose said, turning to Father. "I am sure I saw nice little green things coming up in my field when I looked out today."

"Weeds."

Morrie gazed around the table at the lot of us as if we were a tribe with no ears. "Since when is it impossible for a man to depart a job he did not seek out in the first place? I tell you, I am resigning. Ceasing to be a teacher. Chucking it in."

Father stopped in mid-chew. "You're serious."

"As I have been telling you. I am afraid I am out of my element, posing as a teacher." Morrie seemed composed, although he had to blink considerably to maintain that. Across from him, Rose's cheeks were coloring up like the rise of mercury in a thermometer, not a good sign. Gorging ourselves as we watched all this, Damon and I were the only ones not on record, up to this point. My hope was that Father or Rose or both of them together could talk Morrie out of quitting and everyone would brighten up again, and then I could speak my little piece about some kind of a comet commemoration, and Morrie could do with it or not as he chose, and that would be that. In short, all I wanted was a miracle.

"Out of your element?" Rose sounded incredulous. "You've *always* been—"

"Now, now, Rose," Father headed that off. "Please, let me." He swung around to face Morrie. "You can't leave the school in the lurch like this. The inspector might be here any day."

Morrie was as adamant as Father. "That's precisely the point. What if he had been on hand when that wolf-hunting cretin dragged his son out of school? Wouldn't that have been pretty." He drew in a sharp breath. "Who knows what he might walk in on, if I'm in charge of things."

"Good grief, Morrie, we don't have time to find another teacher. My fellow school board members will strangle me if we have to tell that inspector we've had another case of turnover. Like it or not, we're stuck with—"

"FATHER!" issued forth from the bedroom down the hall. "CAN I SHOW MORRIE MY BIG TOE YET?"

We all swore Toby's voice had grown to the size of Enrico Caruso's during his weeks in bed.

"Tobe," Father called back to the autocrat of the bedroom, "not until we've finished supper, I told you that."

Silence. Then: "ARE YOU ABOUT DONE?"

"Almost." Turning toward Morrie again, Father gave him a strong looking-over before starting in. "I can't ever get a straight line on you." He glanced aside at Rose, who should have known the ins and outs of Morrie if anyone did, but she chose that moment to spear a shred of pork with her fork. Father returned to the Morrie puzzle himself. "I move heaven and earth to land you into the teaching job, which at first you don't at all want. Then you take to it, and by all reports, you're a ring-tailed wonder in the classroom. Now all of a sudden you let Brose Turley buffalo you. Next thing, when we need you to merely be on the premises when the inspector—"

"I am not 'buffaloed' by Brose Turley," Morrie replied stiffly. "I just do not want to invite any more trouble onto the school. It would be on my conscience, if my methods were to—"

Rose suddenly put in: "What is it you intend? To pack up from Marias Coulee? I'm just asking."

"Perhaps I will become a homesteader. That seems to be in fashion around here."

Rose looked as if she wanted to clobber him one. The rest of us at the table stirred, doing whatever we bodily could to draw off a brother–sister spat. I was restlessly trying to get over the horrible thought that if Morrie went, Latin went, when Damon kicked my chair hard enough to send a jolt up my spine.

"Ah, Morrie?" Damon's reminder triggered the words out of me rapid-fire. "Remember the Christmas play?"

"Pull your head out of the clouds, Paul," Father said impatiently. "What does Christmas have to do with anything?"

"Well, I was thinking—Damon and I were thinking—actually, a whole bunch of us at school were thinking—"

"Spit it out, we don't have all night," this from Father again.

"A Halley's comet something-or-other, the school ought to put on some sort of program when it comes, is what we thought.

Like at Christmas." I looked hopefully at Morrie, then at Father and Rose, then back to Morrie. Encouragement seemed to be asleep at the switch.

But Father got hold of the moment. "You are, after all, the one who spouted comet to them until it's running out their ears," he reminded Morrie pointedly. "Just when is the thing due, anyway?"

Morrie shrugged. "Any night now."

"Any night?" Father's voice went way up. "That's the best you can predict?"

"Oliver, Halley's comet travels an elliptical orbit across most of our solar system and arrives to our sight on an approximate schedule of every seventy-five years, it does not pull in on the minute like a train." He brushed a hand through the air as if to erase Father's obvious doubt. "It will come. It always has." Morrie turned his attention to the two of us on the edge of our chairs at the far end of the table. "Paul and Damon, I appreciate the school's wish to celebrate the comet. But even if I were to stay on and preside over that, time is short, and there is not a comet Nativity play."

"Wouldn't need to be a play," Damon improvised cagily.

"No, not at all, huh uh," I fumbled out. "Could be a—" I tried to think of anything sufficiently celestial. Where was blindsight when I needed it, Rose? Across the table from me, she watched me as if I could not fail, the archway of eyebrow that coaxed out unexpected thoughts ready and waiting. The only thing that came to my mind were these mornings of gazing up from the dark in the field to the light of the stars and then trooping in here to this kitchen to the whispery anthem of her whistling. "Music. Could be a music program, couldn't it?" Scratching for words, I came up with: "Harmony of the spheres, you told us about that, Morrie, remember?"

I was simply reaching desperately. You never knew what little boost would send Morrie's thoughts escalating, though. The next thing any of us knew, he was stroking the precincts of lip where his mustache used to be and musing out loud very much as if he were at the front of the classroom.

"Actually, there was a rather nice point about harmony that I did not get around to making to the students. That flaming idiot Brose Turley got in the way of it that day and I never—"

"There now, you see? Comet night, music, that's that," Rose said to us all as if she had neatly bundled up the answers to everything herself. Father looked at her with what might have been startled admiration.

"And besides music, you could make a talk, that night," Damon was busy reeling Morrie in. "Old Beetlejuice or something." Morrie's latest leap heavenward in the classroom had taken us into constellations, and so the bright star Betelgeuse, there at the hinge of the shoulder of Orion the giant, he had cited as a hinge of the human imagination as well. *"Notice how its brighter light draws our attention, and then we see—or think we see—the outline of the giant in the other stars arranged around that point of light. This is called a point of reference, by which we imagine onto the infinite ceiling of the night those expanded figures from our world—here a giant, there an archer, over there the dippers from which they take sips of the liquid darkness—"* Damon's promoter instinct was slick as usual. None of us who ever heard Morrie soar off into the sky and its holdings doubted that he could take all of Marias Coulee with him, on any given night.

Morrie had been listening to Damon as gravely as if he was being enshrined in one of the scrapbooks upstairs. Now he found me with his instructive look and intoned, *"Arma trado."*

"He throws up his arms," I informed the uninitiated.

"'I surrender my weapons,'" Morrie corrected severely.

"That's what I meant."

Morrie gave his upper lip a final pat, the kind I had learned to recognize as introducing an announcement. "This may be lunacy, on my part. But perhaps I do owe it to the students to mark the comet's appearance. Comet night"—he accorded Rose a wry bow of his head, before turning to Father—"won't be detrimental to the school inspection, I can at least assure you of that. The students are as ready for the inspector as I know how to make them, even if I am not."

"Morrie, all I ask is that your body be warm and visible to that inspector when he hits the schoolhouse," Father reassured him. "And so"—a locution that had rubbed off Rose onto him—"keep it plain and simple, on comet night. A few songs by the children and a talk from you about the comet and that will do it." Father eyed his newly unresigned school employee across the table. "In other words, spare the budget from harm."

"Of course," said Morrie, although I noticed he was fiddling with his cufflinks, sometimes a signal that an extravagant notion was on its way from up his sleeve.

"Now can I, Father?"

"Tobe has the eighth wonder of the world to show you," Father interpreted for Morrie's benefit.

"Everybody can see it again if they want."

"We're on our way," Father called back, and the bunch of us trooped down the hall to where Toby held court. Any day now—the doctor's predictive powers were on a par with Morrie's for the comet—when the foot stopped being tender, Toby would be eligible for crutches. Until then, his foot was unbandaged, out in the open but within splints. He beamed at us down the length of the bed, as if he hadn't seen most of us twenty times already that day.

"Morrie, look!" Toby directed, impresario that he was on his pile of pillows.

Morrie leaned over and his eyebrows shot up in surprise. "Toby, you are an evolutionary pioneer. It may take the rest of humankind ten thousand years to catch up with you."

"That much, huh?" Toby said with pride. He had lost the toenail off his big toe. He could hardly wait to show that toe off in the schoolyard.

⌒

"*R*OSE! COME SEE!"

I wouldn't have believed a person could shout in a whisper, yet I managed some such feat when I barged into the kitchen and madly beckoned her outside into the dark that had now changed forever.

We went out the door of the house in nearly one person, Rose so close her shawl smacked the back of my neck as she hurled it across her shoulders. I held the bull's-eye lantern up, ushering her across the yard and into the field, the pair of us tightroping between the seeded furrows, somehow watching our step while trying to read the sky in giddy glances. When I judged we were far enough from the lamplight reflected through the kitchen window, I drew us to a halt. "Here goes." I doused the lantern. Maybe as much as a minute passed while our eyes adjusted to the darkness. "There," I whispered, sheer habit. "Over the top of The Cut."

"Is that it, you're sure?" Rose cupped a hand to her brow.

"Has to be. There's the water bearer, and there's the centaur," I pointed out constellations for her, "and see, that one is just as bright but doesn't fit with any of theirs." No, it was beyond doubt, this was a traveling star. As soon as our eyes had night sight, we could pick out the faint trailing smudge of light, like the here-and-gone strike of a match, that marked the visitor amid the standing clusters in that corner of the sky. The tail of the comet would grow and grow as it neared, Morrie had told us in school. Each night would add to its paradoxical cloud of brightness. I already was dazzled, that the nature of things could be vast enough to cast a stray diamond of light across the spaces of night probably just once in our lifetimes, yet one so legible that the blink of an eye brought this single migratory glow home to us out of all the glimmers held by the sky.

"Oh, Paul, it's beautiful," Rose murmured, my heart dancing to her words. Then she said something odd, her tone wistful. "Morrie needs a comet now and then."

I had no time to puzzle that out. "I have to go in and get everybody up to see it. Father and I can carry Tobe out in a chair."

$\approx$

I HAVE THOUGHT BACK MOST OF A LIFETIME ON HOW HALLEY'S comet arrived to our world in 1910—and have come under its aura again time after time in dreams—and the course of it through the atmosphere here below makes me emotional even yet. By the earthly order of things, Marias Coulee and its scattered antecedents through history were granted the visiting star ahead of the populous parts of the world. Goatherds and keepers of sheep and camel drovers and stalkers of hoofed game at predawn water holes, the rural earth's earliest risers—theirs always would have been the first eyes to find the arriving comet. Those and the dream-tossed; others on this planet may have seen the coming of the fresh star earlier than I did that sleep-short morning, but they were not many. Then, having made itself known to the prairies and savannahs and deserts, the fiery traveler showered portent in past the walls of the greatest of cities. Soothsayers prospered. Beggars did better. Crowned heads grew uneasy; Halley's comet was known to carry off kings. Harold II, King of England, perished to the Norman invaders following the comet's passage in 1066. Edward VII, King of England, was laid in his bulky casket our spring of 1910.

Those who looked to heaven for a wrathful king of everything could all too readily read the comet as a flaming writ of doom. Morrie brought to school sensational newspaper stories of panic among sects that were sure the world was coming to an end according to one feverish prophecy or another, and instructively paired those with similar accounts across the past few thousand years. "Mark Twain, our greatest living American writer, once told the press association its report of his death was an exaggeration, and down through the ages these lamentations fit that same category," he left it at. If that wasn't enough, the Delacroix print on the schoolroom wall was always there as a reminder that the Star Dragon had flown before and given alarm to inflamed consciences, and would again.

Passing over our own roof, Halley's comet could hardly have been more auspicious. To universal relief in the household, on his next call the doctor let Toby proceed to crutches. Damon and I made sure to kid him about being Peg Leg Pete the Pirate Man, and he gyrated through the house with a surprisingly sure swagger. Rose allowed him along on her housekeeping swoops through the downstairs rooms, which meant she could keep an eye on him. And Father looked less like a man chased day and night by a swarm of things; he made it downstairs in time to join Rose and me in our comet-watching every one of those mornings. Life somehow smoothed out, under that brightening cloud of comet tail. Morrie one morning wove it into Latin. "There is a line that is tailor-made for Halley's, and you know which one I mean. *Lux desiderium universitatis,* Paul. Kindly come up with an inspired translation before I become too old and deaf to hear it."

"I will. I mean, I am. Next time, maybe."

Yet one thing strangely troubled me as the great comet progressed across the sky of our lives. The particular fragment of thought never did ascend to dream level, but only because my mind could not quite catch hold of a way to dream it. What plagued me was the idea Eddie—One-Punch Milliron's old adversary—might never look upon Halley's comet. On their ride to school the day after Brose Turley had jerked him out of the classroom, the Pronovosts had sighted the pair of them on their way to the mountains, a pack string behind them, swags of traps clanking on the pack saddles. "Eddie looked like a whipped pup," Isidor reported. Plainly Brose Turley was squeezing in another high-country season of pelts and bounties now that he had Eddie to slave for him. Up there in the Rockies, spring and the end of trapping would not come for some time yet, and meanwhile the comet was low on the southeast horizon, blocked from sight in the mountain valleys by the shoulders of the foothills and the front range of peaks. I could not get rid of the thought that a kind of blindness had been put on Eddie Turley, and where did that fit in the beautiful workings of the universe?

*H*OURS AFTER ROSE AND I MADE OUR FIRST SIGHTING OF the traveling star, Morrie laid out comet night for his attentive eight grades of listeners in the schoolroom. Naturally he leapt ahead on the calendar—three weeks seemed to us all like a terribly long time—to the night when Halley's comet would achieve full magnitude, according to his calculations. That particular night, the tail of the comet would extend across the sky from Minneapolis to the Rockies. Marias Coulee School perhaps could not take full credit for that, but at least we could host the event.

"Your parents of course will need to be reminded," Morrie reminded us, "that we will not start until full dark." It shouldn't be too hard to get parents to be nocturnal one night out of seventy-five years, we figured.

"I shall make a talk on matters of the cosmos," Morrie said offhandedly. We had thoroughly expected that. "And all of you—" he paused as if this was almost too delicious to tell us. Then he told us.

A hush fell on the schoolroom. Three weeks seemed like a terribly short time.

Carnelia wasn't saying anything, even between her teeth. I knew better than to speak up, because if I did it would come out something like: "Morrie, have you lost your mind?" Glancing around the room, I caught a gleam in Damon's eye, not exactly a recommendation for Morrie's scheme. Grover looked dubious. Marta put a hand up to her face to see if this was going to set off a nosebleed. Both sets of Drobny twins licked their lips, tasting conspiracy. Milo, oaf among eighth-grade oafs, inexplicably had a grin on him the size of a calf bucket. At last, next to Milo at the back of the room, Martin Myrdal stuck up a meaty hand. "All of us? The little kids too?"

The first grade en masse—Josef Kratka and Alice Stinson and Maggie Emrich and Marija Stoyanov—turned and glowered at Martin. The Robespierre of the second grade, Emil Kratka, stuck his tongue out at him.

"All," Morrie said firmly. "First grade to eighth grade."

The next question in the air was from Sally Emrich. Sally even had a fussy way of raising her hand. "Teacher, is this a secret? Even from our folks?"

"Let's call it a surprise, Sally. And if we want to surprise someone, we do not tell them about it ahead of time, do we?"

If I have learned anything about what happens in a classroom, it is that inspiration does not always follow a straight path. Up in the second row, Inez Pronovost squirmed one way and then the other at her desk, next to Toby's empty one all these weeks, and suddenly piped up: "Spitbath handshake, Mr. Morgan?"

I saw Morrie covertly cock an ear for school-inspector footsteps in the cloakroom. Hearing none, he spat in his hand. "All right, everyone. The bargain will be sealed in the manner Inez suggests. I'll make the rounds, although each of you must provide the rest of the expectoration—I do not have three dozen decent spits in me. We shall discuss the salivary gland when we are finished."

And so we were launched toward comet night.

"Morrie thought up a doozy this time," I confided to Rose insofar as I could. "I wish I could tell you, but it's a—"

"Ah, but I know all about it," she whispered back, delicately fingering her cocoa cup. I kept forgetting how much time she and Morrie naturally spent together, sister and brother, out of our sight. "That man. You just never know what he will pull next, do you." Her little conspiratorial smile seemed to approve of that, this time.

*A*CROSS THE NEXT WEEKS, MORRIE FOUND SCRAPS OF THE day to rehearse us. Last period was always a catchall, and he used it to the fullest for our one purpose now. Several times we voted to stay in from recess to practice. It was an ensemble effort, whatever the results would be.

"So how is your singing voice by now?" Father asked me one morning after he and Rose and I had checked on the progress of the comet. There still were times when he looked like he was being put through life's wringer—a dry springtime will do that to a farmer—but some matters were not pressing on him quite as hard now. Toby still was the pest of all time, but at least he could periodically be dispatched outside to work off energy by pegging around the yard. Even the specter of the inspector dimmed with each passing day; Father and Morrie had practically squinted holes in the calendar and the long list of one-room schools in Montana and come to the conclusion that with any luck now, the school year would wind down before the Department of Public Instruction managed to get past its backlog and reach us. And while Father would not have said so out loud, having Rose in the house all the time gave the place a feel of ticking along to a natural clock that it had not had for a good, long time. She could be heard rummaging around in the parlor that very moment, setting up for what she announced as spring cleaning.

Before I thought, I scoffed, "Oh, we're not bothering with singing. Anybody can sing."

Father stopped whatever he was doing and sent me a long look. Then crossed the room and closed the kitchen door, an exceedingly rare occurrence. He came over close to me and asked anxiously, "Paul. He doesn't have the whole caboodle of you *whistling*, does he?"

"Father, I can't tell you, can I. It's a surprise. That's the whole idea."

"HERE HE COMES!"

Toby's yelp when he spotted the doctor's Model T chugging along the section-line road toward us would have wakened the dead. Houdini chorused in with him.

"Settle down, you two," Father directed, coming out of the barn where he had been mending harness. This was something he was looking forward to as much as Toby was, if it meant the end of careening crutches.

Damon and I got up from where we were lying flat, trying to snare gophers at the edge of the field. If we caught any, Morrie would have the specimen he wanted to illustrate the history of incisors—from the saber-tooth tiger on down, no doubt—in class the next day. It was a big if. Mostly, this was just such a fine, sunny Sunday afternoon we wanted to be out in it. Now we brushed the worst of the dirt off ourselves without Father even having to tell us and headed across the yard, each trying to look more mature and presentable than the other. How often did mighty events coincide like this? Toby was receiving the doctor visit he had been looking for every day all week, and comet night was a mere two days away.

The Model T pulled up to us, vibrated nervously for several moments, and shut down. The doctor from Westwater got out from behind the steering wheel and was instantly set upon by Toby, in one breath wanting to know if he could throw away his crutches yet and in the next wanting a guarantee that his big toenail would never grow back. Another man climbed out the other side of the automobile. This was no great surprise, as the Westwater doctor had said he wanted Toby's one-of-a-kind foot to be looked over by the orthopedic specialist from the Great Falls hospital whenever that worthy made his rounds in our general direction. Certainly Toby would be ecstatic to rate two doctors. Right now his jabbering away had the Westwater one thoroughly distracted, so Father approached the other. "I don't believe I've had the pleasure, Doctor—?"

"Call me Harry," the man said as they shook hands. "Harry Taggart. School inspector."

It was as if Zeus had appeared in our yard. Father froze. I heard Damon gasp, or maybe it was me.

Actually, Taggart did not look like much. He was a long stick of a man, his bowler hat sitting on him about as it would have on a hat stand. His frowsy mustache made it apparent what an achievement Morrie's had been. But he had slitted eyes, as though his vision was everlastingly pinched to a point by watching people try tricks. And the bag he carried, now that we had a second look, was a dark leather briefcase bulging with whatever a school inspector inspected with.

The intruder explained, "I asked around town and caught a ride out with the good doctor here, to find your place." Those eyes with their visors of lids flicked across the homestead and Father in his barn clothes as if reserving judgment.

"Yes, well," Father rallied, "we weren't expecting you on a Sunday and—"

"Excuse us," the doctor called over, "we are going in the house for me to examine the patient," and Toby vaulted along ahead of him on the crutches.

"And these are your other lads." Taggart belatedly dispensed handshakes to Damon and me. As if a switch had been flipped, now he sounded hearty. "Ready to tackle the Standards tomorrow, buckos?"

We hated it when that tone of voice was used on us. Not trusting what we might say, Damon and I stood there as soiled as badgers and dug our toes in the yard as though in search of more dirt.

The inspector breezed right back to Father. "First off, I should make sure our records in Helena are up to date." He instantly delved into his briefcase the way a gunfighter went to his holster. "*Marias Coulee School District*," he pulled out an official-looking piece of paper and read off, "*established 1901, Township 28 North*, so on and so on. *Teacher, Adelaide Trent—*"

Damon couldn't help it. He snickered.

Father dropped a kindly hand on Damon's shoulder and gave a little squeeze meant to carry all the way to the vocal cords. "Miss Trent is no longer with us. That old epidemic, matrimony." Father forced a chuckle. "The school board fortunately found a sterling replacement."

The school inspector frowned.

"This individual's name?" He spread his piece of paperwork onto the skinny hood of the automobile, reached out a fountain pen and scratched Miss Trent into oblivion, and for better or worse, Morrie was entered onto the rolls of the Department of Public Instruction.

Pen still poised, Taggart was saying, "Next there is the matter of this person's——" and I was proud to have enough Latin instinct by then to know the next phrase was going to be *bona fides*.

Just then Rose quick-stepped out of the house, water bucket swinging in her hand, headed for the pump. Wearing satin for Sunday, she looked very nice indeed. Our visitor cast a glance at Father as if he thought better of him. Capping his pen and putting it away, Taggart drew himself up formally, tipped his hat, and called, "Good day, Mrs. Milliron."

"She's not——" Father started and stopped.

"Oh, how do you do," Rose said, swerving over. "Actually, I am more properly called Mrs. Llewellyn," she said in the melancholically musical fashion we had not heard from her for some time now. "I'm the——" She gestured inclusively around, water bucket and all, a sweep that took in our homestead and hers and the fields and evidently the perimeters of things all the way back to Minneapolis.

"Temporary nurse," Father hastily filled in.

"Neighbor next door," I prompted in the same instant.

"Housekeeper," Rose said, looking at both of us.

Damon saved our skins. In back of Taggart, he frantically pantomimed peering through a magnifying glass, Sherlock Holmes style.

"Ah!" Rose let out. "You must be the school inspector everyone has been so looking forward to." She and he shook hands—hers obviously startled him, being as strong from work as any man's—and she sped on with the conversation as if she had been waiting months to confide in him. "I live just across the way, so it's nothing for me to pitch in here on the household chores and see to Toby since his awful accident, and Mr. Milliron is so busy with farming and the school affairs and all, so it works out well for everyone concerned. You see—" Here she halted and bit her lip. Taggart leaned toward her from the waist as if to make sure he did see. "My husband is"—Rose gestured off to far horizons again—"gone for an extended period."

"What can exceed neighborliness as a virtue?" Taggart proclaimed to us all as if it might be on tomorrow's test. Rose beamed at him and went off to pump water.

Father had not fully recovered from Rose's transit through the situation before Taggart turned to him again. "Mr. Milliron—may I call you Oliver?"

"Be my guest."

"Oliver, how I would like to proceed," Taggart went on in a fashion that made it plain it was how they were going to proceed, "is to meet with you and the teacher before school tomorrow. To examine the classroom equipment and the physical state of the schoolhouse, that sort of thing. Say an hour ahead of start of class? That's usually ample."

My face fell. That would crowd out Latin.

Father said in not much voice, "I'll be there."

At that moment, Toby spun out of the house. Crutchless.

"I CAN GO TO SCHOOL! TOMORROW!"

"Hey, wow, Tobe!" Damon congratulated him.

"The more the merrier," Father said, sounding even more peaked. "We'll all see you tomorrow, Harry."

As soon as the Model T was out of sight, the first necessity had to be performed. I was itching to be the one. But on some scale in his own mind Father kept track of these things, and this was not my turn. "Damon," he said wearily. "Saddle up and go tell Morrie, Judgment Day arrives tomorrow."

Rose waited until the last one of us—Toby, bard of the longest-running foot epic since that of Achilles—had the last bite of supper in him before she said it. "And so. I'll need to move back to my place tonight."

Damon and Toby and I looked at each other. This hadn't occurred to us.

Father was a different story. He was behind the fortification of his coffee cup, taking a long, slow drink, before the last of Rose's words were out. When he finally put the cup down, he addressed Toby. "You can climb stairs, tiger, can you?"

"You bet." Too late, Toby realized what he had condemned himself to.

Father looked down the table to Rose now. His expression was harried, not surprising for a day bookended by the arrival of the school inspector and the departure of the presence that had given the household such a lift. He had a little trouble with his voice when he told Rose, "We don't want to seem to be throwing you out. If it's too much of a rush for you to go yet tonight—"

"I'd better." She made sure to share her commiserating smile around to all of us.

An unforgettable twinge went through me. A sense that something major was ending. I knew I was entitled to feel relief at coming home to sleep, out from under the hovering thunderhead of Aunt Eunice, but that was not what I felt. Anticipation of Rose alighting into the kitchen full of whispered cheer again each morning instead of me stumbling in from the field, dream-driven, should have filled me; but that was not it either.

A chair clattered. Father was onto his feet, tugging at

Damon's collar and giving me a look with plenty of pull in it. "We have to wrestle Tobe's bed back upstairs for him."

"I'll get my things together while you're at that," Rose said, just as awkwardly, "and then I'll scoot."

Father paused. "You don't need to run off."

"I'd better," she said once more, and again her smile was carefully equal for each of us but ended with Father. "I thought I'd ride over and see Morrie yet tonight. He may need some bucking up."

⤿

$\mathcal{W}$E WERE A MOTLEY CREW ON HORSEBACK THAT NEXT MORNing. Toby rode double behind me; his foot still was tender enough that he was not supposed to swing up into a stirrup with it, so Father lifted him up behind my saddle and threatened him extensively against falling off or jumping down. By that hour I was bright-eyed as could be, accustomed to riding to school that early for Latin bouts with Morrie, but Damon drooped sleepily on the back of his horse. Father, in his best clothes, looked like an out-of-place pallbearer on top of the pint-size mare Queenie.

Rose had not appeared at the house by the time we left, and that worried me. I'd had the comet to myself that morning, a lonely enough sighting. I could only hope our kitchen sessions would get back to what they were before.

Plainly Father had enough on his mind without us, so on that ride to school we all stayed as close to mute as boys could humanly be. Toby contented himself with snuggling dreamily into my back as he held on to me, as though I were a horseback version of Houdini. The day broke out in pale spring sunshine. I can still see the schoolhouse as it appeared when we rode up out of The Cut, its paint a bit worn from the affections of the wind, its schoolyard trampled bare, its dawn-caught bank of windows a narrow aperture to sky and prairie. Any inspector from the Department of Public Instruction would have seen a thousand such places. We were about to find out if he had ever seen anything like Morrie.

By the time we were dismounting at the school, the dreaded automobile was tottering over the horizon from the direction of Westwater. That longest day was under way, whether we were ready or not. The schoolhouse did not appear to be. Its windows were not showing any lampshine, which meant Morrie wasn't on hand yet. "Damon, get in there and make sure the chill is off the place," Father directed hurriedly as he hoisted Toby down from behind me. "Stoke the stove up good if you have to. Tobe, now listen. Take it easy on that foot. No running, no rough-housing, got that?" Toby promised, cross his heart, and all but tiptoed across the schoolyard to join Damon inside. In my usual role, elder statesman of the boys, I waited beside Father for the inspector's Model T to pull up next to the flagpole.

"Where's Morrie?" Father asked me through gritted teeth.

"Brushing up on pedagogical principles," I said as if I knew.

"He'd better be."

Harry Taggart unfolded out of the car, spoke of the weather, shook hands with Father perfunctorily, and headed into the schoolhouse like a man on a mission. Father and I hastened after him, trying not to be obvious about looking around for Morrie.

Inside, the schoolhouse was not exactly dark, but it was a long way from illuminated. Toby was somewhat ghostly as he wriggled this way and that in his desk to see if it still fit him. Damon was over by the stove, but not feeding it; the school-room already was toasty as could be. As Taggart squinted around in the gloom, Father struck a match and pulled down the nearest hanging lamp. "Notice we do not go in for careless expenditure of kerosene," he said piously and lit the wick.

Even with that first lamp, the schoolroom gleamed. By the time Father had them all lit, the place was practically blinding. Clean windows glistened, the scrubbed pine floor was spotless, the blackboard was the pure dark of obsidian—from its shining rows of desks to its perfectly aligned arrowheads in the display case, Marias Coulee School showed the handiwork I recognized with a jolt. The only thing lacking was the lingering echo of Rose's whistling.

"Tidy," Taggart conceded, plopping open his briefcase and snatching out a sheet of paper to make a check mark.

"We do our utmost to keep the vessel of knowledge ship-shape," Morrie said from the doorway, causing Father's head to jerk around.

Hand casually out, Morrie advanced toward Taggart, looking as tailor-stitched as when he first stepped off the train. "Kindly pardon my tardiness. I presumed you might like a peek around the premises without the instructional incumbent in the way. Good morning, Oliver, you're looking meditative."

Introductions made, Taggart turned back to Father briefly to ascertain the budgeting for such a level of schoolhouse upkeep, and Morrie took up his station at his desk. I edged over to him and whispered, "We were getting worried. Where were you?"

"Throwing up," he murmured.

Taggart arrived to the desk and got down to business. "Mr. Morgan, I understand you are a replacement teacher. Oliver and his board must have been fortunate indeed to find someone sufficiently credentialed, on such short notice." By now the inspector had his fountain pen poised, over another drastic-looking piece of paper. "Where did you take your degree?"

"Yale," Morrie answered with towering dignity.

Father's eyes bugged out.

"No!" Taggart nearly dropped his pen and paper. "Why, that's first rate! What, may I ask, was your field of study?"

"Yurisprudence."

I was afraid the school inspector was going to choke. His lips crimped in while his Adam's apple bobbed.

Then came the burst, a guffaw that would have put any of Milo's to shame. "*Yurisprudence at Yale, by yingo,* eh?" he cackled out. "I never—" Finally his fit of laughter broke off into a helpless snort.

Father seized the opportunity. "We'll, ah, all step outside and leave you to your work in peace, Harry."

Taggart gaily waved us out, shaking his head and moving off in the direction of the orrery.

The instant we were safely in the schoolyard, Father pounced. "Morrie, damn it, this isn't vaudeville."

"He laughed, did he not?" Morrie said with the air of someone who had just broken the bank at a casino. "I would say life approximates a stage quite often, and a bit of low humor may not be amiss. How many times, Oliver, do you suppose an inspector for the Department of Public Instruction gets a chance to laugh?"

"And I say play it straight. If anything goes wrong today, he'll have us fried in butter."

"Never fear," Morrie responded. "Come on over to the teacherage; I have coffee lying in wait. I'll tell our inquisitor."

We killed time in the teacherage—Damon kept Toby occupied in a game of acey-deucey, the pair of them off in one corner furiously slapping down cards; I sat with Father and Morrie and pined for Latin—until Taggart showed up. He was back to looking official, plunking his bulging briefcase down in front of him as if not letting it out of his sight. Even then I had professional curiosity about what was in the thing. As serious now as if he had never had a laughing jag in his life, the school inspector stuck to formalities. Pen in hand, he elicited from Morrie the University of Chicago and the leather trade and vague smatterings of his existence before teacherhood. At last satisfied, more or less, with Morrie's qualifications, Taggart turned to Father. "I find that the school is exceptionally equipped, and yet the budget is in good trim. Nicely managed by your school board, Oliver."

"We're careful with a dollar," Father said, avoiding Morrie's eye.

"GOTCHA!" Toby let out, evidently springing a wild deuce on his opponent. "I win again, Damon."

Taggart contemplated the cutthroat card game over in the corner. "Your littlest lad appears to be well on the way to recovery, Oliver."

An alarm bell went off in Morrie and Father and me all at the same time. "Tobias had a perfect record before his accident," Morrie thrust in, true enough as far as it went, "but he has been out for six weeks. Has not the Department of Public Instruction some method of taking a stroke of fate of that sort into account?"

Taggart had to mull that. Finally he allowed, "In an extreme case, and I can see that his may have been one, I am permitted to excuse a student from the grade-wide tests. Perhaps in this one instance—"

By now, Toby's face registered full dismay at the prospect of being left out of anything on his debut back in school. "I can spell and everything," he protested shrilly. "R-h-i-n-o-"

"That will do, Tobe," Father put a lid on that.

"No, no," Taggart persisted. "A go-getting attitude should be rewarded. I'll test him just on the spelling standard, orally. Otherwise, he can have the run of the schoolyard this afternoon. Thank goodness you are on hand to supervise him, eh, Oliver?"

"Thank goodness."

"As to the rest of the school day, all morning is yours to do with, Mr. Morgan." Morrie smiled wanly in response. Taggart busied himself with something in his briefcase, then flicked a deadly look that took us all in. "I simply observe."

Marias Coulee School was never quieter than at the start of that day. Nor more decorous. A fresh haircut shined on every boy, the strips of white on the backs of necks practically blinding from the seventh-grade perspective. The girls were tightly braided or ribboned. Clothes that were being saved for an occasion made a surprise appearance: the Kratka brothers echoed one another in plaid shirts obviously fresh from the catalog box, the homemade dresses of the Drobny sisters were a particularly witchy gray. Grover and Adele and Louisa and Alice and Verl and Lily Lee, of the other school board families, bore the same signs of recent ruthless hygiene that my brothers and I did, as scrubbed as new potatoes. Anywhere a person looked in the schoolroom, Damon's canny stops at every homestead along the way to Morrie's yesterday had paid off in style.

In his by-the-book manner, the school inspector was informing us we were not to let his presence distract us in any way whatsoever. "This morning I am merely a fly on the wall." Mine was not the only set of eyes that moved to the swatter hanging on the wall behind Morrie's desk.

"Likewise Mr. Milliron," Taggart officiously swept onward. "He is here to lend a hand as needed." From the row behind me came an involuntary creak of acknowledgment. Father was haphazardly seated in the desk left empty by Eddie Turley.

Now Taggart took the spare chair that usually stood in the cloakroom, squared his briefcase on his lap to write on, uncapped his pen, and called out, "Ready to commence when you are, Mr. Morgan."

Morrie outdid himself that morning. He drilled us through arithmetic like numerary cadets, one grade after another popping to the blackboard to smartly do its sums. Reading period was little short of Shakespearean. Morrie called on Toby as one of those to read aloud, letting off some dangerous steam there. And to stand and recite "Ozymandias," he passed right over me and picked Carnelia. That raised my hackles, until I figured out what he was up to: since she was the oldest girl in school and our desk was near enough to the back of the room, Taggart might be fooled into counting her as an eighth-grader instead of our actual woeful ones. Everything proceeded nicely to geography, which was a constant forest of hands raised to answer. Never had so many known what the capital of Paraguay is. Science of course was our trump card, and Morrie played it with full flourish. Every time I peeked over at Taggart, he was making check marks, hardly frowning at all. I believe all would have ended well if, at the end of that last period of the morning, Milo's hand wasn't still hanging high in the air at the very back of the room.

Morrie hesitated. He'd managed beautifully to camouflage the eighth grade so far, taking answers only from Verl or Martin in the mob of big bodies back there that now included Father, and artfully trying to blend Carnelia in with them. In the best of circumstances, calling on Milo was not a promising proposition. *Don't, don't, don't,* I prayed to Morrie.

Too late. Taggart had noticed the sky-high hand, and Morrie was forced to deal with it. "Milo, something quick, then it's noon hour."

"Yeah, I was just wondering. All this going on, when we gonna get to practice for comet night?"

"Comet night?" Taggart spoke for the first time all morning. "Did I hear right? The comet is there every night. Surely these students know Halley's comet has arrived?"

"Absolutely they do," Morrie said in a hurry. "We have been working on a school function to commemorate the event, tomorrow evening. Inspired by the science of the matter, naturally." I darted a glance over my shoulder toward Father. He looked pained, and not just from hard sitting in a schoolboy desk.

Taggart did not take the bait on the word *science*. His narrow eyes narrowed further. "You have been able to spare time during school hours to work on hoopla for the comet? We shall see." The school inspector rose out of his chair and advanced to the front of the room, unbuckling the flaps of his briefcase as he came. He reached in and began pulling out sheafs of printed paper. These he dropped on Morrie's desk, one, two, three, until there were eight stacks.

Every one of us in every grade knew what those were.

The Standards.

The men spent the noon hour in the schoolhouse readying things for the afternoon-long tests, while we ate lunch in the schoolyard. Over by the teetertotter, a crowd was clustered around the spectacle of Toby's big toe. Letting Tobe have his moment, I parked myself on the front steps of the schoolhouse along with Damon and a majority of the sixth grade.

On every mind was the boggling fact that the school could be shut down if it did not come up to standards, whatever those were.

"They sure are out to get us," Isidor observed.

"By a mile," Miles affirmed.

Grover took a bite of a sandwich that looked twice as thick as and three times more tasty than mine or Damon's. He asked me between chews, "What's *dormitory* from?"

"Umm, give me a minute." On either side of me, the Drobny brothers supported me with silent attention. I thought back to my translation of *Noli excitare canes dormientes,* quite plainly *"Do not disturb the canines that are asleep"* to me, although Morrie truncated it to *"Let sleeping dogs lie."* "'Sleep.' A place of sleeping."

Nick Drobny sounded baffled. "They want to send us all the way to town to sleep?"

"No, the dormitory is where we'd live while we go to school, dunce," said Rabrab.

Damon wasn't saying anything. That meant he was really worried.

Lily Lee reported in a quavering voice, "We'd get to come home weekends, my father says."

"Weekends aren't much, in that kind of setup," Sam Drobny summed it up for us all.

We filed to our seats for the afternoon with rare lack of conversation. Standard tests were relatively new in the educational scheme of things then, and those of us on the receiving end were not sure what we were in for. All too soon Morrie and Father were passing out test papers and giving low-voiced instructions to the grades at the front of the room while the school inspector himself did the same at the back. I watched Carl and Milo and Martin and to a lesser extent Verl confront the long sheets of questions Taggart was inflicting on them. Blood rushed to heads. Hearts very nearly stopped. Urgent inquiries were put to Taggart as to how much time they had for their answers. Days apparently would not have been too much.

When he had untangled from the eighth grade and it became apparent to him that Carnelia and I, quiet as kittens, were a principality unto ourselves, Taggart bent over the pair of us and said in a low tone, "This is highly unusual, one class so small in a school this size. Are there others of you, out sick?"

"We're it," Carnelia mourned, and I nodded abjectly.

Taggart frowned. "I see. Something like this can skew the standards. I will need to count you as anomalous, and parcel the testing of the two of you for a truer picture of your standing. We'll begin with you, young lady. You are to write a three-hundred-word essay to demonstrate meaning and knowledge of a scientific topic, by luck of the draw." Taggart randomly yanked out a test paper. "Astronomy." He started to hand her the sheet, then pulled it back to peer at the heading. "No, wait, my error. I apologize, young miss." He looked at Carnelia with a bit of pity. "Your topic is agronomy." Carnelia did her injured princess imitation, just as if she didn't know more about the gospel of deep plowing than any other schoolgirl in America, and began writing.

"And this lad"—he looked at me like a hangman trying to do his job well—"we'll need to examine on penmanship."

Next, Taggart tiptoed up to Toby and took him out to the supply room for his private spelling bee. Whatever the quality of the spelling, the high little voice sounded confident. After that, the skritch of all of us writing was the only sound in the schoolhouse for a long while. Toby and Father were excused to the schoolyard, and busy as I was copying Palmer-method whorls and creating salutations, I looked out a number of times to see one happy boy being pushed in the swing. At least Toby now was out of the picture as an instrument of the school's fate. That left only all the rest of us.

Each half hour, Taggart and Morrie administered some fresh test to us until we came to the last hour of the day. Looking out over the spent faces, Taggart assured us we were very nearly there, only grammar and reading comprehension to go. "For most, that is," he added. "The others shall take an achievement test."

Morrie frowned. "'Achievement'?"

"A departmental term," the school inspector saw he had to translate. "A vocabulary standard, for your upper grades. To measure verbal facility at a significant developmental age."

A fleeting look of panic passed over Morrie. "By 'upper,' you include—"

"Eighth grade, of course"—Taggart swung his head around and eyed the overgrown aggregation at the rear of the room, which stared cowlike back at him—"and the age bracket is inclusive to the sixth." The entire sixth grade, nobody's fools, squirmed at the notion of being lumped in with the eighth. Carnelia and I, the taken-for-granted grade between, tried to look like an even smaller sliver of the student body than we already were.

Taggart passed out the vocabulary test, a sheaf in itself, and presided over us. Among the combined three grades, winces went off like fireflies as people encountered words they had never seen before in their lives. Through most of the allotted hour, student after student did what they could with the stiff exam and ultimately signaled surrender by handing it in to the inspector.

Eventually everyone was done but me. I was aware of Damon casting worried looks in my direction. Carnelia fidgeted impatiently beside me. I didn't care. I had fallen in love with the test sheets. There it was, language in all its intrigues, its riddles and clues. The ins and outs of prefixes and suffixes. The conspirings of syllables. The tics of personality of words met for the first time. *Look to the root,* Morrie's dictum drummed steadily in me. Almost anywhere I gazed on the exam pages, English rinsed itself off into Latin. *Vulpine* brought the clever face of a fox into my mind. *Corpulent* necessarily meant something about a body, likely a fat one. On and on, the cave voices of vocabulary coming to me, and when I had been through every question, I went back over each a couple of times, refining any guesses.

Finally Taggart told the others they could go outside to wait. At the absolute last, when he checked his watch and called "Time," he collected my test with a look at me as if I must be a total dolt to have taken that long.

It was over. Morrie turned loose the weary three dozen of us, looking considerably done in himself, and the school inspector established himself at the big desk at the front of the room to score the tests.

Father came herding Toby in our direction as Morrie and Damon and I walked somberly to the teacherage to wait for Taggart's verdict. "Give me a day of farming over keeping up with Tobe anytime," he stated. "How did the tests go?"

Morrie thrust his hands to the bottoms of his pockets and hunched up as if he were in a hailstorm.

I just shrugged.

"Tough old tests," Damon at least was definitive. "Especially that last thing."

It took more than an hour for Taggart to show up. Those slitted eyes showed nothing as he stepped into the teacherage. Toby and Damon were back at acey-deucey, and I was sitting at the table doodling Roman numerals onto the tablet Morrie had loaned me while he and Father sat across from each other and looked bleak. "You will receive the official report within a week," Taggart said, "but I can tell you in a preliminary fashion what it will contain." He glanced around at the three sets of schoolboy ears in the room.

"They can't be got rid of," Father justified our presence to Taggart. "Believe me, I've tried. Go ahead, we're ready for our medicine, aren't we, Morrie."

"Vocabulary," Taggart reeled off from one of his perpetual pieces of paper. "The sixth grade, I am pleased to report, is very much up to standard." Morrie looked simultaneously relieved and apprehensive. Taggart gave him a metallic gaze. "And your seventh grade rescues your eighth grade."

Suddenly the inspector's eyes were on me. "One test score was the highest on record. This lad bears watching. He'll know every word there is." One word I did not know at that moment was *daedelian,* which takes its name from the maze-maker in Greek myth and implies unpredictability of a particularly intricate sort. Not terribly many years from then, in a daedelian turn of events, school inspector Harry Taggart would be answering to Paul Milliron, the state's new Superintendent of Public Instruction.

Having reached his limit of congratulation, Taggart went back to the list of results. We could scarcely believe his recital. Subject after subject, Marias Coulee School came out at that heady altitude: up to standard.

Our grins filled the teacherage as the school inspector stuffed his paperwork into his briefcase. He glanced aside at Morrie. "Well done, Mr. Morgan." With a poker face he added, "You evidently majored in something more than *high-yinks* at Yale." Before going, Taggart turned to Father. "Oliver, if I may see you alone a moment, there are just a few things to go over."

The two of them stepped outside. There was a dazed silence among Morrie and Damon and me. Toby, fresh as a daisy from his day, began yattering: "That's over, huh? I liked the inspector, didn't you? Hey, what's gonna happen on comet night? Don't I get to know, now that I'm back in school?"

"No," Damon and I said together, then laughed. "We'd tell you if we could, Tobe," I soothed, "but everyone in school that day has to keep the secret. Only until tomorrow."

Morrie banged his fist on the table, startling the three of us. Smiling like a madman, he banged it again, in sheer jubilation. "'The highest on record,' young scholar," he exulted to me, his proud words my wreath of laurels.

"Wait till Rose hears," Damon loyally backed that up.

"Yeah!" Toby contributed.

"Aw," I said, not knowing what else to say. Luckily we heard the grind of a crank and Taggart's Model T coming to life; then Father reappeared.

"There, now," Morrie leaned back in mock grand fashion. "I believe we all acquitted ourselves quite well today, wouldn't you say, Oliver?"

"A little too much so, in your case," Father said grimly. "You made yourself so popular with Taggart he's coming back for comet night."

"Oliver, I simply cannot tell you. I gave the students my word. More than that, I pledged on my salivary gland." Father went at him with everything but a crowbar, but he could not get out of Morrie what manner of mysterious performance to brace himself for that next night. Philosophically fiddling with his cufflinks, Morrie kept looking around the teacherage as if drawing resolve from its confines. "You have vowed to keep a secret on some occasion, surely? And knew you had to stand by it, through thick and thin, fire and flood, shipwreck and avalanche?"

"Damn it, Morrie, I could do without the disaster comparisons. At least promise me this: whatever you and the students are up to, it won't cause Taggart to give us a black mark as a school."

"It shouldn't."

"How about upping that to 'I guarantee it won't'?"

"The public arena is always a risk. That is why it's an arena,"

Morrie said with the air of an impresario. "The one thing I can assure you of, Oliver, is that our students shall do their best. As, may I point out, they did today."

Stormily rounding us up to go home, Father glanced down at Damon, standing there smug, then at me, still somewhere up on the moon with my test score, and lastly at Toby, pouting at the other two of us for not letting him in on the secret either. He shook his head and said, "They'd better."

THE COMET OWNED HALF THE SKY, THAT NEXT NIGHT, WHEN all of Marias Coulee gathered at the schoolhouse. People oohed and ahhed as they climbed down from their wagons, dusk giving way to dark but Halley's phenomenon shedding so much light the night had its own subdued shadows.

I admit, I had mixed feelings about sharing my messenger from the deepest reaches of morning, mine and Rose's, with so many others. As Morrie had said it would, the comet's brightness now equaled that of the North Star; what a thought, that the known sky had a sudden new lodestar. But the most astounding thing about the comet by far was the monstrous tail. In its first few weeks, Halley's comet grew into the shape of a colossal shuttlecock, its feathers of light flying behind. Now the trailing cloud of light had spread out and arched, curving across the ceiling of the sky. That mysterious stardust of the comet was transparent enough that the constellations beyond could be glimpsed, and this seemed the most magical thing yet, that you could read the other stars through it.

Our bunch stopped for a last look before filing into the schoolhouse. The whole lot of us had come in style in George and Rae's big buckboard—Rose and Rae in their finery, three boys scrubbed and polished for the second time in a row, Father and George stuffed into suits generally brought out for marrying and burying. Clustered there with our heads tipped back, we looked like Sunday visitors to a planetarium. We only lacked Aunt Eunice to recite something baleful to us about stargazing.

The night's skeptic among us, Father gawked as thoroughly as any. At his elbow, Rose teased: "Tell me I didn't hear you wishing for rain tonight."

"We always need rain, Rose." I knew that what Father wanted was a deluge that would have scared off Harry Taggart from chancing muddy roads. No such luck. The school inspector's Ford flivver could be seen prominently among the gathered wagons.

"Farming every moment." Rose glanced down from the comet just long enough to bestow a look of mock disapproval on Father. "Rae, is George that bad?"

"At least."

"Now, now, Rae," George said complacently, his head at home in the stars.

The mood of all of us but Father and me could have been bottled and sold as intoxicating spirits. On my mind was the moment I had uttered "the school ought to put on a comet something-or-other." In impetuosity begins responsibility, whatever the Latin for that was. However, Damon was in his element, intrigue. And Toby could barely contain himself since Damon and I relented, just before leaving home, and let him in on comet night; naturally we sealed the secret in him with a spitbath handshake, but even so it was a risk. "You have to pretend, remember, because you didn't get a chance to practice," we told him a dozen times, but with Toby you never knew. I crossed my fingers he wouldn't forget and blurt out what Morrie and the rest of the school were up to. I crossed my other set that students and teacher, all, wouldn't look like fools before comet night was over.

Everyone piled in to the schoolroom. Homesteaders dressed to their eyeteeth for an event no one could put a name on, the throng crackled with curiosity. Some of the men had helped Morrie set up board benches, and people large and small filled those and all our desks. It was something of a shock to look around that room and see our schoolmates magnified in their parents—a family nose here, an unmistakable set of ears there. I had never noticed before, but the stocky mother and father of the Drobny pair of twins were practically replicas themselves. Trying to take it all in, I spotted Isidor and Gabriel and Inez waving for us to come and sit by them and their parents.

I felt more than a few eyes on us as our group trooped along the aisle. Rose had not spared the satin, a shimmering May-time green for tonight. Community amnesty only goes so far. I could tell, from who spoke to us and who didn't, that a pretty housekeeper who had spent nights in the school board president's house did not sit well with some.

There was enough else to worry about tonight. Morrie was up at his desk fending with Taggart, like a man trying to pet a terrier who might bite. For his part, the school inspector looked as if he was thinking up a test for comet night.

Father saw to it that we were settled near the back of the room, and then bolted for his school board place of honor in the front row. In two steps he was back. Squatting next to me, he leaned in and whispered across to Rose: "I've been meaning to say. The schoolhouse is spotless. You must have put in quite a Sunday night on it."

Rose only smiled. She seemed to know something she wasn't telling.

"May we begin?" the ever-so-familiar voice at the teacher's

desk called out. "The comet is on time, which sets the kind of example a schoolteacher likes to see."

Now the night was Morrie's. In knowing how to cut a figure, he and Rose really were a matched pair. Tonight he could have stood in for a mannequin in a high-class clothier's shop, his tweed suit the definition of dapper and his watch chain hanging resplendent across that vest of paisley. Elegantly he welcomed everyone, and singled out Father and then Joe Fletcher and then Walt Stinson and then our prestigious visitor from the Department of Public Instruction in Helena, and I fretted he was going to get carried away with preliminaries.

I needn't have. With a suitable air of gravity, Morrie now placed the orrery on his desk where everyone could see it, gave the crank a spin so that all the planets orbited, just one time, and then quietly pointed to the center window that framed Halley's comet and its trail of light.

"Whatever little else we know about the properties of existence, we map our days and nights by the fires in the heavens," he began in his best voice. "Threads of light traveling to us across tremendous time show us that the stars hang there, beyond high. Sunlight grants us sustenance of life as we know it, moonlight clothes us in our own particular fabrics of quest called dreams."

The packed house was silent, hanging on every word as Morrie swept to the corners of the universe and back. He covered everything from Copernicus to the Mark Twain crack about exaggerated reports of demise, in this case that of the entire human race. When he knew he had gone on long enough, like an acrobat dismounting he returned to the orrery and ever so slowly spun it again, sending off the planets in their stately chase, as he concluded. "The astronomer Johannes Kepler gave us the grand concept of harmony of the spheres"—I had the impression Morrie was speaking directly to me, even though I knew better—"a planetary system of worlds orbiting in orderly agreement. Another harmonious component, discerned by a genius named Edmund Halley two hundred years ago, is manifest in the sky over us at this minute." He gestured to the window that held the cosmic light. "Just once in most of our lifetimes, this comet comes from nowhere and returns to nowhere—but its passage unfailingly strikes a chord somewhere deep in us." He paused. "Harmony can take surprising forms like that. Here beneath the guiding fires of heaven, in the life we pass through, we must imagine our way to our own episodes of stellar harmony. Your schoolchildren, I am proud to say, have done that very thing for this night."

One after another around the crowded schoolroom we got to our feet, Damon in front of me and Toby in front of him, and Izzy and Gabe and Inie beside us, and down the other aisle Grover with his spectacles glinting and Verl and Vivian managing to be next to each other, and Rabrab looking as if she had swallowed the canary and Carnelia as if rose petals were being scattered for her, and little Josef Kratka scared but reporting for duty, and Milo and Carl and Martin doing their clodhopping best to look civilized, and Nick and Sam and Eva and Seraphina, Miles and Lily Lee, Marta and Peter and Sven and Ivo—every last one of us filing to the front of the room and assembling in the natural stairsteps of grades one through eight.

Morrie took his place in front of us, facing us. In back of him I could see Father hunched down in the front row with the other school board members and our school inspector. Nervous as a goose, he scanned the ranks of us. If we were not singers and we were not whistlers, what were we? I knew Father was hoping Morrie had turned us into, oh, maybe a hand-bell choir. There was not a bell in sight.

Morrie waited a minute for the fidgets to get out of us. He put his right hand up to his mouth. We all nodded our readiness.

"Ladies and gentlemen," Morrie announced grandly, still facing us, hand at the ready, "I present to you the Marias Coulee School harmonica band."

Three dozen harmonicas appeared out of pockets. Morrie blew a musical wheeze on his. Every one of us puffed into our own instrument until we more or less found the note. The drone reached an almost paralyzing level. Morrie cut us off with a chop of his nonplaying hand, gave us the beat one, two, three, and in a single combined gust thirty-six harmonicas launched into "O, Eastern Star." Actually, thirty-five, with Toby sometimes remembering to pretend he was playing his and sometimes holding it out to see if he had it right side up.

The music was ragged around the edges, and to the ears out there in the audience it must have sounded something like being assaulted by an accordion as big as the schoolhouse. We didn't care. We were only trying to be harmonic, not philharmonic. Morrie had drilled us enough and we had practiced enough that we knew we could put the basics of the tune into the air, and beyond that, unanimous effort had to carry the night. Little kids and big, we blew into the homeliest instrument in the world, with the harps of our hearts behind it.

The moment of danger came when the last aspiring note vibrated in the rafters. Morrie had warned us not to take it hard if the worst happened. Tapping our harmonicas dry, we tensely waited for the audience reaction.

No one laughed. It only would have taken one. A horselaugh, or a giggle, and our harmony of harmonicas would have been relegated to a cute stunt. Instead, the parents of Marias Coulee pounded out applause for us and shouted out, "More! More!"

"We were hoping for that word," Morrie said happily, bowing for us all. The next number was more of a miracle yet, at least to me. Milo was our virtuoso on it. The mouth organ was the one scale of life he probably would ever master, and right now he did a solo on "Follow the Drinking Gourd" that wafted sweetly off into the night in search of that spiritual constellation, the rest of us coming in as a hurricane of chorus.

Now came our finale. For once Morrie had known not to press luck too far. We had rehearsed only those tunes and this. Turning to the audience, he announced, "We have a confession to make. There is to be singing, after all, this evening. But we of Marias Coulee School are going to ask you to do it. Ah, you say, but you don't know the words?" Stepping over behind his desk, he put up the window-shade map he covered tests with and there were the lyrics on the blackboard in his elegant hand.

"One last thing," Morrie said as he burnished his harmonica to readiness. "A song is always in search of its thrush. Will my esteemed sister, Rose Llewellyn, please come up and lead the singing?"

Her cheeks coloring very fetchingly, Rose made her way to the front of the schoolroom. She stood there with poise, a dainty satin vision to melt any heart. Damon and Toby and I grinned with pride, while Father tried to look nonchalant. Going up on his tiptoes, Morrie conducted us into the one-two-three beat again. The massed harmonicas struck up the old loved tune everyone knew, and Rose in a clear, melodic voice sang for all to follow:

> *When I see that evening star,*
> *Then I know that I've come far,*
> *Through the day, through all plight,*
> *To the watchfire of the night.*

Our music over, Father and Morrie knew they had to face their own from Taggart. I hung at their side as they approached him while the crowd dispersed, stray hums of harmonicas accompanying most families home.

"I certainly have never seen anything like that in a school-house before," the school inspector said, looking from Morrie to Father and back again. His eyes gave away nothing.

Suddenly he reached out and clapped Morrie on the shoulder. "Top mark for initiative." Then swung around to Father and clapped his shoulder twice as hard. "And that Mrs. Llewellyn, what a trouper!"

How DISTANT AND DISTINCT IT ALL IS, THAT COMET OF nearly half a century ago and Morrie's triumph along with it.

And how tear-streaked, today, under the scimitar of Sputnik. My eyes well up and there is nothing I can do about it. At my age now, tears should be saved for times of mortality. For the passing of loved ones and constant friends. For any whose life touched a tender spot in my own. I know that with every bone of my being, and it does no good at all today.

What a sight I must make like this, a man of my position trudging from empty house to plowed field to pothole pond and back again, my cheeks helplessly damp, my fine oxfords and suit pant cuffs filling with dirt. Should anyone come along the road about now—Emil Kratka, who farms this land for me on shares, or one of the other surviving drylanders—I will be seen as the spectacle I am, over this: the death warrant of one-room schools being asked of me, tonight.

Why can't even the fool thicket that is headed by the appropriations chairman see that the countryside purge of classrooms that is on its way, now that mankind has begun to plow the heavens, is so wrong? Sputnik sails no higher over the heads of Marias Coulee than over those of New York and Pasadena. Yet it is the rural schools that are being declared "behind the times."

Consolidated schools. That is their war cry. Which is to say,

do away with one-room schools and put those students to end-
lessly riding buses to distant towns. Dormitories on wheels.

It has crossed my mind that the appropriations chairman
may have invested in school buses. Or he may be sincere in his
panic that the launching of one satellite has turned Nikita
Khrushchev into Albert Einstein. Either way, it amounts to the
same. Just yesterday he slammed his fist on my desk and called
me an old New Deal hack. The man is so dim he did not even
recognize the clash of his modifiers. Morrie would have jumped
all over him.

What is being asked, no, demanded of me is not only the
forced extinction of the little schools. It will also slowly kill
those rural neighborhoods, the ones that have struggled from
homestead days on to adapt to dryland Montana in their farming and ranching. (The better to populate Billings and benefit
its car dealers, I suppose.) No schoolhouse to send their children to. No schoolhouse for a Saturday-night dance. No schoolhouse for election day; for the Grange meeting; for the 4-H
club; for the quilting bee; for the pinochle tournament; for the
reading group; for any of the gatherings that are the blood-
stream of community.

No wonder the tears come. All those years ago, Damon was
ultimately right when he supposed what plagued me was night-
mare: this is precisely it. I have gone over and over my choices—
try to temper what I see as the misbegotten policy of putting
road miles on children instead of nurturing their minds, or resign in protest. Unluckily, I am not the resigning kind. And so
I can already see the faces of the rural school delegates in Great
Falls, a few hours from now, when I pull my prepared remarks
from the inside pocket of my suit. Oh, I am a known master at
taking the sting out of cuts. "Consolidated schools are an irre-
versible trend fostered by change in our state and lack of budge

in budget chairmen . . ." my text establishes. "The Department of Public Instruction will propose as a guideline that no child should have to ride a school bus more than an hour and a half each way to attend a consolidated school . . ." it vows. "Every power of my department will be exerted to see that rural teachers are reassigned to the district of their choice . . ." it offers. If I know anything, it is how to layer cotton words over hard facts.

Whatever the twist of fate, I am the product of what I am being made to do away with. If Marias Coulee didn't hold full session in the school of life, I don't know where it ever is to be found. For all of Morrie's wizardry in catching the heavenly fireball at the height of its magnitude, Halley's comet was not done with us and our educations. Late one afternoon a couple of days later, Walt Stinson on his way home from a trip to town dropped off our mail, along with compliments on Morrie's talk and the harmonica band, which made Father glow in his own right.

While the two men carried their conversation outside as farmers end up doing, Damon—sports-starved as always—immediately plowed into the newspapers. I was trying to help supper along by taking over the potato-peeling Father had just abandoned when I heard the intake of breath across the room.

"We have to tell Morrie right away," Damon said in a hushed voice.

"What," I kidded him, "did Battle-Axe Nelson knock out the Missouri Mangler or somebody?"

"No. Mark Twain died on comet night."

20

"K<small>EEP</small> <small>ME COMPANY TODAY, WHY DON'T YOU THE TWO OF</small> you," Father said out of nowhere the next Saturday morning. "I have to ride over to the Big Ditch, to settle up."

That sounded tiptop to Damon and me. We hurried through our mush while he went upstairs to deal with Toby, sleeping in. Off somewhere, Rose had the first housekeeping chore of the day cornered, whistling "When I see that evening star" at it until it surrendered.

"W<small>HY CAN'T</small> I <small>GO</small>?" we heard next, on schedule.

"Tobe, my man, the boys and I need to make a little speed today, so no riding double," Father's voice carried. "We're not taking any chances with that foot, this far along. You know it's only one more week until the doctor gives you a last looking-over, and you want him to give you a clean bill of health, don't you?"

"Y<small>ES, B-B-BUT</small>——"

Rose flew to the rescue. "Oh, Toby?" she called from the bottom of the stairs. "You can help me ever so much this morning, counting out the knives and forks and spoons when I polish them. Then later I'll help you take Houdini for a swim, how's that?"

"Rose," we could hear the relief in Father, "you are a peach."

"I take exception to being compared to anything that grows on a tree," she said back, lightly enough, and whisked off to what she had been doing.

Father came back into the kitchen grinning for all he was worth. "Don't just sit there with your ears hanging out, you two. Let's go."

The big grin still was on him as we saddled up and strung out, three abreast, onto the road to the Big Ditch with the morning sun warm on our shoulders. Normally it takes rain to brighten up a dryland farmer, but lately, Father's mood was way ahead of the weather. I couldn't help but wonder about him. Mornings now, he popped into the kitchen almost before Rose and I were putting cocoa to our lips instead of whispers. That was just the start. He went around, these days, with the musing expression of a person caught up in a fresh rhythm of life. On the work of the farm—both farms—it was like New Year's all over again: there was no holding Oliver Milliron from any job that put its head up. This seemed to be another morning when he was setting full sail into life, dry crops or not.

The three of us were a picture not seen on these roads anymore. A man above average, a farmer according to the unaccustomed way he sat aboard a saddle horse, with his best hat on and a manner of looking off for castles in the distance. Two boys, deceptively alike in size but in no way anything like twins. Well matched with his spirited pinto Paint, Damon every so often stuck his legs out wide in his stirrups as some thought or another hit him while we went along. I slouched atop Joker not moving an outside muscle, yet tugging and pulling at my latest session with Morrie with everything I had.

"What now?" Morrie had warily eyed the unsolicited piece of tablet paper I slipped onto his desk, no doubt remembering the *phych* episode.

"Working on my numerals." Latin was back to its natural existence, after school, and there were just the two of us.

"You'll end up more Roman than the Romans," he said as if that was a prospect not altogether to be desired. Still, he was in an unbeatable mood ever since the roaring success of the school inspection and comet night. And Father, carried away by it all, had promised somehow to raise his teaching wage next year. I knew I was interrupting the peace, but I had to bring this up.

Morrie put aside the Shakespeare he had been reading and peered at my block printing:

MARK TWAIN

MDCCCXXXV–MCMX

Swiftly, Morrie looked up at me. "The report unfortunately is not exaggerated this time," he had started school off, the day after Damon spied the news. "A great man has passed, apparently with a comet as a pallbearer. But let us examine 'apparently.'" From there, he again went through the sermon about portents being mere coincidences, flukes from the counting house of chance, and so on. The next thing we knew, we were up to our ears in arithmetic. Obviously he was surprised now to find me voluntarily trooping back into numbers, and in Latin at that. Nonetheless he scanned my effort:

"Let's see, eighteen thirty-five to nineteen ten, yes, correctly rendered. Well done one more time, *philologe novissime.*" That "young scholar" commendation from him was not what I was after, however.

"Morrie? That's seventy-five years, on the nose. Back to you-know-what, last time."

He moaned. "I would have made a good Tasmanian, I know I would have." Then an exceedingly level look intended to set me straight came my way. "Don't go superstitious on me, Paul, you of all people. There can be more than one coincidence in a set of circumstances, surely you see that? What is drawn from those is merely a matter of assigning meanings." He flapped a hand at my sheet of paper. "In this case they amount to a chance set of dates when someone famous was born and, sadly, now has died. No more and no less."

He was not telling me anything I didn't know; my dreams had never met a coincidence they didn't greedily invite in. But awake or asleep, there are times when something chews on meanings for everything it can get out of them. I couldn't help it, whatever Morrie said about flukes. The sky-written parenthesis of fact that Mark Twain came into this world with the previous appearance of Halley's comet and departed it with this one made a person think.

"There the thing goes," Damon spoke up as the road brought us out to the Big Ditch.

His eyes always were the quickest. It took Father and me a few moments to register what looked like a distant structure creeping ever so slightly. The steam shovel was being walked across the plain to Westwater and a railroad flatcar there. In its wake, it had left canals and lateral ditches. Already flowing in those was the irrigation water; the regulated rain, in one way of looking at it. Could I have known, even then, how much the future would favor projects such as the Westwater one? Even when the sky relented on our dryland farms and gave the fields a dousing, as it finally would do that spring, it would not be enough. It would never really be enough. Yet dryland life of one kind or another has persisted in parts of Montana like ours, from that day to this. Plow steel dries out slowest of all.

Damon and I wandered the remains of the construction camp while Father was in the office tent settling up. Nearly all the other tents were down, as gone as Brother Jubal's. The Pronovosts had already moved theirs to the agricultural extension station where their father was doing some firebreak plowing until school let out for the year.

"Gonna miss them next year," Damon said soberly.

"I know. But Gros Ventre isn't the other end of the world." Isidor and Gabriel and Inez had given us the news that over the summer, their family was moving to the town at the foot of the mountains. "Maybe we'll catch up with them again."

"Yeah, maybe."

Father came out of the office tent wearing the look of a man with a good deal of cash in his pocket. It seemed to me we were likely to need it. If the bookkeeping of the Millirons had trouble staying ahead of itself when Father had only one homestead on his hands, what was it going to be like now that he was stretched to Rose's as well, in a dry time?

The man sitting companionably in the saddle between Damon and me as we pointed ourselves home showed no such concern, however. Whatever was on his mind today, it weighed about right to him. I rode beside Father, wishing such peace of mind could be handed around in the family. Dead ahead on our route, so to speak, was the cemetery. I avoided looking toward it. Now that I was no longer in the haunted bed at Rose's place, I didn't want to give Aunt Eunice another opening.

We weren't far down the road when Father pulled up on his reins, as if a thought had just occurred to him. "How about a bit of a race? If you'll go easy on an old man."

Damon took a big chance. "We won't do wrong-end-to; will that be easy enough?"

"Impertinent pup," he said, but was grinning again. "All right, the Milliron derby. From here to the section-line road."

We lined out across the road, and when Father said "Go!" three sets of boot heels made firm contact with horses' ribs. We built up to a gallop. I still say, the back of a running horse is the most wonderful place to be when you are the age Damon and I were then. Under me Joker's mane flew in the wind, flag of its breed, as I bent low over his neck. Stride by stride with us, Damon was jockeyed onto Paint as if glued there. Father was giving us a run for our money, but the way grownups do, he jounced up and down in his stirrups more than the other two of us combined. The section-line road gravitated toward us hoofbeat upon hoofbeat.

Damon rode to win, and did. Joker and I pushed him at it, but did not battle Paint and him hoof and tooth as we did Eddie Turley and the steel-gray horse that time. Somewhere along the line that school year—maybe while reading about Fabius Cunctator, the great delayer—it had occurred to me to save some victory, now and then, for when it really counted. I made sure to come in ahead of Father, though.

"Morrie was right," the words jostled out of Father once we reached the section-line road and dropped down to a canter. "Tribe of daredevils on horseback, the pair of you. And pretty quick you'll have Tobe kiyi-ing along with you again. What's a father to do?"

What he did was to turn in at the cemetery. "Since we happen to be passing," he said with a try at nonchalance that did not even come close. "This won't take long."

Damon looked at me, and I was as startled as he was. We had not done this for some time now. In fact, not since Aunt Eunice was laid to rest, if that's what it could be called.

The prairie offered Marias Coulee a slight knoll for its burials, and our horses grunted at this next unlooked-for exertion and took it slow. On the path in, a killdeer zigzagged in front of us, pitiably dragging one wing in the old trick to draw us away from its nest. The grass on the graves moved in the wind, giving the cemetery an odd liveliness. Father leading, we rode single file now so the horses would not step on the graves. Damon appeared uneasy at our slow parade through the tombstones, and marble and granite standing in ranks have never been the pleasantest sight to me either. The patience of stones. How they await us.

Mother's grave marker stood at the far end of a row. There we swung down from our saddles.

Looking determined, Father went over the grave in a caretakerly way, ridding it of dandelions and wild mustard and brushing a bit of lichen off Mother's epitaph. Damon and I stood back, uncertain. Whatever this was about, Father seemed to want no help.

After awhile he straightened up and stood beside the grave, on one foot and then the other. I could see spasms in his cheek. He always chewed an inside corner of his mouth that way when he was anywhere near Mother's grave.

Suddenly he was saying, "Damon and Paul—I have something to get off my chest. Don't say anything until I finish up, all right?"

This did not sound all right at all, but Damon and I blinked agreement.

Father put his face in his hands, as if avoiding the sight of the tombstone in front of us, then slowly dropped them. His voice shook with the effort of getting the words out.

"I've tried like everything to not let it happen, but I've fallen for Rose. Maybe it took for her to be with us in the house all the time while Tobe was laid up. Maybe I'm just slow. But there's no getting around it anymore, I'm in love with her, hopeless as a—" almost too late, he caught himself from saying *schoolboy* to the two of us—"colt."

I don't know what registered on Damon as he stared slack-jawed at our father, but I was seeing the countenance of the man who had taken the giant step west, with all he possessed, in that Great Northern Railway emigrant car. Oliver Milliron drawn by deepest desires to embark from the known world to territory beyond knowing.

Father took another difficult breath. "I'm going to get my courage up and ask Rose to marry me. I brought you here to the hardest place in the world to say that. To see if I could."

Not even the wind made a sound after that. The spell of silence gave Father a chance to compose himself somewhat.

"Well, what do you think about this?" He scanned our faces anxiously. "Rose in the family will be different than it was with Mother."

"I'll say," I said. I had to. Damon uncharacteristically did not seem to trust his voice.

Father shot me a look.

"A lot more whistling."

There was a long pause while Father's face tried to make up its mind, so to speak. Gradually the sniffing sound that announced laughter came. I would not have said my remark warranted it, but Father laughed until tears came.

21

"*M*ORRIE? YOU'LL BE OUR UNCLE AS WELL AS OUR TEACHER next year, won't you."

"What?" He was caught by surprise, grating the chalk against the blackboard where he was concentrating on tomorrow's history test for the sixth grade. "Ah, that. We shall all have to try to not let it show." Letting me know with a strong glance over his shoulder that I should be more engrossed than I was in translating the twelve labors of Hercules—I was up to number three—he advised, "When you have a chance, look up *avuncular*, so you won't be too disappointed by my failure to match the definition." Chalk still poised, he mused a moment more: "Actually, I suppose step-uncle-in-law would be the cumbersome but apt term. There is no word for that. Where is Shakespeare when we need him?"

The circumference of love depends on the angle you see it from, I learned in the course of that madcap week after Father proposed to Rose.

As soon as he took himself over to the Schrickers and, still nervous and giddy, spilled out the news that he and Rose were getting married, Rae said knowledgably, "Well, of course you are." And George managed, "Good for you." At school, Damon and I ranged through each recess wary of opinions trickling into the schoolyard from parents at home. A few times we had to double up our fists at leers and crude comments, but mostly what reached us—the politics I am in today could learn some civility from the playground kind—was a community sigh of relief at the regularizing of things, finally, under the Milliron roof. The Drobny boys thwacked my shoulder in congratulation until it hurt.

Toby's reaction was the most down-to-earth of all. "Rose, can we still call you Rose?"

When she slipped into the house as early as usual the morning after Father popped the question to her, she still was radiant enough to turn a sunflower's head. A bit giddy myself, I watched her stop short in the kitchen doorway, as though the altar were right there. Her dazed smile hung a little crookedly on her while she checked on me across the room, eternal audience of one.

"I pinched myself, first thing when I woke up," she whispered as if I had asked. "To make sure this is really happening to me. It's so much like a dream, don't you think?"

"Cocoa's ready," I dodged off from that.

She came and sat down catercorner from me, scooting into the chair nearest the stove. It dawned on me this would be her place at the table from now on, every mealtime. The place where Mother always sat.

Rose fiddled with her cup, not even taking a perfunctory sip. Crystal ball–gazing into the cocoa, she murmured, "It makes a person wonder, Paul. Am I the right person to take this on?"

Dumb me, I thought she meant things such as breaking eggs and other feats of cooking. "Well, if they turn your stomach too much—"

"I don't know anything about raising boys," her whisper co-incided with mine. "Children, I mean—but especially someone else's." The knit line between her eyebrows was deeper than I had ever seen it. There was a glisten in the corners of her eyes, of the sort Father had at the cemetery.

All at once I felt as if I were in the witness chair. Tongue-tied, clumsy, and without direction. When you have been with-out a mother, how are you supposed to graft your heart to a new one at a moment's notice? I could have prattled out to Rose any number of fancy reassurances, but there still would have been three sets of facts clopping through this house in boys' shoes. Damon tended to be a schemer, that had to be ad-mitted. Toby on his magic carpet of innocent confusion was going to hit things and break bones, that was proven. Then there was me, something like a dream-wrestling monk mum-bling in a foreign tongue half the time. Father was another matter—Rose would have to judge that one for herself—but as far as I could see, we three weren't much of a bargain for her to walk in on. Viewed from our side, adventures in the leather trade and perdition and westbound trains to unknown places weren't the most motherly of attributes, either. Yet we were all ending up with each other, as that oldest utterance of destiny had it, for better or worse.

In the end, the most honest thing I could offer Rose Llewellyn was the benefit of the doubt.

"Father's had enough experience at boys for you both, prob-ably," I whispered. Then thought to tag on: "Anyway, Tobe and Damon and I have it in writing that you don't bite."

Rose let out a kind of a hiccup laugh, relieved to have the conversation go in that direction for the moment. "Morrie put that in the advertisement. Funny man." She shook her head slightly. "I'll have to learn to get along without him, more."

I stirred. Habits of a lifetime were a lot to be sawed through by a wedding ring. At the betrothal news Morrie had declared gallantly, "I would not want to yield her to anyone but you, Oliver." Why did that remind me of his last-ditch testimonial after Rose insisted on buying Aunt Eunice's homestead?

Worse, what if cold feet ran in their family? Maybe I was not much of a diagnostician, but I seemed to be the only one available. "Uhm, Rose," I jittered this out, barely hearable even to myself, "I know this is a big step for you, at least that's what people always say. If you're going to have, uh, second thoughts, Father would want you to have them right away now instead of after—"

"No, no, not one little bit," she whispered back insistently. "Paul, your father is a find." Her cheeks colored up. "A surprise, I mean to say. The best ever."

It has always intrigued me: did Rose know what was up, that day of Father's proposal? As soon as he lured Damon and me into the roundabout route to the cemetery, did her whistling change over to Mendelssohn? If so, she hid all sign of it by the time we came galloping back to the homestead. Each time I go over this in my mind, she and Toby are at the pothole pond taking turns flinging a stick, Houdini giving himself a bath a minute by plunging in to fetch. I see her perfectly there yet, in Father's Lake District, apron bright against nature's colors as if she had been thought up in a poem by Wordsworth. "Back the same day, I see," that young Rose of then calls over to us as if males generally did not have such homing instincts. Her arm draws back and she sends the stick sailing again. The Milliron men, for Damon and I felt quite elevated after Father's conference with us, stride abreast to the pond, grinning like fools. I'd have given skin off an elbow to listen in on Father's proposal to Rose, and probably that went double for Damon. We did our duty instead. Before Toby knew what hit him, he had been swept away from the Lake District on the pretense that the two of us could not possibly snare gophers without him and Houdini. Left alone with each other, a woman who was used to bossing dust around, and a man trying to master emotions he swore he would never have, had to find common ground if they could. Latin was not a hard topic at all compared to romance, from what I could see.

Cold cocoa now brought us to our senses, both a little embarrassed at our kitchen spill of trepidations.

Rose laughed softly. "Do you know, I really am a case this morning. I didn't even think to look at the comet."

"You'll be sorry." I glanced quickly toward the window, but at that time of year, daylight was cutting into the small hours when the comet showed itself. "It's growing a new tail."

"You're a spoofer," she murmured, although she didn't sound sure. "As bad as Morrie sometimes."

"See for yourself tomorrow morning," I whispered airily. "Morrie told us in school what it's about." Tracing a long arc in the oilcloth with my fingernail, I showed her. "Back here at the end of the tail, there's a gas that separates from the comet dust. The sun pulls it away or something, nobody knows. Usually it happens over so many nights people don't really notice. But once in a great while the comet goes bobtail, and has to grow back. This is one of those times."

$$\frown$$

Rose HAD TO TAKE MY WORD FOR IT THAT HALLEY'S COMET was busily sprouting a new tail, because by nightfall clouds had hidden the sky. When I poked my head out in the last of dark, that next morning, up there was what looked like a vast laundry pile, gray mixed in with white, as if the weather had been saving up and here was the heap. My hopes high, I walked out into

Rose's field a little way to listen for the cry of the curlew at dawn, which is supposed to forecast rain. The curlew could not find its music that morning, but that didn't much worry me. It had to rain sometime, didn't it?

Each dark, cloudy day after that we started off to school convinced we would need our slickers—Father put Toby's on him before swinging him up behind my saddle every morning, and Morrie did the same for him before hoisting him aboard behind Damon for the ride home—and every time we trotted back into the yard as dry as when we had left. Always threatening and not delivering, the aggravating weather kept on like that all week. I thought to myself Friday night, *Damn. It's going to do it to us, isn't it.*

Rose skimmed in on Saturday blissful as she had been lately. Anticipation looked good on her. She was over her case of the flutters, and every morning now we sat jabbering in whispers about her life ahead with us. Without it ever quite being said, she and Father thought it wise to get off to a clean start with Marias Coulee general opinion. They had set the wedding date—the first Sunday after the end of school—not terribly far off but far enough to show they were not being pressed into this by, say, a race with the stork. That all went over my head at the time, naturally. I only knew she was on a cloud of her own, or rather she and Father were. This particular morning, the wavy curls bounced fetchingly on her forehead as she quick-stepped through the kitchen doorway and toward me at the table. "It still looks like rain," she reported in a husky whisper, full of faith. "Maybe today it means it."

"There's going to be trouble," I predicted, not bothering to keep my voice down.

Rose froze in mid-slide into her chair, shooting a wide-eyed look of question across at me.

"He's not gonna come, is he?"

The earsplitting wail from Toby in the upstairs bedroom hung in the air of the house like a stuck echo, then was chased by loud sobs.

"There it is now," I said.

Rose raced out of the kitchen and I followed. There was a clatter in Father's bedroom, and he charged into the hallway trying to tuck in his shirttail and slick back his hair at the same time. He pulled up short at the sight of Rose, and gave her the full-of-sap smile a fiancé gives a fiancée with two weeks to go before the wedding.

"Good morning, my dear. It sounds as if we have a crisis with our impatient patient. Come on up; you may as well get in practice for this sort of thing. You too, Paul; we may need all the troops."

When we reached there, Damon had floundered over to Toby's bed, dragging most of the bedclothes from his and mine on the journey, and was sitting with his arm draped around Toby blearily reciting, "What's the matter, Tobe? Tobe, what's the matter?" although the reason was right out the window.

"The doctor!" Indignantly Toby managed to break off crying long enough to loose another blast at the sight of Father and Rose and me and point to the grayed-over window by his bunk. "It's gonna rain, and he won't come! Why couldn't it rain a couple of days ago?"

Toby's agony was justifiable. This was the day set for his last looking-over by the doctor, but if it wasn't a case of life and death, no physician in his right mind would dare to launch a Model T onto Marias Coulee's roads ahead of a deluge. Henry Ford's pride and joy was no match for our mud. Like the rest of us, Toby had seen too many fledgling automobiles in the ditch to hold any

hope for a traveler arriving when the clouds were practically dragging the ground out there. A pang for him went through me.
After all his weeks as a patient, from the look of things Toby was
going to have to keep right on lugging his foot around as if it were
made of glass, and he howled again at the prospect.

"It just isn't fair, is it," Rose at once pitched in, kneeling to
dab away his tears with her handkerchief, a stylish monogramed
RL one, I noticed, rather than the old yellowed thing Aunt Eunice had always put to the same purpose. "But the doctor will
come the first minute he can, I know he will."

I was not going to bawl about it, but I was almost as desperate as my little brother in hoping she was right. As my pas-
senger to school every morning, Toby had nearly worn the skin
off my back and middle with his wiggle-worm restlessness behind the saddle. Damon now woke up enough to look just as
dismayed at any more days of hauling our whirling dervish
home behind him. Wall to wall, there was not a being in our
household, probably including Houdini, who was not more
than ready for Toby to be certified as mended.

Father, however, was in a predicament. Here he was, a
farmer who madly wanted it to rain and rain some more, but
the parent of a terminally disappointed boy marooned by the
prospect of mud. Covertly, I watched him gauge back and forth
from the gray, swollen clouds outside to Toby's stormy little face
and make up his mind.

"Tobe, my man, we'll go to him," he reached the valiant decision. "The team and surrey will take the mud all right, if the
weather does cut loose. I'll throw on a vulcanized tarp to keep
us dry. We'll get you to that doctor in royal style."

"R-r-really?" Toby's sobs ebbed away at the prospect of a
trip to town. He got busy wiping his nose with the back of his

hand, Rose determinedly substituting the handkerchief every swipe she could. Blinking away last tears, he peered at her in adoration. "Rose, can you come too?"

She looked up at Father. "If it would help—?"

"I'd love to have your company," Father shook his head, "but you'd better hold down things at this end. Get your clothes on, Tobe. Damon, you could stand some, too."

I had hopes myself on the matter of town, but as soon as Father and Rose and I were back downstairs he made it clear other duties beckoned me. "Barn chores," he rattled off, his mind mostly elsewhere, "you and Damon, need I say more?"

Then, strangely, he drew quite a breath and turned so he was facing Rose square on. Determination was in his expression, and inquiry in hers. Whatever this was about, I started to edge to the kitchen to leave the two of them alone, but Father crooked a finger at me.

"I have another task for everybody. Florence's things"—his gaze shifted from Rose's face to include me—"Mother's things— need going through."

"Oh, Oliver. I couldn't." Rose, who had never met a chore she couldn't prevail over, appeared flustered. A closet of clothes every stitch of which would remind me of Mother did not appeal to me, either.

"It needs doing," Father said in both our directions. "I haven't been able to face it myself, and besides, I'm no expert on women's garments. I'd ask Rae to come over and help you, but Tobe and I should try to beat the weather to town." He looked more resolved than ever. He put his hands squarely on Rose's shoulders. "You're to have anything you can make use of," he made clear to her, "and Paul can set aside anything in the way of keepsakes, and the rest we give away."

Rose and I glanced at one another. That was all it took. If we had to do it, we had to.

Father was heading for his yellow slicker coat, to go and harness the horses to the surrey, when he thought to say over his shoulder to me:

"Get Damon in on it. Maybe it'll get some of the excavating out of his system."

From taffeta to gingham, Damon and I peered in confoundment at our mother's wardrobe in one end of the closet in the downstairs bedroom when Rose had finished her other chores for the day. I won't say we all put off the task, but none of us was eager for it. Already I had the feeling I would see these garments again, in many a dream.

Lucky for us, Rose saw she had to take charge. She took the first few things at hand from where they were hanging and carefully laid them out on Father's big bed for sorting. "Your mother had some pretty things."

True, but on the other hand she had not been nearly the clotheshorse Rose was. Mother's everyday dresses, faded in that bleached-out-all-over way ones from the catalog do, instantly were as familiar to me as days of the week. The few more elaborate frocks, the ones Father meant when he would say "Put on a pinafore, Flo, we're going dancing at the schoolhouse," on the other hand looked good as new.

I could see why this was too much for Father. Mindful of his instructions, Damon and I tried time and again to give something to Rose, but she only thanked us warmly and declined to take any of it, not even an apron. Eventually she hesitated over a fox fur muff when Damon reached it down from the closet shelf.

"It's from when we lived back east in Wisconsin," he recognized it soberly.

I was awkward about it, but I felt the offer should be made one more time. "Don't you think you should have this, Rose? It can get cold here, winters, honest."

Diplomatically or honestly or even both, she replied, "It's lovely. I'd be honored to have it." When Damon presented it to her, she stroked the fur and smiled at us. "I'll save it for occasions."

The cleaning out went quicker after that. We dispensed and disposed, this for the missionary society bundle, that for the rag bag. A nice patterned dress that Rose thought would suit Rae was carefully set aside. Things flew along that way until Damon reached in way at the back of the closet and pulled out what proved to be Mother's wedding gown.

He and I goggled at it, afraid to say anything. Rose once more stepped into the breach. "We'll want to keep this and put it away for your father. Here, I'll wrap it and find a drawer for it."

I believe that turned the last corner for all three of us. While Rose busied herself carrying the wedding gown over to lay it out for folding, Damon keenly dug into the dresser drawer where Mother had kept handkerchiefs and sachets and such. In my case, enough load was off my mind that my thoughts started to roam. They marched into that timeless procession of men and women coming down the aisle together—in my view of history, from Rome on down. "*Nuptiae primae.* Sorry. Your first wedding, I was thinking about, Rose. I bet you had a spiffy gown like that, too, didn't you?"

Rose happened to be passing the mirror on the dresser, and at my words, she drew to a halt and held Mother's gown up to her shoulders as she looked at herself reminiscently. "It was magical. I had the nicest white satin one," she said dreamily, "and Casper always looked his best in—"

Silence came down on us like an eclipse.

The back of my neck prickled. First I sent an inquiring look toward Damon, but he was staring at Rose in the mirror. She had put her hand to her mouth.

The question leapt out of Damon. "*Casper* Llewellyn was your mister? The Capper?"

He whirled around to face Rose, and I blindly took a couple of steps toward her, too. She had gone as pale as the gown she was holding. "Really, now," she tried, "couldn't there be more than one Casper Llewellyn in the world?"

"He was! I can tell he was!" Damon's eyes went to the size of turkey eggs. My own probably were no smaller. "Rose, why didn't you ever—"

The answer hit us both at once.

"The long walk off a short pier," Damon went on relentlessly. "Rose, did they—were you—"

"Tell us."

That voice was mine, although I scarcely recognized it. Rose appeared to be as overwhelmed as I sounded. Hastily she laid the wedding gown onto the bed and backed away.

"The 'leather trade'?" I pressed.

Cornered and knowing it, Rose was oddly prim in defending her choice of words. She adjusted her sleeves at the wrists, much in the manner of Morrie, as she stipulated, "Casper traded punches with the best of them on his way up to champion. You could call it a bit of a fib if you want, but—"

Damon still was working his mouth, but nothing was coming out now. I had to be the one to say it. "You're on the run."

"Paul, Damon, please, it's not like that." She drew herself up, then slumped. "Well, it is and it isn't. Some people were after me, or at least the betting money they thought I had, and it just seemed best to, what shall I say, evaporate from that situation and come out here and—Paul?" She broke off fearfully, seeing the look on my face. "What is it?"

"Where does Morrie stand in all this?"

A tiny shade of relief passed over Rose, I saw, to have someone else brought into this besides her and her fight-fixing spouse. She pressed her lips together in quick thought. "Morrie, oh well," she gestured a little as if that would help with what she was saying, "Morrie is in the clear, never fear. He was just a, what would he call it, a general factotum. A hanger-on, the fight crowd would say. The thrown fight was something Casper and his manager cooked up."

As if realizing that sounded too pat, she took some blame onto herself. "Naturally Casper let me in on it," she said tiredly. Rose sat down on the edge of the bed, fingering the lace of the wedding gown as though gathering something from it. "He knew I always could read him like a book, so when he came to me and said, 'Rose, boxing is a tough way to make a living but I know how we can make a killing,' I shouldn't have but I went along with it. When you think about it, didn't it serve the gamblers right for—" Listening to herself say this, she gave up.

"Father is not going to like this," Damon supplied.

He could say that again. There was a side of Father—maybe any man—that did not like to be made a fool of, even in his own best interest. If the sum of Rose's fibs upset him (and why wouldn't it?) and he felt compelled to go to the cemetery for another conversation with Mother's grave, he readily enough could come back with the opposite conclusion from last time, we all knew.

Whatever Capper Llewellyn had been, Rose was a fighter who did not quit. Appalled as I was at the catastrophic story she had just owned up to, I had to admire the combative light that came into her eyes as she looked squarely at me and then at Damon, and at me again. "Conference? In the kitchen?"

Wordlessly the three of us filed downstairs and to the waiting table.

Having seen Rose at this before, I planted my elbows as if anchoring myself into the tabletop. Damon was restless in his chair. Together we looked across at the woman ready to be our prized new mother five minutes ago, sitting there now with her past spilled all over her.

Rose scrubbed a thumb on a windmill in the oilcloth while collecting her thoughts. A serious indent took place between her eyes. Damon and I waited, skeptical, apprehensive, everything.

When she had her words lined up, her voice dropped to the vicinity of the whisper she and I always used.

"Damon is all too right. This would not look good to your father at this late date. But when would it ever have? 'Housekeeper On the Run Seeks Hideyhole'? That kind of advertisement doesn't inspire much confidence, does it? Then once I was here, it never seemed to make any sense to tell on myself. And Morrie." Her hand came up from the table in a helpless little tossing gesture. "Paul, Damon, really, truly, I didn't set out to get your father to marry me, it wasn't like that at all. I'd had enough husband. But your father and I grew on each other and—" There was the helpless gesture again. "He is beloved to me, please believe me. I wouldn't hurt him for all the world."

"Rose, can't you see?" I said numbly. "You can love Father to pieces, and there's still a problem here. Isn't the law after you?"

"Of course it isn't," the prim defense again. "The gamblers were the only ones who ever figured out the fixed fight"—she fanned the air dismissively as if shooing those off—"and that was only because they were stupid enough to guess right."

Hard as that was to follow, somehow it put a different light on things. Drumming in my head ever since the words *the betting money* came into this conversation was Aunt Eunice's prophecy that household help always stole. But that had no way of coming true any further in this case, did it? Whatever temptation had done to her in the days of fight-fixing perdition, no one as clever as Rose could possibly be out to swipe a dryland homestead. Something else grappled in me. If Rose hadn't had one slip of the tongue, Damon and I and Toby—Toby!—would have gone right on prizing her to take Mother's place, and Father would never have need to doubt that he had given his heart to the right woman. Were all our lives supposed to trip over that? Honesty maybe was the best policy, but was it ever costly.

"Any of that, back there," Rose plunged on, "there's no chance of anything like it happening ever again. I know that wouldn't necessarily make it sound any better to some people"— we knew who she meant: Father—"what Casper, well, he and I were up to. But he paid for it with his last breath. And I climbed on that train for good, all that behind me. You have to believe me, on that." Did we? "Paul," she rounded on me, recognizing that of the two stones at the table I was the flintier, "the people in this room are the only ones who would ever let this out."

Suddenly Damon clucked his tongue sympathetically. He appealed to me with an agonized gaze. I could not have put it into words then, but some part of me grasped that a scheme of necessary silence about Rose's past, if I would go along with it, would become an organizing principle for him from then on. He would do whatever it took, leagues beyond any spitbath handshake there ever was, to keep utter secrecy for what he believed to be the right outcome. I could see in my brother's face that for him, Rose was too much to let go of.

And what did he read in mine?

I sat there with my brain nearly cracking, working so hard to think through what was right and what was simply righteous. Damon squirmed some more. How did the two of us get in this situation? The desperado Milliron brothers, One-Punch and Slick. There was the distinct possibility we were way, way in over our heads, plopped there negotiating a marriage for our father or not, a stepmother for ourselves or not. Yet the power of word had fallen to us, out of somewhere.

High color in her cheeks, the warm brown eyes misty with all the emotion she had poured into this, Rose never looked more memorable as I studied her, trying to make up my mind.

"You mean it, about putting all that behind you? You swear?"

"I do."

"Up, down, and sideways?"

"May lightning strike me twice if I don't mean every word. Paul, what more can I say?"

Damon practically wheezed in relief. "That's settled, then. Don't you worry, Rose, we know to keep our traps shut. Right, Paul?"

I nodded the slowest nod of my life.

We still had to deal with the barn. Every now and then a raindrop big as a half dollar pocked the dust in the yard, just enough to make us put on our slickers but not delivering any true moisture, as Damon and I trudged there from the house.

"Sonofabitching weather," I spat out. Damon kept watch on me from the corner of his eye.

Neither of us spoke while we mucked manure out of the horse stalls and freshened up the straw on the barn floor and, last thing, climbed to the haymow. Damon pitched his hay delicately straight down into the manger and I did mine practically a stem at a time, all the effort in me still on the question of Rose and Father. Accuracy plainly was on both our minds when we met in the middle of the haymow and resigned from our pitchforks. I kicked together a mound of hay and sat in it. "Let's think this out, some."

"We better," Damon agreed. "Capper Llewellyn, holy smoke!" He savaged the air with a pantomime left hook that would have sent any Capper opponent through the barn wall. "Practically in the family. How about that."

"Damon, the man was some kind of crook."

"Well, yeah. Except for that." He sobered. "Morrie found out they fixed that fight, right?"

"For crying out loud, he'd have to. A person's sister can't be married to the lightweight champion of the world who throws a fight and gets knocked off for it and that person not find it out."

"That's what I thought," Damon said defensively. "But then why didn't he—when I showed him my scrapbook—"

"I don't know why that didn't set him off. I wish I did. But you heard Rose: he's in the clear. That's what counts." A thought occurred to me. "Where was the short pier, anyway?"

"I think Chicago."

"Lake Michigan, brrr. But there, you see? Morrie and the University of Chicago and all—" I peered intently out the loft door of the haymow as if I could see all this written on the clouds. It still was not raining to amount to anything, and at this rate it never would. "He's there, Rose tells him she needs his help because the gamblers are after her, they get away to Minneapolis. They hole up, but she still has to quit the country because the guys who took Casper on the long walk might track her down back there. Morrie watches over her while she waits to hear on her advertisement, then he comes along with to protect her. That's how it must have been."

"You always hit the nail on the head, Paul," Damon marveled.

We had been so busy at this we didn't hear the surrey until it was almost to the barn door. Toby came bounding out of the carriage, which told us even before he could shout it:

"Paul, Damon! I can ride! My foot's all healed." He bolted for the haymow ladder to join us.

Father wrapped the reins and swung down from the surrey, smiling up at Damon and me. "I hope you counted the rain-drops for Morrie's weather ledger," he bantered to the two of us, just as if a little dry weather was the only thing doing mischief to his destiny.

$\frown$

$\mathcal{T}$HE WIND CAME UP IN THE NIGHT AND THE HOUSE GROANED with it like an arthritic creature turning over. I writhed in bed. It had been an emotional day, there was no getting around that; but Damon and I had done what we hoped was the right thing, hadn't we? Rose had promised up, down, and sideways she was honest now, hadn't she? Morrie had been the noblest Roman of us all in shepherding her out here and sticking with her, hadn't—

Somewhere in the dizzying revolutions of all this in my mind, I dropped off to troubled sleep.

In the immense annals of my dreams, that night's even yet stands alone. Everyone in Marias Coulee, it seemed like, had come to gawk at a short pier. The pier was over the Big Ditch— my notion of a pier was rather approximate at the time—and a boxing ring had been set up on it. A figure in fighting trunks and gloves stood waiting at the far side of the ring, his arms resting on the ropes. And on the near side here Father was, in charge of sending out our boxers, however that came to be. I did not know whether to cheer or not when Eddie Turley, squint-ing like fury, advanced on the other boxer and was dispatched with one blow, *wham!* "Will you look at that!" people kept saying, and I was trying, but it was hard. Because while all this was going on I was being quizzed by Harry Taggart, the school inspector. "Pay attention, bucko." I was trying to, in all directions. I had a black slate on my lap, and I chalked words onto it as Taggart reeled them off to me. *Lux. Desiderium. Universitatis.* "Nasty," I heard Taggart say, and I looked up to see Milo, the next knockout victim, being dragged out of the ring feet first by Father. Where was Rose? How could she miss something like this? Suddenly Father hovered in front of me, looking distraught. "Paul, we need you in the ring. I know what I told you about fighting. But it would be just one punch." Taggart folded his arms and went into a huff. Damon came and put the boxing gloves on me, left one first for good luck, he told me. Anxiously looking past him, I could see the other boxer was bigger than I was, but not as much as I expected. Damon gave me a push out onto the pier and through the ring ropes. "The next challenger, Paul Milliron!" an announcer somewhere was saying. "Versus the lightweight champeen of the world!" His back to me, the champ shadowboxed at the end of the pier. He resembled somebody but I couldn't quite see who, until he threw a final flurry of punches and then did a very odd thing. He shucked off a boxing mitt, then the other. Still turned away from me, he dropped the gloves off the pier into the water. Where he got these I don't know, but now he ever so casually slipped some gleaming things past his fingers onto either hand. Brass knuckles.

"Morrie?" something cried out in my mind, and I sat bolt upright in bed.

Cocoa didn't help, that shivery extra-early hour in the kitchen. Pressing my brow against the night-cold glass of the window as

I tried to see out into the unfathomable world beyond Marias Coulee didn't either. The clouds had blown away and if I hadn't been so disarranged in my head I would have been tingling to see that the comet was back, lower in the sky but still a phosphorescent fireball against the dark. Its new tail swept behind it like a glowing gown. How was it possible for something a million miles from earth to be clearer than anything within my mental horizon? *Morrie? He couldn't be*—

By then I had been up for what seemed an uncountable amount of time; when you break out of a dream like that in the small hours of the morning, sleep isn't coming back. My mind absolutely refused to clear. Blindsight, hindsight, perception by any other name, I had it to contend with to a desperate degree. How could Casper Llewellyn be dead, entombed in blackest newspaper headlines that I had seen with my own eyes in Damon's scrapbook, and yet be up and around in the recognizable figure of Morrie? Was I losing my mind? Had my dream habit finally delivered me to the crazyhouse?

The kitchen clock chimed softly, and I took a frantic look at it. Half an hour, at the most, before Rose showed up for the day. I couldn't face her one more time blind to whatever she and the late Mr. Llewellyn—if he truly was late rather than current—amounted to. I had to know. I flung myself out to the mud room for the bull's-eye lantern.

It took me a couple of shaky tries to light it, but my nerves steadied a bit as I started upstairs. The stairs were no problem, I had such long acquaintance with their every tread and creak. The tricky part waited at the bedroom. There I needed just enough light to find Damon's scrapbooks but not so much that it would wake either of my brothers.

I sneaked up on the bedroom doorway as though it might run off. With excruciating care I set the lantern down outside a corner of the door frame, its bull's-eye pointing to the floor so there was a cast of glow for me to go in on, like a throw rug of light. So far so good, but I was not really anywhere yet, was I. Damon's scrapbooks always were a logjam atop the dresser. I crept in, trying to breathe silently. Not for the first time was I grateful Damon was basically a hibernator; Toby was the concern. If he shot awake and asked what I was doing, and that roused Damon, and the racket brought Father up here grimly demanding explanations as only a father could do, everything was sunk.

I was within a foot of the dresser when Toby snuffled, rubbed his nose with the palm of his hand, and yawned. Frozen on tiptoes, I waited. After forever, Toby turned over and went back to rhythmic breathing.

One by one, I lifted the scrapbooks up to my eyes, peering desperately in the dimness to pick out the right one. Making out the typeface letters on the pasted-in newspaper articles was like trying to read an eye chart in a coal mine, but thank goodness boxing headline writers so loved K.O. in big letters. Mentally apologizing to Damon, I slipped from the bedroom with his prizefighting scrapbook.

Back at the kitchen table, I paged madly through for any article with LLEWELLYN atop. Even so, I almost missed the pertinent one.

WOLGER UPSET WINNER OVER 'CAPPER' IN LAST ROUND!

My eyes swept past the headline. The photograph of the boxing ring at the end of the fight, the victor with an arm raised gladiatorially and the vanquished climbing down through the ropes in the opposite corner, his face half turned away, only puzzled me all the more. That indistinct figure in dark boxing trunks looked so much like Morrie—build, height, weight—but was the hair quite the right color? A black-and-white picture on newsprint isn't much for tint.

I blew out an exasperated breath and sat there no less baffled than I had been. Any print put in front of me will find its way to my eyes, so before I knew it I automatically was reading down through the story of the fight and on into the fine print of the round-by-round scoring of the judges. Even below that, I saw, there was a crowd of type, about like there would have been for baseball box scores. What I did not know about prizefighting would fill a newspaper page, obviously. Father would not have been alone working the ring corner in the dream, I saw right away; it took quite a population of corner men and officials. Here were the judges' names. The referee. The timekeeper. Wolger's manager and seconds and trainer and so on, listed first now that he was the champion. Then like the lead sinker at the end of a futile fishing line, the paragraph clump of ex-champion Casper Llewellyn's retinue. I didn't really imagine a factotum brother-in-law rated inclusion, but my finger trailed down anyway. And stubbed against the last tiny irremovable engravure of type.

Manager: Morgan Llewellyn.

22

"NOW THEN, PAUL." MORRIS MORGAN, SO-CALLED, BRUSHED the day's chalk dust off his hands and settled to his desk, looking like a man with not a thing on his mind except Latin.

Here we were, the usual after-school two of us. Except that nothing was usual since my dream and the fine print after it. *How does he do it?* I wondered from behind what bastion I had, my desperately propped-open primer. *Names are mighty things.* Hadn't he brazenly said that himself, the first morning he stood there at the front of the room taking roll? What a bundle of meaning the shift of one word carried, I was finding out. Morgan Llewellyn as far inland as he could get from fate's short pier; a world of difference, between that version and the pretender stepping down from a train at Rose's side with apparently no more at risk than his hat. I'd gone through that entire school day with my head on fire. Her loving brother, hah, what a stunt that was. Brother-in-law and a different kind of loving, the awful truth was, and it made me so mad for Father's sake I could hardly see straight.

"Now then, or did I say that." Morrie was fussing with my

homework. "I do not see *Lux desiderium universitatis* standing out among these translations."

"I—I'm still working on it."

My heart thumping so hard I was afraid he might hear it, I stayed bent over my Latin primer. As badly as I wanted to jump all over the cool-tongued masquerader parked there at the teacher's desk, masking my own emotions was the first order of business. Rose was at stake in this; that much was clear to me if nothing else was. I had to watch my step if I didn't want to cost Father a wife. And cost Toby and Damon—and there was no denying it, the part of me that was always going to be helplessly smitten with Rose and her whispered confidences—a new mother. The prospect of disaster hammered in me alongside my heart. One wrong word to Morrie and everything could go to pieces. All day now I had been watching him for any sign Rose had told him the cat was out of the bag about the Capper and her, at least to a pair of us. But no, I finally figured out, why would she? As long as Damon and I stayed pledged, it was to her advantage to keep Morrie in the brotherly pose, wasn't it, so no ugly questions would raise their heads to Father as they were sure to if her devoted sibling inexplicably disappeared back onto that train. All safely quiet on that front, I was convinced, as Morrie at last tore himself away from the pages I had handed in and glanced up at me.

"Paul, I am naturally concerned about this situation." The gravity in his voice forced me to struggle into a more upright position at my desk and face him straight on. "If word of this were to get back to Chicago —"

He sighed so heavily it catapulted me up even more. Good grief, had I underestimated him again? Could the man somehow read my mind?

"—my old mentors at the university would question my supposed proficiency in the classics." He critically held my homework up to the light as if that might improve it, while I whooshed a breath of relief. "In my day, I was credited with quite an ability at translation," he continued. "Why then have I not been able to transmit that knack to my prize student? Here, watch."

Abandoning his chair, he whipped off his suit coat—it was almost summerlike in the schoolroom these late spring afternoons—and hung it on the picture hook that held the comet woodcut. Next he pulled his shirt cuffs back a fraction and adjusted his sleeve garters the same minute amount, his version of rolling up his sleeves for blackboard work. I had watched him do this so many times in our Latin sessions together. Never before did the thought accompany it, *Pretty fastidious for a fight fixer.*

"Let us consider *Caesar omnia memoria tenebat,*" Morrie called over his shoulder as he rapidly chalked the sentence on the board. "You have rendered it, 'Caesar held all things in memory,'" chalking that below in elephantine letters. "I grant you, that is grammatically correct. But how many times have I told you, you needn't be so literal if the meaning can be brought out better another way. Why not say," the chalk flew again and the words emerged white and compact, "'Caesar remembered everything.' It's stronger." He made a fist to show so as he turned to me. "It carries the point more forcefully, yet has a nice, easy ring to it. I am at a loss, Paul, as to why someone with your imagination wouldn't come up with that?"

"Maybe it's because I'm not really good at pseudonyms—I mean, synonyms."

Morrie never so much as blinked.

Shaking his head, he trudged to his desk and sat down in the sad company of my translation homework again. "Substitute words exist for a purpose," he said as if it were a main rule of life, "there are times they fit the context better." I couldn't argue with him on that. Ready-made words such as *impostor* and *fraud* wore out in a hurry in my fit of anger with him, and I had sat there most of the day mentally trying more elaborate ones on him (*prevaricator* and *mountebank* and *casanova* were a few) off the great spelling list of deceit. He was looking back at me in his usual tutorial fashion. "I want you to put that imagination of yours to work on Caesar tonight."

"I'll try," I said listlessly.

"You know, Paul, you seem a bit out of sorts today."

"Spring fever."

"In that case, I know just what to prescribe." Reaching for his edition of Caesar's adventures in Gaul, he pulled up short. He tipped his head to one side. "Is your father stopping by, for some reason?"

That sat me up straight as a rod. "Not that I know of."

"That's funny. I thought I heard—"

Smash! Morrie hardly had started up out of his desk chair to check outside before window glass shattered and something flew into the room, plummeting into one of the rows of desks between us. A sage hen, the most blundering bird in the world, immediately popped to mind. But the frightening clatter of the thing across the floor said different. The rock spun to a stop against the far wall of the schoolroom.

I was gaping at the broken window, and Morrie was not much better off, when the door crashed open. Pink gums in a furious face, although no sound issued from Brose Turley as he surged into the schoolroom. He was as fast as he was big. He pounced on Morrie, the desk chair going over backward with a thud like something dead. Grappling Morrie up as if he weighed nothing, in an instant Turley had him pinned against the blackboard, a skinning knife an inch from his throat. It all happened before I could get halfway down the aisle toward the two of them, the crystal grains of glass crunching under my helpless feet.

"Stand still, teacher man." As an alternative to having his throat cut, Morrie stayed perfectly motionless. "Don't you get any ideas, boy," Turley spoke to me as if I was the merest kind of an afterthought. "Go put yourself against that wall."

I backed away toward the section of the wall where Morrie's suit coat was hung. If I could reach around to the brass knuckles that I hoped were in the pockets—

A headlock around my windpipe answered that. Eddie's voice nuzzled my ear.

"Daddy just needs to ask him something. Hold still and behave, and nothing much is gonna happen to you." Nothing much? What did that amount to when a knife was loose in the room? I tried to struggle, and Eddie simply squeezed the attempt out of me.

"All right, hoosier," Brose Turley spoke into Morrie's frozen face. "You listen to me now." The knife twitched to suggest what would happen if he didn't. "Why's the year off like it is? We come out of the mountains for fresh grub, and everything's changed," the words tumbled from him in his chomping way of speaking. "Nothing's right, for this time of year." Turley drew a ragged breath and licked his lips, the sentences an obvious ordeal for him. "Grass going brown already. Creeks are low, weather can't make up its mind to rain. The wolves ain't come down to the river bottom yet. I been here my whole life and I never seen that before." He leaned in harder and Morrie winced. I made a strangled protest and Turley's head snapped around for an instant. "Keep hold of that kid, can't you," he rasped to Eddie.

"I've got him," Eddie answered a little resentfully. Maybe it was my imagination, but the pressure of his arm around my neck seemed to have let up a bit since my gurgle.

Brose Turley hung his whiskery contorted face practically atop Morrie's clean-lipped one. "You answer me straight. There's anybody knows, it ought to be you." He licked his lips again, and I realized it was from fear. He was breathing heavily through his opened mouth, the hard-used teeth atop and the bottom gum line showing like what was under a snake's fangs. I became even more afraid for Morrie. The knife threatened again at the very surface of his throat as Turley demanded to know:

"That comet do this? The world ending in fire? *Is it?*"

Hearing that, I just knew we were sunk. If Brose Turley was crazed with the notion of Judgment Day, the instrument of judgment was apt to be that skinning knife. Three times now I had seen this monster of a man invade this schoolhouse. Surely no one could expect to survive that. Eddie shared my sense of doom in that room, I could tell. He still had me in a clinch to the point of helplessness, but I could feel him trembling, the same as I was. Wide-eyed as could be, we both helplessly watched the white-faced figure rigid against the blackboard.

Pinned there stiff as a dried pelt, how Morrie managed it I will never know. He choked out, "Light is the desire of the universe."

I was thunderstruck. I prayed Morrie would not go on, fatally pedantic, and utter to an unlettered wolf hunter teetering on the brink of insanity, "Or as the Romans would have said, *Lux desiderium universitatis.*"

There was not a movement in the room and the only sound was Eddie's heavy breathing in my ear. At last Brose Turley blurted, "Meaning what?"

Morrie mustered mightily for a person whose toes were barely in contact with the floor. "You carry a lantern when you go into the darkness, don't you? The traveling bodies of the cosmos do the same. The impulse to illumination somehow is written into the heavenly order of things. The sun, stars, they all carry light, that seems to be their mission in being. Are you with me so far?"

"That comet ain't any of those," Turley said ominously.

"It is a celestial body nonetheless," Morrie literally risked his neck in contradicting his interrogator. "One that happens to follow a course we see roughly once in a lifetime."

"Why's it come now, then?" Turley raged. He hulked over Morrie, the knife always ready. "The country burning up along with it!" Bits of spittle flew as he shouted into Morrie's grimacing face. "None of this happened before you showed up. And you and this hoodoo kid, whatever you're up to with ungodly languages. Maybe it'd turn things around if I rid the world of the two of you." At that, Eddie's gripping arm tightened on me, although I couldn't tell if it was voluntary. "Toss what's left of you in the badlands when I get done," his wild-eyed father raved onward. "I know places there, people never would find you."

"Mr. Turley, the world is not ending, believe me," Morrie panted out. "The comet sends us light, not fire. It's too far away for the earth to feel any heat whatsoever from it—you can see a lantern for miles but you have to be up next to it to catch any warmth, am I right?" He paused infinitesimally in the hope that would sink in, then plunged on. "This area is in a drought, true. The dry spell set in months before the comet showed up—Eddie can tell you, the school has measured the precipitation all winter and there's hardly been any. That is merely a matter of weather, not the heavens on fire." Morrie's voice still was a bit high, but steadying all the time. "The comet, you will see fade as it passes by the Earth. In a couple of weeks it will only look like the flare of a match in the sky. A night soon after that, it will vanish. And then you will never lay eyes on Halley's comet again."

Turley licked his lips, more slowly this time. He eyed Morrie dubiously. "How can you tell the way it's gonna behave?"

"Books as old as the Bible," the answer cascaded out of Morrie. "They tell of the comings and goings of this comet, regular as clockwork. The ancient Greeks, the Romans, the chronicle of the Battle of Hastings, medieval monks—the record is long. The period between reported sightings is infallibly seventy-five years. That is how Sir Edmund Halley was able to deduce—"

"Shut your gab." Turley seemed to think over the idea of a regular messenger of light from the universe, not the easiest thing for a man constructed of instinct.

"Daddy?"

Eddie's voice startled us all. He sounded as if he was forcing the words through a trap door in his throat, but they came. "Could be the truth. He told us in school the thing in the sky won't come back practically forever. Showed us on the machine"—Eddie meant the orrery—"where it goes. It'd take a while." His mouth was so near to my ear, I could hear the depth of the gulp he took before saying the next. "No need bothering with the teacher and Milliron then, is there, Daddy? End of the world is one thing—dry weather's another." The last sentence quavered out of Eddie almost as if he were whispering it in schooltime. "We got no call to get rid of people just for that."

Nothing happened for some moments, the Turleys holding the two of us like about-to-be-pelted wolves in my worst dream.

"Maybe not."

No two words ever came more grudgingly. Probably Brose Turley did not loathe the schoolhouse pair of us any less, but he had to take a fresh run at it. He sent a lightning glance over his shoulder at his son and me, then back to the sleeve-gartered figure pressed against the blackboard. "Maybe these're just educated fools. Couldn't make anything happen if they tried." He twiddled the knife next to Morrie's Adam's apple one more time for good measure. "For sure it's going away?"

"If the comet does not, Mr. Turley, I will slash my own throat."

Turley gave a strange acknowledging growl. Over his shoulder he ordered, "Bring him over here."

Eddie frogmarched me over.

Brose Turley jerked his head toward the blackboard, and the next thing I knew I was standing plastered against it next to Morrie. Turley backed away from us a couple of steps. He glared from one to the other of us and underlined it with a kind of snort. Evidently by long habit, he wiped the knife on the thigh of his trousers before putting it away. "Wouldn't say anything about this, if I was you two."

Morrie straightened his tie, possibly to make sure his neck was still there. "Fear not, Paul and I know when discretion is the better part of valor," he said as if addressing a question of etiquette, and I wished he didn't talk that way. "*Silentium aureum,* silence is golden, shall be our creed in exchange for your permanent departure from these premises."

Brose Turley's hand moved back to where he had sheathed the knife, hovering there. He took a step toward us and I held my breath. Seconds dragged by as he stared at Morrie, baffled. Then he spun on a booted heel and headed out the door.

Backing toward that doorway on one slow foot after the other, Eddie gave us a last long look—was it beseeching or simply squinty?—and followed his father.

The schoolhouse felt suddenly bigger. A bit of a breeze whisked in through the broken window. It was going to take more than that, though, to revive me. I was so drained I could hardly shove away from the blackboard. I lurched over to the water bucket. Gulped a dipperful, then retched it right back into the slop pail.

Morrie pounded my back with the flat of his hand to help me through the gagging and coughing. I made it to my desk with his support. When I had told him enough times I was all right, he gave me one more pat on the back and went to his own desk, righted the chair, and collapsed into it for a minute. His fine clothes were disheveled and his hair was tousled. I watched him draw heaving breaths that seemed to come all the way from his shoe tops. Finally he squared himself up in his chair. In a scratchy voice he said, "I believe we will adjourn Latin for the day. We have a window to board up, don't we."

My own voice was none too steady, but I had to get the words out if it was the last thing I ever did.

"Morrie? You managed really well. He could have skinned us alive."

After a moment he gave his mustache some strokes, if it had been there. "I may need to have Rose iron my stomach out, but other than that—thank you, Paul. It was nothing."

"No? Maybe not for a fight manager."

His face went as immobile as when Brose Turley's knife was at his neck. Our eyes locked across the rows of desks. If his redoubtable watch had been out on his desk, a good many seconds would have ticked into the stillness. As things were, there was not a sound in the schoolroom until at last Morrie let out wearily:

"Paul, *Paul,* PAUL. I do believe you are the oldest thirteen-year-old in captivity."

That wasn't how I felt, with everything churning wildly inside me. There were so many ways this could go wrong, I simply sat there and let them race one another behind my eyes, under the shield of what I hoped was a gladiatorial glaze. At last Morrie nodded, a short dip of the head that I somehow realized was a salute, and spoke again as if trying out the words to himself.

"My destiny is in your hands now."

"I didn't ask it to be!" Hot tears flooded my eyes.

"Invited or not—" He let that trail off. "So. Time to tot up. My beloved talkative sister-in-law—"

"Rose didn't tell me. Who you really are, I mean." I stopped. How could I tell him I had pieced together Morgan Llewellyn from a dream and a flyspeck line of type?

"This may be worse than I thought," Morrie was saying, glancing toward the door as if he might bolt for it. "Who else—?"

When I told him Damon had caught on about the Capper and Rose but that was all, something sparked in his gaze.

"I have to say, kudos to Damon and his pernicious scrapbook," Morrie or Morgan or some nominal combination in between managed to husk out. By now he was thinking at top speed, I could tell. I blew my nose and wiped my eyes and waited. At least he still was sitting there instead of making a dash for his saddle horse and the Westwater train depot.

He did, however, cut another glance toward the doorway where Brose Turley only minutes ago had reluctantly left our lives behind. "We came through by the skin of our teeth once already today, Paul. Let us not be precipitous now just because we have the blood left to do it with." I braced. He was reaching his highest pedagogical tone of voice.

Looking intently at me, Morrie put up three fingers and began counting off on them.

"Number one. I recognize that I have not been able to entirely shed the identity of Morgan Llewellyn, although Morris Morgan has been a marked improvement in quite a few respects."

I couldn't quibble with any of that, so I nodded.

He moved on to finger number two. "By some manner of calculation that ought to be beyond anyone of your years, you have thoroughly figured out who I am."

I nodded harder.

The final finger, he paused over.

"Then, inevitably, there is Rose. Far be it for me to see into that attractive head of hers. But from what you say, for reasons of her own she is not breathing my real name even to you." He glanced at me for confirmation and I gave it with body English.

That third finger, he folded down. Leaving the two, side by side, there in the air. "Given our relatively few numbers, isn't it possible that we might negotiate our way out of this uncomfortable situation?"

"Not until I know the whole thing. From the start."

Morrie sat there so long and so still that I was afraid I had messed up entirely. Then he rose from his chair, trailing his fingertips across the desk as he stepped away from it. "That's what I'd say in your place," he granted with a slight slant of smile. There at the front of the classroom, he walked the tight little turn of route, back and forth, where his flights of inspiration had so often taken off from. I waited, achingly hoping he would reach for the last resort of the guilty, the truth. When he began, "The prospect of that much money turned the three of us as crooked as a dog's hind leg," I heard the words with a strange sense of relief.

As he talked on, chimes of midnight out of a tale by Poe could not have resounded more fully in me. "My brother was a thing of beauty in the ring," Morrie, or rather Morgan, said at the outset. Quick as greased lightning, from the sound of it, and a natural left-hander who trained to fight as a righty. Sometime in the course of a bout he would suddenly shift stance and out of nowhere would sail a wicked left hook. It was generally good night for Casper's opponent after that. Twenty knockouts in twenty-two bouts, and capping off his fights that way—"Sportswriters fell all over themselves to be the first to dub him 'the Capper.'" Morrie shook his head as he paced the schoolroom floor. "Casper was the kind of brother I wouldn't have traded the world for, or wanted any more of. On the street, people could scarcely tell the pair of us apart, the fancy-dan boxer and the dandified manager. There were times, though, when the reflection in the mirror was our only resemblance." As he said that, I guiltily thought of some of my times with Damon.

Making the acquaintance of Rose was one of those cloudy times between brothers. "Casper could have had his pick of swooning socialites." From the slight smile on Morrie, he seemed to be reviewing the parade of them. "But no, he has to walk off a case of nerves before the Swenson fight in Minneapolis, and there's Rose on her day off. Down from Lowry Hill, strolling the shore of Lake of the Isles, tossing rusk to the ducks.

"It was love at first wink." His pacing slowed thoughtfully. "You can guess the rest. I tried to cool down Casper with older-brother advice—I sounded as creaky as Polonius, even to myself—but in no time he and Rose were holding hands in front of a justice of the peace." He cut a sharp look at me. "Please believe me, Paul, I had nothing against Rose herself. She was delightful. Too delightful for a man to keep his mind entirely on becoming lightweight champion of the world, was my concern. But I soon came around from that. In every way but one, she was good for Casper."

"The perdition part?"

That stopped him in his tracks. "One might say so," he said drily, "and I gather Rose already has. So, yes, I am afraid extravagance was our middle name there for awhile. She and he went through money as if it came with the morning newspaper. I have never been able to find the handle on a dollar myself. It didn't matter as long as the purses kept growing while Casper fought his way up."

Then came the top rung. Casper defeating the over-the-hill old champion. Setting up the fight between the top-ranked lightweight boxers in the world, Casper Llewellyn versus Ned Wolger. The fixed fight.

"It was Casper's brainstorm, to throw the bout to Wolger the first time they fought. And then wipe the floor with him in the rematch." Morrie wore a speculative expression. "Oh, we thought we knew the risk. Wolger was no slouch. But Casper never doubted for a moment he could handle him, in any fight that was on the level. The oddsmakers were of the same mind. Casper was a three-to-one favorite when we started getting our bets down. Rose achieved most of that with a trip back to Minneapolis"— the reminiscent little smile twitched on him again—"where every housekeeper on Lowry Hill placed money on Wolger for us."

Morrie paced back and forth. "Casper put up enough of a scrap to make it look good." One-Punch Milliron could barely even imagine such a surplus of fistfighting prowess. I listened with my every pore. "We collected the payoffs on our bets, hand over fist," Morrie related. "I began making noise to the newspapers about the public's burning desire to see a rematch, as a good fight manager does. We seemed to be home free." His voice grew tight, reined in hard. "The one thing we didn't count on was how touchy the gambling mob turned out to be. They had no proof the fight was thrown, but they decided suspicions would do. And so they set out to make an example of Casper."

"You and Rose, though," I whispered. "How'd you get away?"

He smoothed the good cloth of his shirt and finicked with his sleeve garters again. "Haberdashery saved our lives, would you believe." His constrained telling of it has stayed with me with the crazy-quilt logic of a dream.

The money burning a hole in her pocket, Rose is at a dress fitting; for some reason I see her in sky-blue silk.

Bird of the same feather, Morrie simultaneously visits his tailor.

Freshly outfitted and doubtless whistling, Rose alights home and finds the place in shambles, with Casper conspicuously missing. Frantic, she rings up the tailor shop, catching Morrie as he is about to stroll out the door.

They duck for cover, bombarding the police and newspapers with telephone calls but refusing to show themselves; in Chicago, according to Morrie, the underworld and civic sentinels tend to merge. That precaution proves necessary; in no time, the mobsters take the Capper for his long walk, his last ever, off the short pier.

Morrie broke in on himself. "Paul? Do you know the saying about how an imminent hanging wonderfully concentrates a person's mind? Casper's fate had that effect on Rose and me. We decided we had to stick together, come what may."

Knowing they are running for their lives now, they hop a boxcar out of town. To Minneapolis, where sanctuary awaited, under the wings of those housekeeping staffs of Lowry Hill.

"Rose was a whiz at catching on at her old haunts there," Morrie concluded the tale and sank into the chair at his desk as if having reached the end of a journey, "but we knew it would be healthier to have much more distance between us and Chicago. Montana seemed to abound in distance." He shrugged. "I believe you know the rest from 'Can't Cook But Doesn't Bite.'"

"You changed your name. Why didn't Rose?"

"She absolutely would not." He flung up a hand in exasperation. "Casper had insurance. If matters were ever to settle down and she could prove her identity, she might be able to claim it. I repeatedly pointed out to her that the entire gambling mob and probably half the Chicago police department would need to go blind, deaf, or deceased for that to happen, but you know how Rose can be."

"The bezzle. What happened to that?"

"The—? Ah, the loot from embezzlement, you mean. Top mark, for looking to the root." He gazed into space, contemplating my choice of word. "Technically, however, what Casper and Rose and I were engaged in does not qualify as embezzlement, I believe. 'Theft' probably says it better. A charge of fraudulence could be thrown in, no doubt. Felonious conspiracy might be on the list in some jurisdictions."

If the list was any longer, he would need to count off on his fingers again. My leaden stare must have finally registered on him. He sighed.

"What's left of the money is moldering in a biscuit tin somewhere. Casper did not trust banks. When he took over the swag, to call it that, because Rose and I were spending it like water, we lost sight of it for good." Morrie sat forward suddenly. "You must understand. The money was merely what might be called the proximate cause of our scheme. Oh, we enjoyed what you call 'the perdition part,' no mistake. But Casper and Rose and I all three mostly liked the plan for its own sake." He pressed his palms against the top of his desk, firming himself to say the rest of it. "When I'm tripping over myself like this it may not sound like it, but we meant no harm to anyone who didn't willingly put that money at risk. The prizefight game draws gamblers as syrup draws flies." He paused as if thinking back. "The prizefight game. I suppose we got carried away with that last word."

The acid of boredom. I sat there trying to comprehend how it had eaten into those three people, so near the tiptop of everything. Maybe a nightly jolt of dreams was no bad thing.

Shadows had lengthened across the worn wood of the schoolroom floor and the window smithereens. Morrie put his hands to his temples and rubbed there as if to erase whatever of this he could. "It's late," he said, barely hearable. "Your father will be coming looking for you."

"Let him." I had to finish this, all the way. "Morrie?" I made myself look at him, although I was seeing beyond to Oliver

Milliron and the world he thought he was gaining in the person of Rose. "I have to tell."

"You don't at all."

"You and Rose—"

"—have done what a man and a woman do. That's so. Nights are long here." His eyes steadied on mine. "But we are not—what you might think, together. Paul, listen to me. Rose is genuine in the feelings she has for your father. She's made me know that. Hard as it is to admit, that's a match I have lost, and on the level."

That fact seemed to make him restless. The next thing I knew, he was on his feet and plucking up a piece of chalk from the blackboard. Only his nerves had anything to say with it, though, as he jiggled the stick of chalk in a one-handed juggle while he paced the front of the room.

"Let us consider one possible outcome," he mused out loud. "If you were to keep silent, matrimony would take its course and your father and Rose would gain the considerable pleasure of each other's company unto eternity. And Toby and Damon and you would have a mother." He gave the wan smile once again. "Although the Milliron household might have to quit paying a housekeeper and hire a cook." The chalk took a higher hop in his hand, was caught and clenched. Morrie went perfectly still as he looked at me over his gripping hand. "As for me, I would finish up the school year and move on."

I said the hardest thing I ever had. "I—I think that's a good idea."

He exhaled, gave me the kind of nod he did when I got a difficult conjugation right, and deposited the chalk—in pieces now—at the blackboard. Before he could move from there I called out:

"There's one thing more."

Slowly Morrie turned around to me, the lightning-rod glint

in his eyes. "I swear, you've caught something from reading Caesar's tactics."

"I want you to give Rose away. At their wedding."

His mouth came open, but before he could manage words I said:

"And you have to mean it."

$\backsim$

AND SO, AS ROSE WOULD HAVE SAID. WHAT STAYS AND WHAT goes. Doctors who work in the mind may offer explanations why certain watershed events do not ever leave us—a first love, death of a parent, moving away from home. Nothing explains the other molecules of time that endure. At the end of that afternoon, tuckered out yet vibrant with purpose, I rode away from the schoolhouse more than half aware that I was traveling into the next chapter of the life of us all.

Where Rose and Father very soon stood in front of a minister and spoke the vows that lasted them the rest of their lives.

Where Morrie kept his promise and gave Rose away and then in that whirl-about way of his was gone from us for good, or better just say forever; Tasmania, if the telegram from a Pacific dock a few months later could be believed.

Where, far-fetched as it then seemed for young centaurs like us, in the fullness of time Damon and I and even Toby would end up tamed and married, napkined and patriarchal.

Those stand like continental divides in my rumpled mind, yet no more clearly than this. That day, I rode down through The Cut and out onto the section-line road across Marias Coulee still trying to gather myself, to put on the face—the one that has lasted to this day—behind which I could seal away Rose's past, and Morrie's, for the sake of the next of life for all concerned. The sky was bare blue; it would be the best possible night to say good-bye

to the comet. There was just enough wind to muss Joker's mane
now and then. I let Joker have his head most of the way home,
until suddenly the reins came alive in my hand and I headed him
at a gallop out into the field between Rose's homestead and our
own. At the spot where I could see to the pothole pond, I pulled
up. There at the Lake District, a flurry had replaced the stillness
of the water. A commotion of wings, a dapple of white against
the prairie. The swans had come in their seasonal visit. Beautiful
as anything, I could hear their whistling.

⌒

*E*VEN WHEN IT STANDS VACANT THE PAST IS NEVER EMPTY.
In these last minutes here, in this house with its kitchen doorway that overheard so many whispered confidences, with its calendar that holds onto Octobers forever, something has found its
way into a corner of my mind. A finding, in more ways than
one. For it has come to me, amid the many jogs of memory
today, that the contingency authority that we so feared from
school inspector Harry Taggart, back then, still exists. I cannot
even guess how far back from modern times it was last used, but
there it stands, I am sure of it, obscurely tucked away in the
powers of my office. And so: what if I now were to resort to
the political instincts and administrative wiles—and, admittedly
and immodestly, the reverse—that have kept me in office all
these terms, to freshen up that dusty capacity of the superintendent of public instruction to take charge of a rural school in
trouble? And if the appropriations chairman is determined to
treat Sputnik like the starter's gun in a race to the school bus, I
would have no qualm in issuing a finding that all rural schools
in the state thereby are in trouble, would I.

I must not show my hand too soon. First it will require an
enabling clause, a phrase, innocent as a pill with the potion deep

in the middle, put before his legislative committee. A house-keeping measure, I will say when I present this; I must make sure to call it that in honor of Rose. Something that can be read more than one way. *Regarding contingent appropriation within the purview of the Department of Public Instruction pursuant to the matter of 'findings'...,* perhaps. Or *In matters of appropriation pertaining to rural schools, the Superintendent shall determine....* Some verbose foliage of that sort above the crucial root, so that while the chairman thinks I am fiddling ineffectually with the rural school appropriation funds lingering in my budget, I will be in fact appropriating—yes, taking; glomming onto, in the translation even Morrie approved of—the sole say for the continued existence of those one-room schools. My schools. I can see the slack faces of the chairman and his pack even now, when the matter goes up to the state supreme court and I as the author of the troublesome meaning can quite happily testify that I meant *appropriate* as the verb of possession.

Oh, there is still a touch or two needed to perfect this, some apt stretch of the imagination to do full justice to the chairman and his ilk in the political infighting. The dream kind, that goes in for brass knuckles. That, too, will come, I know it will. As surely as night.

And so my course is clear and my heart is high. When I pull in to Great Falls to the convocation waiting for word from me about the fate of their prairie schools and rise in front of that gathering and toss away my prepared remarks, I can now say to them the best thing in me: that I will sleep on the question appropriately.